David Fallon

Palgrave Studies in Nineteenth-Century Writing and Culture

General Editor: **Joseph Bristow**, Professor of English, UCLA

Editorial Advisory Board: **Hilary Fraser**, Birkbeck College, University of London; **Josephine McDonagh**, Kings College London; **Yopie Prins**, University of Michigan; **Lindsay Smith**, University of Sussex; **Margaret D. Stetz**, University of Delaware; **Jenny Bourne Taylor**, University of Sussex

Palgrave Studies in Nineteenth-Century Writing and Culture is a new monograph series that aims to represent the most innovative research on literary works that were produced in the English-speaking world from the time of the Napoleonic Wars to the *fin de siècle*. Attentive to the historical continuities between 'Romantic' and 'Victorian', the series will feature studies that help scholarship to reassess the meaning of these terms during a century marked by diverse cultural, literary, and political movements. The main aim of the series is to look at the increasing influence of types of historicism on our understanding of literary forms and genres. It reflects the shift from critical theory to cultural history that has affected not only the period 1800–1900 but also every field within the discipline of English literature. All titles in the series seek to offer fresh critical perspectives and challenging readings of both canonical and non-canonical writings of this era.

Titles include:

Eitan Bar-Yosef and Nadia Valman (*editors*)
'THE JEW' IN LATE-VICTORIAN AND EDWARDIAN CULTURE
Between the East End and East Africa

Heike Bauer
ENGLISH LITERARY SEXOLOGY
Translations of Inversions, 1860–1930

Laurel Brake and Julie F. Codell (*editors*)
ENCOUNTERS IN THE VICTORIAN PRESS
Editors, Authors, Readers

Colette Colligan
THE TRAFFIC IN OBSCENITY FROM BYRON TO BEARDSLEY
Sexuality and Exoticism in Nineteenth-Century Print Culture

Dennis Denisoff
SEXUAL VISUALITY FROM LITERATURE TO FILM, 1850–1950

Laura E. Franey
VICTORIAN TRAVEL WRITING AND IMPERIAL VIOLENCE

Lawrence Frank
VICTORIAN DETECTIVE FICTION AND THE NATURE OF EVIDENCE
The Scientific Investigations of Poe, Dickens and Doyle

Yvonne Ivory
THE HOMOSEXUAL REVIVAL OF RENAISSANCE STYLE, 1850–1930

Colin Jones, Josephine McDonagh and Jon Mee (*editors*)
CHARLES DICKENS, *A TALE OF TWO CITIES* AND THE FRENCH REVOLUTION

Jarlath Killeen
THE FAITHS OF OSCAR WILDE
Catholicism, Folklore and Ireland

Stephanie Kuduk Weiner
REPUBLICAN POLITICS AND ENGLISH POETRY, 1789–1874

Kirsten MacLeod
FICTIONS OF BRITISH DECADENCE
High Art, Popular Writing and the *Fin de Siècle*

Diana Maltz
BRITISH AESTHETICISM AND THE URBAN WORKING CLASSES, 1870–1900

Catherine Maxwell and Patricia Pulham (*editors*)
VERNON LEE
Decadence, Ethics, Aesthetics

Muireann O'Cinneide
ARISTOCRATIC WOMEN AND THE LITERARY NATION, 1832–1867

David Payne
THE REENCHANTMENT OF NINETEENTH-CENTURY FICTION
Dickens, Thackeray, George Eliot and Serialization

Julia Reid
ROBERT LOUIS STEVENSON, SCIENCE, AND THE *FIN DE SIÈCLE*

Anne Stiles (Editor)
NEUROLOGY AND LITERATURE, 1860–1920

Caroline Sumpter
THE VICTORIAN PRESS AND THE FAIRY TALE

Ana Parejo Vadillo
WOMEN POETS AND URBAN AESTHETICISM
Passengers of Modernity

Phyllis Weliver
THE MUSICAL CROWD IN ENGLISH FICTION, 1840–1910
Class, Culture and Nation

Paul Young
GLOBALIZATION AND THE GREAT EXHIBITION
The Victorian New World Order

Palgrave Studies in Nineteenth-Century Writing and Culture
Series Standing Order ISBN 978–3–333–97700–2 (hardback)
(*outside North America only*)

You can receive future titles in this series as they are published by placing a standing order. Please contact your bookseller or, in case of difficulty, write to us at the address below with your name and address, the title of the series and the ISBN quoted above.

Customer Services Department, Macmillan Distribution Ltd, Houndmills, Basingstoke, Hampshire RG21 6XS, England

---

Charles Dickens, *A Tale of Two Cities* and the French Revolution

Edited by

Colin Jones, Josephine McDonagh and Jon Mee

palgrave
macmillan

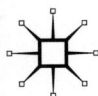

First published 2009 by
PALGRAVE MACMILLAN

Palgrave Macmillan in the UK is an imprint of Macmillan Publishers Limited,
registered in England, company number 785998, of Houndmills, Basingstoke,
Hampshire RG21 6XS.

Palgrave Macmillan in the US is a division of St Martin's Press LLC,
175 Fifth Avenue, New York, NY 10010.

Palgrave Macmillan is the global academic imprint of the above companies
and has companies and representatives throughout the world.

Palgrave® and Macmillan® are registered trademarks in the United States,
the United Kingdom, Europe and other countries.

ISBN-13: 978–0–230–53778–1   hardback
ISBN-10: 0–230–53778–2   hardback

This book is printed on paper suitable for recycling and made from fully
managed and sustained forest sources. Logging, pulping and manufacturing
processes are expected to conform to the environmental regulations of the
country of origin.

A catalogue record for this book is available from the British Library.

Library of Congress Cataloging-in-Publication Data

Charles Dickens, a Tale of two cities and the French Revolution/
    edited by Colin Jones, Josephine McDonagh and Jon Mee.
        p. cm. — (Palgrave studies in nineteenth-century writing and culture)
    Includes bibliographical references and index.
    ISBN-13: 978–0–230–53778–1
    ISBN-10: 0–230–53778–2
    1. Dickens, Charles, 1812–1870—Criticism and interpretation.
    2. Dickens, Charles, 1812–1870. Tale of two cities. 3. France—History—
Revolution, 1789–1799—Literature and the revolution. 4. Dickens, Charles,
    1812–1870—Characters. 5. English literature—French influences.
    6. English literature—19th century—History and criticism. I. Jones,
Colin. II. McDonagh, Josephine. III. Mee, Jon.
    PR4571.C47 2009
    823'.8—dc22

                                                                    2008042644

10 9 8 7 6 5 4 3 2 1
18 17 16 15 14 13 12 11 10 09

Printed and bound in Great Britain by
CPI Antony Rowe, Chippenham and Eastbourne

In memory of Sally Ledger

Contents

List of Illustrations

List of Abbreviations

DSA   *Dickens Studies Annual*
Letters   *The Letters of Charles Dickens*, ed. Madeline House, Graham
           Storey and others, 12 vols. (Oxford: Clarendon Press,
           1965–2002).
           References in text to volume and page.
Slater   *The Dent Uniform Edition of Dickens' Journalism*, ed. by
           Michael Slater and John Drew, 4 vols. (London: Dent,
           1994–2000). References in text to volume and page.
TTC   Charles Dickens, *A Tale of Two Cities*, ed. Richard Maxwell
           (London: Penguin Books, 2003). References in text to book,
           chapter and page.

Acknowledgements

This volume began life as a conference, jointly organised by the editors, entitled 'Charles Dickens and the French Revolution: Crowds and Power', and held at the Maison Française, Oxford, 14–15 July 2006. We thank Alexis Tadié, then Director of the Maison Française, and his staff for their help. Funding for the conference was provided by the British Academy, University of Warwick's History Department and Humanities Research Centre, and the English Faculty of Oxford University. A screening of the 1958 film version of *A Tale of Two Cities*, directed by Ralph Thomas, was held at the Phoenix Cinema, Oxford, and introduced by Michael Wood. At very short notice, Judith Buchanan also screened Frank Lloyd's 1917 film version during the conference.

Besides thanking the above, we also acknowledge our debt to all the contributors to the conference, especially David Paroissien and Carolyn Steedman for their masterly summing up; Beth Palmer, Adelene Buckland, Rosey Dunleavy and Greg Tate, for helping; as well as the audience at the conference for their helpful comments and general support.

In regard to the production of this volume, we also extend our thanks to Anthony Cummins and David Fallon for research assistance; to colleagues who have read and commented on parts of the manuscript, notably Harvey Chisick, Peter Mandler and David Paroissien; and to Joseph Bristow, who as general editor has been generous and scrupulous in his support of this book.

An earlier version of Gareth Stedman Jones's chapter appeared in *History Workshop Journal* 65(1) (2008), pp. 1–22.

Any faults remaining are our own.

As this volume went to press, we learnt of the tragic death of one of our contributors, Sally Ledger. Sally, who was our friend and colleague over many years, died ludicrously young, and just as she had established herself as one of Britain's foremost Dickens scholars.

This volume is respectfully and lovingly dedicated to her memory.

Colin Jones
Josephine McDonagh
Jon Mee

1
Introduction: *A Tale of Two Cities* in Context

Colin Jones, Josephine McDonagh and Jon Mee

A British icon

On 15 October 1859 Charles Dickens wrote to his friend, the French actor François Régnier, giving advance warning of a parcel that he was sending him. It would contain 'the Proof sheets of a story of mine that has been for some time in progress in my weekly journal, and that will be published in a complete Volume about the middle of November'. The 'story' was *A Tale of Two Cities*. 'I want you to read it for two reasons', wrote Dickens:

> First because I hope it is the best story I have written. Secondly, because it treats of a very memorable time in France; and I should very much like to know what you think of its being dramatized for a French theatre. If you should think it likely to be done, I should be glad to take some steps towards having it well done. The Story is an extraordinary success here, and I think the end of it is certain to make a still greater sensation.
>
> (*Letters*, IX, 132)

By this time, Dickens was already the best known and most successful writer in Britain, the author of a dozen novels and an established literary celebrity, whose work had begun to achieve international renown. He had recently launched a series of public readings of his works – for the first time, for his own profit. These were beginning to consolidate his celebrity across Britain and Ireland and in America.[1]

If Dickens's letter to Régnier sounds a note of triumphalism at his 'extraordinary success', it was doubtless mingled with personal relief. The success of the novel in Britain was closely tied to Dickens's new magazine venture, *All The Year Round*, on which, as editor and as majority shareowner, Dickens had staked his professional identity and personal finances.[2] The highly popular *Household Words*, which he had edited for nine years, had just been dissolved following an acrimonious dispute with its publishers. Dickens sought to overcome this setback with a new enterprise, which he accompanied with a nationwide advertising campaign. *All The Year Round* was launched in April 1859 with *A Tale of Two Cities* as its lead item, serialized from the first issue.

The gamble paid off. The novel achieved overwhelming success from the outset, thereby establishing the new magazine commercially. Issued on a weekly basis between April and November 1859, it both met and stimulated further demand by being produced in parallel in monthly parts from June to December. It was published by Chapman & Hall as a single volume in December 1859. By then its serialized form had already secured it a vast readership, numerically outstripping sales figures of all Dickens's previous novels. Dickens also sold the rights in America, where it was published in *Harper's Weekly* between May and December 1859. The German publisher Tauchnitz produced a two-volume English-language edition in the same year. On the back of its growing fame, *A Tale* was adapted for the London stage in 1860, and played to appreciative audiences.[3] Commercial triumph was, moreover, matched by positive critical reception: reviews were mostly favourable. One, for example, claimed that it showed 'every promise of taking high rank among [Dickens's] happiest master pieces'.[4] Dickens's correspondence contains laudatory letters from luminaries, including the historian and social thinker Thomas Carlyle, whose *The French Revolution* (1837) Dickens credited as his main inspiration and source.

Dickens's relief at the success of *A Tale of Two Cities* must have been all the more intense in that it suggested that he had surmounted a particularly severe period of turbulence in his private life. He had recently separated from his wife, Catherine, with whom he had nine surviving children (eight of whom stayed with Dickens and his wife's sister, Georgina Hogarth). The separation had been very public, and, as Dickens's biographers have noted, its consequences seeped into Dickens's professional endeavours.[5] Indeed, it was this that provoked his split from the publishers of *Household Words*. In June 1858, aware of damaging gossip that was circulating about his domestic situation, Dickens had taken the unprecedented step of publishing a 'statement' in *The Times* and other newspapers, as well as in *Household Words*, explaining the separation and denying unspecified rumours about his private affairs. When his publishers, Bradbury and Evans, refused to place the announcement in *Punch*, another magazine they owned, Dickens was so incensed that he decided to split from them too.[6] Many of the rumours in circulation linked Dickens romantically to his sister-in-law, who remained platonically loyal to the charismatic writer. Some – more accurately – alleged a liaison with an unidentified young actress. Ellen Ternan, the woman in question, had met Dickens two years earlier when she and her family had acted with him in Wilkie Collins's play *The Frozen Deep*, about an ill-fated Arctic expedition that had taken place in 1845.[7] Dickens had played the part of Richard Wardour, a man who dies rescuing his rival in love. Dickens confidentially admitted to Angela Burdett Coutts that his initial idea for *A Tale* originated while acting in the play, and parallels between Wardour and the character Sydney Carton are clear.[8] It is only one step – and it is a step that certain Dickens biographers have taken – to seeing the exploration of masculine sacrifice in both *The Frozen Deep* and *A Tale* as an imaginative working through of the knotted relations linked to the breakdown of Dickens's marriage and his love affair with Ternan.[9] In this biographical reading, all the principal male characters in *A Tale* are seen as projections of the author: Manette, 'recalled to life', as Dickens had been by a young woman; Charles Darnay, the accepted lover of Lucie Manette, and who even shared his initials with Charles Dickens; and Sydney Carton (originally named Richard or Dick[10]), who makes the ultimate sacrifice for the greater good of society. Accordingly, the theme of resurrection that reverberates throughout the novel comes to stand for Dickens's own sense of personal resurrection.[11] Ellen Ternan is seen as Lucie Manette and, more controversially, one critic has even suggested that traces of Catherine Dickens can be detected in the character of Mme Defarge.[12]

The 'extraordinary success' of the novel, Dickens's satisfaction with it as 'the best story I have written' and the depiction of it as a multifaceted projection of his own character at a difficult moment in his life are perhaps surprising, given that *A Tale of Two Cities* is in some ways the most 'unDickensian' of Dickens's novels. The most compact and plot-driven of his works (alongside *Hard Times*, 1854), it lacks the expansive cast of Dickensian characters whose personalities are expressed in imaginatively invented idiolects, such as, for instance, Mrs Gamp's famously 'owldacious' eccentricities in *Martin Chuzzlewit* (1844). In *A Tale*, the French in particular are depicted as melodramatic types who speak in a predictable stage French and lack the linguistic inventiveness usually associated with Dickens's characters. Some features may be explained by the original form of publication. Although Dickens was an established master of serial fiction, *A Tale of Two Cities* was produced for a weekly, rather than his preferred monthly, format. These 'teaspoon' parts (a term he echoed back to Carlyle[13]) contributed to the novel's emphasis on plot over character. In a letter to his close friend John Forster, he claimed that in writing the novel he had 'set [himself] the task of making a picturesque story, rising in every chapter with characters true to nature, but whom the story itself should express, more than they should express themselves, by dialogue' (*Letters*, IX, 112–13).

In addition, *A Tale* is exceptional in being one of only two historical novels that Dickens wrote, despite the prestige and popularity of the genre. The other is *Barnaby Rudge*, conceived at least as early as 1836 but not published until 1840, Dickens's novel about the Gordon 'No-Popery' Riots, which erupted in London in 1780. The two novels have much in common. Both cover the final decades of the eighteenth century, and, as Mark Philp points out in his essay, the pivotal events of the Gordon Riots foreshadow those of *A Tale*. The 'incessant footsteps' that echo ominously in the Manettes' Soho house, for instance, during the hot and thundery afternoon in June 1780 (*TTC*, II, vi) could well have been the footsteps of Gordon rioters.[14]

Both novels are preoccupied with collective violence and the mentality of the mob, and in their explicit treatment of political themes may be thought to depart from the more familiar domain of the Dickensian novel. This aspect of both novels obviously shows the influence of Carlyle, but, as the essays in this volume by Philp and Stedman Jones suggest, is far from being totally determined by it. *Barnaby Rudge* engages with the Victorian fears of popular revolutionary violence, which had been given forcible expression in Carlyle's *The French Revolution* (1837) and *Chartism* (1839). In both books, Carlyle represented popular revolutionary action as the expression of a latent inner fury in the people at large, part of an unconscious struggle between order and anarchy, rather than an expression of political aspirations or discrete historical processes. Dickens often uses a similar language of huge natural forces at work, and in *A Tale of Two Cities* takes many of his incidents from Carlyle's history, but he is also willing to explore socio-historical causes of the phenomena he describes. Although by the time Dickens returned to Carlyle's history of the Revolution as one of the key sources for *A Tale of Two Cities* the two celebrity authors had become friends, Carlyle was much more obviously a conservative opponent of the democratic principles he attacked in his apocalyptic *Latter-Day Pamphlets* (1850). Dickens and Carlyle shared a suspicion of political economy and utilitarianism – expressed brilliantly in *Hard Times*, the novel Dickens dedicated to Carlyle (1854) – and a sense of impending social upheaval, but they did not share a philosophy of history or even a political vision. Dickens's brand of populist radicalism shows very little of the later Carlyle's longing for the strong leader or his nostalgia for the past, but instead often maintains a more modernizing view of the future, expressed as the glittering vision of the metropolis of Paris at the end of *A Tale of Two Cities*.[15]

What differentiates *A Tale* from most of Dickens's other work is its balanced Anglo-French location: sixteen chapters are set in London and three in other English locations, as opposed to eighteen in Paris and six in the French provinces. These dual international locations, plus the novel's world-historical theme, give it a different ambiance and cultural reach from the principally London-bound domestic dramas for which Dickens was famous.

Despite its exceptional status within Dickens's *oeuvre*, *A Tale* has never failed to charm Dickens enthusiasts. By the time of his death, it was well on the way to being established as one of his most extensively published as well as most popular works. At the turn of the twentieth century, Sydney Carton, the tragic hero of the tale, had become a stock figure in the national imaginary, a place which Martin-Harvey's barn-storming theatrical adaptation, *The Only Way* (1899), helped to consolidate. As Joss Marsh notes, Carton's elegiac guillotine speech ('It is a far, far better thing...') was used to maintain morale among besieged British troops at Mafeking in the Boer War, while in the First World War it was similarly popular among Tommies in the trenches. *A Tale of Two Cities* had become an icon of British national identity.

Frequent new editions, theatrical performances and, from 1911, film versions have helped to relay throughout the twentieth and twenty-first centuries the flying start the novel immediately won in the nation's affections. Its wide use as a classroom text in English schools has endorsed this position. For many English schoolchildren, *A Tale of Two Cities* is the only Dickens novel they have read in its entirety (its relative and unDickensian brevity helps). This has established Carton's guillotine speech as well as the pithy opening lines of the novel as some of the most frequently quoted, misquoted and mimicked of Dickensian aphorisms.

The iconic status of the novel has allowed it to accommodate a great variety of often wildly divergent readings. It has been read as a reference point for Franco-British relations, a representation of mob violence, a fable about Christian sacrifice or a psychological emanation of the author's troubled sexuality. These interpretations have tended to be taken in isolation, and there have been relatively few attempts to bring together the novel's diverse contexts and spheres of influence. Moreover, it has invariably been viewed within an exclusively British context, with little attention paid to the French aspects of the work. In this volume, in order to achieve a more broadly informed assessment of the novel's place in political and cultural life, we bring to bear on it a spectrum of approaches and points of view by historians of British and French political ideas, literary critics, and historians and critics of film and theatre. Their essays explore and highlight the richness of the novel and its adaptations into other media, and underline the limitations of viewing it solely as a national icon. In these introductory remarks, we seek to contextualize the essays by sketching out the French and British milieux in which Dickens composed his novel and in which it subsequently circulated.

A Tale of Two Cities in France

Dickens does not appear to have thought that it was unreasonable to have high hopes for strong cross-Channel interest in his account of 'a very memorable time in France', an interest that would match *A Tale of Two Cities*'s reception in England. By 1859, his work was already popular in France. The *Revue britannique,* edited from 1839 by Dickens's acquaintance and sometime translator, Amédée Pichot, ran morsels from British journals, including, in 1842, much of *Barnaby Rudge*. *Nicholas Nickleby* (1839) had been staged as a melodrama at the Paris Ambigu-Comique theatre in 1842, while in the 1850s *Martin Chuzzlewit* was serialized in the official government newspaper, *Le Moniteur*.[16] Under an agreement brokered in 1856, moreover, the French publishing house Hachette secured the rights for French translations of all Dickens's major fiction.[17] In May 1860 – in advance of the novel appearing as a single volume in England – Dickens wrote (in unaccented French) to thank Hachette for the decision to translate *A Tale of Two Cities*: 'Voila un de mes espoirs les plus ardents, en l'ecrivant' (*Letters*, IX, 249).[18]

On first encountering Paris in 1844, Dickens had fallen in love with the city ('the most extraordinary place in the world') and his Parisophilia never faltered.[19] He resided there in 1846–7, and was a frequent visitor thereafter, sometimes for lengthy spells. He knew figures from the French literary establishment, and indeed by the mid-1850s had even achieved the status of minor celebrity in Paris. He was stopped in the street by admirers; by 1862 he would proudly observe how his novels were 'to be seen at every railway station, great or small' (*Letters*, X, 151). Yet his hopes for a parallel triumph with *A Tale of Two Cities* in the second of the novel's eponymous cities were to be sadly disappointed. On 16 November 1859, Dickens replied to a non-extant missive from François Régnier, thanking him for his 'kind and explicit' reply to his earlier letter and accepting the impossibility of the French theatrical adaptation to which he had aspired. 'I very much doubted', Dickens added, 'whether the general subject would not be objectionable to the Government, and what you write with so much sagacity and with such care convinces me at once that its representation would be prohibited' (*Letters*, IX, 163).

The French translation of *A Tale of Two Cities* duly appeared in 1861 under the title *Paris et Londres en 1793*, translated by Henriette Loreau, but signally failed to spark enthusiasm among the French reading public.[20] Unsurprisingly, when Dickens took his public readings to Paris in the early 1860s, he chose not to break with his programme of selections. No extracts from *A Tale* were included: *David Copperfield* (1850), *Dombey and Son* (1848), *A Christmas Carol* (1843) and *The Pickwick Papers* (1837) were adjudged more to the taste of his French audiences.[21]

The French in the nineteenth century tended to like their Dickens full of character, individualism and 'English' eccentricity. The 'unDickensian' *Paris et Londres en 1793* did not catch on in France. The politics of the novel in particular were invariably seen as unfathomable, reactionary or even Francophobic. Liberals and radicals were appalled at his depiction of revolutionary characters, while conservative nostalgics for the *ancien régime* took cold comfort from *A Tale*'s pre-revolutionary scenes. In terms of its reception and the meanings ascribed to it over time, *A Tale of Two Cities* thus presents something of a conundrum. Though Dickens avowed it to have been written for French as well as English audiences, the novel has had a highly contrasted inheritance. Francophilic to a tee, Dickens would have been much distressed that his novel should thus become a source of discord, disharmony and misunderstanding between the populations of the two cities and the two nations at which he appears to have targeted it. A runaway success in England, where its status as a national icon stimulated its reproduction beyond the novel form on stage and in film, in France it has been generally poorly known, neglected and often dismissed as pure English jingoism.[22] French writers, literary critics and historians have thus viewed the novel merely as a way-station on the reactionary and xenophobic English political trajectory as regards the French Revolution, leading from Edmund Burke's *Reflections on the Revolution in France* (1790), through Dickens and the Baroness d'Orczy's *Scarlet Pimpernel* (1903) to the *Citizens* (1989) of Simon Schama.[23]

Certainly, the novel has been poorly served by the French publishing industry, and its print history across the Channel is a sombre record of neglect and misunderstanding, which has justified indifference and encouraged hostile readings.[24] Symptomatically, down to the 1930s there were only two re-editions of Hachette's *Paris et Londres en 1793*, in 1873 and 1881. This compares poorly even with the re-editions of other translations by Henriette Loreau (*A Tale*'s first translator), whose *Bleak House* (1857) has had four re-editions, and Charlotte Brontë's *The Professor* (1858) a surprising six, the most recent in 2001. The dozen or so other translations and adaptations of *A Tale* from 1861 until the present compare very unfavourably with *David Copperfield*, for example, which has managed in excess of 100.[25] Moreover, critics have agreed that the quality of the French adaptations and translations of *A Tale* has tended to be mediocre. This is true of the more popular, boiled-down versions, which are full of misunderstandings and errors.[26] But even Loreau's 1861 translation – which remained the standard version for over a century – is criticized for flattening Dickens's style.[27]

Strikingly, if comically, even the title of *A Tale of Two Cities* has proved a stumbling block.[28] The obvious and literal translation – *Un Conte de deux villes* – was not employed for over a century, until 1970 in fact.[29] The dysphonic effect caused by literal translation (notably over '*de deux*') may be a factor in explaining this reticence; so too the apparently general tendency of nineteenth-century publishers to prefer eponymous titles. The most utilized alternative title has been *Le Marquis de Saint-Évremont*. First employed as a subtitle to re-editions of the 1861 translation, *Paris et Londres en 1793*, it was later boosted by the success in France of the 1935 Hollywood film version of *A Tale of Two Cities*, starring Ronald Colman as Sydney Carton, and discussed in this volume by Charles Barr. This was shown under the title *Le Marquis de Saint-Évremont* and triggered a minor flurry of interest in the novel, leading to print adaptations in 1937 and 1938.[30] Other adaptations have been even more imaginative with their titles: *Un Drame sous la Révolution* (1914); *Le Jour de Gloire* (a 1937 stage version, whose authors, André Bisson and Meg Villars, prided themselves on bringing to the attention of the French public 'an English novel which today is rather forgotten' ['un roman anglais qui est aujourd'hui assez oublié']; and *Espoirs et passions* (1989).[31]

To English ears, the French predilection for *Le Marquis de Saint-Évremont* as a title is bizarre. The Marquis is a minor and hardly heroic character – on the contrary, he is the archetypal melodramatic villain, the wicked uncle of the major protagonist, Charles Darnay. Presumably the reference is to the latter, though as Kamilla Elliott discusses, he renounces it completely and never uses it as a means of self-identification. Moreover, *Le Marquis de Saint-Évremont* promotes Darnay at the expense of Carton, whom most English readers regard as the principal male character around whom the themes of redemptive sacrifice cluster most thickly, as opposed to Darnay, his bland and less interesting French lookalike.

Problems with the novel's title in French are symptomatic of more profound misapprehensions. The novel's events occur over more than two decades, whereas the title of the original translation (*Paris en 1793*) highlights one, albeit climactic, moment. Adaptations of the novel for a young or popular audience have tended to follow this lead and to telescope the events of the 1770s and 1780s into brief chapters or else treat them in flashbacks. Adaptations have also tended to omit Dickens's first chapter and start with 'La Malle-poste' – 'The Mail'.[32] We can be absolutely certain that Dickens attached great importance to his opening chapter and in particular to the famous opening paragraph: 'It was the best of times, it was the worst of times . . . '. In 'The Bastille Prisoner', the highly abbreviated version of *A Tale* which he prepared for public reading – which condensed a 400-page novel into three-quarters of an hour of spoken English – Dickens retained the opening paragraph in its entirety.[33] This omission in French adaptations and translations is thus a major step, as is the decision in some versions to omit altogether Carton's final scaffold speech as well (as in the 1959 translation). To English readers, this appears a perverse, not to say incomprehensible, excision of the work's most memorable lines.

National and international contexts

Because *A Tale* has been so little and so poorly known in France and so cursorily studied in French, it has been easy for French readers to dismiss it out of hand. The tendency has been facilitated by the fact that for many the novel appears to equate French popular political radicalism with terroristic and bloody violence, which is condemned from the allegedly superior vantage point offered by British political gradualism. The novel appeared at what now seems the high-water mark of Victorian political stability and seems to express the political complacency of the era. Dickensian critics have sometimes, perhaps unwittingly, endorsed such a view. Puzzled by the choice of the French Revolution as the theme for this historical novel, Philip Collins observes that 'nothing comparable was happening in England in the middle or late fifties to give topicality to (or to inspire) the crowd scenes in the tale'.[34] Radical opposition to the state had receded from public view since the suppression of the Chartist mass rally on Kennington Common in April 1848, inaugurating what appears to be a phase of stability, an 'age of equipoise', in British politics, in contrast to the French revolutionary tradition which had flared up yet again in Paris in the same year. Moreover, from some angles of vision, *A Tale of Two Cities* appears to be invested in a kind of anti-politics, in which only family and close human interrelationships count in a cosy world on which ideology has no purchase. In such readings, the French Revolution provides a backdrop and an analogue to the personal and domestic revolution in Dickens's biography.

Yet in fact *ex post facto* political readings made across the vista of apparent Victorian stability from the 1850s onwards underestimate the significance of the international context of Dickens's political vision at this time. The 'Indian Mutiny' in 1857 provided a particular point of reference in this respect. As Patrick Brantlinger and others have observed, the lurid representations in the British press of atrocities and bodily violence of the Indian mutineers kept popular violence in the mind of the Victorian reading public.[35] They resonate strongly with the events in *A Tale*. Dickens's savage condemnation of the Indian rebels in his letters – were he Indian Commander-in-Chief, he told Angela Burdett Coutts, 'I should do my utmost to exterminate the Race upon whom the stain of the late cruelties rested'[36] – have been seen partly as fuelled by concern for his son Walter, who at the time of the first reports of the violence was en route to India as a cadet in the East Indian Army, where he fought the revolutionaries at Cawnpore and Lucknow as a member of the 42nd Highlanders.[37] Yet Dickens's fiction tells a more nuanced tale. His Christmas story of December 1857, 'The Perils of Certain English Prisoners', written at the time of his concern for his son and set in a South American mining colony, was a deliberate attempt to express solidarity with Britons in India during this period.[38] Interestingly, as in *The Frozen Deep* and *A Tale of Two Cities*, the story includes a love triangle between a woman and two men, including one Captain Carton (*sic*), the hero of the story, whose rescue of a child thought dead is greeted as the act of a Christian saviour, and prefigures his namesake, Sidney Carton's ultimate act of salvation. As Dickens told Henry Morley, the story concerns a 'set of circumstances . . . in which a few English people – gentlemen, ladies and children – . . . find themselves alone in a strange wild place and liable to hostile attack'.[39] Such a description might pass as a description of the final chapters of *A Tale of Two Cities*, while his added comment that 'I want to shadow out . . . the bravery of our ladies in India' strikes a faintly chivalrous but distinctly Prossian note, especially in the encounter of the English 'wild woman' with the 'tiger' Mme Defarge.[40]

The interpersonal intrigues of *A Tale of Two Cities* are thus foreshadowed in this story, as is Dickens's concern with popular violence. 'The Perils of Certain English Prisoners', however, champions a broader political vision. In particular, Dickens highlights issues of bad government in the person of Commissioner Pordage, whose benevolent but misplaced trust of the Indian population reflects the attitude of Lord Canning, Governor-General of India. The latter had controversially called for clemency to be shown to those Sepoys who had not been actively involved in the Mutiny, yet had shown no concern for British expatriates.[41] Articles in Dickens's *Household Words* around this time buzz with similar concerns, including the belief that a corrupt and neglectful government in India had triggered the uprising in the first place and consequently left British citizens exposed to popular fury.[42]

The political parable that Dickens extracted from the 'Indian Mutiny' – as evident in his journalism, correspondence and, imaginatively, in 'The Perils of Certain English Prisoners' – resonates not only with the nakedly emotive concern over popular violence in *A Tale of Two Cities,* but also with the novel's ideological undertow. A neglectful and uncaring government could spark insurrection. Dickens's anxieties in this respect were, moreover, magnified by the current scene in Europe. Napoleon III's aggressive foreign policy – which prompted invasion scares in the late 1850s – was a particular concern. The French emperor seemed itching to start a policy of European expansion as his uncle had – bad in itself for British interests, but worrying for those who thought in terms of neo-Jacobin ideological contagion reaching these shores. For Dickens, however, French aggression also risked giving the British ruling classes a pretext to put reform on the shelf for a generation or more, as had been the case in the 1790s and 1800s.

As a number of the essays in this volume show, Dickens's anxieties about the possibility of popular violence focused far more than has generally been thought on England than on France, and on the future rather than the past. In Mark Philp's terms, Dickens was as much concerned about the future of the 'bloody English' as the past of the 'bloody French'; the 'violent, brutal disorder and arbitrary justice of the novel's narrative of the past', according to Sally Ledger, act as a warning for the future of British society. For Stedman Jones, Dickens's debts to Carlyle were less connected to the latter's notorious anti-democratic attacks on the Paris mob in his *The French Revolution* than with his quasi-apocalyptic anxiety that the potential for violent rebellion was a universal characteristic of the lower orders. *Sans-culotterie* was not an exclusively French phenomenon; it could be for export, especially in the context of heartless insouciance on the part of the ruling classes. As Stedman Jones notes, by dedicating *A Tale of Two Cities* to Lord John Russell, Dickens highlighted the importance of the reform agenda to which the Liberal statesman subscribed, but which seemed to be missing by the late 1850s.[43] If the ruling classes in England were to fail to respond to social distress, major political turbulence loomed. 'There is nothing in the present time at once so galling and so alarming to me', Dickens wrote in a letter (cited in Bowen's essay) to Austen Layard in 1855, 'as the alienation of the people from their own public affairs ... I believe the discontent to be so much worse for smouldering instead of blazing openly, that it is extremely like the general mind of France before the breaking out of the first Revolution ...'.

Despite an apparently more comic approach to crowd violence in London in *A Tale of Two Cities* – the funeral procession, for example – such representations nevertheless retain, as Sally Ledger shows, many elements of the fearful, visceral quality of Parisian violence as evidenced in the storming of the Bastille and the dancing of the Carmagnole. The depiction of the latter episodes also acts as a reminder of the excesses of London's Gordon Riots of 1780, recounted in lurid detail in Dickens's earlier *Barnaby Rudge.*

In *A Tale*, the violence of class relations is less evidently visible in London than in revolutionary Paris, but nevertheless still exists. Heads might roll in the Place de la Concorde, for example, but the novel acknowledges that similar kinds of retributive violence had taken place in London, its traces vividly etched in the very fabric of the city. Temple Bar, for instance, one of the central London landmarks in *A Tale* and the location of Tellson's bank, was the site on which the heads and limbs of executed rebels had been displayed in the seventeenth and eighteenth centuries. Although the practice had ended in 1746 and the last heads had been blown off the monument by the wind in 1772, this vestige of the 'bloody code' which so exercised legal reformers is directly recalled in the novel.[44] The denizens of Tellson's bank, we are told, were 'but newly released from the horror of being ogled through the windows, by the heads exposed on Temple Bar with an insensate brutality and ferocity worthy of Abyssinia or Ashantee' (II, i, 56). The description is comical, yet it cleverly draws together the bank's business with both the 'insensate brutality and ferocity' of an English *ancien régime* practice of exposing heads on Temple Bar and iconic acts of indigenous revolts against British colonial rule. In the Ashanti wars in western Africa in the 1820s, for instance, the Ashanti king had notoriously drunk from the skull of the British governor. In its management of financial affairs, the bank itself, Dickens tells us, is also responsible for taking lives, for indeed, 'putting to Death was a recipe much in vogue with all trades and professions'; 'so many lives that if the heads laid low before it had been ranged on Temple Bar ... they would probably have excluded what little light the ground floor had' (II, i, 56–7). And, lest the metonymic moral be lost on readers, Tellson's, we are told – 'old-fashioned' and 'the triumphant perfection of inconvenience' – was 'much on a par with the country' (II, i, 55).

Earlier, in 1848, at the heart of the international political crisis caused by serial European revolutions, Dickens had argued powerfully that the original French revolutionaries of 1789 had been pushed into rebellion by appalling social conditions: 'an infamous feudality and a corrupt government had plundered and ground them down year after year until they were reduced to a condition of distress which has no parallel'.[45] The picture he presents of France in 1789 in *A Tale of Two Cities* is of a piece with this vision. If its inspiration seems Carlylean, Philp and Stedman Jones also show the extent to which it was grounded in close and wide reading from the political and social writings of the late eighteenth century. From that reading, Dickens concluded that the originators of revolutionary violence were not the savage and vengeful radicals of the Faubourg Saint-Antoine, but the *ancien régime*'s ruling classes, who had made them what they were. The novel is unequivocal in casting ultimate blame on the French aristocracy, an aspect that Dickens defended against Edward Bulwer-Lytton's criticisms in June 1860.[46] Dickens insisted on the authority of 'the tremendous testimony of men living at the time' rather than 'enquiries and provings by figures' (a suggestive phrase in the context of John Bowen's discussion of the obsession with numbering that we witness in the novel).[47] Such 'tremendous testimony' seemed to demonstrate that the French ruling class had shown shameful neglect towards the 'cold, dirt, sickness, ignorance and want' which were the tutelary deities of the incendiary Faubourg Saint-Antoine and which were responsible for the violence with which the French popular classes protested. The 'poverty, nakedness, hunger, thirst, sickness, misery, oppression and neglect of all kinds' (*TTC*, III, ii, 279) – another of those litanies of abstract nouns of deprivation that reverberate throughout the novel – are ultimately most to blame for the upsurge of bloody violence. Moreover, with heavy, unmistakable irony, the narrator corrects both French *émigrés* in Britain and 'native British orthodoxy,' for whom it was

> too much the way . . . to talk of this terrible Revolution as if it were the one only harvest ever known under the skies that had not been sown – as if nothing had ever been done, or omitted to be done, that had led to it – as if observers of the wretched millions in France, and of the misused and perverted resources that should have made them prosperous had not seen it inevitably coming, years before and had not in plain words recorded what they saw.
>
> (II, xxiv, 246–7)

'British orthodoxy' thus comes to participate in the guilt of the French aristocracy in a generalized picture of blinkered vision and neglect.

The last passage highlights particularly forcefully the extent to which, rather than contrasting the situations in Britain and France, Dickens is concerned to draw a comparison between the two. 'The Grindstone' (II, ii) that whets the blades of the blood-crazed revolutionaries may well stand for a huge machine against which the domesticity of the Manette family and their English are deliberately pitched, but the image has already had a complex trajectory in the novel by this stage. Earlier the sufferings of the people of the Faubourg Saint-Antoine under the *ancien régime* are described as 'a terrible grinding and re-grinding in the mill' (I, v, 32). The same metaphor captures the potential injustices of the English legal system when Dickens describes the attorney-general eagerly rising in court to 'spin the rope, grind the axe and hammer the nails into the scaffold' (II, ii, 67). The machine of society that grinds and mills its people is a familiar part of the literal and metaphorical repertoire of Dickens's fiction. Mangles and millstones are manifestations of it in various novels, as with Mr Jaggers in *Great Expectations*, who seems to Pip to be 'grinding the whole place in a mill'.[48] Grinding the innocent is an English and not merely a French preoccupation.[49] Even Lorry describes himself working for Tellson's bank as part of 'an immense pecuniary Mangle' (I, iv, 26). And indeed the French revolutionaries' grindstone stands outside Tellson's Parisian offices.

Furthermore, if 'British orthodoxy' was blind to the distress of the poor in France, it was equally blind to popular sufferings in Britain. The accusation of neglect chimes loudly with Dickens's analysis of the popular emiseration in Britain, especially in London, and expressed repeatedly in the pages of *Household Words*. 'Cold, dirt, sickness, ignorance and want' were not exclusively part of *le vieux Paris* ('Old Paris'). Dickens was a famous London night-walker, and his quotidian odysseys had taught him that the stigmata of popular misery were all too visible on the streets and backways of Old London. In this prism, *A Tale of Two Cities* is less a complacent celebration of alleged British political superiority – as generations of French readers and many English critics have assumed – than a shrill wake-up call to the English ruling classes.

Paris or London?

It is conceivable, if strange to consider, that Dickens did more research for the scenes of urban poverty set in the Faubourg Saint-Antoine in London's East End than in the Faubourg itself. Though he styled himself a 'superior vagabond' during his stays in Paris,[50] Dickens encamped himself almost wholly on the fashionable north-western boulevards of the city. The furthest east his 'vagabondage' took him was to the theatres of the Boulevard du Temple in the north-east of the city, the more centrally located Palais Royal, where his favourite restaurants were to be found, and – satisfying his taste for the ghoulish which, as Keith Michael Baker suggests, he nurtured at Madame Tussaud's in London – the Paris morgue on the Left Bank. All three locations were half a mile or more from the Faubourg Saint-Antoine in the east of the city. Nothing in his correspondence suggests first-hand knowledge of the poverty of the most destitute parts of Paris. The social distress he knew best was on his doorstep in London's East End, not in Paris's workers' suburbs.

The hypothesis that the sites of the kind of social conditions which instigated popular violence in *A Tale of Two Cities* were modelled on London rather than Paris helps explain the depth of political anxiety which Dickens experienced about his English home. He found London frustrating: it was, he muttered on one occasion, 'a vile place'.[51] The moral he drew from his analysis of the French Revolution was that a cruel or uncaring ruling elite could produce revolution by driving the people into revolt out of desperation. In the late 1850s, that seemed more of a danger in London than in Paris. Furthermore, just as Dickens appears to have based his analysis of violence-producing distress in late eighteenth-century Paris on his empirical observations of the streets of mid-nineteenth-century London, so his recipe for political change in contemporary London was based on his extensive knowledge of contemporary Paris. Whilst Dickens had little cognisance of the Faubourg Saint-Antoine which is the villain of *A Tale of Two Cities*, he knew – and knew really well – the 'New Paris' in process of gestation.

Here life could be agreeably characterized, as Dickens once expressed it, by 'pleasantly breakfasting in the open air in the garden of the Palais Royal or the Tuileries, pleasantly dining in the open air in the Elysian Fields [Champs-Élysées], pleasantly taking my cigar and lemonade in the open air on the Italian boulevards towards the small hours after midnight'.[52]

This beautiful city was indeed *the* 'beautiful city' that poor Sydney Carton foresaw on the scaffold:

> I see a beautiful city and a brilliant people rising from this abyss, and in their struggles to be truly free, in their triumphs and defeats, through long years to come, I see the evil of this time and of the previous time of which this is the natural birth, gradually making expiation for itself and wearing out.
>
> (III, xv, 389)

By placing such prophetic words in Carton's mouth, Dickens seems to signify that the tragic hero predicted the modernization of Paris by Napoleon III's prefect of Paris, Baron Georges Haussmann, as the desired *terminus ad quem* to which the French people would arrive two generations after the concluding guillotine scene.[53] Urban transformation in Paris was already in train before 1853, when Haussmann was appointed, but his coming to power accelerated things mightily and dramatically. Paris was 'wonderfully improving', Dickens could report in 1855 of the realignment programme around the Rue de Rivoli. In November of the same year, *Household Words* published 'Paris Improved', an article by Dickens's collaborator W. H. Wills, which eulogized the changes. New Paris was becoming 'a stone and sculptured paradise'. By the early 1860s he would rhapsodize about the 'astounding new work, doing or done'. Paris was thus a model that London should follow: 'I want to show our ridiculous Corporation how improvements are made in Paris', he noted in the mid-1850s.[54] The main obstacle to reform in London was the complex and diffuse networks of political power that had developed as the city expanded exponentially over time. Unlike in Paris, there was to be no central or unified government until the establishment of London County Council in 1888, almost two decades after Dickens's death.[55] As Dickens notes, the vested interest of the Corporation of the City of London was a particular sticking point against change, especially over attempts by public health reformers to establish an effective and centralized mode of regulation. And Temple Bar, that all-important, yet often unnoticed, landmark in *A Tale*, standing on the boundary between the City of London and the City of Westminster, was a 'symbol of the problems facing the reform and modernization of the metropolis', as Lynda Nead has put it.[56] Accordingly, the 'shabbiness of our English capital' and its administrative and jurisdictional chaos stood in pathetic contrast to Dickens's beloved New Paris, in the throes of transforming itself into the very quintessence of urban modernity.[57]

Dickens and Haussmann in fact shared a secret affinity – and a political target. Certainly, Haussmann's aim was to make Paris comfortable for the French ruling classes (and, incidentally, also attractive to superior foreign 'vagabonds' such as Dickens himself). But urban transformation was predicated on the erasure of the 'cold, dirt, sickness, ignorance and want' of the Faubourg Saint-Antoine and its like, and *a fortiori* on the popular political radicalism it underwrote. Dickens must have found such a parallel mildly discomforting, for the notorious authoritarianism of the 'Alsatian Attila' (as Haussmann was known) was not at all to his taste. It is noticeable – as well as quite remarkable – that Haussmann's name does not appear in the lengthy 1855 article on 'Paris Improved'. Perhaps the turbulent international situation and the Napoleonic threat precluded laudatory comments about French public figures. Yet the English writer could not fail to admire the prefect's efficiency, nor to envy the prophylactic impact on poverty and revolt which his reforms were effecting. A new city was bidding to erase the miasma of urban poverty and discontent which had instigated the French revolutionary tradition. A New London could learn from the example of the New Paris which Sydney Carton had imagined on the scaffold.

The individual and the crowd

The question of urban reform touches on a deeper issue in relation to Dickens's politics. Is his interest in reform more a question of regulating or even disciplining the lower classes or genuinely to do with the idea of their liberation? The influence of Michel Foucault and the New Historicism on recent literary studies means that critics are apt to look with a rather jaundiced eye on these matters and read in Dickens a distinctly 'bourgeois' radicalism more concerned with 'improving' or controlling the masses than with their political consciousness.[58] Yet as Patrick Brantlinger and others have suggested, Dickens often exhibits a populist identification with the people that cuts across familiar political boundaries in complicated ways.[59] Sally Ledger points out the extent to which Dickens's novel appropriates the genres of popular culture, especially political satire and stage melodrama, and thereby situates it more firmly in the traditions of popular radicalism than critics have been minded to remark. Indeed, the notorious critic of trade unions (in *Hard Times*) could also thrill to the power of the crowd. He famously wrote to John Forster about his excited self-identification with the rioters in *Barnaby Rudge*: 'I have let all the prisoners out of Newgate, burnt down Lord Mansfield's, and played the very devil' (*Letters*, II, 385). In *A Tale of Two Cities*, Dickens often recycles Carlylean tropes of the revolution as an oceanic force of nature, expressive of the historical inevitability of the Revolution as the creation of a kind of world spirit. (Dickens's refusal even to mention Robespierre and other revolutionary leaders accords with this principle.) Nevertheless, Dickens does not render the political crowd as a collectivity without individuality. The Revolution has human causes and the reactions of the crowd are given socio-historical origins, personalized in terms of individual narratives.

As John Bowen shows, the relationship between the individual and the group is complex and, moreover, thematically central to *A Tale*. As he argues, the preoccupation with enumeration in this novel about two cities, in three sections, in which people's identities are sometimes reduced to numbers, and in which doubles of various kinds abound, is related to the irresolvable problem presented by the competing claims of individuals within a democracy. (1859 saw the publication of John Stuart Mill's *On Liberty* as well as Dickens's *A Tale of Two Cities*.) Counting, Bowen argues, is presented as a self-protective response to unbearable trauma. The originary trauma of *A Tale* initiating events is the rape and murder of Madame Defarge's sister; but Bowen reads outwards from this to see a more general concern with the 'traumas' of competing claims that are structural to all modern democratic societies. In this reading, Carton's sacrifice, his substitution for Darnay, 'the gift of death', provides a resolution to the novel's wounds. Kamilla Elliott, in contrast, in her equally innovative essay, concludes that the novel – and the sacrifice – offer a more pessimistic take on politics: *A Tale* describes a modern, bourgeois notion of identity, which 'ushers in a perpetual identity theft' and in which the 'crimes of ruling males not only pass unaccounted for, but also figure as innocence and heroism'.

The essays by both Elliott and Bowen highlight the representational strategies of the novel. As Bowen points out, Dickens eschews the techniques of the historical novel established by Sir Walter Scott, and later analysed by Georg Lukács, as the presentation of representative 'types' whose lives bear the burden of historical circumstances. Dickens switches easily between a broad historical canvas and focalization from the points of view of individuals, but these individuals are rarely the 'typical characters under typical circumstances', to use the phrase of Friedrich Engels that inspired Lukács.[60] Instead, he develops a narrative technique which cuts between the actions of the mob and the private dramas of particular individuals. The storming of the Bastille, for instance, is not simply a grand historical set-piece. The whole scenario is focalized around the struggle of Ernest Defarge to discover the secret of Manette's cell (where, significantly, the doctor's dreadful experiences have been reduced to a number, 105 North Tower), and is a key episode in the unfolding of the Defarge family drama. This individualizing impulse has a quasi-cinematic aspect. At the end of this chapter, for example, when we briefly learn of the liberation of the seven figures released from imprisonment in the Bastille, the narrative camera zooms in on their puzzled responses:

> But, in the ocean of faces where every fierce and furious expression was in vivid life, there were two groups of faces – each seven in number – so

fixedly contrasting with the rest, that never did sea roll which bore more memorable wrecks with it.

(II, xxi, 229)

Such close-up effects are a familiar part of Dickens's narrative method and they represent one of the reasons why he has so often been described as a 'cinematic' writer.[61] The idea that Dickens the novelist anticipates much about the cinema has become a cliché, reaching back to Sergei Eisenstein's famous essay (and before him, according to Eisenstein, D.W. Griffith).[62] Although Eisenstein gives most of his attention to *Oliver Twist* and to the use of 'parallel montage sequences' that cut between plot strands, as Charles Barr points out in his essay, the Russian does notice one dissolve at the opening of the final chapter of *A Tale*. Eisenstein's essay takes the view that what is particularly suggestive about Dickens for film-makers is his use of 'viewpoint and exposition'.[63] Immediately after commenting on the dissolve in *A Tale*, Eisenstein exclaims: 'How many such "cinematic" surprises must be hiding in Dickens's pages!' Considering cinematic technique in relation to the novels often reveals aspects of Dickens's writing that are not exploited by film adaptations themselves. Garrett Stewart, for instance, has complained that movies frequently ignore the shared basis of the two media and do not exploit what 'Dickens secretly willed to film', that is, a 'whole new mode of kinetic sequencing in which juxtaposition is submitted to continual synthesis'.[64]

In this regard, it is worth noting the extent to which Dickens uses 'eye' as a verb in *A Tale* – as indeed elsewhere in his writings. People and things are constantly being 'eyed' (as Lorry is 'eyed' by his fellow passengers [I, ii, 11]). Things rarely simply *are*. They are being looked over or looked at from somebody's point of view, often askance and usually not straightforwardly. In *A Tale*, we often cut from a larger point of view – it is tempting to call it an 'historical' perspective – to a closer more individual or domestic perspective, but this does not mean there are two entirely separate narrative strands in the novel. It is not simply a question of the 'mob' versus the personal perspective of the Manette circle nor, as we have suggested, the tempestuous French versus the domestic English.

Even at its most terrible, Dickens's crowd contains human faces and potentially positive human instincts. His use of a kind of proto-close-up technique enables him to open up new narrative worlds, which, while not developed further in terms of plot, offer readers a new viewpoint on events. In *A Tale*, this technique helps to interlace the larger historical canvas with the plot of the novel. The Defarges are the instruments of the Revolution, but they are also playing out the plot of a far more intimate family romance of the kind familiar from the Gothic novel. In the process, the novel dramatizes the fundamental democratic question, discussed by Bowen, of the relationship between individuals, more intimate groups and larger collectivities of 'the people'. The puzzlement on the faces of the mythic seven released from the

Bastille asks precisely the question of the relationship between these individuals and their situation: what have their individual stories to do with these larger changes in human history and the human collectivities they involve? The question also highlights the extent to which Dickens's prefigurative role as regards Eisenstein has a political as well as a cinematic dimension. The Bolshevik film-maker's concern not to allow the masses to lose a sense of individual trajectories finds early exemplification in the liberal-radical perspective of *A Tale of Two Cities*.

As one might expect, this political dimension to Dickens's analysis of the relationship between the individual and the crowd receives only passing and uneven reference in film versions of the novel. Certainly, there is enough in the novel to license counter-revolutionary adaptations, as it has sometimes done, and Dickens retains his appeal to Hollywood and the BBC as part of a culture industry, legitimizing what they do by association with cultural 'tradition' and literary value, as several of the essays here show. Yet some adaptations have also exposed the complex cross-currents of Dickens's view of the French Revolution. Essays in this volume suggest that the 1917 and 1935 films of *A Tale of Two Cities* are not unaware of the problem, and this is partly true even of aspects of the more workmanlike 1958 British adaptation. In the now largely inaccessible 1917 film, close-up does not just bring us 'up close' to individuals, but, as Buchanan and Newhouse suggest, leads us into the unconscious fantasies and dreams of its characters. Charles Barr shows how the 1935 David O. Selznick production sought to exploit the radical potential of the novel, while keeping the studios and censors happy, even smuggling into the movie echoes of Eisenstein's own revolutionary cinema. The visionary conclusion of the novel may suggest to some readers the transcendent authority of the domestic sphere, where Carton's name lives on in the children of the Darnays, but Sidney is also the name of one of England's great republican heroes, Algernon Sidney, continually lionized throughout the eighteenth and nineteenth centuries as a martyr to liberty, as he was in Dickens's own *Child's History of England* (1852–54), and the child Sidney, at the end of *A Tale*, remains caught up in a larger narrative imagined in Carton's prophecy.

The exploration in this volume of *A Tale of Two Cities* and its cultural and political impact thus reveals the extent to which those readings of the novel contriving to make it an icon of British national identity often miss the complexity and subtly deployed force of this haunting novel. The essays which follow offer no single, overarching interpretation. Rather, they examine the variety of responses which the novel and its filmic and theatrical avatars have stimulated. They suggest that the 'anti-revolutionary' and 'anti-French' interpretations of the novel which have contributed to the making of a national symbol sell the novel short – aesthetically, ideologically, culturally, politically. The volume will have succeeded in its aims if readers return with renewed eyes to a landmark text in British cultural history.

Notes

1. For details of the readings, see *Charles Dickens: The Public Readings*, ed. Philip Collins (Oxford: Oxford University Press, 1975). For an extended analysis, see Malcolm Andrews, *Charles Dickens and his Performing Selves: Dickens and the Public Readings* (Oxford: Oxford University Press, 2006).
2. See the discussion in Slater, IV, pp. xi–xxiii.
3. Taylor's adaptation ran from 30 January to 24 March 1860. For details of contemporary reviews, see *Letters*, IX, p. 198, n. 4. See also Joss Marsh's essay in this volume.
4. *Letters*, IX, p. 109, n. 2; but see also James Fitzjames Stephens's famously critical review published in *Saturday Review*, 17 December 1859, in which he writes: 'No popularity can disguise the fact that this is the very lowest of low styles of art', and complains about the novel's reliance on the techniques of popular melodrama. Reprinted in *The Dickens Critics*, ed. George H. Ford and Lauriat Lane Jr (Ithaca, NY: Cornell University Press, 1961), pp. 38–48, 43.
5. See, for instance, Peter Ackroyd, *Dickens* (London: Sinclair-Stevenson, 1990), pp. 807–30; and Michael Slater, *Dickens and Women* (Stanford, CA: Stanford University Press, 1983), pp. 135–62.
6. *Letters*, VIII, p. 577n. The statement was made initially in *The Times,* also in June.
7. On Ternan, see *Dickens and Women*, pp. 202–17, and Claire Tomalin, *The Invisible Woman: The Story of Nelly Ternan and Charles Dickens* (London: Penguin Books, 1991).
8. Slater, *Dickens and Women*, pp. 432, 608n and 700ff. See Wilkie Collins, *The Frozen Deep and other Tales* (London: Hesperus, 2004) and *Under the Management of Charles Dickens: His Production of 'The Frozen Deep'*, ed. R. L. Brannan (Ithaca, NY: Cornell University Press, 1966).
9. See, for example, F. S. Schwartzbach, *Dickens and the City* (London: Athlone, 1979), p. 175. '*A Tale* . . . often appears to be more of a crude personal psychodrama re-enacting the events of 1857–8 than a polished work of art.'
10. See Andrew Sanders, *Charles Dickens* (Oxford: Oxford University Press, 2003), p. 34.
11. For the ways in which the novel oscillates between the private and the political, see Catherine Gallagher, 'The Duplicity of Doubling in *A Tale of Two Cities*', *DSA*, 12 (1983), 125–45.
12. See Linda M. Lewis, 'Madame Defarge as Political Icon in Dickens's *A Tale of Two Cities*', *DSA*, 37 (2007), 31–50, 46: 'I do not say that Madame Defarge is a version of Catherine Dickens, but rather that the involvement of middle-class English women in feminist and political causes [in the 1850s] prompted the outlandish satire [Mrs Pardiggle] in *Bleak House* and that Dickens chose to raise the stakes in his horrible nightmare of Madame Defarge and her female army.'
13. *Letters*, IX, p. 145 and n. 1. Other weekly productions were *The Old Curiosity Shop* and *Barnaby Rudge*. But Dickens preferred a less punishing writing schedule.
14. See also Jeremy Tambling, *Dickens, Violence and the Modern State: Dreams of the Scaffold* (London: Macmillan, 1995), pp. 133–54.
15. The standard account of their relationship remains William Oddie, *Dickens and Carlyle: The Question of Influence* (London: Centenary Press, 1972). The role of popular radical thinking in differentiating Dickens's thought from Carlyle's is a recurrent theme in Sally Ledger, *Dickens and the Popular Radical Imagination* (Cambridge and New York: Cambridge University Press, 2007).

16. *Letters*, III, pp. 399, 502n; VII, pp. 726–7. *The Pickwick Papers* was in translation from as early as 1838. For the impact of Dickens's writings about his 'night walks' in the *Revue britannique* on the poet Gérard Nerval, see Karlheinz Stierle, *La Capitale des signes: Paris et son discours*, trans. Marianne Rocher-Jacquin (Paris: Éditions de la Maison des Sciences de l'homme, 2001), pp. 390ff.
17. See *Letters*, VIII, pp. 39–40.
18. 'This was one of my most ardent wishes in writing it.' For a sympathetic view of the quality of Dickens's French, with specific regard to *Little Dorrit*, see Trey Philpotts, *The Companion to Little Dorrit* (Mountfield: Helm Information, 2003), pp. 506–15.
19. *Letters*, IV, pp. 166–7. It is of a piece with his attacks on Podsnapian English chauvinism and complacency. See, for example, his 'Insularity', *Household Words*, 19 January 1856 (Slater, III, pp. 342–3). Our thanks to David Paroissien for this reference.
20. In passing, the title certainly seems to have baffled the bookbinder who prepared the volume for the shelves of the Bibliothèque Impériale (today's Bibliothèque Nationale de France): the spine reads 'Paris et Londres en 1813'!
21. None of the later works, *A Tale of Two Cities* included, was read publicly in England either. See *Public Readings*. For the reading version of *A Tale*, see Slater, '"The Bastille Prisoner": A Reading Dickens Never Gave', *Études anglaises*, 23 (1970).
22. The 1989 Anglo-French television adaptation, mentioned by Charles Barr in his essay, may be a sign of change.
23. For a recent example of this, see the polemical asides of historian Jean-Noël Jeanneney against 'Anglo-Saxon' dominance of the electronic media relating to the French Revolution in his *Google and the Myth of Universal Knowledge: A View from Europe*, trans. Teresa Lavender Fagan (Chicago and London: University of Chicago Press, 2007), including side-swipes at Dickens, Orczy and Schama; and cf. Jeanneney, 'Quand Google défie l'Europe', *Le Monde*, 24 January 2005, p. 13.
24. For the translation history of the work, we are drawing heavily on the witty, amusing and erudite article (now inevitably outdated) by Anny Sadrin, 'Traductions et adaptations françaises de *A Tale of Two Cities*', in *Charles Dickens et la France. Colloque international de Boulogne-sur-Mer, 3 juin 1978*, ed. Sylvère Monod (Lille: Presses Universitaires de Lille, 1979).
25. The catalogue of the Bibliothèque Nationale de France provides the basis for a comparative study of the popularity of Dickens's works in French.
26. In the 1959 translation, for example, during the epic confrontation between Miss Pross and Mme Defarge, for example, we are told that the former 'leva les poings dans l'attitude d'un boxeur'. Similarly, the upturned cart outside the wineshop in Dickens's Chapter 5 becomes a 'camion'. (Loreau had had 'voiture'.)
27. Translation work was not well paid in the nineteenth century, and, moreover, Loreau was still relatively a debutante in her career. On Dickens's translations, see Floris Delattre, *Dickens et la France. Étude d'une interaction littéraire anglo-française* (Paris, 1927), esp. 38ff; Sylvère Monod, 'Translating Dickens into French', in *Dickens, Europe and the New Worlds*, ed. Anny Sadrin (Basingstoke: Macmillan, 1999), esp. pp. 230–6; and Anny Sadrin, *Dickens ou le roman-théâtre* (Paris: PUF, 1992), esp. pp. 93–4 and 94n. On the same theme, see Pichot's comments on translating *David Copperfield*, cited in Delattre, p. 62.
28. *David Copperfield* had already had some perplexingly cavalier treatment in this respect: it first appeared in French in Pichot's translation in 1851 as *Le Neveu de*

ma tante, resurfacing in a new translation in 1853 as *La Nièce du pêcheur.* Sadrin, 'Traductions et adaptations françaises', p. 6; Sylvère Monod, 'Une curiosité dans l'histoire de la traduction: *Le Neveu de ma tante* d'Amédée Pichot', *Études anglaises,* 4 (1961).

29. *La Petite Dorrit. Un Conte de deux villes,* trans. Jeanne Metifeu-Béjeau, ed. P. Leyris (Paris, 1970).

30. *Le Marquis de Saint-Évremont. Paris et Londres en 1793,* Bibliothèque de la Jeunesse (Paris, 1937); *Le Marquis de Saint-Évremond, illustré de 47 photos,* trans. Mme Tissier de Mallerais (Paris, 1938; revised edn 1959). Note that the latter work placed a 'd' rather than a 't' at the end of Saint-Evrémont. Nearly all translations placed the acute accent on this name in a more comfortably French location.

31. André Bisson and Meg Villars, 'Le Jour de Gloire', *La Petite Illustration,* no. 811. Théâtre, no. 207, 27 February 1937; *Espoirs et passion: un conte de deux villes,* trans. L. Terelli (Paris, 1989). There are two other modern translations which show the eventual triumph of the literal title: *Le* [sic] *Conte des deux villes,* trans. C. Derblum (Monaco, 1989); *Un Conte de deux villes,* trans. E. Bove, intro. Olivier Barot (Paris, 1991).

32. This the case with *Le Marquis de Saint-Évremont,* 1937 and 1938 translations noted above, note 33. But the mailcoach adventure which starts the 1937 translation begins 'c'était un vendredi soir de la fin de novembre en l'an de grâce 1785' [*sic*: not 1775].

33. 'The Bastille Prisoner', in *Charles Dickens: The Public Readings,* pp. 279–94. Only one word was in fact changed in the paragraph – presumably by mistake: 'noisiest' became 'loudest'.

34. Philip Collins, 'A Tale of Two Novels: *A Tale of Two Cities* and *Great Expectations* in Dickens's Career', *DSA,* 2 (1972), 336–52, 344: 'Nothing comparable (to Chartist demonstrations of the 1840s) was happening in the middle of the late fifties, to give topicality to (or to inspire) the crowd scenes in the *Tale*'. See also Hilary Schor, 'Novels of the 1850s: *Hard Times, Little Dorrit* and *A Tale of Two Cities*', in *The Cambridge Companion to Dickens,* ed. John O. Jordan (Cambridge: Cambridge University Press, 2001), pp. 64–77, 73. Both are cited in Deborah Wynne, 'Scenes of "Incredible Outrage": Dickens, Ireland, and *A Tale of Two Cities*', *DSA,* 37 (2006), 51–64. Wynne argues that the crowd in *A Tale* is modelled on Protestant revivalists whom Dickens may have encountered in Belfast.

35. Patrick Brantlinger, *Rule of Darkness: British Literature and Imperialism, 1830–1914* (Ithaca, NY and London: Cornell University Press, 1988), pp. 199–227; William Oddie, 'Dickens and the Indian Mutiny', *Dickensian,* 69 (1972), 3–17; and Grace Moore, *Dickens and Empire: Discourses of Class, Race and Colonialism in the Works of Charles Dickens* (Aldershot: Ashgate, 2004). On the representations of violence in the accounts of the Mutiny, see Jenny Sharpe, *Allegories of Empire: The Figure of Woman in the Colonial Text* (Minneapolis, MN: University of Minnesota Press, 1993), pp. 57–85.

36. *Letters,* VIII, p. 459: phrases more or less repeated to Emile de La Rue shortly afterwards (p. 473). Moore balances these expressions by pointing out the more nuanced responses published in *Household Words* under Dickens's direction. See Moore, p. 108.

37. Dick Kooiman, 'The Short Career of Walter Dickens in India', *Dickensian,* 98 (2002), 14–28.

38. See Dickens to Henry Morley, 18 October 1857, *Letters,* VIII, pp. 468–9.

39. Dickens to Henry Morley, 18 October 1857, *Letters,* VIII, p. 469.

40. Dickens to Henry Morley, 18 October 1857, *Letters*, VIII, p. 469. See, for example, Moore, p. 141 and passim on Madame Defarge's 'orientalism'. Moore offers Ulricka Wheeler, the British heroine dubbed the 'Judith of Cawnpore', as a possible model for Miss Pross.

41. Dickens to Emile De La Rue, 23 October 1857, *Letters*, VIII, pp. 472–3.

42. Such views were widely held at the time, and even expressed in Parliament in July 1858 by Disraeli, then Chancellor of the Exchequer. See Moore, pp. 135–6. They are not in fact far removed from Dickens's notorious attacks on liberal reactions to the Governor Eyre controversy of 1865.

43. Since June 1859 Russell had been Secretary of State for Foreign Affairs. Dickens's political vision thus took cognisance of the delicate relationship between national and international affairs.

44. In the words of an anonymous commentator in 1853, Temple Bar constituted 'an enduring record of the power of the crown, and of the passions of the people – a memorial of a period, when, to insure the security of the throne, the terrors of the law were alone relied upon, and humanity and compassion for human imperfection constituted no part of the criminal jurisprudence of the country'. *Temple Bar: the City Golgatha by a member of the Middle Temple* (1853), p. 1. Subsequent references in the text. Tellson's was actually modelled on Child's Bank, which occupied 1 Fleet Street, and used storage space in Temple Bar, which was located in the road opposite the main door of the bank.

45. Charles Dickens, 'Judicial Special Pleading', repr. Slater, II, pp. 137–42 (p. 140).

46. *Letters*, IX, pp. 258–60.

47. *Letters*, IX, p. 259.

48. Charles Dickens, *Great Expectations* (London: Penguin Books, 1996), ed. Charlotte Mitchell, intro. David Trotter, p. 202.

49. The novel does not fit easily, therefore, into the 'French theory' versus 'English common sense' critical paradigm that David Simpson has so brilliantly traced back to the anti-revolutionary rhetoric of the 1790s in his *Romanticism, Nationalism, and the Revolt against Theory* (Chicago: University of Chicago Press, 1993). Strangely, Simpson does not discuss *A Tale*, even though he does give some consideration of the issue beyond the Romantic period.

50. *Letters*, VII, p. 742.

51. *Letters*, VI, p. 287.

52. Charles Dickens, 'A Little Dinner in an Hour', *All the Year Round*, 2 January 1869, repr. Slater, IV, pp. 364–70, p. 365. See Michael Hollington, 'Dickens, *Household Words* and the Paris boulevards', in Sadrin, *Dickens, Europe and the New Worlds*.

53. For an overview of Haussmannization, see Colin Jones, *Paris: Biography of a City* (London: Penguin Books, 2004), esp. ch. 9; and the classic text of Walter Benjamin, *The Arcades Project*, trans. Howard Eiland and Kevin McLaughlin (Cambridge, MA: The Belknap Press of Harvard University Press, 1999).

54. [W. H. Wills], 'Paris Improved', *Household Words*, 12 (November 1855), pp. 295, 304; *Letters*, VII, pp. 163, 695, and X, p. 151.

55. Roy Porter, *London: A Social History* (London: Hamish Hamilton, 1994), chs. 10 and 11.

56. Lynda Nead, *Victorian Babylon: People, Streets, and Images in Nineteenth-Century London* (New Haven, CT: Yale University Press, 2000), p. 203.

57. Slater, IV, p. 279.

58. The by now classic account of Dickens as an agent of disciplinary culture is D. A. Miller's *The Novel and the Police* (Berkeley, CA, and London: University of California Press, 1988).

59. Patrick Brantlinger, 'Did Dickens Have a Philosophy of History? The Case of *Barnaby Rudge*', *DSA*, 30 (2001), 59–74. Brantlinger underscores this aspect of Dickens's politics by referring to it as 'grotesque populism' (p. 62), deliberately distancing himself from Bagehot's description of Dickens as a 'sentimental radical'.
60. Frederick Engels, Letter to Margaret Harkness, April 1888. www.marxists.org/archive/marx/works/1888/letters/88_04_15.htm [accessed 15 February 2008].
61. The fullest discussion of this issue is to be found in Grahame Smith's *Dickens and the Dream of Cinema* (Manchester and New York: Manchester University Press, 2003). See also *Dickens on Screen*, ed. John Glavin (Cambridge: Cambridge University Press, 2003).
62. Sergei Eisenstein, 'Dickens, Griffith, and the Film Today', in *Film Form*, ed. and trans. Jay Leyda (New York: Harcourt, Brace, 1949, repr. 1977).
63. See Eisenstein, pp. 195–255.
64. Garrett Stewart, 'Dickens, Eisenstein, Film', in Glavin, *Dickens on Screen*, pp. 122–44 (p. 122).

2
The New Philosophy: The Substance and the Shadow in *A Tale of Two Cities*

Mark Philp

How does Dickens understand the events of the French Revolution? Given that the events are so much contested ground, such that what happens, and how and why it happens, are melded into often starkly contrasting and deeply ideologically inflected interpretations of the period, we should not think that Dickens's position is likely to be either simple or naive.

Understandably, there is a tendency to contextualise Dickens by referring to Thomas Carlyle's politically conservative account, since Dickens himself signals his respect for *The French Revolution* (1837) in his Preface and signs of his indebtedness to Carlyle are evident in his correspondence. But this does not mean that this is the only historical source or the dominant interpretative and literary lens through which Dickens viewed the Revolution. Another way of reading *A Tale of Two Cities*, which depends less on Carlyle, recognizes a wider range of influence at work and takes Dickens's own sympathies and leanings more seriously. Through such a reading, France becomes less an exceptional case and more merely another example of a corrupt monarchical and aristocratic regime; less too an attack on the bloodthirsty French, more an assault on bloody privilege. If we see the focus of the work as being relations of privilege and subordination, of power and domination against impoverished weakness and sullen resentment, and treat the particular historical setting as the background for that more fundamental theme, then *A Tale of Two Cities* can be read as a sympathetic representation of the 'new philosophy' of the late eighteenth century and of its critique of power and privilege.

That 'new philosophy' – which was 'the talk of the salons and the slang of the hour' – ought not to be associated solely with the French Enlightenment *philosophes* and their associated coteries, even if they played a major part initially in spawning it.[1] Although Dickens shares some of Carlyle's and the social commentator Louis-Sébastien Mercier's cynicism towards the pretensions of French cultural and intellectual life,[2] at the same time he articulates a critique of manners which is no great distance from Jean-Jacques Rousseau's *Discourses* and which is in direct sympathy with Dr Manette's and Charles Darnay's sense of the world and of their stoic reasonableness in facing its demands. Both, in different ways, may be taken as exemplifying a change in eighteenth-century manners that is sympathetic to aspects of enlightenment thinking but that issues in a more practical attitude and orientation to the world and those they encounter.[3] Their view is one of fundamental decency, coupled with an application of reason and common sense to the impositions of the aristocratic and monarchical orders of Europe. That critical reflection issues in a moralism among the middling orders that repudiates the libertinism of the rich, and looks to aid, comfort, enlighten and reform the experiences of those less well placed. Their 'new philosophy' widely evident in English liberal circles at the outbreak of the Revolution certainly marshals Dickens's sympathy; indeed, he is very much a product of it.

Just as this new philosophy is wider than any country, so too do Dickens's concerns in the book assume a wider view. The book is called *A Tale of Two Cities*, and while Paris overshadows the presence of London, London has a crucial importance. Moreover, there is a third player in the background: America. Dickens consciously situates the action in a triangle, between the oppressive history of France *and* the oppressive history of England, with the example of America as an independent and free republic ready to hand. This triangle encapsulates the struggle between the old orders of Europe and the new philosophy, one central part of which was the 'Revolution controversy' of the 1790s over how to understand – and evaluate – the opening stages of the French Revolution. In this essay I want to show the extent to which Dickens's *Tale of Two Cities* intentionally reproduces the themes of the new philosophy and its critique of privilege, and in doing so substantially echoes the reformist perspectives of the controversy. Moreover, in this way the text is left with a very similar set of difficulties to those faced by supporters of reform in the mid- and late 1790s – difficulties that influence also the shape of middle-class radicalism in the nineteenth century.

I

The novel's action opens on the eve of the American Revolution (1775): 'Mere messages in the earthly order of events had lately come to the English Crown and People, from a congress of British subjects in America: which, strange to relate, have proved more important to the human race than any communications yet received through any of the chickens of the Cock-lane brood' (I, i, 5–6). Darnay is tried on suspicion of treason, where the treason relates to the provision of information to 'Lewis, the French King' concerning 'what forces our [King] had in preparation to send to Canada and North America' (II, ii, 66). The focus is on French aid to the American Revolutionists, and the emphasis of the chapter is on the draconian character of the law of treason (had it been a lesser offence the fascination for the crowd would have been proportionally reduced) and the use of spies by the British government (and, it later transpires, the capacity of the French state to manipulate the British government into the prosecution and destruction of its enemies). If America plays little part in the subsequent unfolding of events, it reappears as a reminder in Manette's defence of Darnay, 'tried for his life as the foe of England and the friend of America' (III, vi, 295). The implicit link between America and France and England is equally a feature of the opening debate on France, notably in the suggestion, which runs throughout the reporting of the initial stages of the Revolution, that France has been brought to this pitch because of the contagion of American republicanism or, more commonly, because the costs of the war have produced the fiscal crisis that resulted in the calling of the Estates General. The link also featured in the millenarian enthusiasm which yokes the two revolutions together, as in Richard Price's *Discourse on the Love of Our Country* (1789):

> After sharing in the benefits of one Revolution, I have been spared to be a witness to two other Revolutions, both glorious. And now, methinks, I see the ardour for liberty catching and spreading, a general amendment beginning in human affairs, the dominion of kings changed for the dominion of laws, and the dominion of priests giving way to the dominion of reason and conscience. . . . Behold, the light you have struck, after setting America free, reflected to France and there kindled into a blaze that lays despotism in ashes and warms and illuminates Europe.[4]

The echoes are not accidental. Dickens is fully aware of the extent to which the fortunes of the three nations were seen as connected. We need to understand much of the rest of the work as inflected with this understanding, so that his portrayal of France is not innocent of his portrayal of England, and neither is untouched by the implicit counterfactual of American liberty. This is clear from the way he understands the initial events of the French Revolution in July 1789, which might be characterized as follows:

> four or five persons were seized by the populace, and instantly put to death; the Governor of the Bastille, and the Mayor of Paris, who was detected in the act of betraying them; and afterwards Foulon, one of the new ministry, and Berthier his son-in law, who accepted the office of Intendant of Paris. Their heads were stuck upon spikes, and carried about the city . . . Let us then examine how men came by the idea of punishing in this manner.
> They learn it from the governments they live under, and retaliate the punishments they have been accustomed to behold. The heads stuck upon spikes, which remained for years in Temple-bar, differed nothing in the horror of the scene from those carried about upon spikes at Paris: yet this was done by the English government . . . *Lay then the axe to the root, and*

teach governments humanity. It is their sanguinary punishments which corrupt
mankind . . . by the base and false idea of governing men by terror, instead of
reason, they become precedents.[5]

This view does not come from Carlyle. Indeed, Carlyle's reading of these
summary executions is quite different, generating a set of comments that sit
somewhat uncomfortably alongside Dickens's account of events (see *TTC*, II,
xxii, 233–4):

> Surely if Revenge is a 'kind of justice,' it is a 'wild' kind! O mad Sans-
> culottism, hast thou risen, in thy mad darkness, in thy soot and rags;
> unexpectedly like an Enceladus, living-buried, from under his Trinacria?
> They that would make grass be eaten do now eat grass, in *this* manner?
> After long dumb groaning generations, has the turn suddenly become
> thine? – To such abysmal overturns, and frightful instantaneous inversions
> of the centre of gravity, are human Solecisms all liable, if they but knew
> it; the more liable, the falser (and top heavier) they are![6]

For all that Dickens suggests in his Preface to *A Tale* that 'no one can hope
to add anything to the philosophy of Mr. CARLYLE'S wonderful book', it
seems clear that he is not operating with Carlyle's philosophy and that he
has a more rational and sympathetic account of a number of its principal
events. This is partly because Carlyle is far from being Dickens's only source.
Dickens's essays 'Judicial Special Pleading' (1848) and 'A Flight' (1851) both
show evidence of the influence of Adolphe Thiers's *History of the French Revolu-*
tion (translated in 1838), which Dickens read and which certainly influenced
his judgement. Thiers's view that the opening violence of events in France
had to be understood as a legitimate response to oppression was echoed in
A Tale of Two Cities. 'It was a struggle on the part of the people for social
recognition and existence', Dickens wrote. 'It was a struggle for vengeance
against intolerable oppressors. It was a struggle for the overthrow of a system
of oppression, which in its contempt for all humanity, decency, and natural
rights, and in its systematic degradation of the people, had trained them to
be the demons that they showed themselves, when they rose up and cast it
down for ever.'[7] The harvest that is reaped has sometimes been sown;[8] or as
he puts it in conclusion to *A Tale of Two Cities*, 'Crush humanity out of shape
once more, under similar hammers, and it will twist itself into the same
tortured forms' (III, xv, 385). Interestingly, however, Thiers's work, unlike
Carlyle's, is almost free of commentary of this type; indeed, so much of it
is a narrative of events that it is not easy to see Dickens using it as a source
of interpretation – perhaps not least because the first English edition added
a number of footnotes from more sanguinary and less sympathetic sources,
such as Archibald Alison's *History of Europe at the Time of the French Revolution*
(1833).

In part Dickens's interpretation differs because he is not thinking solely of the bloody French. 'Judicial Special Pleading' is directed against Sir Edward Hall Alderson, the judge presiding over the trials of Chartists in 1848, who claimed in his opening remarks that the people in the French Revolution were far worse off after the event than before. Dickens's message is that the British judicial system simply cannot hope to maintain its sway by fraudulent claims such as these: 'The grade of education and intellect [the Chartist agitators] address is particularly prone to accept a brick as a specimen of a house; and its ready conclusion from such an exposition is, that the whole system which rules and restrains it is a falsehood and a cheat.'[9]

The implicit parallels between France and England are central to the action in *A Tale of Two Cities*. Beyond the calm of the Manette household, not far from Soho Square, as Mr Lorry visits Miss Pross, 'hundreds of footsteps' reverberate in the night (II, vi, 95–108) – echoes of the Gordon Riots (footsteps that are then re-echoed in the novel on the nights of July 1789 [II, xxi, 218]). This parallel had already been drawn:

> There is in all European countries, a large class of people of that description which in England is called the '*mob*'. Of this class were those who committed the burnings and devastations in London in 1780, and of this class were those who carried the heads upon spikes in Paris . . . How is it then that such vast classes of mankind as are distinguished by the appellation of the vulgar, or the ignorant mob, are so numerous in all old countries? The instant we ask ourselves this question, reflection feels an answer. They arise, as an unavoidable consequence, out of the ill construction of all old governments in Europe, England included with the rest. It is by distortingly exalting some men, that others are morally debased, til the whole is out of nature. A vast mass of mankind are degradedly thrown into the background of the human picture, to bring forward with greater glare the puppet-show of state and aristocracy. . . . These outrages are not the effect of the principles of the Revolution, but of the degraded mind that existed before the Revolution . . .[10]

Dickens's explanation for the violence in France is essentially of this character. The system before the Revolution was one of brutal monarchical rule, aristocratic tyranny and priestly indulgence and fraud, which by its inhumanity and intransigence oppressed the people, deprived them of the means of living, and drove them to the point of demented fury. Once so bent and broken, the cracks that then appeared in the imposing edifice of the state inevitably became channels for the expression of people's grievances. That elemental response and reaction on occasion break into a rhythm and a pulse of their own – as in the summary justice meted out to Foulon and Berthier (II, xxii, 232–5) during the September Massacres (III, ii, 271–4) and in the madness of the Carmagnole (III, v, 288–9). Yet in contrast to Carlyle, these moments of irrationalism do not, in Dickens, become the animating force of a revolutionary process that comes completely to override individual wills and individual actions. The forces that drive the multiple, enumerated Jacques are not at all mysterious; they are rooted in the tyrannies of the old order. 'Sow the same seeds of rapacious license and oppression over again, and it will surely yield the same fruit according to its kind' (III, xv, 385). Indeed, the entire plot is an expression of – a working out of – the outrages of the old order, drawing into its path first Manette and then Darnay. This explanation is cogent and simple – revenge for the miseries inflicted and endured by those who are so brutalized by their conditions that they come to lack a capacity to feel for the humanity of their victims (although M. Defarge wobbles slightly on this),[11] just as their tormentors lacked the capacity to see them and treat them as human.

That understanding of French revolutionary violence is hardly original to Dickens – but nor is it something he simply absorbs from Thiers's *History*. And while he may have found some comfort in the view from Carlyle, Carlyle's is an altogether darker picture (G. K. Chesterton writes that in Carlyle's text 'we have . . . a curious sense that everything is happening at night. In Dickens even massacre happens by daylight').[12] Dickens has a perspective on French events that others have had, but it is not one he is drawing wholly from contemporary historians, and it is one that encompasses reflection on parallel British institutions and practices and that emphasizes the link with the American Revolution.

Indeed, if one wants to find strong parallels between Dickens's views and those of others, one need look less at those who adopt a *post-hoc* reflection on events courtesy of historical distance and more at individuals who reacted to events at the time, whose concerns he echoes. This is not a criticism of Dickens; rather, it is to recognize that he identifies himself with that part of the 'new philosophy' that he associates in the novel with a new groundswell of enlightened opinion, which animated the opening stages of the Revolution in France and was a profound influence on many of those who greeted it in Britain. That philosophy involves an essential egalitarianism and humanitarianism and an understanding that there are certain fundamental features of human beings that demand respect, since without it they can be ruled only by force and fraud. It issues in claims for fundamental rights, but equally in demands for general standards of justice in the management of government and in the assignment of benefits and burdens. It has an implicit populist edge in that it sees the people as capable of enlightenment and reason when not subjected to imposture or ground down by brutality. Moreover, this new philosophy is not just the product of France, nor is it identified wholly with that articulated by the *philosophes*, whom Dickens himself criticizes and whom Edmund Burke casts as the schemers against an order that demands our submission to necessity, without which 'the law is broken, nature is disobeyed, and the rebellious are outlawed, cast forth and exiled, from this world of reason, and order, and peace, and virtue, and fruitful penitence, into the antagonist world of madness, discord, vice, confusion and unavailing sorrow'.[13] It is equally the philosophy of America (as Dickens signals). Indeed, it is not unconnected with the fact that there are very strong links between the early constitutionalist and liberal wing of the French Revolution and the American revolutionists (most notably, but by no means exclusively, through the Marquis de Lafayette, Thomas Jefferson and Thomas Paine) and with the philosophy of those in Britain who responded warmly to the opening stages of the French Revolution, who had been opposed to the war against America and who sought a reform of the franchise and electoral abuses in the House of Commons through the reform societies of the early 1780s and 1790s.

Dickens is clear that this is a philosophy for the British – one that many in England aspire to (although that is clearer in *Barnaby Rudge* than in *A Tale of Two Cities*) and that helps us to comprehend the potential impact of the brutalities of the old regime in England. Thus Dickens meditates on the transition from the heads modelled on spikes and visible through the windows of the Barmecide Room of Tellson's – itself responsible for so many heads that, had they not been privately disposed of would have blocked the light from the ground floor – to a more civilized age (II, i, 56). Moreover, Dickens's narrative voice commits him to this philosophy and against those, like Burke, who refuse to see the justice of the cause of reform: 'it was much too much the way of native British orthodoxy, to talk of this terrible revolution as if it were the one only harvest ever known under the skies that had not been sown – as if nothing had ever been done, or omitted to be done, that had led to it – as if observers of the wretched millions in France . . . had not seen it inevitably coming, years before' (II, xxiv, 246–7). And, as we have seen, when he challenges other readings of France he does so in the context of the rise of Chartism and its physical force advocates – not to support them, but to worry that the judicial system is providing them with the same ammunition of grievance through imposture as mobilized the French in 1789.[14] This sympathy is equally strong in his 'The Fine Old English Gentleman' (1841),[15] which is specifically directed against the repression of the 1790s:

> The good old times for cutting throats that cried out in their need,
> The good old times for hunting men who held their fathers' creed,
> The good old times when *William Pitt*, as all good men agreed,
> Came down direct from Paradise at more than railroad speed . . .
>
>
> In those rare days, the press was seldom known to snarl or bark,
> But sweetly sang of men in pow'r, like any tuneful lark;
> Grave judges, too, to all their evil deeds were in the dark;
> And not a man in twenty score knew how to make his mark. . . .

Those were the days for taxes, and for war's infernal din;
For scarcity of bread, that fine old dowagers might win;
For shutting men of letters up, through iron bars to grin,
Because they didn't think the Prince was altogether thin ... [16]

For Dickens, then, Britain in the 1790s is part of his context for understanding events in France. Not only is he aware of the repression that Pitt unleashed, I would suggest that he is also alert to the Revolution controversy that the opening events in France sparked, and is fully cognisant of the position of those who greeted events in France and looked for signs of change at home.

The two long quotations I have used to summarize Dickens's position are from the first part of Thomas Paine's *Rights of Man* (1791). That text is Paine's counter to Burke's *Reflections*, and, as in a number of other such replies, a part of the case is that Burke mischaracterizes the narrative of events, turning occasional episodes of violence in response to oppression into a story of wild and licentious anarchy. The first part of *Rights of Man* has been interpreted as a Fayettist tract, dramatically less democratic and radical than the second part issued a year later. [17] That reading is certainly plausible in that the first part does seem to evince a more traditional, liberal-constitutionalist doctrine, and it is more concerned with presenting the reasonableness of the French process. But it is far less clear how far this is a rhetorical ploy on Paine's part, masking his more democratic principles so as to render his text more plausible and acceptable to his English readership, as against expressing his real commitments. It is true that in the opening pages of the second part Paine turns away from Lafayette, but he does so as Lafayette himself moves away from the Revolution and its republican possibilities. The more central development in part two is Paine's own turning away from the details of French affairs to allow him to develop his conviction that the American experience can provide an example and method for the reform of the corrupt monarchies of Europe. But, from the point of view of Dickens, and from the point of view of the generality of English readings of the opening bouts of revolutionary violence in France, whether Paine really meant what he wrote in the first part of *Rights of Man* is less relevant than that he wrote it, that it chimed to a considerable degree with the response of other sympathizers with France, and that it offered its readers (including, plausibly, Dickens) a way of reading French events that countered the reactionary denunciation of Burke and the loyalist presses. By 1792–3, the growing sense of the depth of ideological divisions encouraged Paine to look for a more radical response from his English audience, and further polarized a controversy that was becoming a battle over reform in Britain. But what Paine provides in his opening salvo, and what Dickens would certainly have recognized in his account, is a powerful and seminal statement that lays at the door of the aristocratic orders of Europe the evils of populist violence. That statement is echoed in Dickens's portrait of the Marquis's philosophy: 'Repression is the only lasting philosophy.

The dark deference of fear and slavery, my friend...will keep the dogs obedient to the whip, as long as this roof...shuts out the sky' (II, ix, 128).

The parallel between Dickens and Paine is important. The position that underlies Dickens's interpretation of events in France also informed many reformist responses to Burke's *Reflections*. (The suggestion that there is much difference between James Mackintosh and Paine on this is not, I think, wholly tenable.)[18] But that position took a beating in subsequent years and did so in large part because events in France were seen as spiralling out of control, resulting in a Jacobin bloodbath, making it harder to present the violence as an initial and short-lived reflexive urge for retribution. At the same time, in Britain, the loyalist reaction against reformers and sympathizers with France caricatured their position as excusing, and thereby condoning, welcoming and inciting, the extremes of revolutionary violence. That meant that those who in the opening years had sympathized with France and welcomed the change in the political order subsequently found themselves accorded responsibility for the bloodbath of the September Massacres, the execution of the king and the Terror. Moreover, it was their 'new philosophy' or 'new morality'[19] that was increasingly pilloried for unleashing the most monstrous of impositions and the most fatal of errors on the population. Indeed, as described by the complacent loyalist Stryver, they are 'infected by the most pestilent and blasphemous code of devilry that ever was known' (II, xxiv, 248). And just as Darnay finds it impossible to confront Stryver and challenge the falsehoods he is spreading (conscious as he is of having left his responsibilities in France to what are now agreed to be the mercies of the 'ruffian herd'),[20] so too many of those in the 1790s found themselves effectively silenced, not by the reasonableness of their opponents, but by the closing down of reasonable debate through wild exaggeration, reaction and prosecution. Effectively, the dispute over the understanding of events in France became a dispute over the principles of the new philosophy and their 'effects', and in that dispute, as loyalism becomes ascendant, backed firmly by local magistrates and the sanction of the law, those principles are increasingly distorted, traduced, and attributed responsibility for events in ways that forestall a reasonable defence. The new philosophy is portrayed as a commitment to reason so abstract that it loses contact with the substance of human life until it turns back upon it and consumes it. Indeed, so polarized does the debate on France become that the attribution of rationality, purpose and justification to those acting in France is tantamount to sedition – and those who espouse the new philosophy, who recognize this rationality and see the parallels in England, are increasingly driven, either to silence or to see in the prevailing order a more tyrannical design that justifies more practical and potentially fatal resistance.

What is surprising about Dickens's novel to someone steeped in 1790s England is that it charts a path – both tells a story and gives an account of the forces that lie behind that story – that, after 1792, becomes unavowable for many of those English reformers who initially responded so warmly to events in France, as the scene in Telson's bank when Darnay collects the letter for Evrémonde exemplifies. Dickens, as we have seen in his concerns about Chartism, is far from being a revolutionary enthusiast, but he has, as did many of those who welcomed the changes, a sense of where the Revolution came from and a sense of the forces that drove it. He acknowledges that it is difficult to prevent the old order from reaping its own whirlwind – 'the sense of being oppressed, bursting forth like fire' (III, x, 337)[21] – a whirlwind that Britain's practices and institutions, by implication, might equally have sown – and indeed could be seen as having done in 1780. That sense of France, and the corresponding sense of England's situation, becomes denounced as Jacobinism, the infection of French principles, the tincture of the new philosophy. Dickens drinks pretty deep in this philosophy. Even the Church receives a Painite reading with its rejection arising 'from years of priestly imposters, plunderers, and profligates' (III, ix, 326).

Nor should we think that Dickens is merely taking the obvious and reasonable view. It seems clear, for example, that one of his sources was Arthur Young's *Travels in France during the years 1787, 1788, 1789* (1792).[22] Although Dickens's editor suggests that Mercier is the source for the story of the child being killed by the coach dashing through the narrow Parisian streets, Young offers an essentially similar picture:

> The coaches are numerous and, what are much worse, there are an infinity of one-horse cabriolets, which are driven by young men of fashion and their imitators, alike fools, with such rapidity as to be real nuisances, and render the streets exceedingly dangerous...I saw a poor child run over and probably killed, and have myself been many times blackened with the mud of the kennels...[23]

But when Young comes to talk of the opening events of the Revolution his is a much more anxious judgement than Dickens's or of many who responded to Burke:

> He who chooses to be served by slaves, and by ill-treated slaves, must know that he holds both his property and his life by a tenure far different from those who prefer the service of well treated freemen; and he who dines to the music of groaning sufferers, must not in the moment of insurrection, complain that his daughters are ravished, and then destroyed; and that his sons throats are cut. When such evils happen, they surely are more imputable to the tyranny of the master, than to the cruelty of the servant.... The excesses of the people cannot...be justified; it would undoubtedly have done them credit, both as men and Christians, if they had possessed their new acquired power with moderation. But let it be remembered, that the populace of no country ever use power with

moderation; excess is inherent in their aggregate constitution: and as every government in the world knows, that violence infallibly attends power in such hands, it is doubly bound in common sense, and for common safety, so to conduct itself, that the people may not find an interest in public confusions.[24]

Young sits uncomfortably on what quickly becomes a fence dividing those responding to France, at once compassionate and sharing Dickens's sense of the plight of the people and yet fearful of the populace, resistant to political innovation (as against turning to England for an example), and very much a supporter of order. His *Example of France a Warning to England* (1793) moves him firmly off that fence and into the loyalist camp. In 1792, when the *Travels* were published, what separated Young from Paine was Paine's enthusiasm for the larger process and for the principles that he took to underlie these events. What separates Dickens from Young is a weaker version of both points – a sense that the seeds of these events have been sown and that the principles that should underlie the political and social order are those of right and equity, fairness and justice.

That Dickens's reading of events bears this resemblance to Paine's in 1791 raises the obvious question of how far he may have drawn from Paine's work. He expressly mentions as influences Carlyle and Louis-Sébastien Mercier's *Tableau de Paris* (published 1782–8). Paine certainly met Mercier, definitely by 1801, but he may also have known him through Thomas Holcroft in London before 1792, and they both became deputies to the National Convention in 1792.[25] Moreover, Dickens tells John Forster in May 1860 that, when working on the book, he 'read no books but such as had the air of the time in them' (*Letters*, IX, 245), which suggests he may well have gone back to the pamphlet literature of the 1790s (as he went back to the periodicals of the time, such as the *Annual Review* and possibly *Gentleman's Magazine*, even though their take on events is strikingly less sympathetic than his). And in going back to that literature it would have been impossible to ignore the conflict between Burke and Paine.

II

For all the parallels with the early readings of events in France we might nonetheless think that Dickens has little in common with the more speculative side of the new philosophy, either in its Paineite cult of individual rights or in its Godwinian aspirations for political justice and impartiality. Indeed, we might think of Dickens as part of the critique of abstract reason, through his sentimental radicalism, centred on the family relations of Darnay and Lucie and their family, and in that sense, and in very sharp contrast to Godwinism and the new philosophy, essentially centred on private affections.[26] But that interpretation of his position does not withstand closer scrutiny.

In Dickens's novel the family is a nightmare as well as a refuge. Darnay repudiates his family, while Mme Defarge, as we discover, is the real zealot for family feeling – revenging the deaths of her parents and brother and sister to the full. Manette, in contrast, accepts Darnay/Evrémonde as his son-in-law, thus overriding the ties of family and particularity in favour of a wider value of humanity and the right of each generation to make its own destiny (Paine's 'Every age and generation must be as free to act for itself, *in all cases*, as the ages and generations which preceded it'[27]). Carton's sacrifice is, of course, partly for love and redemption, yet it is also partly the ultimate sacrifice for justice – a justice that demands a terrible price because of the weight of history that drives events forward, but that realizes a higher value and truth. His substitution is a truly Godwinian moment,[28] albeit not exactly in keeping with Godwin's principle of sincerity (although, interestingly, it is not something that Godwin ever realizes in his own novels as these focus resolutely on the way that the flawed understandings and misapprehensions of his protagonists generate disaster).

For Dickens, the bloody French are not dramatically different from the bloody English. Out of these national histories spin cycles of oppression and resistance, together with the occasional isolated individual who breaks out – albeit rarely completely, but who then has no natural connections. Indeed, the connections they have are almost unnatural: we do not know quite what Darnay's mother requires of him, but it does not seem that his connection with Manette is based on any knowledge of the ties that secretly bind them, but the Marquis does take active pleasure in his knowledge of that relationship – 'a Doctor with a daughter. Yes. So commences the new philosophy' (II, ix, 131) – as if he sees the superb irony of locking up the father and subsequently being in a position to bed the daughter by proxy – history repeating itself. Pross and Barsad are an unnatural pair of siblings; indeed, the whole coterie – Lucie, Manette, Darnay, Lorry, Carton, Pross and Cruncher, son, and flopping wife – is an ill-assorted bunch, and do not form a family in any traditional or natural sense of the word. And as they recognize the connections resulting from the capriciousness of their personal histories, they are dumbfounded, barely grasping the web that connects them.

In that web, the pressure of the French crowd is almost incidental. It is not the driving force behind events so much as a chorus that attests and reacts to the unfolding narrative driven by the aristocratic injustice that infects the past and, through it, the present. When the revolutionary crowd release Darnay at his first trial (just as he was released in London), they are responding to history (Manette's good name and his vouchsafing of Darnay); just as the crowd that condemns him 24 hours later does so on the basis of the testimony of Manette concealed in the Bastille and revealed by Defarge; it is one piece of history against another. Manette's personal testimonial will in turn be trumped by his long-silent but infinitely more powerful denunciation of the infamy of the Evrémonde family and by the imperative of holding aristocracy to account for its misdeeds. In neither case is the crowd's response irrational. To break out of that history, in a way that the heroes of Godwin's novels are characteristically unable to do, is to break free from the forces that drive that history. It is to take one's place as a fragment in a relatively alien and atomized world – hidden in a corner of Soho, away from the footsteps that mark London's own terror, thrown up against and clinging to other victims of that historical process – linked by affections, to be sure, but also by principles of decency, honesty, humanity – a set of liberal personal virtues and philosophical values that are as deeply critical of the British state and its institutions (especially the eighteenth-century British state) as they are of France before the Revolution.

So Dickens's novel in part articulates the new philosophy of the 1790s, and in doing so continues an essentially liberal, Enlightenment tradition that is individualist, critical of imposition and humanitarian. In doing so, he espouses a philosophy that caught the imaginations of radicals and reformers in France, America and England at the end of the eighteenth century, but was quickly swamped by events in France, systematically pilloried in England, and came to be regarded with wide suspicion and as evidence of a kind of European corruption in America. Moreover, Dickens's own position reflects the impasse that many reformers in Britain came to experience under Pitt. They knew that the system needed to be changed, but were unwilling to countenance what seemed to be the only means by which such change could be effected. It was one thing to see the violence of the crowd as a reaction to appalling repression, quite another to lead such violence or to know how to break out of that cycle. Furthermore, Dickens's silence about the key players in events in France in 1793 and 1794 equally matches that of the vast majority of those in Britain who had sympathized with France between 1789 and 1792. There is little engagement with Robespierre and Saint-Just.[29] Above all, in sharp contrast to loyalist propaganda, Dickens's silence involves an implicit refusal to see them or the events that they came to epitomize and that finally consumed them as in any sense the natural progeny – the fault – of the new philosophy.

III

The chapter 'The Substance of the Shadow' contains Manette's letter and the crowd's reaction to it. Central to the chapter is Darnay's mother's presentiment 'that if no other innocent atonement is made for this, it will one day be required of him' (III, x, 343). The substantive injustice carries its own shadow – shadows that stalk the novel in the form of the multiple Jacques – and those shadows themselves become substance, a repressed that can no longer remain repressed, and that, in coming to expression, mirrors with a vengeance the brutalities inflicted on them. In this way, history plays out: substance generating shadow, shadow made substance, and the substance of the old order cast into the shadows. In the press of history, that cycle is not easily broken; Dickens himself is silent on how it could be broken. What he offers is a refuge that many who welcomed events in France in 1789–92 took, namely, to step aside from that process, partly by finding in friendship and domesticity a locus of value, and partly by taking a more aloof, almost Archimedean standpoint, from which the immediate troubles of the world may be viewed more benignly:

> I see a beautiful city and a brilliant people rising from this abyss, and, in their struggles to be truly free, in their triumphs and defeats, through long years to come, I see the evil of this time and of the previous time of which this is the natural birth, gradually making expiation for itself and wearing out.
>
> (III, xv, 389)

But the puzzle remains of how to get from the abyss of the present to this future – a puzzle that equally faced those with such high hopes of reform and progress in the 1790s. The blank refusal on the part of the authorities to countenance reform and the accusation of gross irresponsibility in even considering reform at such a time prompted William Windham's 'What, would he recommend you to repair your house in the hurricane season?'[30] Faced with this, many of those who supported reform faced an increasingly difficult choice as to how far they were prepared to go in securing the rights that they saw as essential to a free society. By the end of the 1790s a number had become committed to countenancing more extreme and direct measures and joined the sister societies of the United Irishmen to plot for the overthrow of Britain's *ancien régime*. But the vast majority of those who first greeted 1789 in France and understood the forces that drove the changes there were rendered increasingly silent and impotent. The loyalties of some turned against France when she launched her policy of international revolution in November 1792, since this seemed to be a case of returning to the traditional pattern of French foreign policy and could be justifiably resisted as a result. Others saw the Terror unfold with puzzled incomprehension, their philosophy proving inadequate to explain this seemingly apocalyptic turn, which was taken as evidence that their initial identification with France and the understanding they showed to its early excesses were mistaken and ill-judged. Yet still others had a sense of the fragility of political order, the difficulty of ensuring consensus on the principles that underlie political rule and the unpredictable effects of poverty and misery on those most expected to take the order on trust. For such men and women history had to be ridden out as best they could, with some compensating sense that over time progressive change would occur, but with a profound uncertainty as to how to act and whom to support to ensure that change occurred in the most peaceful manner possible, and with some sense of the risk they ran of appearing complicit with the violence or with the existing order. For those who took this view, who make up the circles around Joseph Johnson, Horne Tooke, Godwin and many others in the capital and throughout the provinces, there is a willingness to demand, as Dickens does from Sir Edward Hall Alderson, that power speak the truth, that constitutional principles and practices be used as procedural rules on whose equity and fairness people should be able to rely, and that literature and art be permitted to comment on the political world in less direct and contentious but nonetheless deeply felt ways. But the twenty years of the Revolutionary and Napoleonic Wars is a long time in politics and few of the generation of the 1780s and 1790s survived to play prominent parts when reform returned to the agenda after the end of the war. A new generation, with distant memories of France, Ireland, the English reform movements and, still further back, the American Revolution, pick up the threads of reform and campaigning. But the legacy of France (and Ireland) was to provide an abiding fear of change descending into blood-bath. Where the middling orders of England in 1789 were for the most part convinced that France was reaping a harvest that she had sown, that sense dims as events gather pace. It loses many in September 1792, and still more in 1793 and 1794. Darker, more malicious and more conspiratorial explanations are offered, and the innocent reasonableness of thinking that people were reacting to the brutality of their oppression becomes less confidently assumed. The more tolerant perspective of Paine's early writing, which we find mirrored in Dickens, is a perspective on France that re-emerges only as a result of the obsessive return to events by historian after historian in the first half of the nineteenth century. Dickens finds this more tolerant perspective gestured to but rejected in Young, narrativized in Thiers and seen through a glass darkly, if at all, in Carlyle, but increasingly confirmed as he reads himself back into the period. But his reading is also influenced by his sense that his own political system is not free from force and fraud, its church not free from hypocrisy and imposture, and his fellow English not spared poverty and misery. And his characters reflect his own sense that, while one cannot approve of the recourse to violence against an intransigent state, one cannot deny their very real grounds for complaint. In that sense *A Tale of Two Cities* is a classically liberal text reflecting a classically liberal position. It has a sense of an order that could command people's consent, coupled with a clear recognition that the current order does not meet such criteria, which situation demands sympathy for those exploited and downtrodden by it, without finding it possible to countenance positive support for agitation and resistance. That position is not an inevitable one; rather, it is in part an effect of the rhetoric and reaction of the 1790s that constructed the French Revolution as the bogeyman of political and social change. On this view, it is not difficult to see that Dickens was drawn to the events not simply as a dramatic setting but also as an open sore for those like him who felt for the poor, exploited and oppressed, who could understand their reaction when unfettered, but who could not countenance taking a more active role that might issue in another Terror.

Notes

1. Dickens to Sir Edward Bulwer-Lytton, 5 June 1860: *Letters*, IX, p. 259. My thanks to the editors and contributors and to Delia Da Sousa Carrea for advice on Dickens's resources.
2. See 'Monsieur the Marquis in Town', in which the reception includes 'unbelieving philosophers who were remodelling the world with words, and making card towers of Babel to scale the skies with . . .' (*TTC*, II, vii, 110–11).
3. One of Dickens's Burkean characters describes Darnay as 'infected with the new doctrines . . . [and as having] set himself in opposition to the last Marquis, abandoned the estates when he inherited them, and left them to the ruffian herd' (II, xxiv, 248).
4. Richard Price, *Political Writings*, ed. D. O. Thomas (Cambridge: Cambridge University Press, 1991), pp. 195–6.
5. Thomas Paine, *Rights of Man, Common Sense, and other Political Writings*, ed. Mark Philp (Oxford: Oxford University Press, 1995), p. 108, emphasis added.
6. Thomas Carlyle, *The French Revolution: A History* (London: Chapman & Hall, n.d.). Volume 1 of the *Standard Edition of Thomas Carlyle's Works*, Book V, chapter 9, p. 176. The reference to Enceladus is to the myth of a giant lying beneath Sicily, often associated with volcanic eruptions. Carlyle too, however, reserves a component of judgement on the grounds of provocation: 'Horrible in Lands that had known equal justice! Not so unnatural in Lands that had never known it' (p. 177). The reference to grass concerns the crowd's revenge on Foulon, who had suggested that the poor could eat grass (TTC, II, xxii, 231).
7. 'Judicial Special Pleading', *The Examiner*, 23 December 1848, repr. Slater, II, pp. 137–42 (p. 141). Dickens makes this claim shortly after citing Thiers's view that the burdens of the society fell entirely on the mass of the people.
8. See Dickens's 'The Flight', in *Dickens on France*, ed. John Edmondson (Oxford: Signal, 2006), p. 9.
9. Edmondson, ed., *Dickens on France*, p. 234.
10. *Rights of Man*, pp. 109–10.
11. See *TTC* III, xii, p. 352: ' "Well, well", reasoned Defarge, "but one must stop somewhere . . ." '
12. G. K. Chesterton, *Appreciations and Criticisms*, Chapter 19, at http://www.dickens-literature. com/Appreciations_and_Criticisms_by_G.K_Chesterton/18.html
13. Edmund Burke, *Reflections on the Revolution in France*, ed. Conor Cruise O'Brien (Harmondsworth: Penguin Books, 1969), p. 195.
14. Essentially, that the system is being unreasonable. Chesterton notes that: 'There was, above all, a certain reasonable impatience which was the essence of the old Republican (Dickens), and which is quite unknown to the Revolutionist in modern Europe. The old Radical did not feel exactly that he was 'in revolt'; he felt if anything that a number of idiotic institutions had revolted against reason and against him.' *Charles Dickens*, Chapter 9, at http://www.lang.nagoya-u.ac.jp/~matsuoka/CD-Chesterton-CD-2.html#IX
15. See Patrick Brantlinger, 'Does Dickens Have a Philosophy of History? The Case of *Barnaby Rudge*', DSA, 30 (2001), 59–74.

16. Charles Dickens, 'The Fine Old English Gentleman' New Version. (To be said or sung at all Conservative Dinners)', ed. Philip V. Allingham. www.victorianweb.org/authors/dickens/pva/pva352.html

17. See Gary Kates, 'From Liberalism to Radicalism: Tom Paine's *Rights of Man*', in *Journal of the History of Ideas*, 50 (1989), 569–87; and Richard Whatmore, ' "A Gigantic Manliness": Paine's Republicanism in the 1790s', in *Economy, Polity and Society*, ed. Stefan Collini, Richard Whatmore and Brian Young (Cambridge: Cambridge University Press, 2000), pp. 135–57.

18. See Kates, 'From Liberalism to Radicalism', p. 576. Kates sees Mackintosh as endorsing universal suffrage where Paine does not. (It is true that Paine does not fully develop a defence of universal manhood suffrage much before 1795.) But Paine and Mackintosh's accounts of what went on in Paris and how we should understand the outbursts of violence are more or less the same. On the explanatory front there is little or nothing between them. It is also worth recalling that the political careers of these two men took very different directions as the reaction increased. Mackintosh's 'principles' may seem more radical than Paine's careful rhetorical strategy, but they were also more easily jettisoned under pressure.

19. See James Gillray, *New Morality* (London, 1798).

20. It is difficult to believe that 'ruffian herd' (II, xxiv, 248) is not informed by Burke's 'swinish multitude'.

21. Manette's description of the young dying boy (Madame Defarge's brother).

22. See *Letters*, IX, p. 41, n. 4.

23. Arthur Young, *Arthur Young's Travels in France during the years 1787, 1788, 1789*, ed. Miss Betham-Edwards (London: George Bell, 1906) p. 103. The relevant scene in *TTC* is II, vii, 114.

24. Young, *Travels in France*, pp. 322–3.

25. See John Keane, *Tom Paine: A Political Life* (London: Bloomsbury, 1995), p. 449, which repeats the story of Lewis Goldsmith being at dinner with Mercier from Alfred Owen Aldridge, *Man of Reason: The Life of Thomas Paine* (London: Cresset Press, 1960), p. 266. The suggestion of earlier connections via Holcroft comes from the mentions of Mercier in William Godwin's Diaries in the early 1790s, with Holcroft marrying one of Mercier's daughters. Paine was also in London at the time and certainly met Godwin.

26. The role of the private affections (or, more accurately, the absence of a role in moral judgement for them) is a central theme in Godwin's *Enquiry Concerning Political Justice* (London, 1793) for which Godwin was roundly attacked, especially after 1797. His concessionary defence is in his *Thoughts Occasioned by the Perusal of Dr Parr's Spital Sermon* (London: G. G. and J. Robinson, 1802).

27. Paine, *Rights of Man*, pp. 91–2.

28. Godwin asks in *Political Justice* what we should do if a fire occurs and we can only save one of two persons: the Archbishop Fénelon, author of *Telemachus*, a seminal book of moral and political education in France (1699), or his serving woman, who happens to be my mother. Impartial justice demands the greater good and Fénelon must be saved.

29. Perhaps especially from the generation that witnesses the American war – Coleridge writes a verse drama, and others of his generation are less reticent. But those ten years older are less forthcoming.

30. Albert Goodwin, *The Friends of Liberty: The English Democratic Movement in the Age of the French Revolution* (London: Hutcheson, 1979), p. 118.

3
The Redemptive Powers of Violence? Carlyle, Marx and Dickens

Gareth Stedman Jones

Among the many questions raised by the French Revolution of 1789, one in particular haunted the imagination of the nineteenth century: its violence. No one could deny that the Revolution had produced momentous and lasting changes. The Europe of the *ancien régime* had been destroyed and all attempts to restore it had foundered. But these changes appeared to be inseparable from the violence that had brought them about. Violence, it seemed, had not been incidental to the Revolution, but inherent in its popular character. Popular sovereignty had gone together with crowd coercion and a reign of terror. Hunger, long-held grievances and the provocations of the Old Order were among its precipitants. But, by any measure, it had been excessive, and its legacy had been an unforgettable cluster of images of the burning of chateaux, of the destruction of the Bastille, of angry crowds, summary justice and the hanging lamppost (the *lanterne*), of the execution of a king and queen, and most of the leaders of the Revolution itself, of the Terror and the guillotine, of women with the ferocity of 'tigers' – the *tricoteuses*, knitting while heads fell, of revolutionary armies, of the desecration of churches and the mass drownings (*noyades*) of Jean-Baptiste Carrier.

Interest in the Revolution of 1789 was not dislodged by the occurrence of revolutions in 1830 and 1848. Politicians and historians from Croker to Acton continued to be preoccupied with 1789, while its perennial popularity as a theme in popular consciousness was suggested by its central place in Madame Tussaud's Chamber of Horrors. In 1830 in France, significant liberal gains had been made without undue loss of life. But a succession of riots, uprisings and conspiracies in its aftermath suggested that the changes were but a stage in an ongoing process.[1] In 1848, the successes of the people had been short-lived. Only in the first great revolution had epochal change, mass political participation and violence run together.

It was this equation that remained so disturbing; and in many studies beginning with Madame de Staël's *Considerations on the Principal Events of the French Revolution* (1818), historians tried to distinguish the 'good' years of the liberal revolution of 1789–91 from the 'bad' years of Jacobinism and the Terror of 1792–94. But even in the 'good' years, it was impossible to separate the achievements of the legislature from violence and crowd action. The storming of the Bastille and the burning of the chateaux took place near the beginning of the Revolution in 1789. Was it therefore possible to detach the Revolution from the violent and assertive actions of the people? In the English-speaking world, the person who had posed this question in its sharpest form was Thomas Carlyle.

Carlyle's *French Revolution* was arguably the first of a new type of history in which a collective entity, the French People, were conceived as the active protagonist of the historical process.[2] This approach had only been made possible by Carlyle's intimate acquaintance with a tradition of thinking, until the 1820s little known outside Germany – the aesthetic and religious theories of *Sturm und Drang* (Storm and Stress) and German Romanticism.

Back in the 1820s, John Stuart Mill had perceived that the novelty of the Revolution required a new sort of history. To understand 'how a people acts', it was necessary to know how its 'civilisation, morals, codes of thought and social relations' were shaped. As he wrote in his review of Sir Walter Scott's *Life of Napoleon* in 1827,

> heretofore, when a change of government had been effected by force in an extensive and populous country, the revolution had been made always by and commonly for, a few; the French Revolution was emphatically the work of the people. Commenced by the people, carried on by the people, defended by the people with a heroism and self-devotion unexampled in any other period of modern history, at length terminated by the people when they awoke from the frenzy into which the dogged resistance of the privileged classes against the introduction of any form whatever of representative government had driven them; the French Revolution will never be more than superficially understood, by the man who is but superficially acquainted with the nature and movements of popular enthusiasm. That mighty power, of which, but for the French Revolution, mankind perhaps would never have known the surpassing strength – that force which converts a whole people into heroes, which binds an entire nation together as one man, not merely to overpower all other forces, but draw them into its own line, and convert them into auxiliaries to itself . . . The man who is yet to come, the philosophical historian of the French Revolution . . . will draw his philosophy from the primeval fountain of human nature itself.[3]

But promising though these remarks sound, Mill could never have written Carlyle's book, for he was still too wedded to eighteenth-century notions of historical writing in which the aim was to abstract, to stand as far as possible away from the drama and to draw lessons in the calm of reflection. This was certainly the approach adopted by the major British academic authority on the Revolution from the 1810s to the 1840s, William Smyth, Regius Professor of History at Cambridge and Whig protégé of Holland House. Like Voltaire, Smyth considered that the historian should in so far as possible sift out details, ephemera and peculiar events from his consideration of the past. Such a position had also been enjoined upon him by one of his patrons, Sir James Mackintosh, the erstwhile defender of the French Revolution and admired Whig theorist. It was an approach that had already been successfully employed by de Staël in her widely read *Considerations on the French Revolution*.[4] Congratulating Smyth on his appointment in 1808, Mackintosh urged him to produce a 'universal history':

> all occurrences of local and temporary importance are excluded; all events, merely extraordinary or interesting, which leave no permanent effects, can only be mentioned as they illustrate the spirit of the times. Nothing becomes the subject of universal history, but those events, which alter the relations of the members of the European community, or its general condition, in wealth, civilisation and knowledge. The details of national history no more belong to this subject than the peculiarities of English biography to the history of England.[5]

For Smyth, the French Revolution was a failed attempt to imitate England in 1688. It was besmirched by crime and folly in each of its stages.[6] Its most terrifying aspect was its theory. It was an object lesson of the folly of attempting to apply the doctrines of utility and perfectibility.[7] These beliefs had led to an inhuman moral code, which had produced the Terror, and to the false idea that good could come through evil. Tory historians like Archibald Alison and John Wilson Croker did not basically depart from this approach, except to offer slightly differing sets of concluding maxims.

As Hevda Ben-Israel has argued, the use of Edmund Burke to elaborate a romantic conception of history, to construct an organic history of the national past, was a phenomenon more of the European mainland than of England itself.[8] In England, admiration for Burke was generally tempered by moderate liberalism or an ongoing Whiggism. No one endorsed his roseate description of the *ancien régime*. The prevalent view – by the 1820s, shared also by many Tories – was that Burke had exaggerated the evils of the Revolution and had temporarily lost his judgement. Even supposed romantics like de Staël in her *Considerations on the French Revolution* or Sir Walter Scott, who attempted to follow Robert Southey's *Life of Nelson* (1813) with a *Life of Napoleon* (1827), remained wholly rationalist in their approach to historical analysis and moderate liberal in their historical interpretation.

Carlyle's *French Revolution*, therefore, could only have been written by someone drawing on a cultural position quite distinct from anything to be found in Britain at the time. Carlyle's insistent analogy between history and poetry originated in Johann Gottfried von Herder, though the sense of ominous tragedy he brought to it did not. Carlyle believed that history was 'the sole Poetry possible' in the disbelieving modern world, that the grandest of fictions faded before 'the smallest historical *fact*', that history was 'an inarticulate Bible; and in a dim manner reveals the Divine Appearances in this lower world. For God did make this world, and does forever govern it; the loud-roaring Loom of Time, with all its French Revolutions, Jewish Revelations, "weaves the vesture thou seest him by" '.[9] The historian was the successor to the epic poet; that was why Carlyle prepared for his writing of *French Revolution* by reading the *Iliad*, Dante and Milton, and why, like the ancient bards and Hebrew prophets, he composed his history in a semi-trance.[10]

It was this belief that history was a form of bardic poetry and thus a narrative of 'facts, facts, no theory' without the distance that enabled reflection or abstraction, that made Carlyle's history so novel and powerful.[11] Carlyle may have learnt certain of his techniques of identification, dramatization and of the sympathetic portrayal of character from Scott's novels, but his idea of history as divine Revelation and of the historian's task as diviner and seer could not have originated in a country where the Lockean approach to the origin of ideas was still the order of the day.[12]

Carlyle's major preoccupation was with spiritual crisis, with the terrors of the loss of faith and with the urgency of its recovery. This was a central feature of all his major texts – not just *Sartor Resartus* (1838), but *The French Revolution*, *Chartism* (1840) and *Past and Present* (1843) as well. The trauma of despair and rebirth, which Carlyle associated with his experience in Leith Walk around 1821 or 1822, remained the defining imaginative experience of his life.[13] Thereafter, he compulsively repainted that experience or the differing fragments from it on larger and larger canvasses until it engulfed the central event of modern history, the French Revolution, which he tried to describe as an eye-witness to the Apocalypse.[14] It also coloured his vision of the still uncertain future of his own society, hollow in faith and, in the 1830s and 1840s, sunk in mammonism and do-nothingism. Just as he demonstrated extraordinary inventiveness in populating his histories and fictions with different emanations of himself with whom he could conduct dialogue – Teufeldröckh and his editor, Sauerteig, Dryasdust, Hofrath Heuschrecke and others, so, long before *The Strange Case of Dr Jekyll and Mr Hyde* (1886), the Darwinian thought experiment of Robert Louis Stevenson, Carlyle was able to draw on his own chthonic depths and acute sense of the uncertain boundary between human and animal to populate his epic and warning tale of revolution.

How fragile and precarious civilization was! Carlyle's personal nightmare of loss of faith described in *Sartor* became the waking nightmare of a whole faithless people in *The French Revolution*. The point of Teufeldröckh's clothes philosophy, the moral of *Sartor*, is reiterated at the beginning of his history: 'Of man's whole terrestrial possessions and attainments, unspeakably the noblest are his Symbols, divine or divine-seeming; under which he marches and fights, with victorious assurance, in this life battle; what we can call his Realised Ideals.' Thus, 'strong was he that had a church . . . the vague shoreless universe had become a firm city for him, and dwelling which he knew. Such Virtue was in Belief: in these words well spoken: I believe.'[15]

Similarly, the ancient monarchy was 'a symbol of true guidance in return for loving obedience; properly if he knew it the prime want of man. A symbol which might be called sacred.'[16] But this faith had been desecrated and lost. Under Louis XV, 'Louis the Well-beloved', the response to petitions of grievance had been the erection of a gallows, 40-foot high. Now 'twenty five dark savage millions' looked up 'to that ecce signum of theirs forty foot high'.[17] It was the tarnishing and fading of these symbols of faith in France through the frivolous and irresponsible pleasures of the court and the idle aristocracy that made the Revolution possible.

The appearance of 'philosophism' – Carlyle means the epoch of the *philosophes* – was a sign that 'faith is gone out; scepticism is come in . . . that a Lie cannot be believed . . . Philosophism knows only this.'[18] Now into 'the Paper Age', the last years before the Revolution, the French had become 'an unbelieving people'.[19] The state survived so long as no attempt was made to reform it. 'It is singular', Carlyle observed, 'how long the rotten will hold together, provided you do not handle it roughly . . . so loath are men to quit their old ways'. But to attempt change in these circumstances was fatal. 'Our whole being is, an infinite abyss, *overarched* by Habit, as by a thin Earth-Rind, laboriously built together.' And as if to emphasize the interconnection between the personal and the historical, it is Teufeldröckh from *Sartor* 'our Author' whom Carlyle allows to address the reader at this crucial stage of the narrative. 'Let but, by ill chance, in such ever-enduring struggle, your thin "Earth-rind" be once *broken*. The fountains of the great deep boil forth; fire fountains, enveloping, ingulfing. Your earth-rind is shattered, swallowed up; instead of a green flowery world there is a waste wild-weltering chaos; – which has again, with tumult and struggle, to *make* itself into a world.'[20]

Finally, Carlyle in *The French Revolution* evokes a peculiarly gruesome and disturbing vision of revolution as a war between rich and poor born out of the loss of faith and habit. It was disturbing because, unlike Benjamin Disraeli's picture of 'the two nations', whose ancient feud could notionally be removed by the marriage between Sybil and Egremont, Carlyle's picture was drawn from a notion of the conflicting forces which reside within the self. The primitive, the instinctual, the murderous *is not* reassuringly projected onto another class or race, but remains in a state of suppressed but ever-smouldering rebellion within each individual self. The vision of revolution found in the book is inspired by the uprising of the Titans against the Olympians, by Lucifer's rebellion or by a picture of primeval Holocaust. It is, as Philip Rosenberg has suggested, nearer to Freud's *Totem and Taboo* (1913) than Marx's *Communist Manifesto* (1848).[21] For 'every man', Carlyle believed – and he had already made the point in *Sartor* – 'holds confined within him a *mad*man' and with the breakdown of order following the fall of the Bastille, the *mad*man escapes. Joseph-François Foulon, who had once advised the Parisian people to eat grass, is discovered in Paris. The crowd forthwith hurry him to the *lanterne* at the corner of the Place de Grève and, having hanged him, put his head on a pike and stuff his mouth with grass.[22] Dickens was particularly impressed by this passage and devotes a whole chapter to the Foulon episode in *Tale of Two Cities* (II, xxii). Carlyle wrote of it, 'surely if revenge is a kind of justice, it is a wild kind. O mad sansculottism, hast thou risen, in thy mad darkness, in thy soot and rags; unexpectedly, like an Enceladus, living buried, from under his Trinacria? They that would make grass be eaten do now eat grass in this manner? After long dumb groaning generations, has the turn suddenly become thine?'[23]

Carlyle wasted few pages on the constitution-making of successive assemblies. For him the Revolution was 'sansculottism':

> the open violent rebellion, and victory of disimprisoned anarchy against corrupt worn out authority: how anarchy breaks prison; burst up from the infinite deep, and rages uncontrollable, immeasurable, enveloping a world; in phasis after phasis of fever-frenzy – till the frenzy burning itself out, and what elements of new order it held (since all force holds such) developing themselves, the Uncontrollable be got, if not reimprisoned, yet harnessed, and its mad forces made to work towards their object as sane regulated ones.[24]

Sansculottism rises mysteriously and terrifyingly from the deep:

> When the age of miracles lay faded into the distance as an incredible tradition, and even the age of conventionalities was now old; and Man's existence had for long generations rested on mere formulas which were grown hollow by force of time; and it seemed as if no Reality any longer existed but only Phantasms of Realities and God's Universe were the work of the Tailor and the Upholsterer mainly, and men were buckram masks that went about becking and grimacing there, – on a sudden, the Earth yawns asunder, and amid Tartarean smoke, and glare of fierce brightness, rises Sansculottism, many headed, firebreathing, and asks: What think ye of *me*? ... The Age of Miracles has come back. Behold the World Phoenix ... It is the Death-Birth of a World.[25]

Those who have written about Carlyle and 'The Condition of England Question', focusing especially on *Chartism* and *Past and Present*, rarely connect these writings with his *French Revolution* and even less with the German inspiration of his thought. More specifically, historians have failed to notice how much of the impact made by Carlyle's *Chartism* or *Past and Present* was the result of the continuity of themes and concerns carried forward from his work on France. Yet for readers in the 1830s and 1840s, the scenario sketched in Carlyle's contemporary pamphlets looked alarmingly similar to his description of the build-up to revolution in 1789.

In *Chartism* Carlyle observed that 'revolt, sullen revengeful humour of revolt against the upper classes, decreasing respect for what their temporal superior command, decreasing faith for what their spiritual superiors teach, is more and more the universal spirit of the lower classes'.[26] Furthermore, he ominously reminded his readers of signs of the motif of class revenge, which had driven forward uprisings in the past and had ultimately produced the Terror in France. He referred to the case of the Glasgow cotton spinners who allegedly had sentenced and executed a strike-breaker. 'Glasgow Thuggery speaks aloud too, in a language we may well call infernal ... like your old Chivalry *Femgericht*, Secret Tribunal ... suddenly rising once more on the astonished eye, dressed now not in mail shirts, but in fustian jackets'.[27] And once again he referred to the personal nightmare of *Sartor*: 'If men had lost their belief in a God, their only resource against a blind no-God, of necessity and mechanism, that held them like a hideous World-Steam-Engine, like a hideous Phalaris Bull, imprisoned in its own iron belly, would be, with or without hope, *revolt*.'[28]

This situation might be dangerously near. For Britain in the 1840s was 'the heyday of semblance', with even religion becoming mechanized. 'Depend upon it, Birmingham can make machines to repeat liturgies and articles; to do whatsoever feat is mechanical.' So was 'God, as Jean Paul predicted it would be, become verily a force; the Aether too, a gas. Alas that Atheism should have got the length of putting on priests' vestments and penetrating into the sanctuary itself.'[29] In France, the foolish Girondins had called up the whirlwind by urging the Revolution on in its early years. Perhaps a similar fate awaited the Parliamentary Radicals. 'The speaking classes speak and debate, each for itself; the great dumb deep-buried class lies like an Enceladus, who in his pain, if he will complain of it, has to produce earthquakes.'[30] With grim delight, Carlyle wrote of the Terror in *The French Revolution*: 'it was not the Dumb Millions that suffered here; it was the speaking thousands, and hundreds and units; who shrieked and published, and made the world ring with their wail'.[31]

If English historians have not generally understood how important Carlyle's *French Revolution* was in fuelling a literature of social fear in the 1830s and 1840s, they have been even less aware how important his German proto-romantic inheritance was in shaping the peculiar definition which he gave to the social question and its resolution. Three aspects of his approach should be briefly mentioned: his definition of the social realm and its attendant downgrading of the political; his conception of religion or faith as the binding force of society; and finally, the role he assigned to 'the people', the 'sans-culottes' or the 'working classes' in his providential conception of history.

On the first point, no commentator could miss Carlyle's hostility to democracy.[32] What has attracted less attention has been the subordinate and in some sense degraded position he assigned to the *political* as such. In *Past and Present*, he despised political reform as a mere tinkering with machinery. Fundamentally, his distrust was similar to that of Johann Georg Hamann or Herder and related to the vanity of the pretensions of reason when it aspired to legislate in abstraction from any social embodiment.[33] Hamann had protested against Kant that reason could not be 'pure', that is, it could not claim any right to existence as a disembodied entity. In Carlyle, this scepticism appeared clearly in a definition of what would later be called *ideology*. 'Man's philosophies are usually the supplement of his practice; some ornamental logic varnish, some outer skin of articulate intelligence with which he strives to render his dumb instinctive doings presentable when they are done.'[34] The 'true law code and constitution of society' were unwritten and rested on 'its system of habits ... the only Code, though an Unwritten one, which it can no wise disobey'.[35] Man's 'civilization' was only a 'wrappage, through which the savage nature of him can still burst, as infernal as ever'.[36] Moreover, unlike Coleridge, Carlyle attributed no divinity or eternity to the state and its political symbols. Symbols were formed by 'sacred combinations of men' in society, but like all human creations, lost their force in time.[37] Thus, as Catherine Gallagher has shown, unlike Coleridge, Carlyle was able to treat political symbols as targets for irony – like the 'champion of England' in *Past and Present* almost too fat to mount his horse at the coronation.[38]

What Carlyle pitted against Benthamite or mechanical conceptions of society was Herder's idea of culture. Society was a living tissue, an organism, held together by what *Sartor* describes as the 'organic filaments' – language and custom, the living landscape, dress, climate, a shared past.[39] Man is spirit, he wears clothes; this is a visible emblem of the bonds that tie him to other men. It was 'in society that man first feels what he is; first becomes what he can be'. This is why Carlyle was so alarmed by the fear that in the England of his time, persons were held together by nothing except 'the cash nexus'. Better, as he asserted in *Past and Present*, the intimate feudal interdependencies of 'Garth and Cedric' 'related indissolubly' than the vaunted empty liberty of the present age in which the continued reality of interdependence only resurfaced in the ravages of contagion.[40] In a much-repeated example in *Past and Present*, Carlyle cited the case of the Irish widow who killed seventeen of her neighbours with typhus, because help had been refused to her at the proper time.[41] This was the inspiration behind Dickens's use of smallpox as the tie which binds together Lady Dedlock, Esther Summerson and Joe, the crossing-sweeper in *Bleak House* (1853). The thinning out of interconnection between individuals under the impact of mammonism lessened the capacity of society to produce symbols, and the loss of symbols was tantamount to a loss of humanity.[42] The decay of symbols had produced a descent into animality, that condition in which trousers had allegedly been made out of the skin of the victims of the guillotine at the tannery at Meudon and in which in the unemployed England of 1842, a poor couple in Stockport had began to kill their children, to claim death insurance and also to eat them.[43]

The second aspect of Carlyle's approach, the conviction that a society not held together by religious belief would dissolve and fall apart, came from France rather than Germany. In 1830 Carlyle had translated Saint-Simon's *Nouveau Christianisme* (1825). He was tempted by the Saint-Simonians; some of their beliefs resembled his own. But he was finally warned off by Goethe from having further contact with them.[44] Many of the religious convictions of the Saint-Simonians had been taken from the so-called 'Theocrats', the main philosophical proponents of the French counter-revolution, Joseph de Maistre, and especially Louis de Bonald, whose main contention was that without religion, society would dissolve, as the history of the French Revolution had supposedly proved.[45] Unlike de Maistre, Bonald or Chateaubriand, however, the Saint-Simonians did not believe that social cohesion could be secured by the return of medieval Catholicism. Their search was to find a new version of a *pouvoir spirituel* ('spiritual power') capable of taking the place of the Catholic Church. Hence 'the Religion of Saint-Simon'.[46]

Carlyle was not sympathetic to the details of this creed. Indeed, within a few years the Saint-Simonians had made themselves the laughing stock of Europe with their call for the 'rehabilitation of the flesh' and their search for the female messiah. What Carlyle shared with the Saint-Simonians was their diagnosis of religious need and the search for a new source of *pouvoir spirituel*. In Carlyle's case, this took the form of 'hero worship' or 'the gospel of work'. In *Chartism*, he referred to the destruction of the Church by the Revolution:

> that one whole generation of thinkers should be without a religion to believe, or even to contradict; that Christianity in thinking France, should as it were fade away so long into a remote extraneous tradition, was one of the saddest facts connected with the future of that country. Look at such political and moral philosophies, St Simonisms, Robert Macairisms and the 'literature of desperation'. Kingship was perhaps but a cheap waste compared with this of the priestship.[47]

The third important point about Carlyle's German inheritance was the way in which it shaped the role he assigned to the *sans-culottes*, the *people*, the *working classes*, in the past and in the present. Here what is especially noticeable is that while the main protagonists of Carlyle's social and historical dramas make sounds and create a noise, they do not speak. Carlyle describes the French people whose grievances were met by Louis XV's gallows as 'a dumb generation; their voice only an inarticulate cry'.[48] By the time Carlyle gets to *the Assembly of Notables*, the people were ceasing to be dumb, but had not quite achieved true utterance. The people 'speaks through pamphlets, or at least bays and growls behind them, in unison – increasing wonderfully their volume of sound'.[49] At the siege of the Bastille, once again the people achieves sound, maybe even speech, but not thought: 'Great is the combined voice of men; the utterance of their instincts, which are truer than their thoughts.'[50] In fact, although at certain points in the narrative the people appear to be on the point of breaking into articulate speech, they never actually do so.

In the case of the English working classes, the inarticulacy becomes threatening and deafening. Carlyle first introduces them in *Chartism* by bemoaning a lack of understanding among the upper classes, 'what it is that the underclasses intrinsically mean; a clear interpretation of the thought which at heart torments these wild inarticulate souls, struggling there with inarticulate uproar, like dumb creatures in pain, unable to speak what is in them. Something they do mean; some true thing withal, in the centre of their confused hearts – for they are hearts created by heaven too.'[51] As for the supposed demands of the Chartists, the demands of the Charter, Carlyle comments: 'what is the meaning of the five points, if we will understand them? What are all popular commotions and maddest bellowings, from Peterloo to the Place de la Grève itself? Bellowings, *in*articulate cries as of a dumb creature in rage and pain.' But Carlyle goes on, 'to the ear of wisdom they are inarticulate prayers: Guide me; Govern me. I am mad and miserable and cannot guide myself'.[52]

But it was not simply the underclasses who could not speak their meaning – who could only act it – it was also the English, who were praised as a dumb race. 'Not the least admirable quality of Bull is ... of remaining insensible to logic.' Long after the logical argument is settled, for instance the repeal of the Corn Laws, Bull will see whether nothing else *illogical*, not yet spoken, not yet able to be spoken, do not lie in the business, as there so often does.'[53]

At a more metaphysical level, this emphasis on silence and inarticulacy touched the core of Carlyle's vision of history and reality. 'The cloudy-browed thick-soled opaque Practicality, with no logic utterance, in silence mainly, with here and there a low grunt or growl, has in him what transcends all logic-utterance: a congruity with the unuttered.' On the other hand, 'the Speakable, which lies atop, as a superficial film, or outer skin, is his or is not his; but the doable which reaches down to the world's center, you find him there'.[54] Or, as he stated elsewhere, 'Speech is time, Silence is eternity'.[55] Speech related to the visible universe. But the poet, 'the seer penetrates the visible universe to reach the invisible, but truly real universe, of which the visible is indeed the garment or symbol'.[56]

It is at this point – that of the silence or inarticulacy of the people, the English, the oppressed, the working classes – that the affinity between German proto-romanticism and the subsequent marxian tradition appears at its clearest. In 1844, the young Friedrich Engels wrote an enthusiastic review of Carlyle's *Past and Present* for *Deutsch-Französische Jahrbücher*, edited in Paris by Karl Marx and Arnold Ruge. Carlyle's book, according to Engels, was the only work in England to show 'traces of a human point of view'. Discounting a few phrases which 'derived from Carlyle's particular standpoint, we must allow the truth of all he says'. Engels agreed that the evils from which England suffered were social not political and that democracy would only be a 'transitional stage', whether, as Carlyle thought, on the way to true aristocracy, or as Engels thought, to 'real human freedom'.[57] Engels also agreed with Carlyle about the religious roots of the social crisis. 'We too are concerned with combating the lack of principle, the inner emptiness, the spiritual deadness, the untruthfulness of the age ... We want to put an end to atheism, as Carlyle portrays it, by giving back to man the substance he has lost through religion.'[58] Finally, Engels agreed with Carlyle about 'the revelation of history'. Carlyle's position represented the first step towards the position of Marx's and Ruge's journal. The disagreement, as Engels saw it, was between Carlyle's 'pantheism', which Engels likened to that of David Friedrich Strauss or the early Friedrich Schelling, and Feuerbachian humanism, the position espoused at that moment by Engels and Marx.[59]

This review of *Past and Present* was followed a year and a half later by Engels's celebrated account of *The Condition of the Working-Class in England* (1844). In that book, the basic stance remained that of Feuerbachian communism, but now conceived as the outcome of a revolution, 'in comparison with which the French Revolution and the year 1794 will prove to have been child's play'.[60] The text resonates with Carlylean references. Engels was impressed not merely by Carlyle's denunciation of a society in which all forms of connection have been reduced to that of 'the cash nexus'. Like others among Carlyle's admirers in the 1840s and 1850s, Engels was fascinated by his highlighting of violence as the primitive vehicle of the struggle between what he called the 'upper' and 'under' classes, or what Engels called the proletariat and the bourgeoisie. Thus crime, whether against person or property, was the first stage of the existential choice between enslaved animality and rebellion as the expression of humanity. Similarly, Engels – and Marx after him – eagerly adopted Carlyle's analogy between the violent justice allegedly meted out to blacklegs by the Glasgow cotton spinners and the vengeance once wreaked on high-living miscreants by the old *Femgericht* of medieval Germany.[61]

The clearest indication that Marx owed something of his conception of the role and activity of the proletariat to Carlyle came in a speech he gave on the anniversary of *The People's Paper* in April 1856. After speaking of the 'heroic struggles' the English working class had gone through since the middle of the eighteenth century, he went on: 'to revenge the misdeeds of the ruling class, there existed in the middle ages in Germany, a secret tribunal, called the Vehmgericht. If a red cross was seen marked on a house, people knew that its owner was doomed by the Vehm. All the houses of Europe are now marked with the mysterious red cross. History is the judge – its executioners the proletariat.'[62]

Carlyle had changed the representation of the working classes. They were henceforth no longer just the volatile city crowd, the playthings of demagogy, the reincarnation of the Roman mob or the oppressed and childlike equivalents of West Indian slaves. They had been made into the powerful sphinx-like symbol of the age. In place of the passive, dependent and predominantly feminine image of pauper apprentices, indentured children and white slaves, Carlyle substituted a more sullen, angry and threatening picture, centred on the resentments, confusion and choleric temper of grown men. The looming and swelling presence of the working classes now portended something – a warning to the governors of the need to rule, a still barely moving yet faintly stirring Enceladus, who might suddenly arise from the fiery deep, as he already had in France, toppling the flimsy superstructures of Anglo-Saxon civilization in his wake. The novelists strove to weave tragedies, romances, melodramas and sentimental fiction from Carlyle's warning tale. They faithfully reproduced his primal obsession with violence, his contempt for formal politics and even his tartarean metaphors.[63]

But the greatest affinity between the Marxian position and that of Carlyle is suggested not by a presence, but an absence. In Engels's *Condition*, as later in *Capital* (1867) or Marx's political writings, despite the wealth of descriptive detail about the condition of the proletarians in town and country and about the history of the emergence of the proletarian class, no proletarian was offered a speaking part. As in Carlyle, so here speech was only a masquerade. What mattered was action. As Goethe – a hero for both Carlyle and Marx and Engels – had stated, *'Erst war der Tat'* ('first came the deed'). Marx and Engels had written only a few months before, 'it is not a question of what this or that proletarian, or even the whole proletariat, at the moment *regards* as its aim. It is a question of *what the proletariat is* and what in accordance with this being, it will historically be compelled to do.'[64]

It was the idea of a dissonance between speech and action, between subjective intention and objective effect, which inspired Marx's scattered judgements of the Terror in 1844. If there was tragedy in the Terror, its source was not the sufferings of the victims or the arbitrary justice which accompanied the process, or even the excess of violence, but a misrecognition on the part of the main participants – the Jacobins and the sansculottes – of the task which history had assigned to them. The period of the Convention represented 'the *maximum of political energy*, *political power* and *political understanding*'. Yet 'Robespierre, Saint-Just and their party fell because they confused the ancient *realistic-democratic commonweal* based on *real slavery* with the *modern spiritualistic-democratic representative state*, which is based on *emancipated slavery, bourgeois society*.' Their 'terrible illusion' was to have sanctioned in the *rights of man* 'modern bourgeois society, the society of industry, of universal competition, of private interest freely pursuing its aims, of anarchy, of self-estranged natural and spiritual individuality' and at the same time to have attempted afterwards 'to annul the *manifestations of the life* of this society' in 'the manner of antiquity'.[65] Or, as he explained in 'On The Jewish Question', 'at times of special self-confidence, political life seeks to suppress its prerequisite, civil society and the elements composing this society, and to constitute itself as the real species-life of man devoid of contradictions. But it can achieve this only by coming into *violent* contradiction with its own conditions of life.' And so, just as war ends in peace, 'the political drama necessarily ends with the re-establishment of religion, private property, and all elements of civil society'.[66]

In the case of 'the mass', the sansculottes, their misrecognition resulted not from anachronism, but from the fact that their 'real conditions of emancipation' were different from those of the bourgeoisie'. This meant that if 'the material conditions' for 'the abolition of the bourgeois mode of production' did not yet exist, proletarian overthrow of the rule of the bourgeoisie could only be temporary: in fact, 'only an element in the service of the *bourgeois revolution* itself'. A few years later, in a polemic against the German radical Karl Heinzen, Marx wrote of 1794, 'the terror in France could thus by its mighty hammer blows only serve to spirit away, as it were, the ruins of feudalism from French soil. The timidly considerate bourgeoisie would not have accomplished this task in decades.'[67]

In *The German Ideology* of 1845–7, Feuerbach was repudiated and the theme of political alienation receded. The pathos attaching to Marx's original explanation of the Terror disappeared, alongside his earlier notion of democracy sketched out in his critique of Hegel's theory of the modern state in 1843. There was no longer any reference to the juxtaposition between the realities of bourgeois civil society and the doomed Jacobin attempt by force to constitute 'the real species life of man devoid of contradiction'. All that remained – memorably spelled out in the opening pages of Marx's 1852 *Eighteenth Brumaire of Louis Bonaparte* – was a notion of the necessary false consciousness, which had accompanied the great bourgeois revolutions of the past. 'Just when they seem engaged in revolutionizing themselves and things, in creating something that has never yet existed, precisely in such periods of revolutionary crisis they anxiously conjure up the spirits of the past to their service and borrow from them names, battle cries and costumes in order to present the new scene of world history in this time honoured disguise and this borrowed language.' The leaders of the French Revolution 'performed the task of their time in Roman costume and with Roman phrases, the task of unchaining and setting up modern *bourgeois* society.' Once 'the new social formation' was established, 'the antediluvian Colossi disappeared and with them resurrected Romanity'. In its place there appeared 'bourgeois society in its sober reality'. 'Its real commanders sat behind the counter, and the hog-headed Louis XVIII was its political chief.'[68] Brilliant though this invective is, the once substantive contrast between human emancipation and material reality had disappeared. The point of contrast was now with 'the social revolution of the nineteenth century', 'which cannot draw its poetry from the past, but only from the future' and would not require 'recollections of past world history in order to dull themselves to their own content'.[69]

What Marxism took over from German proto-romanticism was a pronounced scepticism about the role of subjective reason and individual intention in history. The rationality of history inhered, not in the individual agents who composed it, but in the process as a whole. For Carlyle, history possessed a redemptive and purgative function because it was made into a manifestation of divine justice. For Marxism, history possessed a teleological goal, unconsciously powered by a class struggle, which hastened the onward march of the forces of production. In Carlyle, a ruling class is doomed once it loses faith, in Marx and Engels once it loses the ability to drive forward the productive forces.[70] In both cases, these were processes that took place behind the backs of historical agents. They were decipherable only by the seer or the philosopher. History itself, as Hegel once claimed, advanced through its bad side – through wars and destruction, through violence and unreasoning passions, through the obscure and subterranean movements of aversion and desire. If, therefore, there was a relationship between individual activity and the movement of history, speech or rational discourse was not its medium.

Something very similar to the Vehmgericht theme appears in Dickens's *A Tale of Two Cities* as a crucial element in the hitherto hidden narrative of Dr Manette explaining the origins of his incarceration in the Bastille. The Doctor had been called to attend a dying peasant girl, raped by one of the aristocratic Evrémonde brothers. The brother of the violated girl had been fatally wounded when he had attempted to avenge his sister: 'Marquis', said the boy, turned to him with his eyes opened wide, and his right hand raised, 'in the days when all these things are to be answered for, I summon you and yours, to the last of your bad race, to answer for them. I mark this cross of blood upon you, as a sign that I do it.' And after similarly cursing the other brother, Dr Manette's account continued: 'Twice, he put his hand to the wound in his breast, and with his forefinger drew a cross in the air. He stood for an instant with his finger raised, and, as it dropped, he dropped with it, and I laid him down dead' (III, x, 339). Mme Defarge, the later leader of the revolutionary women of Saint-Antoine, was this boy's younger sister.

Dickens was a fervent admirer of Carlyle's *French Revolution*, and used it as the basis of his historical narrative. His hope was to 'add something to the popular and picturesque means of understanding that terrible time', but added, 'no one can hope to add anything to the philosophy of Mr. Carlyle's wonderful book' (Appendix II, 398–9). Yet, although many episodes in the book draw on Carlyle for the sequence of events and for much of the local detail in particular scenes, Dickens's debt to Carlyle was shallower than might at first appear.

From the time of Humphrey House's *The Dickens World* in 1941, there is still a lingering tendency to consider Dickens as politically naive and historically 'vague'. Such accusations – particularly in relation to *A Tale of Two*

Cities – are ill founded. There was nothing 'vague' about the efforts he made to align his fictional narrative with the historical course of the Revolution.[71] Furthermore, his treatment of revolutionary violence, despite some superficial resemblances, was not at all akin to Carlyle's. In Carlyle, 'sansculottism' or the terrifyingly awoken 'Enceladus' is summoned up from the deep by the *ancien régime*'s loss of faith and therefore of its will to rule or lead. In Carlyle, the violence is purgative and all-consuming like the lava from a huge volcano, enveloping, destroying and cleansing everything in its path. The people, so long deserted by their rulers, are the bearers of this violence, the agents appointed by history to cleanse and punish. But the people are never given individual stories to tell or indeed, as I mentioned earlier, the power of articulate speech.

In *A Tale of Two Cities*, on the other hand, the fall of the *ancien régime* is the result of a neglected and pitifully meagre agriculture, for which Dickens had turned to the account of Arthur Young, the arrogance and cruelty of the aristocratic ruling order and the unwillingness of the *ancien régime* to reform. It was a regime enveloped in 'the leprosy of unreality' (II, vii, 111).[72] In the poverty-stricken district of Saint-Antoine, 'cold, dirt, sickness, ignorance and want, were the lords in waiting on the saintly presence'. Hunger was palpable. 'The children had ancient faces and grave voices'. Hunger in turn generated a smouldering rage. 'Depressed and slinking though they were, eyes of fire were not wanting among them; nor compressed lips, white with what they suppressed . . . in the hunted air of the people there was yet some wild beast thought of the possibility of turning at bay' (I, v, 32–3). Far from 'vague', Dickens's evocation of the life of the rural and urban poor in the last decades of the *ancien régime* and his eye for significant detail were at least as sharp as those of the best twentieth-century social historians. His historical account makes it entirely credible that, when the opportunity finally arose and the Bastille was besieged, the regime found itself at the mercy of a 'remorseless sea of turbulently swaying shapes, voices of vengeance, and faces hardened in the furnaces of suffering until the touch of pity could make no mark on them' (II, xxi, 229).

But it was not solely poverty that fuelled their anger. Something even stronger also drove their hatred: their abuse, the gross iniquities of unequal laws and uncontrolled punishment, being treated with contempt, being socially excluded and sexually abused. When Evrémonde's coach runs over a child, the irritated Marquis frets at the noise the dying child makes. He tosses a coin into the crowd. But the reaction is silence and the coin is thrown back. The Marquis in turn is later murdered by the child's father, who is then made subject to a barbarous form of punishment reminiscent of that meted out to Damiens in the 1750s. The Defarges and the habitués of the wine shop in Saint-Antoine await their chance. Revolutionary violence is not indiscriminate. The violence of the Bastille crowd led by Mme Defarge and 'The Vengeance', directed at Foulon and de Launay, are not indiscriminate.

It is retribution for their past abuse of the people of Paris. Conversely, when the Revolutionary Tribunal in its first hearing of the case against Charles Darnay hear the testimony of Dr Manette, they set him free. However terrifying the trial, this was not a kangaroo court. Mme Defarge forces the reopening of the case. But even she, sometimes thought to contain echoes of Lady Macbeth in her delineation, had adequate reasons for her hatred. As she explains to Darnay's wife, Lucie, '[i]s it likely that the trouble of one wife and mother would be much to us now? She resumed her knitting and went out' (III, iii, 279); and, as Dickens explains, 'It was nothing to her, that an innocent man was to die for the sins of his forefathers; she saw not him, but them' (III, xiv, 376).

But even when the excesses of the crowds could not be ignored, as they could not at the time of the September Massacres, they were made rationally explicable. War – the imminent danger of the invasion of Paris by the army of the Duke of Brunswick in the autumn of 1792 – created widespread suspicion. 'In the universal fear and distrust that darkened the time, all the usual harmless ways of life were changed.' 'What private solicitude could rear itself against the deluge of the Year One of Liberty?' The hearts of prisoners failed them when they heard 'the thronging feet'. 'For the footsteps had become to their minds as the footsteps of a people, tumultuous under a red flag with their country declared in danger, changed into wild beasts, by terrible enchantment long persisted in'.

Compare Mary Wollstonecraft's approach to the same incidents in her 1794 history of the Revolution. 'When justice or the law is so partial, the day of retribution will come with the red sky of vengeance, to confound the innocent with the guilty. The mob were barbarous beyond the tiger's cruelty: for how could they trust a court that had so often deceived them, or expect to see its agents punished?'[73] Dickens's language for the description of the crowds and the violence of the French Revolution was not that of Burke and Carlyle, or later of Hippolyte Taine, but of the radicals of the 1790s, Paine and Wollstonecraft, or advanced Whigs like Charles James Fox and James Mackintosh; or indeed Arthur Young, who in 1792 wrote of the Revolution:

it is impossible to justify the people on their taking up arms. But is it really the people to whom we are to impute the whole; or to their oppressors who had kept them so long in a state of bondage? He who chooses to be served by slaves, must know that he holds both his property and life by tenure far different from those who prefer the service of well-treated freemen, and he who dines to the music of groaning sufferers must not, in a moment of insurrection, complain that his daughters are ravished, and then destroyed, and his son's throat are cut. When such evils happen, they are surely more imputable to the tyranny of the master, than to the cruelty of the servant.[74]

The political difference between Dickens and Carlyle did not consist solely in their different readings of the past. It very directly concerned their reading of their own epoch. When revolution broke out once again in Europe in 1848, Carlyle wrote: 'everywhere immeasurable Democracy rose monstrous, loud, blatant, inarticulate as the voice of Chaos'.[75] Compare that with Dickens writing from Paris to his friend John Forster on 29 February 1848: 'Mon ami, je trouve que j'aime tant la République, qu'il me faut renoncer ma langue et écrire seulement le langage de la République de France – langage des dieux et des Anges – langage, en un mot, des Français' ('My friend, I find that I like the Republic so much that I must renounce my own language and only write in the language of the French Republic – the language of gods and angels – the language, in a word, of the French people': *Letters*, V, 256).

There is yet another tenacious myth about the period in which Dickens was writing, which has led commentators to discount the seriousness of his politics. That is that the 1850s was 'an age of equipoise' and therefore that in *A Tale of Two Cities* a 'soothing distance' separated the novelist from his subject. This was certainly not how Dickens experienced that decade. Like other Whigs and Radicals, he was appalled by the 'iron tyranny' brought about by the 1851 *coup d'état* by which 'the cold-blooded scoundrel' Louis Napoleon declared himself Emperor of France.[76] Such a usurper with such a fragile basis of support was only too likely to imitate his uncle and plunge Europe back into war. Furthermore, with the general defeat of the 1848 revolutions, Britain was left as the only defender of liberty in Europe.

But how secure was the future of liberty and social progress in Britain itself? Dickens dedicated *A Tale of Two Cities* to Lord John Russell, the Whig prime minister between 1846 and 1852, and reinforced this dedication by naming the hero of his story 'Sydney Carton', a clear reference to the great Whig martyr Algernon Sydney, who had been executed in 1683 for his defence of English liberties in the Rye House Plot against the oncoming Catholic tyranny of James II. Like Russell, Dickens believed in active reforming government, both to improve the standard of life of the people and in particular to provide them with education, and abroad to police the abolition of the slave trade and support the principle of liberal government.

But after 1848, Russell had found himself thwarted by a change in the climate of opinion. Anxiety about Chartism and revolution gave way to complacency and self-congratulation, immortalized in Mr Podsnap. There was no longer energetic support for active reforming government. Instead, public opinion concurred in believing that taxes could and should be further reduced, since Britain's liberal principles would triumph without any active intervention on the part of government.[77]

A Tale of Two Cities was therefore intended as a warning. Britain could suffer the fate of France in 1789, not because of loss of faith, but because of a *laissez-faire* complacency, lethargy and the lack of any will to engage in serious reform. As Dickens wrote to the radical and archaeologist Austen Layard in 1855,

> there is nothing in the present time at once so galling and so alarming to me as the alienation of the people from their own public affairs. I have no difficulty in understanding it. They have had so little to do with the Game through all these years of Parliamentary Reform, that they have sullenly laid down their cards and taken to looking on ... And I believe the discontent to be so much the worse for smouldering instead of blazing openly, that it is extremely like the general mind of France before the breaking out of the first Revolution, and is in danger of being turned by any one of a thousand accidents – a bad harvest – the last straw too much of aristocratic insolence or incapacity – a defeat abroad – a mere chance at home – into such a Devil of a conflagration as has never been beheld since.
>
> (*Letters*, VII, 587)

*

In this chapter, I have compared the ways in which the historical and political significance of revolutionary violence was explained and assessed by three of the most powerful writers and historical observers of the nineteenth century – all, as it happens, living within a few miles of each other in London in the 1850s. The great strength of the account put forward by Carlyle, and to some extent followed by Marx, at least in relation to the Revolution of 1789, was that it grasped the undeniably world-changing significance of the actions of the crowd. As Marx put it in *Capital*, force was 'the mid-wife of every old society, pregnant with a new one'.[78] It was 'the instrument with the aid of which every social movement forces its way through and shatters the dead fossilised political forms'.

But the danger of such an approach, particularly when generalized by Marx, was its assumption that there was a general equation between revolution and progress, and that the putative long-term social effects of the action of collectivities could be divorced from their immediate and individual human costs. The indecisive and often disenchanting experience of the 1848 revolutions undermined for many the sense that revolution of itself provided a royal road to progress, even if it reinforced for a few the notion that violent change was necessary and must be organized.

After the gargantuan scale on which revolutionary violence was practised in the twentieth century, the view espoused by Dickens and the English radicals of the 1790s – often then dismissed as naive and apolitical – may now be seen to have more to be said for it. Revolutions as revolts of the people against manifest injustice and oppression have justification. But that justification consists in the fact that the anger, which emanated from 'the cold, dirt, sickness, ignorance and want' produced by an oppressive or tyrannical regime, could find no other expression except in violence and a cycle of revenge. In this perspective, revolution is sometimes a regrettable necessity, but understandable though it may be, there is no redemptive value in violence in itself. Is, then, revolution still to be automatically associated with progress? In the light of twentieth-century experience, we might prefer the more interrogative note adopted by the lowly seamstress in her final remarks to Carton, before facing the guillotine. 'I am not unwilling to die, if the Republic which is to do so much good to us poor, will profit by my death, but I do not know how that can be' (III, xiii, 368).

Notes

1. In 1832, John Stuart Mill commented that it was 'the vainest of fancies to look for any improvement in the government or in the condition of the people when even honest men are apt to consider any misconduct on the part of the Government a full justification for civil war, and when every King, every minister, considers every act of resistance to Government a justification for suspending the constitution and assuming dictatorial power'. Cited in Georgios Varouxakis, *Victorian Political Thought on France and the French* (Basingstoke: Palgrave Macmillan, 2002), p. 60.
2. Thomas Carlyle, *The French Revolution*, 3 vols. (London, 1837). References in this essay will be to the World Classics one-volume edition, ed. K. J. Fielding and David Sorensen (Oxford: Oxford University Press, 1989).
3. Anon. (J. S. Mill) review of Walter Scott, *Life of Napoleon Bonaparte*, *Monthly Review*, n.s. V1 (September 1827), pp. 92–5, in 'Essays on French History and Historians', ed. John M. Robson, *Collected Works of John Stuart Mill*, XX, pp. 58–9.
4. James Mackintosh, *Vindiciae Gallicae* (Dublin: [n. pub.], 1791), p. 195; Madame de Staël stated, 'My ambition will be to speak of the age in which we have lived, as if it were already remote'. *Considerations on the Principal Events of the French Revolution*, 3 vols. (London: [n. pub.], 1818), I, p. 2.
5. R. J. Mackintosh, *Memoirs of the Life of Sir James Mackintosh*, 2 vols. (London: E. Moxon, 1835), I, pp. 413–14.
6. Introducing his French Revolution lectures in 1832, Smyth stated: 'During all these lectures, the lesson that I am constantly endeavouring to enforce, is the duty in politics, of moderation'. 'After all', he had written earlier surveying the situation in 1792, 'it is possible, that war might have been avoided by both countries, if the popular party in France (that guilty party), could but have behaved with any tolerable moderation, and justice to their fallen monarch'. W. Smyth, *Lectures on History: Second and Concluding Series on the French Revolution* (Cambridge: J. and J. Deighton, 1842), pp. 46, 269.
7. These were aspects of what Smyth called a 'new morality'. 'Measures of injustice, systems of confiscation and plunder, proscriptions, insurrections, the murder of a king, the murder of each other, the destruction of a large part of the population, of a whole town, of the inhabitants of a whole district or province, all these outrages on humanity were always announced to the public and to the world, as acts of patriotism in the actors, as necessary to the Revolution, as evils that would be compensated by the future freedom and happiness of France, as calamities that must be overlooked, for the present, on account of the future consequences.' Smyth, *Lectures on History*, VIII, p. 252.

8. Hedva Ben-Israel, *English Historians in the French Revolution* (Cambridge: Cambridge University Press, 1968), pp. 116–19.
9. Carlyle, 'Goethe', in *Critical and Miscellaneous Essays*, 5 vols. (Chicago and New York: Belford, Clarke & Co., 1899), I, pp. 172–223. Carlyle owed this idea to one of his main sources of inspiration, the German romantic writer Jean Paul Richter. Richter wrote, 'die Geschichte ist ... die dritte Bibel'. Cited in John D. Rosenberg, *Carlyle and the Burden of History* (Oxford: Clarendon Press, 1985), pp. 7–8.
10. See Rosenberg, *Carlyle and the Burden*, pp. 16–17.
11. Cited in Ben-Israel, *English Historians*, p. 136.
12. See Gareth Stedman Jones, 'The Return of Language: Radicalism and the British Historians 1960–1990', in *Political Language in the Age of Extremes*, ed. W. Steinmetz, forthcoming 2009.
13. Carlyle described his experience fictionally in *Sartor Resartus* as the culmination of the 'Sorrows of Teufelsdrökh' [*sic*] in the Rue St Thomas de l'Enfer in the chapter entitled 'The Everlasting No'. He later recalled that this crisis was based on his own life and took place on the road leading from Edinburgh to the beach and seashore at Leith. See John Morrow, *Thomas Carlyle* (London: Hambledon Continuum, 2006), pp. 16–17.
14. On Carlyle's vision of the French Revolution as a 'modern apocalypse', see Rosenberg, *Carlyle and the Burden*, p. 13.
15. Carlyle, *French Revolution*, pp. 10–11.
16. Carlyle, *French Revolution*, p. 11
17. Carlyle, *French Revolution*, p. 55.
18. Carlyle, *French Revolution*, p. 16.
19. Carlyle, *French Revolution*, pp. 31, 38.
20. Carlyle, *French Revolution*, pp. 39–40. As John Burrow has pointed out, one of Carlyle's early passions was geology. Indeed, the original reason why he first learnt German was in order to read the geologist Abraham Gottlob Werner. Carlyle's image of the earth-rind and his picture of the material (and cultural) world as an endless cycle of decay, cataclysm and renewal derived from the geology of James Hutton, whose *System of the Earth* (1785) was strongly advocated by Carlyle's Edinburgh teacher, John Playfair. See John Burrow, 'Images of Time: from Carlylean Vulcanism to Sedimentary Gradualism', in *History, Religion and Culture: British Intellectual History 1750–1950*, ed. Stefan Collini, Richard Whatmore and Brian Young (Cambridge: Cambridge University Press, 2000), pp. 206–10.
21. Rosenberg, *Carlyle and the Burden*, pp. 93–4.
22. Carlyle, *French Revolution*, p. 216.
23. Carlyle, *French Revolution*, p. 216. Carlyle frequently used the image of Enceladus to evoke the people, the crowd or the working classes. See, for instance, Carlyle, *Chartism* (London: Chapman & Hall, 2nd edn. 1842), p. 89. Enceladus was one of the Titans who fought against the gods of Mount Olympus. As Enceladus was fleeing, Athene threw at him the island of Sicily, which landed on top of him.
24. Carlyle, *French Revolution*, p. 221.
25. Carlyle, *French Revolution*, p. 222.
26. Carlyle, *Chartism*, p. 41.
27. Carlyle, *Chartism*, p. 41.
28. Carlyle, *Chartism*, p. 37.
29. Carlyle, *Chartism*, pp. 44, 103.
30. Carlyle, *Chartism*, p. 89
31. Carlyle, *French Revolution*, p. 443.

32. 'Democracy is, by the nature of it, a self-cancelling business; and gives in the long-run a net-result of *zero*. Where no government is wanted, save that of the parish-constable, as in America with its boundless soil, every man being able to find work and recompense for himself, democracy may subsist; not elsewhere, except briefly, as a swift transition towards something other and further'. Carlyle, *Chartism*, p. 53: 'Democracy, which means despair of finding any Heroes to govern you, and contented putting up with the want of them, alas, thou too, *mein Lieber*, seest well how close it is of kin to *Atheism*, and other sad *Isms*.' Carlyle, *Past and Present* (London, 1843), p. 289.
33. See Frederick C. Beiser, *The Fate of Reason: German Philosophy from Kant to Fichte* (Cambridge, MA and London: Harvard University Press, 1987), pp. 38–43.
34. Carlyle, *Past and Present*, p. 253.
35. Carlyle, *French Revolution*, p. 40.
36. 'Nature', Carlyle continued, 'still makes him; and has an Infernal in her as well as a Celestial'. Carlyle, *French Revolution*, p. 376
37. 'As time adds much to the sacredness of Symbols, so likewise in his progress he at length defaces, or even desecrates them; and Symbols like all terrestial garments, wax old'. Carlyle, *Sartor Resartus* (1831; London, 1870), pp. 137, 133–8.
38. Carlyle, *Past and Present*, p. 190; Catherine Gallagher, *The Industrial Reformation of English Fiction 1832–1867* (Chicago and London: University of Chicago Press, 1985), pp. 195–200.
39. Carlyle, *Sartor Resartus*, pp. 149–55.
40. Carlyle, *Past and Present*, p. 328.
41. Carlyle, *Past and Present*, p. 202.
42. 'It is in and through *Symbols* that man, consciously or unconsciously, lives, works, and has is being: those ages moreover, are accounted the noblest which can the best recognize symbolical worth, and prize it the highest'. Carlyle, *Sartor Resartus*, p. 136.
43. Carlyle, *Past and Present*, pp. 4–5; Carlyle, *French Revolution*, p. 376. The human skin tannery at Meudon was almost certainly a myth. But see the discussion in Rosenberg, pp. 94–5.
44. 'Von der Societe St Simonienne bitte sich fern zu halten' ('please keep your distance from the St Simonian Society'). Cited in Georg Bernhard Tennyson, *Sartor Called Resartus: The Genesis, Structure and Style of Thomas Carlyle's First Major Work* (Princeton, NJ: Princeton University Press, 1965), p. 143. The Saint-Simonian 'apostle' Gustave d'Eichthal visited England in an effort to convert Mill and Carlyle. See Richard K. P. Pankhurst, *The Saint-Simonians, Mill and Carlyle: A Preface to Modern Thought* (London: Sidgwick & Jackson, 1957). Although Carlyle's embrace of a post-Christian religion resembled the starting point of the socialists, his residual Calvinism with its emphasis on man's capacity for evil separated him from the optimistic Pelagian or Lockean assumptions which underpinned most varieties of socialism before 1850.
45. On the 'theocratic' critique of the Revolution, see de Bonald's critique of Condorcet in 'Supplement aux deux premières parties de la Théorie du Pouvoir politique et religieux', in *Oeuvres complètes de M. de Bonald*, ed. l'Abbé Migne (Paris: [n. pub.] 1864), I, pp. 722–42; more generally, see Joseph de Maistre, *Considerations on France* (1797), trans. and ed. Richard A. Lebrun (Cambridge: Cambridge University Press, 1994).
46. See *The Doctrine of Saint Simon: An Exposition: First Year, 1828–1829*, trans. Georg G. Iggers (Cambridge, MA: Harvard University Press, 1958).

47. Carlyle, *Chartism*, p. 57.
48. Carlyle, *French Revolution*, p. 37.
49. Carlyle, *French Revolution*, p. 122.
50. Carlyle, *French Revolution*, p. 202.
51. Carlyle, *Chartism*, p. 6.
52. Carlyle, *Chartism*, p. 52.
53. Carlyle, *Past and Present*, pp. 212, 215, 218–19.
54. Carlyle, *Past and Present*, pp. 214–15.
55. Carlyle, *Sartor Resartus*, p. 134.
56. Cited in Tennyson, *Sartor Called Resartus*, p. 90.
57. Friedrich Engels, 'The Condition of England. *Past and Present* by Thomas Carlyle' (London, 1843), in *Karl Marx and Friedrich Engels Collected Works*, (hereafter *MECW*) (London, 1975), III, pp. 444, 450, 455, 464.
58. *MECW*, III, p. 463.
59. *MECW*, III, pp. 460–1.
60. Friedrich Engels, 'The Condition of the Working-Class in England', *MECW*, IV, p. 323.
61. Carlyle's reference was made to support his argument that it was not 'nakedness, hunger distress of all kinds, death itself' that man found intolerable. It is the feeling of *injustice* that is insupportable to all men'. Carlyle, *Chartism*, p. 36.
62. Karl Marx, 'Speech at the Anniversary of *The People's Paper*', *MECW*, XIV, pp. 655–6.
63. See Gallagher, *Industrial Reformation*, chs. 5 and 8.
64. Karl Marx and Friedrich Engels, 'The Holy Family' (1844), *MECW*, IV, p. 37.
65. Karl Marx, 'Critical Marginal Notes on the Article by a Prussian', *MECW*, III, p. 197; 'The Holy Family', p. 122; and see also François Furet, *Marx et la Révolution française* (Paris: Flammarion, 1986).
66. Karl Marx, 'On the Jewish Question', *MECW*, III, p. 156.
67. Karl Marx, 'Moralising Criticism and Critical Morality: A Contribution to German Cultural History contra Karl Heinzen', *MECW*, VI, p. 319.
68. Karl Marx, 'The Eighteenth Brumaire of Louis Bonaparte', *MECW*, XI, pp. 103–4.
69. Marx, 'Eighteenth Brumaire', p. 106.
70. Karl Marx, 'Preface to the Critique of Political Economy', *MECW*, XXIX, p. 263.
71. Although Dickens may have relied on Carlyle for crucial aspects of his picture of the *ancien régime* and of the sequence of revolutionary events leading up to the September Massacres and the king's death, he took care to complement this account with other sources – primarily, the *Annual Register* for England in the 1770s, Sebastian Mercier for the changing life of Paris and Arthur Young for the state of the French countryside in 1789. Invaluable on this and many other points is Andrew Sanders, *The Companion to* A Tale of Two Cities (London: Unwin Hyman, 1988).
72. 'Military officers destitute of military knowledge; naval officers with no idea of a ship; civil officers without a notion of affairs, brazen ecclesiastics of the worst world worldly, with sensual eyes, loose tongues and looser lives' (II, vii, 110).
73. Mary Wollstonecraft, *An Historical and Moral View of the Origin and Progress of the French Revolution* (London: [n. pub.], 1794), pp. 234–5.
74. Cited in Sanders, *Companion to* A Tale, p. 395.
75. Carlyle, *Latter Day Pamphlets* (London: Chapman & Hall, 1850), p. 6.

76. See Dickens to F. O. Ward, 14 January 1852, *Letters*, VI, p. 575.
77. On the climate of opinion in the 1850s and the frustrations of the Whig radicalism of Lord John Russell, see Jonathan Parry, *The Politics of Patriotism: English Liberalism, National Identity and Europe 1830–1886* (Cambridge: Cambridge University Press, 2006), esp. ch. 4.
78. Karl Marx, 'Capital', *MECW*, XXXV, p. 739.

4
A Genealogy of Dr Manette

Keith Michael Baker

The aim of this essay is to explore some possible sources for Dickens's portrait of Dr Manette.[1] When it came to this central figure in his novel, Dickens's imagination was evidently fed by several springs, not least his memories of prisoners he had seen in Philadelphia.[2] Perhaps, too, recalling a famous passage in Laurence Sterne's *Sentimental Journey Through France and Italy* (1768), he also saw in his mind's eye the Bastille prisoner Sterne's Yorick fancied he might become, pale and feverish after thirty years in chains, hopelessly engaged in 'work of affliction' to mark the passage of his days, his body 'half wasted away with long expectation and confinement'. In emphatically sentimentalist mode, Sterne had invited his readers to share with his protagonist in this imagined prisoner's despair, feeling to the point of tears 'what kind of sickness of the heart it was which arises from hope deferr'd'.[3]

To unravel the literary skein further, one might ask whether Sterne in his turn had encountered the innocent young Huron of Voltaire's *L'Ingénu* (1767), carried into the Bastille 'like a corpse being transported to the cemetery'.[4] (It turns out, though, that imprisonment afforded this Voltairean hero the opportunity to mix his tears with a lengthy tutorial in theology, philosophy and history from the persecuted Jansenist who became his cellmate. He is closer to Candide than the solitary, despairing prisoner imagined in *A Sentimental Journey*.) Sterne had surely discussed with Diderot and Baron d'Holbach and others, during his Paris visits earlier in the 1760s, the fortress that had in its time welcomed so many dissidents, men of letters and other unfortunates, that 'hideous château, palace of vengeance' Voltaire had evoked throughout the many editions of his *Henriade* (1723).[5] And since an obvious place to search for a prototype of Dr Manette is among the more historical accounts of these other former prisoners of the Bastille, that is where the search will begin. It may turn out, though, that these accounts are no less imaginative than their more obviously literary counterparts.

I

I shall begin by pointing to the broader context in which Bastille prisoners were discussed in pre-revolutionary France and eventually liberated in 1789. Dr Manette is a victim, a victim of what might be called aristo-despotism, the repressive force of aristocracy and despotism combined, the fusion of social oppression and arbitrary political power into the principle of an entire social order. There were many such victims of aristo-despotism, real and fictitious, to be found in the political imaginary of eighteenth-century France. Indeed, the modern discourse of victimization found its origins precisely in that period. This is not to say that there were no victims before the eighteenth century. But the French developed a particularly powerful and sentimental discourse of victimization that formed part of their construction of the modern self. It is not surprising, from this perspective, that Sterne's *Sentimental Journey* was rapidly translated into French and frequently imitated thereafter, often in a Rousseauian vein.[6]

Rousseau, poor persecuted Jean-Jacques, is a key figure here. He offered himself up in his *Confessions* (1782) and other writings as the quintessential victimized self, wronged not just by a tyrannical political power but by the generalised system of oppression some dared to call 'society'. Rousseau socialized despotism, made it social as well as political, saw it running through the entire social order. He subjectivized victimhood, transforming virtue – at least, the only virtue possible in modern society – into the sentimental identification of the self with the oppressed other. In the new secular imaginary of suffering, the victim replaced the martyr.

Nowhere was this sentimentalized language of victimization put to better use than in the lawcourts, an institution as central to the political culture of the French *ancien régime* as it would be to the plot of *A Tale of Two Cities*. Sarah Maza has written an excellent book on the judicial *causes célèbres* of the *ancien régime*, highlighting the ways the published pleadings in these cases offered everyday melodramas of intimidation and social violence in which the innocent fell prey to arrogant courtiers, exploitative aristocrats, ministerial despotism or a harsh judicial system.[7]

One case of this kind, not discussed by Maza, was pleaded in Arras in 1786. The young barrister's name was Maximilien Robespierre. The future Incorruptible defended an old couple detained pending trial on charges of usury, during which time of imprisonment the husband had lost his mind. 'His unhinged imagination saw only chains, cells, guards and executioners, and his senseless and incoherent speech recovered only frightful images', Robespierre laments in his printed *mémoire* appealing the wife's harsh eventual sentence. Indeed, he finds the sight of this distracted old man so moving that he cannot continue. 'I suppress these overwhelming reflections ...', he writes. 'I stifle the cry of grief ...'.[8]

This same language of sentimentalized outrage also found its way into the dramatic pamphlet literature that made the Bastille a symbol of despotism in the last two decades of the Old Regime. Rolf Reichardt and Hans-Jürgen Lüsebrink have provided a rich analysis of the appearance of this literature, as of the growing gap between the legendary Bastille and the actual conditions within the prison.[9] Clandestine memoirs of Bastille prisoners had appeared intermittently throughout the century, but the anti-Bastille pamphleteering began to take on a more radical political focus in the 1770s. One of its central works, published as *Remarques historiques et anecdotes sur le château de la Bastille,* first appeared at the time of Louis XVI's accession in 1774 among the flood of clandestine publications protesting against the arbitrary rule of Louis XV's last ministers.[10] Attributed to Brossais du Perray, it was translated into English in 1780 on the initiative of the prison reformer John Howard. Reprinted again in French a few years later, together with another classic of the anti-despotism pamphlet literature, *Le Gazetier Cuirassé,* it was recycled several more times in 1789.[11] Written to inspire hatred of despotism by denouncing the mental and physical horrors inflicted on those arbitrarily detained in this most fearsome of fortresses, it gathered descriptions of cases of prisoners confined in the Bastille over the preceding decades. The series of cases was radically enlarged when the pamphlet was reprinted in 1789.

The cries of this pamphlet paled, though, in comparison with the most famous and commercially successful work in the anti-Bastille literature, the *Mémoires sur la Bastille* published from London by the journalist and former barrister – and recent Bastille prisoner – Simon-Nicolas-Henri Linguet in 1783 and circulated rapidly and widely throughout Europe in the years thereafter. Unrivalled for the immediacy and emotional urgency of prose already honed in his judicial briefs, Linguet in effect opened the Bastille to all with his descriptions of its 'tortures of the soul, its prolonged convulsions, its perpetual agony that renders eternal the miseries of death'. Linguet's Bastille prisoner, languishing there because he has displeased a minister or his subaltern, or one of their valets, finds himself 'abandoned without resource of any kind, with no other distraction but his thoughts and anxieties, to the most bitter sentiment that can affect a heart that crime has not degraded, the sentiment of outraged innocence as it sees itself perishing with no way of making itself known …'. He lies isolated and forgotten in his cell, held 'in this absolute silence … this nothingness more cruel than death … this universal abstraction'. 'He senses his existence being daily extinguished, and at the same time feels he is being kept alive only to prolong his punishment.' Linguet does not demand justice for the wretched prisoners of the Bastille. Instead, he calls for the demolition of the entire structure. 'Speak', he adjures Louis XVI, 'at your voice the walls of this modern Jericho will fall. This would be the glory of your reign.'[12]

Other pamphlets followed. In 1787, Henri Masers de Latude scored a distinct success with his *Histoire d'une détention de trente-neuf ans, dans les prisons d'état. Ecrite par le prisnnier lui-même.* As much dramatic narrative as it was political protest, this novelistic work charted Latude's imprisonment by order of Mme de Pompadour, his vain efforts to secure his release, his several attempts at escape and his eventual release in 1784 after a long public campaign on his behalf. Latude claimed that he had spent 12,163 days in different prisons, sleeping on straw, devoured by disgusting insects, reduced to bread and water, his hands and feet in chains for 1,218 of these days, or rather 'these perpetual and hideous nights'. Could anyone, after reading these memoirs, 'refuse ... a tear of pity?'[13]

In the meantime, Mirabeau had fuelled the anti-Bastille fire with his incendiary *Des lettres de cachet et des prisons de l'Etat* (1782), the cosmopolitan adventurer Cagliostro had fought publicly to save himself from imprisonment in the Bastille for his involvement in the Diamond Necklace Affair, and Beaumarchais's Figaro wittily had boasted of the six months of free lodging he had enjoyed within its walls (a joke with a long history). By 1789, there was a rich reservoir of words and images that gave symbolic meaning to the taking of the Bastille and the liberation of its prisoners. We know, of course, that only seven prisoners were left in the Bastille by 14 July 1789. But their symbolic significance did not depend on their numbers, and descriptions of their liberation became crucial in the newspapers and pamphlets heralding the moment of transition from an old regime to a new.[14]

As Reichardt and Lüsebrink suggest, the stereotypical prisoner portrayed by the Bastille literature was an old man, white-haired, often to the waist. He first emerged from his cell in Louis-Sébastien Mercier's report of prisoners liberated in celebration of Louis XVI's ascension in 1774.

> Among their number was an old man who, for forty-seven years, had groaned in detention within four thick, cold walls. Hardened by adversity, which strengthens a man when it does not kill him, he had endured the boredom and horrors of captivity with a firm and courageous constancy. His white, thin hair had acquired almost the rigidity of iron, and his body, buried for so long in a coffin of stone, seemed to have contracted its compact solidity.[15]

Delivered from his tomb, the prisoner 'believes this is a dream. He hesitates, he rises, he walks with trembling step, he is astonished by the space he traverses. To him, the prison staircase, its hall, its courtyard, all seem vast, immense, almost endless. He stops as if disoriented and lost; his eyes can scarcely stand the full light of day; he cannot weep.' Led to his former home, he finds that it has been demolished and replaced, that nothing and no one in this city is familiar to him after his decades of imprisonment. Weeping, he longs to return to his cell. He is brought to a frail former servant, from whom he learns that 'his wife had died thirty years ago, from grief and misery; that his children had left for unknown climes; that all his friends were no more'.[16]

In 1789, the same account of this old man was included verbatim in the catalogue of past Bastille prisoners in a much enlarged version of the 1774 *Remarques historiques et anecdotes*.[17] Other descriptions of those freed on 14 July 1789 often included one or more old men weakened in mind and body by long imprisonment. There was

> a beautiful man, at least five feet and eight inches tall, who according to his own statement had been imprisoned for thirty years; he is around sixty-five to seventy years old …. Supported, he was led through all of Paris; at the Palais Royal, an unusual and very memorable scene met the eye: on the one side this courageous old man among his liberators, on the other side the speared heads of the governor, his deputy, and a warder, who had tyrannized this miserable old man for thirty years.

Several other reports singled out a prisoner grown old while long behind bars. He was variously 'a harmless old man', a man whose 'beard reached down to his stomach', a man with 'a massive grey beard … more than a foot long', a man 'whose hair had grown white in a captivity of forty years'.

Délivrance de M. le Comte de Lorges, prisonnier à la Bastille depuis 32 ans.

Illustration 4.1   The freeing of the Comte de Lorges, prisoner in the Bastille (courtesy, Bibliothèque Nationale de France)

Although his name initially varied from account to account, this pathetic figure was soon identified as the comte de Lorge (or Lorges). This was the name he was given in yet another 1789 edition of the 1774 *Remarques historiques et anecdotes*, revised and expanded to provide a description of the taking of the Bastille and the liberation of its prisoners.[18] In a further account, *Le langage des murs, Ou les cachots de la Bastille devoilant leurs secrets*, de Lorges's now empty cell was quickly shown to a visitor by a workman as the entire prison was being demolished. An inscription on its wall called out for revenge. 'Yes, you are avenged', exclaimed the visitor, 'avenged not by a single man but by a whole nation, impatient for liberty, which has conquered in a single night a prejudice of twelve centuries, by the blows of the French who have united to lay low the dreadful monster of despotism that, covered with the liveries of the highest power, devoured victims without number.'[19]

Jean-Louis Carra described seeing de Lorges for the first time among the liberated prisoners taken to the Hôtel de Ville on 14 July 1789. 'One saw with surprise an old man whose beard reached down to his belt, worthy of respect for the ills that he had suffered and the length of his captivity.' Carra recalled that he visited the former prisoner again: 'he told me the history of his imprisonment and promised details of the other circumstances of his life'. Carra quickly published the details of the count's imprisonment, first in a separate pamphlet and then as part of his widely circulated *Mémoires historiques at authentiques sur la Bastille*.[20]

II

What relationship might there be between this Bastille literature and the character of Dr Manette? It seems highly likely that Dickens found a copy of the *Tableau de Paris*, with its vivid portrayal of the white-haired, disoriented prisoner freed from the Bastille in 1774, among the 'two cartloads' of books on the French Revolution he borrowed from Carlyle as he was preparing to write his novel.[21] And there are enough similarities between this unnamed prisoner and Dickens's character – beginning with the date of their release at the beginnning of Louis XVI's reign – to suggest a strong connection. But is it possible that the later accounts of the Comte de Lorges also offered Dickens a germ of the idea of Dr Manette? It is a long way from Paris in 1789 to London in the 1850s though and it would be reasonable to ask how, if at all, Dickens could have known specifically of de Lorges, either directly or indirectly. This prisoner makes no appearance in Dickens's obvious source of inspiration, Carlyle's history of the French Revolution. So eloquent in describing the fall of the Bastille, Carlyle was relatively restrained when it came to its prisoners. We could surely have expected more of him on this subject.[22] Dr Rigby, an English traveller to Paris in the days immediately following 14 July 1789, reported being driven to tears at the sight of a Bastille prisoner released after 42 years (Rigby remembered the name, perhaps misheard by his foreign ear, as 'Count d'Auche'), but his letters to his family during this period, wonderful as they are, were not published until 1880.[23]

Fortunately, we do have another, well-documented and quite specific source for the transmission of the story of the comte de Lorges to Britain. It comes in the person who did every bit as much as Dickens and Carlyle to shape the British view of the French Revolution in the nineteenth century and beyond, namely Marie Grosholz, later Madame Tussaud. In her *Memoires*, Tussaud recalled that this 'most remarkable' among the former prisoners of the Bastille was brought to her immediately upon his release, 'that she might take a cast from his face, which she completed, and still possesses amongst her collection. It is a whole length resemblance taken from life. He had been thirty years in the Bastille, and when liberated from it, having lost all relish for the world, requested to be re-conducted to his late prison, and died a few weeks after his emancipation.'[24] This figure was immediately exhibited in the famous Paris waxworks of the man Mme Tussaud called her uncle, Philippe

Illustration 4.2 Madame Tussaud, The Comte de Lorges (courtesy of Madame Tussaud's)

Curtius, and it was one of the objects she brought with her to England when she escaped France in 1802.[25]

De Lorges, victim of that 'horrid despotism that had prevailed [in France], and might, at any future time, be renewed in that kingdom', was described at length in the first catalogue of Tussaud's show in 1803, though the details given there drew heavily on the narrative of the life of Latude.[26] The description was changed in subsequent catalogues and suspicious details eliminated. 'The existence of this unfortunate man in the Bastille, has by some been doubted', visitors were told after 1823. 'Madame Tussaud is a living witness of his being taken out of that prison, on the 14 July 1789. Madame Tussaud was then residing in the house of her uncle, No. 20, Boulevard du Temple, Paris. The Count was brought to the house, but his chains had been taken off. The poor man, unused to liberty for upwards of 20 years, seemed to be in a new world: 'freedom had no joys for him:– he had lost his relatives – and habit made him repine for the solitude from which he had been taken. He frequently with tears, would beg to be restored to his dungeon. The unfortunate Count lived but six weeks after his liberation. The cause of his confinement was his having given offence to a Minister.'[27]

De Lorges remained in what became the Chamber of Horrors far longer than he ever languished in the Bastille – throughout the nineteenth century and for the better part of the twentieth. And this is where the author of *A Tale of Two Cities* made his acquaintance. We know that Dickens was a great fan of Madame Tussaud's and he left us a vivid prescription for a visit to the Chamber of Horrors in *All the Year Round*. 'To enter the Chamber of Horrors rather late in the afternoon, before the gas is lighted, requires courage', he warned.

> Let the visitor enter this very terrible apartment at a swift pace and without pausing for an instant, let him turn sharply to the right, and scamper under the scaffold, taking care that this structure – which is very low – does not act after the manner of the guillotine it sustains, and take his head off. Let him thoroughly master all the circumstances of the Count de Lorge's imprisonment, the serge dress, the rats, the brown loaf – let him then hasten up the step of the guillotine and saturate his mind with the blood upon the decapitated heads of the sufferers in the French Revolution – this done, the worst is over.[28]

It seems reasonable, then, to conclude that at least one of the lines in the genealogy of Dr Manette runs from the comte de Lorges, via Madame Tussaud's and Curtius's waxworks, back to the anti-Bastille publications of 1789, and beyond that to the *ancien régime* pamphlets upon which those writings drew. But there is an additional wrinkle to this story, which is that de Lorges never actually existed. We can admire Madame Tussaud's brilliance in taking a cast from a nonexistent face. But the fact of the matter is that de Lorges was invented by Carra, who recycled earlier narratives of Bastille imprisonment to produce the memoirs of its quintessential prisoner. He was endowed with bodily form by Curtius, who had him on exhibition in Paris almost as soon as the ink was dry on Carra's pamphlet. And he was smuggled to Britain, and most brilliantly merchandised there, by that most enterprising counter-revolutionary impresario of the nineteenth century, Madame Tussaud.

Nineteenth-century conservatives famously blamed the free-thinking of Voltaire and Rousseau for the outbreak of the Revolution: it was, it was said, *'la faute à Voltaire, la faute à Rousseau'*: 'Voltaire's fault', 'Rousseau's fault'. At risk of a bad pun, and whatever Dickens's genius in the matter, one might say of the creation of his quintessential Bastille prisoner that, at least in part, *C'etait la faute à Tussaud.*

Notes

1. I wish to thank John Bender and Dan Edelstein for helpful comments on earlier drafts.
2. Andrew Sanders, *The Companion to* A Tale of Two Cities (London: Unwin Hyman, 1988), pp. 48–51.
3. Laurence Sterne, *A Sentimental Journey through France and England,* ed. Melvyn New and W.G. Day, in *The Florida Edition of the Works of Laurence Sterne* (Gainesville, FL, 2002), vol. 6, pp. 97–8.
4. Voltaire, *L'Ingénu,* ed. Richard A. Francis, *Les Oeuvres complètes de Voltaire,* vol. 63C (Oxford: Voltaire Foundation, 2006), p. 249. Unless otherwise noted, translations from the French are my own.
5. On Sterne's visits to France, see Arthur H. Cash, *Laurence Sterne: The Later Years* (London and New York: Methuen, 1986), pp. 124–51, 176–88. In addition to radical men of letters Sterne enjoyed an acquaintance in Paris with the Prince de Conti, secretly the patron of Jansenist dissidents and their protector from the Bastille.
6. Lana Asfour, 'Movements of Sensibility and Sentiment: Sterne in Eighteenth-Century France', in *The Reception of Laurence Sterne in Europe,* ed. Peter de Voogd and John Neubauer (Bristol: Thoemmes Continuum, 2004), pp. 9–31.
7. Sarah Maza, *Private Lives and Public Affairs: The Causes Célèbres of Prerevolutionary France* (Berkeley, CA: University of California Press, 1993).
8. *Oeuvres complètes de Maximilien Robespierre,* ed. Victor Barbier and Charles Vellay (Paris, 1910), vol. 1, pp. 283, 286 ('Affaire de François Page').
9. Rolf Reichardt and Hans-Jurgen Lüsebrink, *The Bastille: A History of a Symbol of Despotism and Freedom,* trans. Norbert Schürer (Durham, NC: Duke University Press, 1997).
10. *Remarques historiques et anecdotes sur le château de la Bastille* ('Historical Remarks and Anecdotes on the chateau of the Bastille') (n. pub., 1774). To push the pamphlet's sales, the *Mémoires secrets* remarked on its clandestine availability on 19 March 1775, intimating that it was written 'by some of the unfortunate prisoners detained at the end of Louis XV's reign in relation to the troubles excited in the state by the last revolution' – meaning by the latter phrase the suppression of the *parlements* by Maupeou in 1771 (they were restored at Louis XVI's accession). The newsletter added another pitch on 23 March, by insisting that 'the [Bastille] plan and the

details concerning the organization, discipline, and assaults that the prisoners have to suffer in the château; the interrogations, shocks, and violence to which they are exposed, are extremely exact and curious'. *Mémoires secrets pour servir à l'histoire de la république des lettres en France,* etc., 36 vols (London [Amsterdam], 1777–89), vol. VII, pp. 311, 313.

11. Le *Gazetier Cuirassé, ou Anecdotes scandaleuses de la Cour de France ... Auxquelles on a ajouté Des Remarques historiques, ou anecdotes dur le Chateau de la Bastille & l'inquisition de France. Le Plan du Château de la Bastille* ('Imprime à cent lieus de la Bastille, à l'enseigne de la Liberté', [1785?]).

12. *Mémoires sur la Bastille et la détention de l'auteur dans ce château royal depuis le 27 septembre 1780 jusqu'au 19 mai 1782* (Paris, Libraire des Bibliophiles, 1889), quotations from pp. 65, 94, 134.

13. [Henri Masers de Latude], *Histoire d'une détention de trente-neuf ans, dans les prisons d'etat. Ecrite par le prisonnier lui-même* ['History of an Imprisonment of 39 Years in State Prisons, Written by the Prisoner Himself': Amsterdam, 1787, p. 99. An English version appeared the same year.]

14. See especially Reichardt and Lüsebrink, *The Bastille.*

15. Louis-Sébastien Mercier, *Tableau de Paris,* ed. under the direction of Jean-Claude Bonnet, 2 vols. (Paris, [1794?] 1998), vol. I, pp. 725–6.

16. Mercier, *Tableau de Paris,* I, pp. 725–6.

17. *Remarques historiques sur la Bastille; sa demolition, & Revolutions de Paris, en juillet 1789. Avec un grand nombre d'anecdotes interessantes & peu connues* ('A Londres', 1789).

18. *Remarques et anecdotes sur le château de la Bastille, suivies d'un detail historique du siege, de la prise & de la demolition de cette Forteresse, Enrichies de deux gravures analogues* (Paris, 'De l'imprimerie de Grange. Et se trouve chez Goujon, Marchand de Musique, au Palais Royal', 1789), pp. 81–2.

19. [Mauclerc], *Le langage des murs, Ou les cachots de la Bastille dévoilant leurs secrets* (Paris, 1789) ['The Language of the Walls, Or, the Dungeons of the Bastille revealing their Secrets': a reprint from the *Révolutions de Paris*], p. 133.

20. [Jean-Louis Carra], 'Précis historique de la détention du Comte de Lorges à la Bastille pendant trente-deux ans; enferme en 1757, du temps de Damiens, & mis en liberté le 14 Juillet 1789', in *Mémoires historiques at authentiques sur Bastille, Dans une Suite de près de trois cens Emprisonnemens, détaillés & constatés par de Pièces, Notes, Lettres, Rapports, Proces-verbaux, trouvés dans cette Forteresse, & rangés par époques depuis 1475 jusqu'à nos jours, &c.,* 3 vols. ('A Londres et se trouve à Paris', 1789), vol. II, pp. 357–73 (quotations, pp. 357–8). The details of de Lorges's ordeal in this account appear suspiciously similar in a number of respects to those in the story of Latude's captivity, as published in the very successful *Histoire d'une détention de trente-neuf ans* of 1787 and in this same volume of Carra's *Mémoires historiques et authentiques,* pp. 286–320.

21. See J. A. Falconer, 'The Sources of *A Tale of Two Cities*', *Modern Language Notes,* 36 (1921), 3; Sanders, *Companion to* A Tale, pp. 48–51.

22. But Carlyle did draw on Linguet's *Mémoires* and Pierre-Louis Manuel's *La Bastille dévoilée* to recall to life another former inmate, writer of a letter cast up in 1789 with the dust of that prison. 'Likewise ashlar stones of the Bastille continue thundering through the dusk; its paper archives shall fly white. Old secrets come to view; and long-buried Despair finds voice. Read this portion of an old Letter: "If for my consolation Monseigneur would grant me, for the sake of God and the Most Sacred Trinity, that I could have news of my dear wife; were it only her name on a

card, to show that she is alive! It were the greatest consolation I could receive . . . ."
Poor Prisoner, who names thyself *Quéret-Démery,* and has no other history, – she is
dead, that dear wife of thine, and thou art dead! 'Tis fifty years since thy breaking
heart put this question; to be heard now first, and long heard, in the hearts of
men.' Carlyle, *The French Revolution,* vol. I, Book 5, ch. 7. Sanders identifies this
passage as a possible source for the idea of the fateful testament Dr Manette hid
in the walls of his cell. See Sanders, *Companion to* A Tale, p. 155.

23. *Dr. Rigby's Letters from France &c in 1789. Edited by his Daughter, Lady Eastlake*
     (London, 1880), pp. 66–70.

24. *Madame Tussaud's Memoirs and Reminiscences of France, Forming an Abridged History
     of the French Revolution. Edited by Francis Hervé, Esq.* (London, 1838), pp. 94–5.

25. David Bindman, *The Shadow of the Guillotine. Britain and the French Revolution*
     (London: British Museum Publications, 1989), pp. 40, 92. On the history of Mme
     Tussaud's, see Pamela Pilbeam, *Madame Tussaud and the History of Waxworks* (New
     York and London: Hambledon, 2003).

26. *Biographical Sketches of the Characters Composing the Cabinet of Composition Fig-
     ures Executed by the Celebrated Curtius of Paris and his Successor* (Edinburgh, 1803),
     pp. 40–1. I wish to thank Lela Graybill for this information on the description of de
     Lorges in Tussaud's 1803 catalogue and in the later catalogue cited in the following
     note. My understanding of Tussaud's representations of figures from the French
     Revolution more generally has also been informed by Graybill's study, 'The Wound
     and the Weapon: The Virtual Culture of Violence in the Age of Reform, 1757–1832'
     (PhD dissertation, Stanford University, 2006).

27. *Biographical and Descriptive Sketches of the Whole Length Composition Figures and
     other Works of Art Forming the Unrivalled Exhibition of Madame Tussaud* (Bristol,
     1823), pp. 38–9.

28. Charles Dickens, *All the Year Round,* 7 January 1860, p. 252, quoted in Bindman,
     The Shadow of the Guillotine, p. 92.

5
From the Old Bailey to Revolutionary France: The Trials of Charles Darnay

Sally Ledger

Dickens's novels and journalism are peppered with trial scenes: highlights include the hilarity of the Breach of Promise suit in *The Pickwick Papers*, Oliver Twist's poignant appearance before a magistrate, the Artful Dodger's comic bravado as his sentence is passed, the bullying judgment passed on Barnaby Rudge by a gentleman country magistrate, the extended satire on a Chancery suit in *Bleak House* and the high melodrama of the trials of Charles Darnay in *A Tale of Two Cities*.

In developing set-piece trial scenes, Dickens borrows from both official texts, such as the *Annual Register* and Howell's *State Trials*, and from unofficial texts, such as broadsides and prison calendars. Generically, the trial scenes lean heavily on both satire and melodrama, in each case drawing on an aesthetic grammar that was comprehensible to elite and non-elite classes alike. Melodrama was forged as a form during the French Revolution, its anti-aristocratic temper well adapted to Dickens's own political temperament and to the subject matter of *A Tale of Two Cities*. Boutet de Monvel's *Les Victimes cloitrées* ('The Cloistered Victims'), written and performed in 1791, is generally agreed to have been the first stage melodrama; characteristic of the genre during the Revolution is Sylvain Maréchal's *Le jugement dernier des rois* ('Last Judgement of Kings'), first performed, to great acclaim, in Paris in October 1793, two days after the execution of Marie Antoinette. The play's melodramatic denouement enacts the swallowing up of a whole crowd of European monarchs by a volcano, which 'consumes their very bodies'.[1]

What was it, though, that drew the nineteenth century's most successful novelist to the law in general and to the set-piece trial scene in particular? The answer is partly rooted in biography. In Peter Ackroyd's words, Dickens 'carried hatred enough for all forms of the law itself', and one cannot argue with his reflection that '[t]here is only one good judge in the whole of Dickens's work, few good solicitors, and really nothing but loud-mouthed barristers'.[2] At the same time, though, the novelist had a professional connection with the English legal system that endured even beyond the publication of his most extended satire on the law, *Bleak House*. He became a lawyer's clerk in

75

1827 and then a shorthand reporter in Doctors' Commons near St Paul's in 1829 (where he reported trials).[3] In 1834 he wrote to the Steward of New Inn stating that he intended 'entering at the bar, as soon as circumstances will enable me to do so', and there even came a time when he applied (more than once) to become a magistrate.[4] At the end of 1839 he joined Middle Temple with the idea of one day being called to the Bar; it was only in 1855, two years after the publication of *Bleak House*, that he finally withdrew his application. So, although he 'detested and pilloried the Law', he was also magnetically drawn to it.[5]

The repetition of the set-piece trial scene in Dickens's fiction can be attributed not only to his personal interest in law, but also – and simultaneously – to his lifelong passion for the theatre. In the late 1820s, by his own account, he went to the theatre every night for at least three years. Not much of a success as a playwright, he was an excellent actor, and arguably did not take to the stage as a professional only because he was ill on the day of his audition at Covent Garden.[6] The trial is the most theatrical arena of the law, full of melodramatic exaggeration and gesture, and admirably well adapted both to a staging of the legal process and to exposing its abuses.[7]

A Tale is the most theatrical of Dickens's novels, and this is in no small part due to its subject matter as well as to Dickens's liberal deployment of trial scenes. The inherent drama of the French Revolution was immediately apparent to London's theatre managers, with the fall of the Bastille inspiring a number of dramatic performances, including John Bent's *The Bastille*, performed for 79 successive nights at the Royal Circus from August 1789.[8]

Set-piece trials were a long-established staple of popular culture in the nineteenth century: theatrical melodramas such as *Black-Eye'd Susan* (1829), *Sweeney Todd* (1847), *The Colleen Bawn* (1860) and *The Bells* (1871) all thrived on the inherent dramatic conflict of the courtroom scene.[9] Middle-class culture, and the novel especially, readily absorbed the melodramatic trial set-piece which had its roots in popular culture: Elizabeth Gaskell and George Eliot, for example, incorporated highly dramatic trial scenes into their novels.[10] It is in Dickens's novels alone, though, that set-piece trial scenes contribute to a critique of the legal process: in other mid-nineteenth-century fictions trial scenes are used more simply as generic supports to melodramatic plotlines.

It was not only in the theatre and the middle-class novel that trial scenes gripped the cultural imagination of the nineteenth century: street literature was similarly in thrall to the trial set-piece. The prolific broadside and ballad industry of the first half of the nineteenth century was fuelled by the trial, sentence, dying words and execution of a string of infamous murderers, among them William Corder, François Courvoisier and Maria Manning. Broadside and ballad accounts of their trials, as well as accounts that he read in the middle-class newspaper press, would have contributed significantly to the shaping of Dickens's representation and critique of the legal process in his novels. The Swiss-born Maria Manning, who had shot her lover, Patrick O'Connor, in the head, erupts from the pages of *A Tale* in the shape of the pistol-wielding Mme Defarge: one of the moments of high drama in the novel is her semi-comic life-and-death struggle with the doughty and all too English Miss Pross. Victor Gatrell has remarked that broadsides were not exclusively read by common people in the streets, but had a wider cultural purchase,[11] and it seems likely that these texts would also have partly shaped Dickens's own fictional engagement with law and justice. He had an intense interest in the trial and conviction of such criminals, and in some instances attended executions, most memorably those of William and Maria Manning whose lifeless bodies grimly haunt his *Household Words* essay 'Lying Awake'.[12]

Show trials and accounts of the sentencing and execution of convicted prisoners held, then, a central place in the popular cultural imagination of the first half of the nineteenth century, and the trial scenes in *A Tale*, like those in his other novels, are both shaped by and contribute to the formation of this textual field. Dickens would also have been intensely aware of the long sequence of political trials strewn across the first half of the nineteenth century: the trials of radical Regency activists such as Henry Hunt and Samuel Bamford, and of radical Regency journalists such as William Cobbett, Thomas Wooler, William Hone and Leigh Hunt; the dramatic conviction and execution of the Cato Street conspirators in 1820; and the Chartist trials of 1839 and 1848. These, as well as the trials of Thomas Hardy and of John Horn Tooke in 1794 and 1795, were recorded in the *Annual Register*, long runs of which Dickens owned and drew on liberally in his fiction.[13]

There are no fewer than four trial scenes in *A Tale*. Tried once for treason in the Old Bailey (he is accused of being a spy), and three times before the French Revolutionary Tribunal as an aristocrat, the trials of Charles Darnay exploit the melodramatic potential of the trial scene to the full. An apotheosis of Dickens's embroilment with both theatre and law, *A Tale* plays off the loquaciousness and legalese of London's Old Bailey justice against the more cursory justice of the French Revolutionary Tribunal. Both are found wanting.

In the first trial of Darnay, at the Old Bailey, the viciousness of the mob of spectators is barely distinguishable from the mob attending his subsequent trials before the Revolutionary Tribunal in France. Baying for blood, fickle and incontinent, the spectators in each case are concerned with spectacle and sensation rather than with justice. The English mob of 1780 is, as is ever the case in Dickens's historical novels, very much a reflection on the volatility of contemporary British culture: he never regarded the 1850s with the equanimity of subsequent historians.[14] Following Carlyle, Dickens explicitly posits the 'The Terror' to be a direct consequence of poverty and oppression, the novel protesting passionately against the 'unspeakable suffering' and 'intolerable oppression' of the French people (*TTC*, III, xiii, 360). As in his other novels from the 1850s, Dickens's feeling is that British culture could produce its own Terror if the sufferings of the poor were not addressed. In the very first chapter of *A Tale* its author reflects on the extent to which the years before the French Revolution were 'so far like the present period' (I, i, 5).

Darnay's trial at the Old Bailey on suspicion of being a spy in the pay of the French king is presented as a commercial theatrical event rather than as a process focused on the dispensation of justice: 'For, people then paid to see the play at the old Bailey, just as they paid to see the play in Bedlam – only the former entertainment was much dearer', he tells us (II, ii, 63). The ironic, alliterative juxtaposition of Bailey and Bedlam economically discloses to the reader the narrator's stance towards the former. There is a carefully staged parallel scene in the first French section of the novel in which Mr Lorry angrily demands of the wine shop owner, Defarge, whether he 'make[s] a show' of the deranged Dr Manette: that the Frenchman's motivation in displaying the abject condition of Lucie's father is to inspire revolutionary feelings in his cohorts arguably gives his spectacle a moral force that the Old Bailey 'play' lacks (I, v, 40).

In his account of the trial of Darnay at the Old Bailey, Dickens reveals his knowledge of the spate of late eighteenth- and early nineteenth-century treason trials in an ironically phrased exchange between Lorry's messenger, Jerry Cruncher, and a member of the ghoulish crowd outside the court room awaiting the verdict. The latter reflects on the probable fate of accused:

> '. . . and then his head will be chopped off, and he'll be cut into quarters. That's the sentence.'
> 'If he's found Guilty, you mean to say?' Jerry added, by way of proviso.
> 'Oh, they'll find him Guilty,' said the other. 'Don't you be afraid of that.'
> (II, ii, 64)

As well as prefiguring the death sentence that will later be meted out to Darnay by the Revolutionary Tribunal, this brief exchange confirms the more likely fate of a Darnay in England's Old Bailey in the late eighteenth century. John Barrell and Jon Mee have remarked that 'By today's standards, most criminal trials during this period were very short, lasting a few hours or, in some instances, even minutes.'[15] Or as Victor Gatrell has reflected, 'Old Bailey Trials were usually conducted at breakneck pace . . . and prejudice against the prisoner usually ruled.'[16]

Dickens's original for Darnay, Francis De la Motte, a French baron resident in England, was summarily found guilty of espionage in 1781, condemned largely on the evidence of a spy. Dickens would have read about this case in the *Annual Register* for 1781, adjacent as it was to the account of the trial of George Gordon, which had provided some of the raw material for *Barnaby Rudge* some eighteen years earlier. De la Motte was hanged, but Dickens spares Darnay the usual kind of Old Bailey justice. Partly, of course, the novelist is preserving Darnay for the summary justice of the Terror at the novel's close, but it is more than simply a matter of needing a plot. For the novel stages a careful comparison of British and French justice in the late eighteenth century. Whilst Dickens does not set up Old Bailey justice in 1780 as a model and contrast to the justice of the Terror, there are some clear distinctions to be made between the legal procedures operating in Britain and in France at this period, distinctions to which the novel is alert. At the Old Bailey Darnay does at least have an advocate, denied to him at the Revolutionary Tribunal; his defence counsel would also have had the right to challenge the selection of jury members; and defendants in British treason trials 'were required by statute to be given, ten days in advance of their trial, a copy of the indictment and full lists of the panel of jurors and the witnesses summoned by the prosecution'.[17] Defence witnesses were permitted in British trials, and a range of verdicts could be reached; and whilst no formal appeal could be made after the sentence was pronounced, a defendant could move for a 'writ of error', alleging that an error of law had been made in the original trial.[18] No such concessions to a fair trial were made in revolutionary France. Whilst speed was of the essence in France as in Britain, the defendant had even fewer rights: Robespierre gradually placed men of his choosing in powerful positions in the Tribunal, whose verdict was without appeal; punishment was meted out within twenty-four hours of the sentence.[19] By June 1794, 'public cross-examination of defendants was abolished, as were defence counsels; . . . defence witnesses did not have to be heard; and the sole verdicts which the tribunal could pronounce were restricted to death or acquittal.'[20] The standard of evidence required was set as 'every kind . . . either material or moral or verbal or written, which can naturally secure the approval of every just and reasonable spirit; the rule of judgement is the conscience of the jurors enlightened by love of their fatherland.'[21]

These significant differences notwithstanding, the bloodthirsty English mob disappointed by Darnay's reprieve is every bit as savage as its French counterpart later in the novel; and the Old Bailey itself is condemned as 'a kind of deadly inn-yard, from which pale travellers set out continually, in carts and coaches, on a violent passage into the other world: travelling some two miles and a half of public street and road, and shaming few good citizens if any' (II, ii, 63). Dickens was infuriated too that in the eighteenth century and well beyond the law was such that 'today [it is] taking the life of an atrocious murderer, and tomorrow of a wretched pilferer who had robbed a farmer's boy of sixpence' (I, i, 7).

In allowing Darnay's defence counsel, Mr Stryver, with Sidney Carton's help, to succeed in securing a not guilty verdict, Dickens is to a certain extent superimposing his mid-century reformist vision of the legal process onto a harsher eighteenth-century legal regime that he would like to purge. In this way his novel from 1859 has a continuous timescale, constantly reflecting on its year of publication whilst narrativizing the historical past.

Dickens had extensive experience as a professional reporter of legal speeches, and this partly accounts for his extraordinary alertness to the lexicon and grammatical trickery of legal rhetoric.[22] In the Old Bailey trial scene he achieves a satirical effect through a startling deployment of the techniques of indirect speech.[23] The reported speech of the opening indictment's unabashed pre-judgment of Darnay (based on the original transcript of the De La Motte trial) is lent pace and drama through its compression of the opening charge:

> Silence in the court! Charles Darnay had yesterday pleaded Not Guilty to an indictment denouncing him (with infinite jingle and jangle) for that he was a false traitor to our serene, illustrious, excellent, and so forth, prince, our Lord the King, by reason of his having, on divers occasions, and by divers means and ways, assisted Lewis, the French King, in his wars against our said serene, illustrious, excellent, and so forth[;]
>
> (II, ii, 65)

The elliptical 'jingle and jangle', as evasive here as Mr Jingle's truncated grammar in *The Pickwick Papers*, and the repetition of pandering, hyperbolic patriotic sentiments, combine to deflate the prosecution's case even as the prosecution itself attempts to puff it up. The text of the novel deftly slips between reported speech and narratorial intervention as it moves from the economical 'jingle and jangle' of authorial condemnation to the 'serene, illustrious, excellent' overstatement of the prosecution counsel. Dickens's lampooning of the original transcript of the De La Motte trial is a *tour de force* of satirical concision: the initial indictment statement in the transcript of the trial runs to approximately 6,000 words; Dickens makes do with just 133.[24]

Darnay is saved from death in the Old Bailey by his barrister's rapidly paced interrogation of Roger Cly, a masterpiece of satirical economy:

> Never [been] in a debtors' prison? – Come, once again. Never? Yes. How many times? Two or three times. Not five or six? Perhaps. Of what profession? Gentleman. Ever been kicked? Might have been. Frequently? No. Ever been kicked downstairs? Decidedly not; once received a kick on the top of a staircase and fell down stairs of his own accord. ... Expect to get anything by this evidence? No. Not in regular government pay and employment, to lay traps? Oh dear no. Or to do anything? Oh dear no. Swear that? Over and over again. ...
>
> The virtuous servant, Roger Cly, swore his way through the case at a great rate. ... He had never been suspected of stealing a silver teapot; he had been maligned respecting a mustard-pot, but it turned out only to be a plated one. He had known the last witness seven or eight years; that was merely a coincidence.
>
> (II, iii, 70–1)

In the first paragraph, a form of free indirect discourse evolves as the narrative shifts between reported speech and narratorial intervention. Cly's monosyllabic negatives are interrupted by the narrator's satirically inflected declarations of the witness's virtue: the repeated phrase, 'Oh dear no' towards the end of the first paragraph moves the passage away from reported speech towards an ironically implied authorial condemnation of the spy. Likewise, in the phrase 'Over and over again' we have the narrator ironically commenting on the quality of the witness's evidence, once again in a shift from the mode of reported speech which generally characterizes the interrogation.

In the second paragraph, Roger Cly's admissions are brought into sharp focus by their 'seeming to be reported without the questions that led to them'.[25] That they almost seem like voluntary statements ('He had never been suspected of stealing a silver teapot') increases their satirical effect.

Satire cedes to unadorned melodrama in Darnay's trials before the Revolutionary Tribunal. Brutally stripped of legal rhetoric and summarily sentencing Darnay to death, French justice is presented without any settled legal lexicon. Dickens is far from happy about this: he never had any problem with law *per se*, but rather with what he regarded as a cumbersome and often unjust English legal process, which he wished to see reformed. His admiration for the newly evolving police force as a mechanism of law enforcement is evident in his *Household Words* essay from 1850, 'A Detective Police Party'.[26]

One of Dickens's major concerns about French revolutionary justice is its apparent fickleness and instability. Whilst initially Darnay is tried as a returning emigrant (a new law is introduced to outlaw this even as he leaves England), in the second French trial he is tried as an aristocrat, and in the final French trial he is convicted on the basis of a denunciation by Dr Manette; the novel is alert to the fact that the Tribunal's procedures and the revolutionary laws that governed them were frequently revised.[27] On his first return to Paris Darnay is interrogated before a Prison Tribunal:

'Your age, Evrémonde?'
'Thirty-seven.'
'Married, Evrémonde?'
'Yes.'
'Where married?'
'In England.'
'Without doubt. Where is your wife, Evrémonde?'
'In England.'
'Without doubt. You are consigned, Evrémonde, to the Prison of La Force.'
'Just Heaven!' exclaimed Darnay. 'Under what law, and for what offence?'
The officer looked up from his slip of paper for a moment.
'We have new laws, Evrémonde, and new offences, since you were here.'

(III, i, 260–2)

Such 'new laws' were increasingly designed to make an acquittal the exception rather than the rule. One British aristocrat who had the good fortune to be freed by the Tribunal, having been arrested in the summer of 1793, subsequently reflected with a degree of *schadenfreude* that 'Our two . . . Conductors convey'd us to the fatal Conciergerie. The entrance therein (at that period) and Death were nearly synonymous.'[28] Robespierre, who was to become synonymous with the Terror, was opposed to the establishment of a Revolutionary Tribunal for much the same reason that he opposed the show trial of Louis XVl: according to him, 'since the people had already overthrown the monarchy and established the Republic, the King's guilt was already proven, and the trial's verdict was already announced.'[29] The same went for those aristocrats such as the fictional Darnay who would be sentenced by the Tribunal. In each case, according to Robespierre, in mounting pre-scripted show trials 'Vous ne donneriez à l'univers qu'une ridicule comédie' (You would do nothing but perform a ridiculous comedy before the universe).[30] Perceiving its disruptive potential, Robespierre was equally intent on purging theatricality from politics – another ground for opposing the Tribunal.[31]

Notwithstanding Robespierre's objections, the Tribunal was established in March of 1793. Dickens's novel is highly conscious of the theatrical potential of the Tribunal's brutal conception of justice, employing in the French trial scenes a full-blown melodramatic aesthetic. *A Tale of Two Cities* conceives that in the revolutionary court there is no emotional or aesthetic space for the nuances of satire that we find in London's Old Bailey scene: good versus evil, right versus wrong – melodrama is itself here stripped bare. The reason for this is that whereas satire, with its desire to correct wrongs through ridicule, can be effective in a context of the rule of law, in the unstable, shifting and seemingly arbitrary law of the Terror it is ineffective as a political aesthetic. Dickens's response to the 'dreadful moral disorder' of the Tribunal (III, xiii, 360) is a melodramatic expression of horror at its disregard for human life and an attempt in the fictional realm to restore partial order. It is interesting that the first contemporary stage adaptation of *A Tale of Two Cities* focused on the French Tribunal, preferring the lucid moral universe – and inherent theatricality – of the melodramatic mode to the moral nuance and more verbal orientation of satire. Tom Taylor's 1860 stage adaptation cuts out the Old Bailey scene altogether and makes much of the novel's melodramatic device of the swapping of identities.[32]

Melodrama, according to Peter Brooks, is an 'intense emotional and ethical' genre 'based on the Manichaestic struggle of good and evil'. Providing moral order at the dawn of the post-sacred moral universe, the purpose of melodrama is 'to recognize and confront evil, to combat and expel it, to purge the social order'.[33] This is precisely the purpose of Dickens's response to the French Revolution in *A Tale of Two Cities*, which also draws on the bodiliness of the melodramatic mode and on its theatrical semiotics of gesture.

Darnay is sentenced to death on the basis of a so-called denunciation by his father-in-law, Dr Manette. Manette's written testimony concerning the events that led to his own imprisonment in the Bastille tells a melodramatic tale of a peasant girl raped by the evil lords of the manor. The melodrama of Manette's story is given bodily expression as his daughter, Lucie, faints when the guilty verdict is pronounced against the father of her child. Her physical collapse interestingly replicates the conduct of many convicted women prisoners in nineteenth-century Britain, whose demeanour when their sentences were read out was a major preoccupation of broadside literature. Typical of these is a broadside from 1821 in which Anne Barber, condemned to hang for murdering her husband, collapses:

> The prisoner did not seem conscious of her situation during the trial; but when the Jury returned and gave their Verdict, she became sensible of her dreadful situation, turned pale, trembled exceedingly, and fell upon the floor of the dock.[34]

The transposition of this device to Lucie Darnay – a beautiful and innocent victim who is mourning the imminent death of her husband – increases its melodramatic effect at the same time as using an instantly recognizable device from street literature.

The form of Dr Manette's forced testimony against his son-in-law is as melodramatic as its content, for we learn that it was written in his own blood whilst incarcerated in the Bastille. Here Dickens seems to draw, consciously or unconsciously, on the political and aesthetic testimony of the Chartist Ernest Jones, whose claim that he wrote poetry using his own blood as ink whilst a political prisoner between 1848 and 1850 was widely circulated in the radical press of the early 1850s.[35] He is also very likely drawing on Alexandre Dumas's novel from 1844–5, *Le Comte de Monte-Cristo*, which he knew and had written about.[36] Jones too may have been borrowing from Dumas in his melodramatic self-presentation as a victimized political prisoner. Dickens was no apologist for Ernest Jones, whom he associated with Physical Force Chartism and dismissed in his 1854 essay 'On Strike'.[37] Characteristically, though, the novelist was greatly concerned by the legal procedure used to sentence the Chartists in 1848, Jones among them. In an essay written for the *Examiner* in 1848, Dickens defended Jones and others against the lack of impartiality in various judges' directions to juries in Chartist trials.[38] One sees here and across Dickens's writings that he was as alert to miscarriages of justice in England as in France.

A Tale closes with Sidney Carton's martyrdom, his death supplying the kind of denouement that the Old Bailey crowd thirsted for in the novel's opening chapters. In the earlier trial scene Dickens describes the frustration of the mob when they are denied the execution and dying words that broadside culture as well as Old Bailey justice had led them to expect:

> The crowd came pouring out with a vehemence that nearly took [Jerry Cruncher] off his legs, and a loud buzz swept into the street as if the baffled blue-flies were dispersing in search of other carrion.
>
> (II, iii, 82)

The French revolutionary mob is every bit as bloodthirsty as its counterpart in the Old Bailey, the jury at Darnay's final trial including a man with a 'craving face', 'A life-thirsting, cannibal-looking, bloody-minded juryman' (III, ix, 328). Unlike the spectators at the Old Bailey trial, though, the French mob gets the blood it craves, a fact that is only redeemed, according to the novel's melodramatic moral structure, by Carton's heroic self-sacrifice. Dickens once again draws on broadside culture in giving the reader an account of Carton's demeanour as he is led to the scaffold. The same is true of the hero's imagined last speech, in which he is said to have reflected on his coming death that: 'It is a far, far better thing that I do, than I have ever done; it is a far, far better rest that I go to, than I have ever known' (III, xv, 390). In combining melodrama with street culture in the final phases of the novel, and in drawing on popular satire in its earlier sections, Dickens characteristically produces a truly democratic as well as a politically alert literary text.

Safely back in England the Darnays' son, the end of the novel tells us, will grow up to become 'the foremost of just judges' in a highly conventional domestic close utterly characteristic of mid-century melodrama (III, xv, 390). The projected establishment of a just legal order beyond the pages of the novel and outside of its chronology is, though, part of Carton's sanitized dream vision as he is led to the guillotine. Such a vision is consonant with Dickens's commitment to legal reform in the 1850s, at the end of which decade *A Tale* was serialized in *All The Year Round*; earlier in the decade, too, *Bleak House*'s Ada Clare had been able to imagine 'an honest judge in real earnest' who would be able to establish justice in Chancery.[39] Notwithstanding these idealized visions of a reformed legal order in the future, it is the violent, brutal disorder and arbitrary justice of the novel's narrative of the past that tells us more, and more powerfully, about the present in which it was written and read.

Notes

1. Peter Brooks, 'Melodrama, Body, Revolution', in *Melodrama: Stage, Picture, Screen*, ed. Jacky Bratton, Jim Cook and Christine Gledhill (London: British Film Institute, 1994), pp. 11–24, 15, 17.
2. Peter Ackroyd, *Dickens* (1990; London: Minerva, 1991), p. 127.

3. Ackroyd, *Dickens*, pp. 123, 135.
4. Dickens to Henry Nethersole, 13 November [1834], in *Letters*, I, p. 43.
5. Ackroyd, *Dickens*, pp. 311 and 776–7.
6. Ackroyd, *Dickens*, pp. 118–19, 128, 148, 149.
7. For the theatricality of political trials, see for example Julia Swindells, *Glorious Causes: The Grand Theatre of Political Change, 1789 to 1833* (Oxford: Oxford University Press, 2001).
8. John Bent, *The Bastille* (London: Lowndes, 1789).
9. Douglas Jerrold, *Black-Ey'd Susan* (1829), in *Nineteenth-Century Plays*, ed. George Rowell (Oxford: Oxford University Press, 2nd edn 1972), pp. 1–43; George Dibdin Pitt, *The String of Pearls (Sweeney Todd)* (1847), in *The Golden Age of Melodrama*, ed. Michael Kilgarriff (London: Wolfe Publishing, 1974), pp. 243–62; Dion Boucicault, *The Colleen Bawn* (1860), in Rowell, pp. 175–231; Leopold Lewis, *The Bells* (1871), in Rowell, pp. 469–502.
10. See, for example, Elizabeth Gaskell, *Mary Barton* (London: Chapman & Hall, 1848); and George Eliot, *Adam Bede* (London: Blackwood, 1859).
11. Victor Gatrell, *The Hanging Tree: Execution and the English People, 1770–1868* (Oxford: Oxford University Press, 1994), p. 169. On ballads and broadsides see also Leslie Sheppard, *The History of Street Literature* (Newton Abbot: David & Charles, 1973); and Robert Collison, *The Story of Street Literature* (London: Dent, 1973).
12. Charles Dickens, 'Lying Awake', *Household Words* 6 (30 October 1852), 145–8, repr. Slater, III, pp. 88–95.
13. See J. H. Stonehouse, *Catalogue of the Library of Charles Dickens From Gadshill Place, June 1870* (London: Piccadilly Fountain Press, 1935), pp. 113 and 7 for details of Dickens's ownership of the *State Trials* and of the *Annual Register* (1758–1860). Andrew Sanders has done important work in bringing our attention to the extent to which Dickens drew on the *Annual Register* in his novels. See Andrew Sanders, *The Companion to A Tale of Two Cities* (1998; Robertsbridge: Helm Information, 2002).
14. For the political tenor of Dickens's writings of the 1850s, see Sally Ledger, *Dickens and the Popular Radical Imagination* (Cambridge and New York: Cambridge University Press, 2007), chs. 6 and 7.
15. *Trials for Treason and Sedition, 1792–1794*, ed. John Barrell and Jon Mee (London: Pickering & Chatto, 2006), p. xliv.
16. Gatrell, *Hanging Tree*, p. 359.
17. Barrell and Mee, *Trials for Treason and Sedition*, p. xlvi.
18. Barrell and Mee, *Trials for Treason and Sedition*, pp. xlvii, xlviii.
19. David Andress, *The Terror: Civil War in the French Revolution* (London: Little, Brown, 2005), p. 289.
20. Colin Jones, *The Longman Companion to the French Revolution* (London and New York: Longman, 1988), p. 113. See also Simon Schama, *Citizens: A Chronicle of the French Revolution* (London: Viking, 1989), p. 837: under the newly established law of Prairial anyone 'denounced for "slandering patriotism", "seeking to inspire discouragement", "spreading false news", or even "depraving morals, corrupting the public conscience and impairing the purity and energy of the revolutionary government" could be brought before the Revolutionary Tribunal. That court could issue only one of two sentences: acquittal or death.'
21. *The French Revolution: A Document Collection*, ed. Laura Mason and Tracy Rizzo (Boston, MA: Houghton Mifflin, 1999), pp. 241–43. Quoted in Andress, p. 310.

22. Dickens had been a parliamentary reporter for the *Morning Chronicle* in the 1830s.
23. I am indebted to Michael Gregory for my understanding of Dickens's manipulation of indirect and direct speech in the Old Bailey scene. See Michael Gregory, 'Old Bailey Speech in "A Tale of Two Cities"', *Review of English Literature* 6 (1965), 42–55.
24. For the original text of the trial see www.oldbaileyonline.org/html_units/1780s/t17810711-1.html [accessed 12 February 2005]. For an account of the trial of Francis Henry De la Motte, see Harvey Peter Sucksmith and Paul Davies, 'The Making of the Old Bailey Trial Scene in *A Tale of Two Cities*', *Dickensian*, 100 (2004), 23–35.
25. Gregory, 'Old Bailey Speech', p. 47.
26. [Charles Dickens], 'A Detective Police Party', *Household Words* 1 (27 July 1850), 404–14, and *Household Words* 1 (10 August 1850), 457–60, repr. Slater, II, pp. 265–82. Well known too are the rather curious incidents when Dickens himself tried to enforce the law. On one occasion he was seen helping a policeman arrest a tramp in St James's Park; on another he threatened to take legal action against a baker's man seen relieving himself outside the gates of Tavistock House.
27. Jones, *Longman Companion*, p. 113.
28. V. T. Harlow, 'An English Prisoner in Paris during the Terror (1793–1794)', *Camden Miscellany* (London: Royal Historical Society, 1929), vol. 15 pp. 1–10, p. 5.
29. Susan Maslan, *Revolutionary Acts: Theatre, Democracy, and the French Revolution* (Baltimore, MD: Johns Hopkins University Press, 2005), p. 133. Maslan argues that 'Robespierre's argument against a trial rests on a set of Lockean assumptions about the relations between people and their rulers. In the *Second Treatise of Government* Locke argues that no earthly judge can adjudicate between a people and their ruler. Thus, when the people consider the government to be tyrannical, they must submit themselves to heavenly judgement by means of a trial of arms.' See John Locke, *Two Treatises of Government*, ed. Peter Laslett (Cambridge: Cambridge University Press, 1963), pp. 425–7.
30. Maslan, *Revolutionary Acts*, p. 134.
31. Danton, though, stoutly defended the establishment of the Tribunal. See Schama, *Citizens*, p. 707: ' "Let us be terrible so that the people will not have to be," Danton told the Convention, defending the establishment of the Revolutionary Tribunal. . . . Danton recognized it was essential that the state take into its own hands the kind of punitive powers needed . . . if the lynch mobs and the improvised murder gangs were to be denied their prey.'
32. Tom Taylor, *A Tale of Two Cities* (London: Thomas Hailes Lacy, 1860).
33. Peter Brooks, *The Melodramatic Imagination: Balzac, Henry James, and the Mode of Excess* (New Haven, CT: Yale University Press, 1976), pp. 12–13.
34. '*A Brief Account of the Trial and Execution of ANN BARBER . . . August 13, 1821, for the Murder of her Husband, James Barber, by Poison*', John Johnson Collection, Bodleian Library, Murders and Executions Folder 2.
35. See, for example, a short item on 'Ernest Jones' in *The Red Republican*, 20 July 1850, p. 1, col. 3.
36. See Sanders, *Companion to* A Tale, p. 155.
37. [Charles Dickens], 'On Strike', *Household Words* 8 (11 February 1854), 553–9, repr. Slater, III, pp. 196–210.
38. [Charles Dickens], 'Judicial Special Pleading', *The Examiner*, 31 December 1848, repr. Slater, II, pp. 137–42.
39. Charles Dickens, *Bleak House*, ed. Nicola Bradbury (1852–3; repr. London and New York: Penguin Books, 2003), p. 78.

6
Face Value in *A Tale of Two Cities*
Kamilla Elliott

A Tale of Two Cities is acutely concerned with lost and changing social identities before, during and after the French Revolution of 1789. Ruptures and
realignments of identity in he novel are expressed largely through ruptures
and realignments of proper names pronounced, renounced, denounced,
hidden, discovered, recorded, altered and blotted out; faces presented,
represented, (mis)recognized, recorded, altered, masked, frozen, distorted,
changed and severed from bodies. The novel's preoccupation with how
names and faces construct, deconstruct and reconstruct social identity is,
I suggest, informed by the rise of mass picture identification between 1789
and 1859. In this period, an increasing proportion of the population gained
access to established cultural forms of picture identification, like portraiture
and passports. New technologies, particularly photography, also made picture identification widely available. In probing the centrality of proper names
and faces to social identity and social identification, the novel also probes
the identity theft that names and faces made possible. Read in the context
of modern modes and means of identification, the novel raises unsettling
questions about the ethics of identification and 'face value'.

Something of the complexity of face–name identification can be seen in
the presentation of the character of Dr Manette. At the beginning of *A Tale*,
Manette's lost social identity is expressed chiefly in terms of a detached proper
name and an illegible, unrecognizable face. He is identified by a process
akin to picture identification, in which a represented face is matched to
an embodied face in order to establish a proper name and social identity.
Mr Lorry travels to Paris 'to identify him if I can'. Following eighteen years
incarcerated in the Bastille, Manette 'has been found under another name; his
own, long forgotten or long concealed' (*TTC*, I, iv, 28). He identifies himself
geographically and institutionally as 'One Hundred and Five, North Tower'
(I, vi, 44), his cell in the Bastille. In taking on the name of his location, his loss
of social identity extends to a subjective inability to delineate himself from his
surroundings. His loss of nominal identity is manifested in 'the scared blank
wonder of his face', through which 'No human intelligence could have read

87

the mysteries of his mind' (I, vi, 51). The blank face of his subjectively lost identity renders him socially unrecognizable. It is only when a glimmer of memory strikes Manette that Lorry recognizes him: 'At first I thought it quite hopeless, but I have unquestionably seen, for a single moment, the face that I once knew so well' (I, vi, 45–6). Only when Lorry recognizes the face does he make a positive identification, matching Manette's embodied face to its representation in his memory. The recalled name, and by extension the recalled social life, here depend on the recalled face.

Lorry's process of personal identification is a prototype of picture identification. As we shall see in more detail below, in increasingly populous areas, in times of immense social mobility, personal acquaintance and personal memory became insufficient to establish social identity. Thus, pictorial and ekphrastic images came to serve as cultural and bureaucratic collective 'memories'.

This essay belongs to a larger study investigating how British fiction informs and is informed by the rise of picture identification from the late eighteenth century.[1] Picture IDs aim to establish unique social identities, as the passport historian Martin Lloyd avers: 'The passport must be unique, signifying a unique individual [and]...the examiner...must...determine if the passport is uniquely identical with the individual.'[2] Dominant theories of identity in the humanities today, however, deny the possibility of the unique, unambiguous identity that picture IDs aim to establish. Developed largely to combat claims that identity is objective, fixed, essentialist and natural, and to oppose uses of such claims to construct and defend social hierarchies and uneven distributions of political power and economic resources, these theories view individualist notions of identity as patriarchal, capitalist, bourgeois and right-wing. They have, therefore, sought to dismiss and dismantle the representational capacities of proper names and physiognomical faces. Individualism, proper nouns and faces have given way to Foucauldian preoccupations with societies, common noun categorizations and bodies.[3] Jacques Derrida and others have deconstructed proper nouns to improper and common nouns.[4] As proper nouns have collapsed into common and improper nouns, so too have faces been severed from discursive, psychoanalytic and performative bodies alike.[5] Gilles Deleuze and Félix Guattari have abstracted individuating, physiognomical faces into machines of 'faciality';[6] psychoanalysts have wiped them into blank sites of projection.[7] In consequence, studies within the humanities generated by these theories are preoccupied with bodies rather than faces, with common rather than proper nouns, with identity at the level of class, gender, sexuality, race and nationality rather than with individual identity. By contrast, in picture identification, the face is to the body as the proper noun is to the common noun: it denotes a particular, as opposed to generic, identity.[8]

Attention to the proper nouns and faces of picture identification, however, need not mark a return to the concepts of identity against which recent and current theories militate. Picture identification by no means purports to identify essentially, absolutely, finally, positively or objectively. Agencies producing and using picture IDs readily acknowledge that they are social constructions that can be forged, falsified and fabricated.[9] That picture IDs must be updated and renewed, together with the ongoing addition of biometric indicators and technologies, attests to institutional and cultural awareness that identities are changing and elusive. Nor does the general public naively or devoutly declare their faith in the veracity of picture identification, as popular jokes clustering around the phrase 'If you actually look like your passport photo ...' attest.[10] Picture IDs further acknowledge the fragmented nature of social identity. They seek to establish unique, unambiguous identity through pieces and fragments: through represented symbols and images interacting with presented body parts and performed signatures. These have no centre, no transcendental signified, but refer only to each other. The modest aims and claims of picture IDs, then, consist of matching and mapping pieces and patches to establish social identity temporarily for specific purposes, such as financial transactions, travel and access to privileges, activities, memberships and spaces. Picture IDs are never once and for all. They are constantly remade, reinscribed with new elements, and must be continually represented.

A study of picture identification need not mandate a return to a definition of individual identity in the terms of bourgeois individualism. Proper names and faces not only individuate, they also attach family, regional, religious and national names and facial resemblances to related others. The proper names and faces of picture identification, then, are not simply reactionary entities requiring suppression, denial, dismissal or dilution to common nouns and bodies. Rather, they warrant serious investigation.

Contemporary academic rejections of individual identity are not far removed from the attitudes and actions of French revolutionaries. Revolutionaries worked not only to overturn hierarchical common noun class categorizations and to redistribute economic resources to bodies. They also strove to destroy privileged, individuated identities represented by named faces, that is, by pairings of upper-class proper names and faces on coins, paper money, portraits, busts and other sculptures. Not only did revolutionaries criminalize common nouns describing the French ruling classes ('aristocrat' and '*émigré*'), rendering them synonymous with criminal categories ('traitor' and 'thief'), they also blotted out aristocratic proper names. As the guillotine severed individuating faces from generic bodies, decapitated heads joined blotted-out names to eradicate privileged, individuated social identities.[11]

Concomitantly, new laws extended individuating inter-semiotic identities to the masses in the ekphrastic facial descriptions required in French passports from 1791. On 5 June 1791, the French Foreign Minister, Montmorin, issued this passport:

> By the Authority of the King
> To all officers, civil and military charged with overseeing and maintaining public order in the different departments of the Kingdom and to all others similarly responsible, greetings. We order and direct that you allow to pass freely the Baroness de Korff, going to Frankfurt with two children, a maid and a personal valet and three servants without giving her or allowing her to be given any obstruction. The present passport is valid for one month only.[12]

Issued 'By the Authority of the King', this passport enabled Louis XVI and Marie Antoinette to escape from Paris disguised as the valet and maid indicated therein. They had nearly escaped France when Louis leaned out of the coach window and was recognized by a retired soldier named Deurne, who raised the alarm. Deurne had never seen the king, but identified him by the resemblance of his face to its depiction on the promissory notes of the period.[13] Deurne, then, made a picture identification of the monarch, matching an embodied face to a represented face, and attached those matched faces to a proper name.

Up to this point, as the historian John Torpey points out, 'descriptions of a person's social standing – residence, occupation, family status, and so on – were generally regarded as adequate indicators of a person's identity for purposes of internal passport controls in France'. But when Montmorin defended his oversight on the grounds that, 'with the large number of passports [he] signs, it is impossible for him to verify whether the name of the persons who request them is true or false', the failure of such information to establish social identity became manifest.[14] The incident further highlighted the failure of common noun categorizations, like 'valet' and 'maid', to establish specific social identity and, concomitantly, the ability of common nouns to disguise individual social identities.

In England, political philosophers increasingly despaired of the ability of proper names to represent persons. In 1830, Jeremy Bentham recommended that each person be legally required to have a unique name. Realizing the impossibility of enforcing such a system, he subsequently suggested tattooing names on bodies.[15] In 1843, John Stuart Mill worried extensively in his *System of Logic* about the semantic emptiness of proper names.[16]

In France, following the king's near-escape, a law was hastily passed requiring passports to contain physical descriptions – descriptions that were primarily facial. This is an example from the period:

> aged forty-eight years – height four feet eleven inches – brown hair and eyebrows – brown eyes – nose like a duck – large mouth – wide chin – round

forehead – round face with a small spot on the right cheek and going a bit grey . . . [17]

In a similar vein, Mme Defarge in *A Tale* keeps a knitted register, 'That she may be able to recognise the faces and know the persons', 'that she may identify them' (III, iii, 276, 277). Her knitted description of the double-agent John Barsad follows the pattern of French passports – and strikingly so:

age, about forty years; height, about five feet nine; black hair; complex-ion dark; generally, rather handsome visage; eyes dark, face thin, long, and sallow; nose aquiline, but not straight, having a peculiar inclination towards the left cheek . . .

(II, xvi, 187)

As Mme Defarge completes the description, she pronounces: 'It is a portrait!' (II, xvi, 184). Ekphrastic descriptions were the poor man's portrait, the every-man's portrait. They had been instituted in France during the 1760s to keep track of vagrants who lacked the customary verbal identifiers of residence and occupation and were not readily recognized by locals.[18]

But the Revolution and Reign of Terror are only one social context for *A Tale*. Practices of mass social identification, both institutional and social, increasingly paired proper names and faces. By the time *A Tale* was published in 1859, photography was becoming the portraiture of the masses. Although photographs were used only intermittently in passports from 1854,[19] the *carte de visite* was widely displacing the purely written calling card. Documents based on the *carte de visite* were used for employee identification, as passes to events and for other social and cultural purposes from the 1850s.

A Tale goes beyond social practices of picture identification, however, to characterize class groups and class conflict through proper names and faces. Aristocrats are reduced to their titles in the expression 'Monseigneur as a class', and in the title (redoubled to shore up the lesser status of) 'Mon-sieur the Marquis', who dances failed attendance on Monseigneur (II, xxiii, 236; II, xxiv, 243). Stripping aristocrats of Christian and family names strips them of the markers of kinship and distils them to an identity of sheer entitlement.

Aristocratic faces join aristocratic names in decamping from expressing reli-gious and socio-biological bonds. The stone face of the Marquis emblematizes both religious and humanist evisceration: body without soul and hardened heart.[20] The depiction of his face as a mask further represents him as con-structed, artificial, unnatural. Monsieur the Marquis's sole point of passion lies in maintaining the entitled prerogatives of the family name (II, ix, 127–9). It is less the family nature of this name than its entitlement that he seeks to protect, evinced by his willingness to sacrifice the sole heir, his nephew,

Charles Darnay to it. Together, impersonal title and stone mask create a picture ID of a class morally, emotionally and physically impervious to others and to its own social danger and impending extinction.

While male aristocrats distil to their titles, male revolutionaries truncate to a shared Christian name, Jacques.[21] Christian names serve a dual function: they make one a member of the Christian Church and distinguish members of the same family from one another. They thus forge bonds beyond the family and create divisions within the family. The newly adopted revolutionary first name revokes the baptismal name, marking a rejection of membership in a religion advocating submission to divinely ordained class hierarchies. The shared name refuses distinctions in the new class family, fusing identities more tightly even than the bonds of the twinned Evrémonde fraternity. The shared name makes the many one and the plural 'People' singular: 'The Republic goes before all. The People *is* supreme' (III, vii, 303; emphasis added). The many must become one in order to overthrow the one 'Monseigneur as a class'. Only numbers, physical descriptions and professions differentiate one Jacques from another. Numbers in place of names indicate a loss of subjective, individual identity here and in Manette's 'One Hundred and Five, North Tower'. However, in the case of the Jacques, they also represent a new order, a new history, a new sequence of swelling numbers pressing horizontally against fixed hierarchies from below: 'Work, Jacques One, Jacques Two, Jacques One Thousand, Jacques Two Thousand, Jacques Five-and-Twenty Thousand; in the name of all the Angels or the Devils – which you prefer – work!' (II, xxi, 224).

In contrast to the impassive stone face of the Marquis, the faces of the revolutionaries are depicted as excessively passionate, as 'faces . . . more horrible and cruel than the visages of the wildest savages in their most barbarous disguise' (III, ii, 272). Intriguingly, both Marquis and mob faces are represented as masks, suggesting that both extreme impassivity and impassionedness are social constructions, contrasting an essentially 'human', 'real', 'authentic', normative, middle-class, middle-ground psyche.

Yet the class lines are not as clearly drawn: they are disrupted by gender lines. The novel's two main female characters, Lucie Manette-Darnay-Evrémonde and Mme Defarge, stand paradoxically ruptured from the males of their common noun class designations and aligned with their enemies in name and face. Like the Jacquerie, Lucie of the many family names is known chiefly by her forename. Like the Jacquerie, she has generated a second Lucie, a namesake undifferentiated from her except by chronological sequence. Like the Jacquerie, Lucie has an immensely emotive face: 'a forehead with a singular capacity (remembering how young and smooth it was), of lifting and knitting itself into an expression that was not quite one of perplexity, or wonder, or alarm, or merely of a bright fixed attention, though it included all the four expressions' (I, iv, 23). Revolutionary faces too are described as 'knitted': 'foreheads knitted into the likeness of the gallows-rope they mused about enduring, or inflicting' (I, v, 33).

In a similar vein, Mme Defarge is nominally and facially differentiated from male revolutionaries and aligned with her arch-enemy, the Marquis. She is never Madame Jacques, nor do we know her Christian name until she is called to witness in a court of law near the end of the novel. The frequent truncation of her name to 'Madame' aligns her with the titular Marquis and Monseigneur. Her 'steady face' (I, v, 35) stands in marked contrast to the savage faces of other revolutionaries and closer to the Marquis's stone face.

But these nominal pieces and facial images are simply a backdrop to the novel's central concern with the social identities of its middle-class or would-be middle-class males. While calling Manette again by his proper name recalls him to life, health, friends and family as well, throughout the novel there is a sense that 'it is better not to name' (III, xi, 349–50). In a political context where hierarchical patriarchy is being levelled by horizontal fraternity, the paternal name is fraught with danger. Naming too often takes the condemnatory and lethal form of denunciation, as indicated in the word-play 'he is denounced – and gravely' (III, vii, 303). For Charles Darnay, the reattachment of a detached name threatens annihilation of life, health, association and identity. Darnay is just one step ahead of the Revolution, on a downwardly mobile quest to dissociate himself from his aristocratic patriarchal heritage. He has renounced his father's name, Evrémonde, and substituted an anglicized version of his mother's name, D'Aulnais. He has refused his title of 'Marquis', placed his wealth in the service of the French lower classes and gone to work among the English middle classes (II, xiv, 159). Darnay has thus already done to his own name and inheritance what the Revolution is doing to those of his peers: 'the nobility were trooping from France by every highway and byway, and their property was in course of confiscation and destruction, and their very names were blotting out' (II, xxiv, 251). But Darnay finds that, in spite of his own nominal blottings and private family revolution, his family name is impossible to cast off. His 'detested family name had long been anathematised by Saint Antoine, and was wrought into the fatal register', 'registered, as doomed to destruction ... the château and all the race ... Extermination' (III, x, 344; II, xv, 178–9). The family name is relentlessly reattached, then attached to a capital sentence (III, xiii, 360).

The old family name joins new condemnatory common nouns. 'Aristocrat' has become synonymous with 'criminal', and 'emigrant' with 'traitor' (III, i, 256–8). In the barrage of old names and new nouns, Darnay experiences a loss of subjective identity: 'I am lost here. All here is so unprecedented, so changed, so sudden and unfair, that I am absolutely lost' (III, i, 262). The subjective, individuating 'I' is lost through re-association with the family name and redefinitions of common noun classifications. On trial for guilt by association with the family name and criminalized common nouns, English pseudonyms, individual innocence, morality, motivation or action are of no avail. Darnay can only attempt interpretive escapes:

> Was he not an emigrant then? What did he call himself?
> Not an emigrant, he hoped, within the sense and spirit of the law.
>
> (III, vi, 293)

But these too are insufficient to save him. At his first French trial, he only manages to throw off guilt by nominal association through affiliation with another family name, Manette's, into whose family he has married. Subsequently, however, the lethal patriarchal name proves more powerful than the salutary effects of Manette's. Manette and his daughter, far from saving Charles by their name, are drawn into guilt by association with the Evrémonde family name and its capital sentence.

The family name condemns people through guilt by association. So too does the family face. Dickens's fascination with family resemblance has been widely discussed. In *A Tale*, Lucie bears and uncanny resemblance to both her father ('The resemblance between him and Lucie was very strong at such times' [II, vi,104]) and her mother ('It is the same. How can it be!' [I, vi, 47]). Her daughter resembles her facially, and nominally. Jerry Cruncher's son shares his name and is described as his father's 'express image' (II, i, 57). The Evrémonde twins are all but identical (III, x, 333). Darnay must resemble twin father and uncle, for Manette regards him with 'an intent look, deepening into a frown of dislike and distrust, not even unmixed with fear' before he learns Darnay's family name (II, iv, 85).

In a context of picture identification, the shared family face functions as corroborating evidence for the family name and reinforces guilt by nominal association. Conjoined in the 'fatal register' of Mme Defarge, family face and name forge a lethal form of picture identification (III, x, 344–5). The family resemblance that proves salutary in other Dickens novels proves fatal in *A Tale*.

Therefore, the novel investigates how far other kinds of shared faces can rescue people from guilt by association. Lucie's sympathetically knitted forehead wars with Mme Defarge's knitted register and the knitted faces of revolutionary revenge to vindicate Charles Evrémonde, called Darnay. At Darnay's English trial for treason, Lucie's emotive face imparts middle-class sympathy to a mostly lower-class, unsympathetic crowd: 'Her forehead had been strikingly expressive of an engrossing terror and compassion'; 'This had been so very noticeable, so very powerfully and naturally shown, that starers who had no pity for him were touched by her' (II, ii, 67). They are more than touched by her; they adopt her facial expression:

> Any strongly marked expression of face on the part of a chief actor in a scene of great interest to whom many eyes are directed, will be

unconsciously imitated by the spectators. [Lucie's] forehead was painfully anxious and intent ... Among the lookers-on there was the same expression in all quarters of the court; insomuch, that a great majority of the foreheads there, might have been mirrors reflecting the witness.

(II, iii, 75)

The facial mirroring here forges resemblances and connections other than those made by familial or class bonds. It even binds together opposed categories, like French and English, and higher and lower classes.

But bonds forged by affective facial resemblances are subject to rapid, bipolar fluctuations in the novel. At Darnay's first trial in France, spectators shift rapidly from one facially evinced emotion to its opposite: 'So capriciously were the people moved, that tears immediately rolled down several ferocious countenances which had been glaring at the prisoner a moment before, as if with impatience to pluck him out into the streets and kill him' (III, vi, 294). Elsewhere,

The mad joy over the prisoners who were saved, had astounded [Manette] scarcely less than the mad ferocity against those who were cut to pieces ... With an inconsistency as monstrous as anything in this awful nightmare, they had helped the healer ... then caught up their weapons and plunged anew into a butchery so dreadful, that the Doctor had covered his eyes with his hands ...

(III, iv, 281)

The sympathetic urge to ameliorate suffering here alternates with a violent urge to inflict suffering. One leads to, feeds on and requires the other.

Even Lucie's sympathy is construed as enmity. The shared face of sympathy proves not only ineffectual to save those condemned as criminals by revolutionaries. but is itself culpable and subject to punishment. When Darnay is sentenced to death, Mme Defarge imagines Lucie 'in a state of mind to impeach the *justice* of the Republic. She will be full of *sympathy* with its *enemies*' (III, xiv, 375; emphases added). Sympathy is not only the enemy of violence, but also of justice. Lucie's middle-class sympathy is the enemy of social justice because it asks the lower classes to yield their claims for social equality and legal recourse and to let wrongs committed against them by ruling-class males pass unpunished, unaccounted for, unrecompensed.

Furthermore, middle-class female sympathy is destructive in being self-sacrificing. Lucie's face works to school the lower classes in sacrificing their interests to ruling-class male interests. To sympathize with Lucie is to join her in self-abandonment to the interests of middle-class men. If middle-class female sympathy does not prove fatal in being a crime against the French Republic, then it works its own suicidal course. Carton's identification with

Lucie's sympathy leads to his own self-abandoning suicide, although I shall qualify and complicate this reading below.

It is not simply its redoubled internal and external destruction that thwarts the ability of the shared emotive face to save. More resolute and fixed than any face-borne emotion is the steady face of Mme Defarge, presiding over condemnatory picture identification: her knitted register of faces and names set against Lucie's knitted face. Mme Defarge remarks: 'it is very strange – now, at least, is it not very strange . . . that, after all our *sympathy* for Monsieur her father and herself, her husband's name should be proscribed under your hand at this moment' (II, xvi, 192–3; emphasis added). Like the picture IDs of Mme Defarge's register, revolutionary faces are symbolic: 'upon them, and upon the grown faces, and ploughed into every furrow of age and coming up afresh, was the sign, Hunger' (I, v, 32). Symbolic power proves stronger than affective power in the novel because the revolutionaries add to symbolic faces rhetoric, logic and law: arguments of cause and effect, hypotheses supported by evidence, rhetorical parallelism and legal balance sheets that demand an eye for an eye, a tooth for a tooth, innocent lives for innocent lives, a family for a family, a class for a class. These mirrorings prove far more compelling, powerful and durable than fluctuating affective facial mirrorings. In their lethal operations, they fix faces forever (II, ix, 134).

If the shared family face and the symbolic face condemn, and if the shared affective face fails to save and even destroys people, another kind of shared face vindicates and saves them. While Lucie's facially expressed sympathy *motivates* Carton to die in the place of Darnay, it does not *empower* him to save Darnay. At both Darnay's English trial and in France, Carton saves Darnay by the shared face of physiognomical resemblance: 'they were sufficiently like each other to surprise, not only the witness, but everybody present, when they were thus brought into comparison' (II, iii, 77). Physiognomical resemblance to Carton twice saves Darnay from execution: once in England and once in France. In the first instance it does so by confusing their identities; in the second by an act of reciprocal identity theft that extends to future generations.

This kind of shared face saves by evoking a physiognomical resemblance that is not the result of a family relationship. In being physiognomical, it manifests none of the instabilities of affective facial mirroring. In being unconnected to family relationships, it brings with it none of the guilt of family, class or national association, for Carton and Darnay hail from different families, classes and nations. It further counters nineteenth-century faith that physiognomy expresses moral character, for the men manifest markedly divergent moralities. The shared face, appearing outside the family, refuses to corroborate the guilt attached to the family name. More significantly, the unrelated, shared physiognomical face subverts faith in picture identification to establish unique, unambiguous social identity, for the shared face attaches itself to two names. It thus unravels eye-witness identifications in the English court and unpicks the stitches of Mme Defarge's knitted identifications in France.

No one, to my knowledge, has observed that their shared face rescues not only Darnay but also Carton from legal, moral, female and lower-class condemnation, allowing the French aristocrat to escape public guilt by family, class and national association and the dissolute English middle-class professional to emerge cleansed of his private moral guilt as a transnational, transgenerational hero.[22] The process by which Carton emerges innocent of his personal, moral, romantic and professional guilt, and Darnay innocent of his family, gender, national and class guilt, depends on a mutual identity theft. Double identities rejected as duplicitous and criminal elsewhere in Dickens's fiction here effect a miraculous exculpation of both individual guilt and guilt by association.

Moreover, the process operates under the rhetorical figure of simile rather than that of metaphor or metonymy, tropes that are more commonly invoked in humanities theory and criticism. Simile maintains difference and coexistence against metaphoric merger and metonymic displacement. Where metaphoric condensation would fuse the sins and crimes of the two men, and where metonymic displacement would require one man to be held accountable for them all, simile allows each man to exchange his guilt for the other's innocence and his innocence for the other's guilt, and both to emerge scot free.

Let us contextualize these procedures and consider them more closely. Both rhetorical and theoretical studies tend to overlook and denigrate simile in favour of metaphor. Critical discussions of metaphor and metonymy greatly outnumber discussions of simile.[23] Moreover, many of the articles that discuss simile and metaphor together argue for simile's inferiority to metaphor. In studies of literary composition and of identity, metaphor is seen as more daring than simile because it claims identity, while simile, with its 'like' and 'as' conjunctions, claims only similarity. Christian Metz's claim that metaphor is 'more striking than its rival [simile]' in that it 'actively supplant[s] ... one word by another', a procedure that 'was only potential in simile', is typical, as is John M. Kennedy's article 'What Makes a Metaphor Stronger than a Simile?'[24]

Nor is simile granted the tremendous semiotic, psychoanalytic, cognitive and cultural theorizing power accorded metaphor and metonymy. Roman Jakobson's association of metaphor with paradigmatic signification, lyrical poetry, Romanticism and Freudian dream symbols, and metonymy with syntagmatic signification, epic poetry, realistic novels and Freudian dream projections inspired many to carry these figures from classical rhetoric and literary studies into theories of mind, language, history and culture.[25] Jacques Lacan's argument that the unconscious is structured like a language, for example, is rooted in psychoanalytic appropriations of metaphor and metonymy.[26] Other theories of mind in philosophy and cognitive linguistics also accord metaphor and metonymy a prime place.[27] One scholar even suggests that metonymy is the symbolism of the soul.[28] Semiotic theorists similarly maintain that metonymy and metaphor go beyond ornamentation to epitomize significatory, cognitive and interpretive processes.[29] Hayden White makes metaphor and metonymy central operations of historical discourse.[30] Cultural scholars accord theorizing power to metaphor and metonymy.[31] While some theorists, like Paul de Man and Hayden White, pursue the heuristic uses of a range of rhetorical figures, simile is never among them.

Metaphoric merger and metonymic displacement are certainly in evidence in *A Tale*, but they tend to govern the identification of women and the lower classes. If Lucie epitomizes metaphoric identification, Mme Defarge pursues a metonymic identity. Lucie's 'magic secret' lies in her ability to merge identities, not only her own identity with theirs, but also to inspire merged identities among the men who love her: in 'being everything to all of us, as if there were only one of us' (II, xxi, 221). But Lucie loses her own identity in the identities of others, a loss of individualism that middle-class male heroes ultimately eschew, in spite of temporary and projective mergers through Lucie. Mme Defarge, by contrast, is preoccupied with metonymic identification, that is to say, identity by association. She associates names with names and names with faces to forge identities and sentences in her knitted register. The attributes and actions of the Marquis St Evrémonde stand, synecdochally, for his entire family and class, so that his whole family and entire class must be punished for them. More than this, she pursues a revolutionary identity of displacement.

The novel, however, rejects both metaphoric merger and metonymic association for its middle-class and would-be middle-class males. Jane Caplan reminds us that 'The term *identity* . . . incorporates the tension between "identity" as *self-same*, in an individualising, subjective sense, and "identity" as *sameness with another*, in a classifying, objective sense.'[32] Simile, a figure of sameness that didactically retains differentiation, maintains individuation for middle-class men against metonymic displacement by, or metaphoric merger with, associated others and eschewed common noun categorizations, such as 'wastrel', 'drunkard', '*émigré*', 'traitor', 'prisoner' – even 'citizen'. It further navigates the competing claims of family, class, gender, sexual, racial, national, age and other group affiliations on higher-class males in the formation of their social identities by giving priority to bonds with other higher-class men.

The 'like' simile governs the identities of socially dominant males in the novel. Darnay, an aristocrat, resembles Manette, a middle-class male, in his efforts to live as a middle-class male in England: '*Like you*, a voluntary exile from France; *like you*, driven from it by its distractions, oppressions, and miseries; *like you*, striving to live away from it by my own exertions, and trusting in a happier future' (II, x, 139).

Lorry's circumnavigations around middle-class male identity are also expressed through simile. Breaking the news to Lucie that her father is alive, he unfolds his identity through simile:

> *Like* Monsieur Manette, your father, the gentleman was of Beauvais. *Like* Monsieur Manette, your father, the gentleman was of repute in Paris. . . . His affairs, *like* the affairs of many other French gentlemen and French families, were entirely in Tellson's hands.
>
> (I, iv, 25; emphases added)

When Lucie seeks to substitute identity for simile ('But this *is* my father's story' [I, iv, 25; original emphasis]), Lorry maintains the differentiations of simile: 'this *is* the story of your regretted father. Now comes the *difference*' (I, iv, 26; emphasis added). Simile here is not simply an indirect approach to a shocking revelation. It defines Manette chiefly through similar males from whom he is subsequently individuated and differentiated. Later, when Manette suffers a relapse of identity loss, Lorry restores his missing fragments of memory through similaic identification.

Simile extends from rhetoric to visual representations. The faces of Carton and Darnay are like each other rather than identical: even the seamstress at the end of the novel can see the seams that the conjunctions of simile resolutely maintain. Their similar faces forge confused rather than metaphorically fused or metonymically associated identities. Facial simile maintains a double identity that allows Carton and Darnay to be confused and distinguished as it serves their interests.

In Victorian prose fiction and theatrical melodrama, double identity is invariably adopted to commit crimes with impunity. Barsad–Pross and English Cly–French Cly take on double identities to commit fraud, perjury, theft, espionage and treason with impunity. The double-agent John Barsad is ultimately discovered and condemned because he has only one face for two names. By contrast, those double-agents of each other, Sydney Carton and Charles Darnay, possess two names and two faces, which allow them to dissociate identities as well as to exchange them.

Nevertheless, in the double agency of double-agent John Barsad–Solomon Pross, *A Tale* finds its template for exonerating Darnay from his guilt by association and Carton from his personal guilt. Pross can plead innocent of the crimes committed by Barsad, just as Barsad can plead innocent of the crimes committed by Pross. In the same way, Darnay is acquitted at his English trial, not because he is proven innocent, but because his identity is perceived to be interchangeable with Carton's. Legal punishment depends on the unambiguous, unique, positive identification of a criminal. Since neither man can be positively identified uniquely and unambiguously by attaching one face to one name, no man can be identified as having committed the crimes. The charges therefore go unanswered. No guilty parties remain. No one is punished.

Simile effects this mutual vindication. After their resemblance has astonished everyone at Darnay's English trial, the two men are represented as 'so like each other in feature, so unlike each other in manner – standing side by side, both reflected in the glass above them' (II, iii, 81). The men stand hinged by similaic conjunctions of rhetoric and mirror: 'side by side', 'like' and 'unlike', the mirror, a visual echo of the verbal rhetoric, yielding an inter-semiotic identification. Like similes, mirror images resist identity and one-way displacements, for mirror reflections are never exact resemblances because they reverse left and right fields. Added to this scopic mirroring, Dickens had devised a nominal left-and-right field, verbal-mirrored reversal when he initially named his characters Charles Darnay and Dick Carton.

The reversal of left and right fields extends to the novel's core concerns with the guilt and innocence of the two men. The description of their reflection in the criminalizing glass that has reflected so many guilty parties before them and in which Darnay was earlier ashamed to see himself reflected is followed swiftly by the verdict, 'ACQUITTED' (II, iii, 82; original emphasis). This moment epitomizes the larger game of mirrors in which guilt and innocence are reversed until only exculpation is possible. Carton is innocent of the nominal and affiliative charges of *émigré*, aristocrat and Evrémonde, under which he dies; Darnay is guilty of them. As Carton dies at the guillotine to save Darnay from his guilt by association, Darnay lies in a carriage under the influence of drugs and Carton's name, falsely accused of the manly incapacity and intoxication that are Carton's characteristic sins. As each is falsely accused of, and subjected to recriminations for, the other's sins, culpability and accountability vanish: crimes and punishments are divided so that neither is punished for his own. Both are refigured as falsely accused innocents, scapegoats for the other's sins. The scapegoat, Mark M. Hennelly tells us, is 'a double and a double, an ambiguous mixture of sameness and difference as it represents *both* sin *and* salvation'.[33] *A Tale of Two Cities*, like the mirror in the English court, redoubles Hennelly's 'a double *and* a double' when each man serves as scapegoat for the other. Neither is an innocent atoning for a guilty other: rather, each is guilty of his own sins, but eludes his own guilt by taking on and passing as innocent of the other's sins.

Such are the mirrored operations of simile, the mutual exchanges of justice and injustice, guilt and innocence, that each figures as both an unjustly punished innocent and a guilty party that goes unjustly unpunished. Where metonymic displacement would require one to be punished in place of the other and metaphoric merger would result in the unjust punishment, or the unjust exculpation, of both, simile succeeds in saving by a double reflection, a double resemblance, a double exchange. The illusion of simile is that each sin has been accounted for, that atonement and expiation have occurred, but it has all been done with mirrors. Similaic identity theft changes personal vice into public virtue and public vice into personal virtue, just as Barsad's betrayal of England figured as patriotism in France, and his betrayal of France figured as heroism in England.

Carton's final prophetic vision extends the mutual identity theft to posterity, creating a joint paternity for future generations expressed inter-semiotically in a rhetoric of faces and names. Carton envisages a future in which Lucie holds 'a child upon her bosom, who bears my *name*' (III, xv, 389; emphasis added). In this scenario, 'Sydney' at last lies on Lucie's bosom and receives her body and love through a nominal and facial interpenetration with Darnay that forges a joint paternity for the boy. If little Sydney Darnay resembles his father, as he must in a Dickens tale, then he will also resemble Carton. Named Sydney rather than Charles, his name and face will create a picture ID that evokes Carton as much as, if not more than, it does Darnay. And if, like Dickens's own sons named after other men, Carton's surname serves as middle name, young Sydney Carton Darnay subsequently solidifies the joint paternity when he names his own son after himself, not his father. Once the name passes from son to grandson, it becomes a patriarchal name.

Carton's own sullied name is sanitized by his namesake, who inherits the moral character and professional industriousness of his biological father:

> I see that child who lay upon her bosom and who bore my name, a man winning his way up in that path of life which once was mine. I see him winning it so well, that my name is made illustrious there by the light of his. I see the blots I threw upon it, faded away. I see him, foremost of just judges and honoured men . . .
>
> (III, xv, 390)

Sydney Carton, debauched wastrel, can never rise from advocate to judge, but his namesake can and, in his vision (which the narrator assures us is prophetic), does. The men who stood charged as traitors, exploiters, plunderers, rapists, murderers, drunks, failures and wastrels incapable of reform or rescue now co-create judges who determine the guilt and innocence of others. The novel avers in the face of all this that 'the Creator . . . never reverses his transformations' (III, xv, 385). Any reversals of mirrored simile would require each man to carry and account for his own guilt. Carton's death, then, is not only for Darnay, but also for himself. Darnay's life, then, is not only for himself, but also for Carton.

In the final analysis, the similaic mode of inter-semiotic identification, far from establishing unique, unambiguous identities to protect society from crimes and acts of terror, ushers in a perpetual identity theft that allows the individual sins and class crimes of ruling males not only to pass unaccounted for, but also to figure as innocence and heroism. It further establishes an inheritance of patriarchal legal power that passes from criminals to judges. At the guillotine, Carton prophesies: 'I see the evil of this time and of the previous time of which this is the natural birth, gradually making expiation for itself, and wearing out' (III, xv, 389). No man makes expiation for his evil; evil makes expiation for itself. In this context, Carton's final words, 'It is a far, far better thing I do, than I have ever done', evoke a definitive shudder.

Notes

1. While picture IDs can contain written information other than names and biometric indices other than faces, these are variable and secondary. Only proper names and faces are universal and primary. Recent political discussions of identity cards in England maintain that, while fingerprint and iris recognition technologies are more accurate than even digital facial recognition technologies, not everyone has fingerprints or irises: only the face is universal. Houses of Commons Home Affairs Committee, *Identity Cards: Fourth Report of Session 2003–4* (Stationery Office, 30 July 2004), vol. 1, p. 45.
2. Martin Lloyd, *The Passport: The History of Man's Most Travelled Document* (Stroud: Sutton Publishing, 2003), p. 130.
3. See, for example, Michel Foucault, *Madness and Civilisation: A History of Insanity in the Age of Reason*, trans. Richard Howard (New York: Pantheon, 1965); and Michel Foucault, *Discipline and Punish: The Birth of the Prison*, trans. Alan Sheridan (New York: Pantheon, 1978).
4. Jacques Derrida, *Of Grammatology*, trans. Gayatri Chakravorty Spivak (Baltimore, MD: Johns Hopkins University Press, 1976); and Jacques Derrida, *On the Name*, ed. Thomas Dutoit, trans. David Wood, John P. Leavey, Jr and Ian McLeod (Stanford, CA: Stanford University Press, 1995).
5. Judith Butler's work on performative bodies is the best known. See her *Gender Trouble: Feminism and the Subversion of Identity* (New York: Routledge, 1990).
6. Gilles Deleuze and Félix Guattari, *A Thousand Plateaus: Capitalism and Schizophrenia*, trans. Brian Massumi (London: Athlone Press, 1988), pp. 187, 194 and passim.
7. See, for example, H. G. Wallbott's discussion of Lev Kuleshov's 1919 experiments with facial expression in film montage. 'Influences of facial expression and context information on emotion attributions', *British Journal of Social Psychology* 27 (1988), 357–69.
8. This concept persists today in the widespread consensus that blurring the face alone in film or video obscures social identity.
9. See, for example, the House of Commons report cited in note 1.
10. These include: 'you aren't well enough to travel'; 'it's time to take a holiday'; 'it's time to go home'; and 'there's something seriously wrong with you'.
11. As with all revolutions, such pairings were reinscribed to establish new hierarchies. See, for example, Sylvia Musto, 'Portraiture, Revolutionary Identity and Subjugation: Anne-Louis Girodet's Citizen Belley', *Canadian Art Review* 20.1/2 (1993), 60–71.
12. Adrien Sée, *Le Passeport en France* (Chartres: Faculté de Droit, 1907), cited in Lloyd, *Passport*, p. 61; translation Lloyd's.
13. Lloyd, *Passport*, pp. 61–5.
14. John Torpey, *The Invention of the Passport: Surveillance, Citizenship and the State* (Cambridge: Cambridge University Press, 2000), pp. 17–32.

15. Jeremy Bentham, 'Principles of Penal Law' (1830), *The Works of Jeremy Bentham*, ed. John Bowring, 11 vols. (Edinburgh: W. Tait, 1843), vol. 1, p. 557. I am indebted to Jane Caplan for this reference (see note 36 below).

16. John Stuart Mill, 'Of Names and Propositions', *A System of Logic Ratiocinative and Inductive, Being a Connected View of the Principles of Evidence and the Methods of Scientific Investigation*, 2 vols., 10th edn (London: Longmans, Green, & Co., 1879), I.

17. Lloyd, p. 66.

18. I am indebted to Colin Jones for this information.

19. Passport photographs were not used consistently until the First World War and even then were accompanied by ekphrastic descriptions.

20. Victorian literary conventions drew on Johann Kaspar Lavater's popular revival of classical physiognomy in the 1770s, which held that both soul and heart manifested in the face.

21. The Jacquerie was a synonym for peasant uprisings in France, stemming from the 1358 peasants' revolt. Peasant revolutionaries received the generic name 'Jacques Bonhomme'.

22. This essay discusses guilt, sins and crimes as they are constructed in the novel and levies no independent moral judgement on these issues.

23. As of this writing, the *MLA Bibliography* yields 9,097 hits in a keyword search for metaphor but only 421 for simile. The latter drops to 355 when one searches for simile apart from metaphor and to 333 when articles in a journal entitled *Simile* not addressing simile are omitted. This yields a ratio of greater than 27:1.

24. Christian Metz, *The Imaginary Signifier: Psychoanalysis and the Cinema*, trans. Celia Britton (Bloomington, IN: Indiana University Press, 1982), p. 176; John M. Kennedy, 'What Makes a Metaphor Stronger than a Simile?' *Metaphor and Symbol* 14.1 (1999), 63–9.

25. Roman Jakobson, *Selected Writings* (The Hague: Mouton, 1966–81).

26. Jacques Lacan, *Écrits: A Selection*, trans. Alan Sheridan (London: Tavistock, 1977).

27. Verena Haser, *Metaphor, Metonymy, and Experientialist Philosophy: Challenging Cognitive Semantics* (Berlin: Mouton de Gruyter, 2005); *Metaphor and Metonymy at the Crossroads: A Cognitive Perspective*, ed. Antonio Barcelona (New York: Mouton de Gruyer, 2000).

28. Susan Nalbantian, *The Symbol of the Soul from Holderlin to Yeats: A Study in Metonymy* (London: Macmillan, 1977).

29. Paul de Man, *Allegories of Reading: Figural Language in Rousseau, Nietzsche, Rilke, and Proust* (New Haven, CT: Yale University Press, 1979).

30. Hayden White, *Metahistory: The Historical Imagination in Nineteenth-Century Europe* (Baltimore, MD: Johns Hopkins University Press, 1973).

31. Zoltán Kövecses, *Metaphor in Culture: Universality and Variation* (Cambridge: Cambridge University Press, 2005).

32. Jane Caplan, ' "This or That Particular Person": Protocols of Identification in Nineteenth-Century Europe', in *Documenting Individual Identity: The Development of State Practices in the Modern World*, ed. Jane Caplan and John Torpey (Princeton, NJ: Princeton University Press, 2001), p. 51; original emphasis. Caplan cites and builds on arguments by Beatrice Fraenkel, *La signature: genèse d'un signe* (Paris: Gallimard, 1992), p. 197.

33. Mark M. Hennelly, Jr., ' "Like or No Like": Figuring the Scapegoat in *A Tale of Two Cities*', *DSA* 30 (2001), p. 220; original emphasis.

7

Counting On: *A Tale of Two Cities*

John Bowen

> If anyone questioned me, indeed, if anyone should ask, 'What are you doing there?' I should reply at once, 'I am counting.'
>
> Jean-Paul Sartre, *Being and Nothingness* (1943)

> It calculates so as not to have to speak, for fear of falling back into nothingness.
>
> Pierre Klossowski, *Nietzsche and the Vicious Circle* (1969)

> – In small numbers, but what is a small number? Where does it begin and end? At one? At one plus one? One plus one man? One plus one woman? Or none whatsoever? Do you mean to say that it begins with all men and all women, with anyone? And does democracy count?
> – Democracy counts, it counts votes and subjects, but it does not count, should not count, ordinary singularities: there is no *numerus clauses* for *arrivants*.
> – It is perhaps still necessary to calculate, but differently, differently with one and with the other.
>
> Jacques Derrida, *Politics of Friendship* (1994)

> But never did Henry, as he thought he did,
> end anyone and hacks her body up
> and hide the pieces, where they may be found.
> He knows: he went over everyone, & nobody's missing.
> Often he reckons, in the dawn, them up.
> Nobody is ever missing.
>
> John Berryman, from 'Dream Song 29'

I

At the end of Book I, chapter 5 of *A Tale of Two Cities*, there is an apparently trivial exchange between Jarvis Lorry and Ernest Defarge, which occurs just before Lucie Manette and Lorry see her father for the first time since his release from eighteen years' imprisonment in the Bastille. Lorry speaks first:

> 'Do you make a show of Monsieur Manette?'
> 'I show him . . . to a chosen few.'
> 'Is that well?'
> '*I* think it is well.'
> 'Who are the few? How do you choose them?'
> 'I choose them as real men, of my name – Jacques is my name.'
>
> (*TTC*, I, v, 40)

Defarge then strikes 'twice or thrice upon the door', drawing 'the key across it, three or four times' (I, v, 40) before they enter the room. In this threshold scene, wrapped in enigma, it is striking how often we are asked to register countable numbers: two, three and four times, as well as the uncounted 'few' who are privileged to witness the still-suffering Manette, and who are both named and unnamed by the generic 'Jacques'. But this is of a piece with the novel as a whole, which is full of counting, and troubled by its relationship with naming. I want to argue that we should be more aware of this distinctive and insistent quality of the book, and should particularly note the ways in which such counting and uncountability represent (or figure, or account for) kinds of political being and obligation in relation to other kinds of more familiarly novelistic action and duty. As Jacques Derrida points out in a number of texts, particularly *Politics of Friendship* (1994) and *The Gift of Death* (1992), the question of democracy has an intimate relationship to matters of counting: of counting votes, at its simplest.[1] But for Derrida, there is a deeply problematic relationship between the impulse to make every vote count and the very different respect for what he calls 'the irreducible singularity' of the other.[2] *A Tale of Two Cities* insistently returns to the conflicted and aporetic nature of that relationship.

There are a number of dimensions to this question of enumeration: narrative, fictional, historical and political. All novels, perhaps all narratives, as Alex Woloch in *The One versus the Many: Minor Characters and the Space of the Protagonist in the Novel* has shown, take a stand on the political question of the relationship between the claims of the one as opposed to the many in their very constitution of what Woloch calls the 'character space' and 'narrative asymmetry' of a particular fiction, in such everyday things as the creation or existence of a named main character or hero, for example.[3] To do so is to single out one from many, or one from few, and to grant him or her a fictional pre-eminence or centrality. The writing of history, in the nineteenth century at least, shares many narrative conventions and their consequences with the novel. The most interesting example of this is the work of Dickens's friend Thomas Carlyle, who famously asserted, in 'On Heroes and

Hero-Worship' (1841), that history was 'but the Biography of great men';[4] but who in a remarkable passage in *The French Revolution* (1837), in a welter of enumeration, contrasted the complexly asymmetrical fate of the uncounted and barely represented many with the remembered and represented few. In the chapter entitled 'A Trilogy', after quoting liberally from the accounts of three men who escaped the July Massacres and lived to tell their tales, 'Brave Jourgniac, innocent Abbé Sicard, judicious Advocate Maton', Carlyle then reflects on those who did not survive, did not narrate and whom we can merely count:

> Thus they three, in wondrous trilogy, or triple soliloquy: uttering simultaneously, through the dread night-watches, their Night-thoughts, grown audible to us! They Three are become audible: but the other 'Thousand and Eighty-nine, of whom Two-hundred and two were Priests,' who also had Night-thoughts, remain inaudible; choked forever in black Death.[5]

The 1850s saw a major contribution to debates about the nature of mass democracy. John Stuart Mill's *On the Nature of Representative Government* (1851) was followed in 1859 (the same year as *A Tale of Two Cities*) by *On Liberty,* a text concerned at its heart with enumeration and the consequences of a change from a political order in which 'a governing One' exercised power to societies endangered by majoritarian tyranny, as in the 'aberrations' of the French Revolution which were, for Mill, 'the work of a usurping few'.[6] Mill's central assertion is that:

> The will of the people, moreover, practically means the will of the most numerous or most active *part* of the people – the majority, or those who succeed in making themselves accepted as the majority; the people may consequently decide to oppress a part of their number, and precautions are needed against this as against any other abuse of power.[7]

The central problem of modern liberty and democracy is constituted by a conflict of numbers and the antimonies of the very small ('The One', the 'few') and the very large ('the most numerous', 'the majority'), whose conflicting claims are most starkly polarized in Mill's central claim that 'If all mankind minus one were of one opinion, mankind would be no more justified in silencing that one person than he, if he had the power, would be justified in silencing mankind'.[8] The ensuing difficulty of reconciling these competing and incommensurable claims, which we can call the question of the 'minus one' for Mill, is also to be answered by a number, another 'one': the assertion of 'one very simple principle ... that the sole end for which mankind are warranted ... in interfering with the liberty or action of any of their number, is self-protection.'[9]

One way to begin to recognize the claims of others is by counting them; another is by naming them. Novels, *par excellence*, are domains of naming and Dickens was a great namer.[10] The depiction of historical action, in history or fiction, raises in acute form the relationship between naming and numbering. *A Tale of Two Cities* is concerned with a small (unusually small for Dickens) group of named characters, but the novel waits some time before it names them – or indeed anyone at all: the first chapter, for example, mentions the king and queen of both countries, the Lord Mayor, the 'City tradesman', and the youth who had 'his hands cut off' (I, i, 5–7); but it is only Joanna Southcott (who never appears again) who is given a proper name. In exemplary contrast, the first sentence of Carlyle's *The French Revolution* (which played so central role in the gestation of *A Tale of Two Cities* that Dickens claimed to have read it 500 times) begins with a name and naming: 'President Hénault, remarking on royal Surnames of Honour ...'.[11] For Georg Lukács, in his seminal Hegelian account of the rise and fall of the historical novel, 'It was the French Revolution, the revolutionary wars and the rise and fall of Napoleon, which for the first time made history a *mass experience*.'[12] Mass history raises acutely the problem of how to represent the many and the unnamed. For Lukács, Walter Scott succeeded in this through the creation of mediocre heroes who represented wider social movements and groups of people through their typicality 'in the sense of the decent and average, rather than the eminent and all-embracing'.[13] In this essay, I want to explore Dickens's more diverse strategies to represent popular or mass action, or rather, to figure the complex relations of prioritization and subordination that exist within historical and fictional narrative between the claims of the many and the few. These include strategic delay, anonymity and non-differentiation in naming; the figuring of popular or mass action through quasi-allegorical figures such as St Antoine and the sea; characterization by profession or type, including 'the mender of roads', 'Monsieur', 'the Vengeance' and the endlessly proliferating semi-anonymous Jacques; and, perhaps above all, through simple and complex forms of enumeration.

When Dickens thinks of the political, in *A Tale of Two Cities* and other writing of the period, he thinks of both very large and very small numbers, between which lies the terrain – classically that of the realist novel – of the few friends or characters whom we are asked to care for particularly, to take particular care of. These three dimensions or members of the sequence – the many, the single, the few – and the tensions or contradictions of their relationship bind together the action of the novel through a constant questioning of the relation of enumeration to fiction and to political and ethical obligation. The numbers of *A Tale of Two Cities* have often been registered in criticism as questions either of triangles – erotic ones, in particular – or doubles of various sorts, but the book may ask us to count higher and more strangely than such twos and threes allow.[14]

II

There is a revealing letter from Dickens to Austen Layard of 10 April 1855, in which he writes about the contemporary political situation in Britain:

> There is nothing in the present time at once so galling and so alarming to me as the alienation of the people from their own public affairs .... I believe the discontent to be so much worse for smouldering instead of blazing openly, that it is extremely like the general mind of France before the breaking out of the first Revolution, and in danger of being turned by any one of a thousand accidents – a bad harvest – the last straw too much of aristocratic insolence or incapacity – a defeat abroad – a mere chance at home – into such a Devil of a conflagration as has never been beheld since.
>
> (*Letters*, VII, 586–8)

The letter comes from a period in which Dickens is both very fully engaged with contemporary political life and deeply pessimistic about the nature and consequences of mid-Victorian political processes. In his 'most sombre and oppressive' novel *Little Dorrit*, which began publication later that year, we have in the Circumlocution Office a very dark, almost Kafkaesque, sense of the constitutive futility and obstructiveness of government and bureaucracy.[15] Such pessimism and anger are even clearer in Dickens's political journalism of the period, which, particularly in response to the misconduct of the Crimean War, is a good deal less good-humoured and buoyant than that of previous decades. Whereas the 1850s are often seen as a relatively settled decade after the 'Hungry Thirties' and 'Angry Forties', Dickens's sense as he lived through it was very different. He perceived a state and political settlement vulnerable in all directions, in which any one of many possible causes – aristocratic 'insolence or incapacity', imperial failure, domestic uncertainty, natural disaster – was capable of overturning an entire social and political order.[16] It was so worrying to him that he made a rare, directly political intervention – 'the first political meeting I have ever attended' – in 1855 in his vigorous support for the work of the Administrative Reform Association founded by Layard, the recipient of the letter.[17]

Dickens, then, saw England at this period as in an essentially pre-revolutionary situation. It is, though, the way in which he makes the analogy between the state of England in the mid-1850s (four years before he wrote *A Tale*) and that of *ancien régime* France that I shall highlight. He does so by asking about the relationship between, on the one hand, the singular event, the one accident that might cause an unprecedented conflagration, and, on the other, the thousand possibilities that might lead to it. Both are questions of numbers, as are the first French Revolution and, slightly later in the letter, 'the disgusted millions' whose suffering 'perhaps not one man in a thousand of those not actually enveloped in it ... has the least idea' (*Letters*, VII, 587). The following week, Dickens published a savage attack on the Palmerston government, entitled 'The Thousand and One Humbugs'. Its title is taken from one of his favourite texts, *The Thousand and One Nights*, in which each story, whose number in principle need have no end, evades a sacrificial death.[18] A thousand and one; one in a thousand; one of a thousand: each time, in thinking of the political, Dickens thinks of numbers, of the very large and the very small. Those numbers, I want to argue, are deeply implicated in the way he thinks about both the socially and politically catastrophic – the disgusted millions, the discontent that might blaze out, the devil of a conflagration that might ensue – and the necessity of a singular relationship to one's duty or responsibility. These three dimensions or members of the sequence – the many, the single, the few – and the tensions or contradictions of their relationship, as in Scheherazade's story, bind deeply together questions of enumeration, sacrifice, narrative and death.

As too does *A Tale of Two Cities*, a novel full of counting and numbers, from the title-page down: 'A Tale of Two Cities / In three books / Book the First / Recalled to Life / Chapter One / The Period'. The three books of the novel are simply numbered, unlike, say, those of *Little Dorrit*, whose two volumes are called 'Poverty' and 'Riches', or *Hard Times*, whose three books are 'Sowing', 'Reaping' and 'Garnering'. Chapter titles include 'Five Years Later', 'Hundreds of Promises', 'Two Promises', 'One Night', 'Nine Days' and 'Fifty-Two'. The first chapter, 'The Period', is characterized both by numbers and by their lack, with what can and cannot be counted: 'It was the year of our Lord One Thousand Seven Hundred and Seventy-five ... Mrs Southcott had attained her twenty-fifth year ... the Cock Lane ghost had been laid only a round dozen of years' (I, i, 5); seven robbers attack the mail, three are shot and the other four shoot the guard. Against these knowable and countable dates, people and things are set on the one hand singular, allegorical presences such as Death and Fate; on the other, the uncountable numbers of the 'mob', the 'long rows of miscellaneous criminals' and the 'myriads of small creatures – the creatures of this chronicle among the rest' (I, i, 7): everything, in short, that is singular, superlative, beyond or below measure, uncountable, uncounted or countless.

I want to argue that the relationship between that singularity, those singularities, those numbers and that immensity should be more central to our understanding of the novel and to emphasize this numerical iteration in order to ask how it represents (or figures, or accounts for) the nature of political being and obligation in relation to other kinds of more familiarly novelistic action and duty. Dickens's *Hard Times* dramatizes this very problem in Sissy Jupe's account to Louisa Gradgrind of her failure to succeed in the M'Choakumchild classroom:

> Then Mr M'Choakumchild said he would try me again. And he said, This schoolroom is an immense town, and in it there are a million of inhabitants, and only five-and-twenty are starved to death in the streets, in the course of a year. What is your remark on that proportion? And my remark was – for I couldn't think of a better one – that I thought it must be just as hard upon those who were starved, whether the others were a million, or a million million. And that was wrong, too. ... Then Mr M'Choakumchild said he would try me once more. And he said ... that in a given time a hundred thousand persons went to sea on long voyages, and only five hundred of them were drowned or burnt to death. What is the percentage? And I said ... it was nothing ... Nothing ... to the relations and friends of the people who were killed.[19]

The whole passage, and a good deal of the weight of Dickens's critique of utilitarianism, rest on the contrast between countable numbers and what lies outside or beyond them. Sissy's behaviour 'was the result of no arithmetical process, was self-imposed in defiance of all calculation, and went dead against any table of probabilities that any actuary would have drawn up from the premises'.[20] M'Choakumchild's reasonable and calculable numbers – five and twenty, a million, a hundred thousand, five hundred – are taken to their limits by Sissy's 'million million' and 'nothing'. Sissy's failure (which is also, of course, a success) to offer the correct statistical response is predicated on her openness to the singular event, the existential 'Nothing' of each death of those who starve or drown. *A Tale of Two Cities* accelerates and intensifies this questioning and limit-testing of enumeration. The novel's quasi-mathesis or numerology asks us to count differently and to question how, if at all, we might number such things as death, sacrifice or secrets, when numbers become incalculable, and if or when we might ever stop counting.[21]

Let me give some examples of some of the different ways that the novel uses numbers, to show how they simultaneously structure and destructure it. In the first court scene, for example, Stryver wants to know if Cly was in prison two or three times, as he claims, or five or six (II, iii, 70). We would feel differently about his veracity if the latter were true. We register the horror of the Bloody Code in the 'dozens' burned in the hand, or the felon executed for 'robbing a farmer's boy of sixpence' (I, i, 7); of the *ancien régime* in Manette's 'eighteen years' (III, iv, 280); of the guillotine and those who witness it in the wood sawyer's proud boast that 'he shaved the sixty-three today, in less than two pipes' (III, ix, 324). The fall of the Bastille ('Two fierce hours ... Four fierce hours ... eight great towers' [II, xxi, 224]) culminates in the spectacle of 'seven prisoners released, seven gory heads on pikes' (II, xxi, 230). The novel, before its famous coda of Carton's quasi-prophetic quasi-utterance 'It is a far, far better thing . . .' ends with a single number: '[t]he murmuring of many voices, the upturning of many faces, the pressing on of many footsteps in the outskirts of the crowd, so that it swells forward in a mass, like one great heave of water, all flashes away. Twenty-Three' (III, xv, 389). The three metonymic manys – voices, faces, footsteps – end in a single similitudinous mass 'like one great heave of water'. The moment of Carton's death and the culminating action of the novel, together with the shift from Carton's focalization to objective narration – the flash or cut to death, knowledge, climax, objectivity and prophecy – are signalled by a number, Carton's number: twenty-three.

Twenty-three does not seem to be accidentally chosen, a single prime number of the next two digits – two and three – that is greater than both, just as this is one tale of two cities in three books, centring on three people: a woman, and two men who look like one. For the question of ones, and twos and threes and what might or could be beyond three is very important to the book and to the fates of its characters. We have learned from René Girard, Eve Kosofsky Sedgwick and others of the significance of triangular desire both to this novel and to Dickens's later fiction in particular.[22] But what one could call the question of the three here – most obviously Lucie, Sydney and Charles – is so saturated with other numbers – the sixty-three or fifty-two who die on the scaffold, the six tumbrels transformed into the huts of millions of peasants, the twenty-five thousand Jacques, the twenty years of life the unbrutalized beholder would give to petrify the mob, the twelve hours of the clock and many more – that we may need to think of it as much in arithmetical as triangular terms. In Book I, chapter 2, for example, 'The Mail', Jarvis Lorry is introduced not by name but by number as 'the first of the persons with whom this history has business' (I, ii, 8). He is both a part of, and apart from, the 'Two other passengers, besides the one' on the coach: 'All three were wrapped . . . Not one of the three could have said . . . what either of the other two was like . . . each was hidden from the eyes . . . of his two companions' (I, ii, 9). There are seven numbers in three sentences in a pattern of one, twos and threes: two, one, three, one, three, two. No names. When one coachman asks the other what he makes of the action we have just witnessed, he replies 'Nothing at all' (I, ii, 14). Those numbers – one, two, three and nothing at all – seem just as important an act of scene-setting, of striking 'the key note' as Dickens sometimes put it, as that of the more celebrated first chapter.[23] These numbers, their sequencing, instability, combination, division and transformation, and the question of what they mean, will echo through the novel, heard and unheard, seen and unseen.

III

There seem to me, caught as I necessarily am in this contagion of enumeration, to be three striking things about all these numbers. First, as I hope to have shown, there is a repetitive and deeply unstable return to questions of ones, twos and threes. The Bible, for example, is called at one point 'the two Testaments' (I, ii, 9): the question of the relation of one thing (or person) that might be two or three or more is one (or two or three or more) that haunts the novel, most notably in the many (or, depending on your scale, the few) pairs and doubles of the book. Secondly, there is both a linking and substitution of numbering and naming in the book, which is often figured through an absence or belatedness of naming. The question whether something is named or counted is intensely important. In the scene of the first meeting of Lucie and her father, he is unable to name himself as anything other than a number and a location:

> 'Did you ask me for my name?'
> 'Assuredly I did.'
> 'One Hundred and Five, North Tower.'
> 'Is that all?'
> 'One Hundred and Five, North Tower.'
>
> (I, vi, 44)

Thirdly, and perhaps most importantly, the novel seems troubled by the relation of quite small numbers to very large ones. In chapter 3, for example, Lorry has two dreams: first of a run on the bank in which 'more drafts were honoured in five minutes than even Tellson's ... ever paid in thrice the time' (I, iii, 16), a dream of a currency of unstoppable momentum and proliferation, and consequent loss. His second dream is that 'He was on his way to dig some one out of a grave', in which he sees a 'multitude of faces' with many different expressions: 'but the face was in the main one face' (I, iii, 17). With the characteristic condensation of dreams, Lorry sees the same face (and this is a novel that constantly returns to the figure of the face) that simultaneously and sequentially represents an impossible multitude.

We see this vividly in 'Hundreds of People' (Book II, chapter 6), set in Manette's house in Soho Square. It is where we learn (although we do not know we learn until later) that Manette has buried what will become the fatal paper in his cell and we hear for the first time the echoes of revolutionary footsteps. A small group, consisting of a father, a daughter and two friends – Manette, Lucie, Darnay, Carton – gather, are named and are numbered: 'Mr Darnay presented himself ... but he was only One ... Mr Carton had lounged in, but he made only Two' (II, vi, 104–6). They hear the 'echoes of footsteps coming and going' which Darnay, having first made the expressive, thematic remark 'a multitude of people, and yet a solitude', imagines as 'the echoes of all the footsteps that are coming by-and-by into our lives' (II, vi, 106–7). Sydney replies prophetically (thus prophesying his later prophetic gift): 'There is a great crowd coming one day into our lives, if that is so' (II, vi, 107). It is an intensely suggestive chapter of echoes, anticipations and numbers, which asks at its heart what the relation (if any, for they may simply be incommensurable) might be between those three kinds of counting: the one, the few, the many; the solitude, the few friends, the multitude. Carton's climactic death will also bring these three kinds of counting together – he dies alone in the sight of the anonymous many while a small group of friends flees to safety. Why should this be? Why these particular emphases on ones, twos, threes; on counting, naming and anonymity; on unstoppable momentum to the extremely large and countless?

The critical attention to numbers in the novel that there has been has seen the book as concerned essentially with doubling: with twos, pairs and halves, with, as Catherine Gallagher puts it in her seminal essay 'The duplicity of doubling'.[24] There is a good deal of evidence to support this: doubles such as Sydney and Charles; the two Lucies; the twin Evrémonde brothers; two Jerry Crunchers; the two non-corresponding halves of Manette's consciousness; the doubled actions; the corresponding pairs such as Miss Pross and Mme Defarge; and the analogues to historical narration in public execution, the Revolution and the resurrection motif. Psychic, social and narrative doubling is constitutive of this novel, in a peculiarly intensive form. It may also be essential to our understanding of representation: as Geoffrey Bennington writes: 'the present presentation of meaning by expression is *haunted* by its repetition. Its reproduction or representation is always possible. The sign is a sign only in this milieu of "re".'[25] This novel too is a milieu of 're', its actions and characters dominated by the power of revolution, revenge, repetition, resurrection and recalling. Yet such repetition, in order to be repetition, can never be identical. Twos in the novel often becomes three and more. Jerry Cruncher follows his father, another Jerry Cruncher, on a graverobbing expedition; who is joined by another man, who then appears to little Jerry 'to have all of a sudden, split himself into two' (II, xiv, 167). Two becomes three becomes four.[26] There are two trials, one in England and one in France, but then a third which reverses the judgment of the previous two. It takes four men to make chocolate, one carrying two watches. At times, this momentum to count one more becomes almost self-parodic: 'Jacques One, Jacques Two, Jacques Three! This is the witness encountered by appointment, by me, Jacques Four. He will tell you all. Speak, Jacques Five!' (II, xv, 173). At the storming of the Bastille, Defarge shouts: 'One drawbridge down! Work, comrades all, work! Work, Jacques One, Jacques Two, Jacques One Thousand, Jacques Two Thousand, Jacques Five-and-Twenty Thousand; in the name of all the Angels or the Devils – which you prefer – work!' (II, xxi, 224).

It is this onward march of numbers, their apparently unstoppable momentum, an incalculable automatism of the arithmetical from one to many millions, that seems both constitutive of fictional and political representation in the novel and profoundly unsettling of it: four incendiaries 'were steadily wending East, West, North, and South . . . and whosoever hung, fire burned. The altitude of the gallows that would turn to water and quench it, no functionary, by any stretch of mathematics, was able to calculate successfully'

(II, xxiv, 242). This reaches its height in the chaotic enumeration and lack of it in the 'Year One of Liberty', which sees 'three hundred thousand men ... rise against the tyrants of the earth' and 'forty or fifty thousand revolutionary committees all over the land' and yet, as an example of 'the strange law of contradiction which obtains in all such cases', there was 'no measurement of time ... count of time was there none' (III, iv, 283). Both novel and characters recognize and enact the vertiginous momentum of this 'law of contradiction', seeking at the same time and often in the same gesture both to accelerate and end it:

> 'It is true what madame says,' observed Jacques Three. 'Why stop? There is great force in that. Why stop?'
> 'Well, well,' reasoned Defarge, 'but one must stop somewhere. After all, the question is still where?'
> 'At extermination,' said madame.
> 'Magnificent!' croaked Jacques Three.
>
> (III, xii, 352–3)

IV

There is a close relationship between what is called modernity and enumeration. As Ian Hacking has shown in detail, an 'avalanche of printed numbers' characterized nineteenth-century life, whose advent coincided with, and was at least in part caused by, the very events that Dickens narrates: 'before the Napoleonic era, most official counting had been kept privy to administrators. After it, a vast amount was printed and published.'[27] It is as central to the project of instrumental and bureaucratic reason – to surveillance, the disciplining of the social and the control of population – as it is to capitalistic enterprise. But there is also a more properly political dimension to the question of counting. The most suggestive, if rather undeveloped, discussion of this topic is that of Jacques Derrida in *Politics of Friendship*, which is concerned with the relationship between the calculability of votes and subjects that must operate within any political democracy and the radical ethical obligation to the singular claim that the other makes upon me. As Derrida writes:

> the question of democracy thus opens, the question of the citizen or the subject as a countable singularity. And that of a 'universal fraternity'. There is no democracy without respect for irreducible singularity or alterity, but there is no democracy without the 'community of friends' (koína ta philōn), without the calculation of majorities, without identifiable, stabilizable, representable subjects, all equal. These two laws are irreducible one to the other. Tragically irreconcilable and forever wounding. The wound itself opens with the necessity of having to *count* one's friends ... More

serious than a contradiction, political desire is forever borne by the dis-junction of these two laws ... There is no virtue without this tragedy of number without number. This is perhaps even more unthinkable than a tragedy.[28]

That wound – between the calculations of M'Choakumchild and Sissy Jupe, as it were – also seems to lie near the heart of the nineteenth-century histor-ical novel, which also is deeply concerned with the question of virtue and the tragic within historical action. It is often said, taking its classic form in Lukács's *The Historical Novel* (1937), that *A Tale of Two Cities* is essentially an apolitical and weak work.[29] Commenting on the failure, as he sees it, of the post-1848 bourgeois novel, Lukács argues that 'even with a writer of Dickens's rank the weaknesses of his petit-bourgeois humanism and idealism are even more obvious and intrusive than in his social novels ... in the historical novel this tendency of Dickens must necessarily take on the character of modern privateness in regard to history.'[30] That opposition – between privateness and history – seems to me something that the novel is wholly unwilling to accept, not least because the stability of the public/private opposition is constantly both structured and undone by the novel's treatment of *friendship* – which may include (and indeed require) the giving up of one's life.

Politics of Friendship points to the deeply unsettling binding together of politics and friendship within a long tradition of thought from Aristotle onwards. The question of friendship within this tradition is deeply linked to the figure of the brother and of the brotherhood that constitutes the third claim of the single yet trinitarian 'dawning Republic One and Indivisible, of Liberty, Equality, Fraternity, or Death' (III, i, 255). *A Tale of Two Cities* seems to me a remarkably acute and sustained dramatization of the competing ethical, narrative and political demands that they make and the consequent con-flict, disjunction or irreconcilability between, on the one hand, the claims of brother- and sisterhood, of friendship and the small group of friends (Lucie, Charles, Alexander, Sydney, Jarvis) and, on the other, the claims of millions. Brothers matter a good deal to both the novel's main and sub-plot: its central action begins with the abduction of the future Mme Defarge's sister by two brothers in a terrible fraternity of rape. Later, the 'sisterhood' (II, xxii, 231) of the Terror will take its revenge, with Mme Defarge refusing the plea by Lucie to her 'sister-woman' (III, iii, 278). In the sub-plot, the key to Carton's substitution for Darnay is Miss Pross's discovery of her lost and idealized brother, Solomon, alias John Barsad. These intimate claims of friendship and fraternity have, to say the least, a problematic relationship with those of the many. Darnay, condemned to death in the cell, learns 'that he was vir-tually sentenced by the millions, and that units could avail him nothing' (III, xiii, 360). Although he is wrong, the incommensurability or incom-patibility between the claims and powers of units and of millions is at the heart of the novel's action and politics, but for Dickens it is not necessarily a tragic incommensurability. As so often in nineteenth-century thought and fiction, the binary logics of melodrama usurp tragic energy, directing it into an essentially redemptive resolution.[31]

Twice in the novel the numbering stops, on both occasions at or close to death. In their final appearance in the novel, as Lucie, Darnay and Lorry flee Paris to safety, they believe that they are being pursued. Not, however, to re-arrest them, as they fear, but simply to ask them yet another question about counting. Their reply, the last words that Lorry speaks in the novel, is another number:

> 'Ho! Within the carriage there. Speak then!'
>   'What is it?' asks Mr Lorry, looking out at window.
>   'How many did they say?'
>   'I do not understand you.'
>   ' – At the last post. How many to the Guillotine today?'
>   'Fifty-two.'
>   'I said so! A brave number! My fellow-citizen here would have it forty-two; ten more heads are worth having. The Guillotine goes handsomely. I love it.'
>
> (III, xiii, 371)

Carton is, of course, one of that number, the one whom we as readers are asked particularly to care about. With his death and substitution for Darnay, the novel commits itself simultaneously, if implausibly, to the claims of friendship, the singular hero and to the prospect of a democratic France that is to come. In a novel haunted by compulsive and violent repetition, it is only such a sacrifice, it seems, that can resolve its narrative and political antinomies and enable the small company of friends to escape to freedom and life. Carton's death is also figured as a necessary sacrifice to redeem Paris, which he imagines or prophesies as 'a beautiful city and a brilliant people rising from this abyss', in whose future he sees the 'evil of this time and of the previous time of which this is the natural birth, gradually making expiation for itself and wearing out' (III, xv, 389). His death draws on and condenses what Derrida, in his analysis of Cicero's *De Amicitia* calls the 'exemplary heritage' of friendship which transports 'the name's renown beyond death. A narcissistic projection of the ideal image, of its own ideal image (*exemplar*), already inscribes the legend. It engraves the renown in a ray of light, and prints the citation of the friend in a convertibility of life and death, of presence and absence, and promises it to the testamental *revenance* . . . of more [no more] life, of a *surviving*'.[32] It would be hard to think of a better description of Carton's final prophetic self-projection, which capitalizes so hyperbolically on the resources of this tradition as, both alive and dead, present and absent, he projects his own simultaneous survival and commemoration, which culminate in the vision of the 'child who lay upon her bosom and who bore my name', making his name 'illustrious' and in turn producing another child 'of my name' to whom his story is told 'with a tender and a faltering voice' (III, xv, 390). Carton dies and lives on, and the footsteps die out for ever in the narcissistic, idealized, exemplary, testamental, sacrificial, redemptive, expiatory act that releases family, generational succession and nature ('of which this is the natural birth' [III, xv, 389]) as both private and public solutions to the potentially tragic, and more than tragic, irreconcilabilities and woundings of the novel's revolutionary violence.

V

Carton's death is, of course, a secret action – secret to everyone but the unnamed seamstress – that is also entirely public. Secrecy is one of the deepest concerns of the novel and deeply linked to counting. Of the three passengers on the Dover coach, for example, 'Not one of the three could have said, from anything he saw, what either of the other two was like; and each was hidden under almost as many wrappers from the eyes of the mind, as from the eyes of the body, of his two companions' (I, ii, 9). Jerry Cruncher's eyes look 'as if they were afraid of being found out in something, singly, if they kept too far apart', with 'a sinister expression, under an old cocked-hat like a three-cornered spittoon' (I, iii, 15). We find secrecy in Tellson's bank and Lorry's mission ('a secret service altogether' [I, iv, 29]), Manette's and Darnay's imprisonments, Carton's secret love for Lucie, the secret conspiracies and spying of the book, and most strikingly in the vision of radical, death-like secrecy that constitutes human individuality or, perhaps better, singularity in the celebrated opening to Book I, chapter 3:

> A wonderful fact to reflect upon, that every human creature is constituted to be that profound secret and mystery to every other. A solemn consideration, when I enter a great city by night, that every one of those darkly clustered houses encloses its own secret; that every room in every one of them encloses its own secret; that every beating heart in the hundreds of thousands of breasts there, is, in some of its imaginings, a secret to the heart nearest it! Something of the awfulness, even of Death itself, is referable to this.
>
> (I, iii, 14–15)

At such moments, there are deep consonances between *A Tale of Two Cities* and Derrida's discussion of Jan Patočka's *Heretical Essays in The Philosophy of History* (1975) in the 'Secrets of European Responsibility' chapter of *The Gift of Death*, which explores the nature of the secret in relation to history and responsibility through 'the figures of death that are necessarily associated with absolute secrecy'.[33] In his paraphrase and discussion of Patočka, Derrida writes:

> History can be neither a decidable object nor a totality capable of being mastered, precisely because it is tied to *responsibility*, to *faith*, to the *gift*. To *responsibility* in the experience of absolute decision made outside of knowledge or given norms, made therefore through the very ordeal of the undecidable; to religious *faith* through a form of involvement with the other that is a venture into absolute risk, beyond knowledge and certainty; to the *gift* and to the gift of death that puts me into relation with the transcendence of the other, with God as selfless goodness, and that gives me what it gives me through a new experience of death ... the gift of death (*donner la mort*) would be this marriage of responsibility and faith. History depends on such an excessive beginning.[34]

It is a remarkable set of claims, but one that take us very close to *A Tale of Two Cities* and which may help us avoid some of the more precipitate or pre-emptive readings of the novel. The whole book, as Dickens's mature reflection on the nature of historical process at a time of intense personal and historical crisis, is akin to the seizing 'hold of a memory as it flashes up at a moment of danger' in Benjamin's phrase, and the memory that it grasps in many ways shadows forth Patočka's/Derrida's insights.[35] The history of responsibility, which embeds or incorporates multiple incommensurable secrets and different demonic raptures within it, takes on a particular form: 'The history of secrecy, the combined history of responsibility and the gift, have the spiral form of these turns [*tours*], intricacies [*tournures*], versions, turnings back, bends [*virages*], and conversions. One could compare it to a history of revolutions, even to history as revolution.'[36]

The conceptual frameworks that have dominated criticism of Dickens's historical fiction (and perhaps also that of historical understanding more generally) are essentially empirical or Hegelian in form.[37] A very different attempt to think the nature of the historical can be seen in the thought of Martin Heidegger's *Being and Time* (1927) and its successors, particularly the work of Derrida and Patočka, which has the potential to take us much closer to the political and ethical forces at stake in *A Tale of Two Cities*. At the heart of Heidegger's questioning of the historical is his distinction between the historical and the chronological. For Heidegger, history is conceived within the western tradition in essentially chronological and metaphysical terms, and only a rethinking of historicity and temporality in terms of a more originary thrownness would enable us to experience a more authentic and true relationship to our historical being.[38] Patočka, following Heidegger's analysis in 'The Question Concerning Technology', sees the history of western thought as both leading to and complicit in an essentially technological or instrumental reason, which is (even now, as we speak) devastating the planet. He adds, however, to Heidegger's account of history, reason and technology another dimension: that of the sacred, orgiastic and secret. For Patočka, the long history of western reason, from Plato to the world of 'rational domination, the cold "truth" of that coldest of cold monsters' that we live in today, entails a complex set of repressions or incorporations of the orgiastic, sacred and secret.[39] He distinguishes between the everyday and 'the exceptional, the holiday' when we do not engage responsibly with the world, 'but are enraptured, where something more powerful than our free possibility, our responsibility, seems to break into our life and bestow on it meaning which it would not have otherwise. It is the dimension of the demonic and of passion'.[40] These forces, argues Patočka, cannot simply be overwhelmed, but must 'be grafted onto responsible life' and for him, the two defining moments of this grafting occur in Plato's allegory of the cave and in the Christian 'inscrutable relation to an absolute highest being in whose hands we are not externally, but internally'.[41] The consequence of these graftings is that the core of historical life consists of everydayness and the orgiastic living side-by-side in an often uneasy coexistence:

> historical life means, on the one hand, a differentiation of the confused everydayness of prehistoric life, of the division of labour and functionalization of individuals; on the other, the inner mastering of the sacred through its interiorisation.[42]

Over recent centuries, those of what is known as modernity, however, there has been a simultaneous radicalization and destabilization of the relation of the demonic and sacred to that of responsible everydayness, as signalled by the occurrence or recurrence of the orgiastic, fetishistic and demonic character in modern life, in the 'new flood of the orgiastic' which is 'an inevitable appendage to addiction to things', and which is shown in extreme form in war and revolution.[43] For Patočka, this duality is both the product of a long history and at the heart of the modern condition:

> War as a global 'anything goes', a wild freedom, takes hold of states, becoming '*total*'. The same hand stages orgies and organizes everydayness. The author of the five year plans is at the same time the author of orchestrated show trials in a new witch hunt.
>
> (Patočka, *Heretical Essays*, p. 114)

Dickens is similarly troubled by the release of the orgiastic, ecstatic and demonic in modernity, as shown in its defining political event, the French Revolution. We can see this most clearly in the 'ogreish' spectators of the guillotine, or, most vividly of all, the episode of the Carmagnole, which begins with an impossible counting:

> five hundred people ... dancing like five thousand demons ... No fight could have been half so terrible as this dance. It was so emphatically

a fallen sport – a something, once innocent, delivered over to all devilry –
a healthy pastime changed into a means of angering the blood, bewilder-
ing the senses, and steeling the heart. Such grace as was visible in it, made
it the uglier, showing how warped and perverted all things good by nature
were become.

(III, v, 288–9)

On the one hand, the novel's value system confronts the orgiastic revolutionary floodwaters with the kind of bourgeois virtues epitomized by Jarvis Lorry:
reliability, punctuality and responsible self-effacing attention to duty. Yet,
with Patočka, it sees the essential weakness of simply opposing the demonic
and orgiastic to the rational, responsible and mundane virtues of the novel's
bourgeois protagonists. For it also wants to imagine a more powerful counter-
magic, as it were, powerful enough to exorcise the demonic rapture of the
revolution. This is the peculiar significance of Carton's life and death. For he
too participates in the orgiastic and demonic in his 'Bacchanalian' drunken-
ness and 'orgies' (II, v, 90) with Stryver, but his orgiastic and demonic drives
or needs are capable of internalizing, overcoming or sublating their ecstatic
rapture in a secret, and essentially mysterious, self-sacrificing choice.

There is, as several critics have noted, something potentially absurd in
Carton's and the novel's ending, ripe for parody and pastiche in its hyperbolic capitalization on the discourses of friendship and dying for the other.[44]
But there is, I want to argue, a second lineage for Carton's actions here in
the work and, perhaps also, the death of Patočka, who, as one of the three
spokesmen for Charta 77, was to die after eleven hours of interrogation by
the Czech police. In the idiom of Sartrean or Heideggerean existentialism,
we could see Carton's death as a way of taking responsibility for an action
'in the sense that we truly bear it, that we identify with its burden' in contrast to the 'avoidance, escape, deviation into in authenticity and relief' of
inauthentic existence.[45] But Carton's death is also a form of secret sacrifice
that supplements the existential pathos of his death with a counterforce
to the destructively orgiastic energies of the revolution. Carton's life/death
seems to draw deeply not merely on the Ciceronian/Montaignon discourse
of friendship and the political, but also on the forces within western thought
that bind together questions of the political with those of the sacrificial, secret
and demonic. It may be its ability to draw on and yet not be defined by these
two traditions that gives Carton's death its singular, non-exemplary force,
poised as it is between the tragic and the absurd, in both senses of that word.

A Tale of Two Cities is a history of revolution, which seeks to understand in
relation to questions of history, responsibility for and secrecy both the kind
of sacrificial and demonic rapture that the Revolution manifests in the insane
fury of the Carmagnole and the Terror, and the version of Christian sacrifice
that is Carton's death. It relates a number of conversions and overturn-
ings, both 'public' like the revolution and 'private', such as Jerry Cruncher's

forswearing of grave-robbing and Carton's sudden sobriety, to tell a history of secrets, gifts and sacrificial death. It begins in an idiom that is close to a parody of conventional historical narrations: 'It was the best of times, it was the worst of times, it was the age of wisdom, it was the age of foolishness ...' (I, i, 5). It dramatizes in the place of these impoverished, interchangeable idioms, feebly grasping after the totality of 'the age', an action that moves to an awakened responsibility, to the question of faith and the transcendence of the other, through the gift of death. The whole of the novel moves towards the death of Carton, which is both a public act – a public execution, a putting to death – and a secret act of substitution and suicide that gives up its life (or death) to save another. Carton dies 'while assuming responsibility for one's own death, committing suicide but also sacrificing oneself for another, *dying for the other*, thus perhaps giving one's life by giving oneself death, accepting the gift of death, such as Socrates, Christ, and others did in so many different ways.'[46] This, it should be emphasized, is not an evasion of the historical but an attempt to think it in a more originary way: for Derrida, this 'discourse on sacrifice and on dying for the other ... this investigation into the secret of responsibility is eminently historical and political. It concerns the very essence or future of European politics'.[47]

On a psychic level, counting is often the sign of, and counterforce to, unbearable or traumatic affect. Lorry, for example, seeking to contain his emotion when telling Lucie that her father is alive, says when she kneels to him: '[y]ou confuse me, and how can I transact business if I am confused? Let us be clear-headed. If you would kindly mention now, for instance, what nine times ninepence are, or how many shillings are twenty guineas, it would be so encouraging' (I, iv, 27). When Darnay is imprisoned, he counts: ' "Five paces by four and a half, five paces by four and a half, five paces by four and a half." The prisoner walked to and fro in his cell, counting its measurement ... The prisoner counted the measurement again ... Five paces by four and a half' (III, i, 267), unconsciously repeating the counting by Manette of the lines he can draw across the window of his cell: 'It was twenty either way, I remember, and the twentieth was difficult to squeeze in' (II, xvii, 196). It is a way of calming the madness, of seeking to contain, know or control the unknown, frightening or mysterious. When Lucie is married and Manette finds out who Darnay is: 'The time went very slowly on, and Mr Lorry's hope darkened, and his heart grew heavier again, and grew yet heavier and heavier every day. The third day came and went, the fourth, the fifth. Five days, six days, seven days, eight days, nine days' (II, xviii, 205). A method of coming to terms – or failing to come to terms – with the fatal or horrific is to count the number of the dead or wounded: the 'eleven hundred defenceless prisoners' (III, iv, 280) of the July days, the 2,973 dead of 11 September 2001 or the estimated 654,965 Iraqi deaths that, the *Lancet* estimates, occurred between the invasion of that country on 20 March 2003 and the end of June 2006.[48]

Not long before Carton's death, we experience the most intense and troubling scene of counting and the ending of counting in the whole novel. At the heart of the novel, or rather beneath its layers of lost and embedded narratives, are the figure and voice of a nameless woman who has been abducted and, it seems, raped. She has been so traumatized by these terrible experiences, which follow the manslaughter of her husband, that she can speak only a few phrases, which are hysterically and endlessly repeated. The revelation of this incident, which is the inaugurating moment of the events that the novel narrates and its defining secret, occurs quite late in the book. We learn of the nameless woman neither through her own voice nor through that of the omniscient narrator, but from the written testimony of Dr Manette, set down during his long imprisonment in the Bastille. Her story is doubly or triply secreted: by her traumatic inarticulacy, in being handed over to the memory of a man given up for dead, and then, when written down by him, buried in the wall of France's most secure prison. She dies shortly afterwards and plays no active or direct part in the novel; yet the novel would not exist without her, for if she had not been abducted, then the entire sequence of events that follows would not have taken place and her sister, Mme Defarge, the embodiment of revolutionary terror, would not have been so vengeful, so long have implacably opposed the aristocracy or so long plotted their destruction. Within the terms of the novel, without this near-silent woman's abduction and rape, the French Revolution would not have taken place.

In narrative terms, we should think of this not so much as a scene or event of the novel but as a kind of narrative *crypt* in the sense that Nicolas Abraham and Maria Torok use the term, to describe a psychic or other kind of presence that is held within another, but is radically inassimilable to it, remaining, in their terms, incorporated rather than introjected.[49] Hers is the founding trauma of the book and, when recovered and recounted, precipitates Darnay's death sentence and Carton's death. Its narration is the novel's most unbearable moment, another sacrifice, another fraternal scene and another moment, many moments, of counting. For more than twenty-four hours the unnamed sister of Mme Defarge, having been raped, after her father and husband have been driven to their graves and her brother fatally wounded, obsessively, compulsively, traumatically names, counts and silences counting: 'She never abated the piercing quality of her shrieks, never stumbled in the distinctness or the order of her words. They were always "My husband, my father, and my brother! One, two, three, four, five, six, seven, eight, nine, ten, eleven, twelve. Hush!"' (III, x, 339). The most moving ethical call of the book, its most powerful invocation to us as readers to respond to the suffering other, foregrounds both the impossibility of such a response (she is both fictional and long dead) and its paradoxical, and more than paradoxical, nature. This is not simply because those who respond most strongly to her death, Mme Defarge and the revolutionary court, become radically unjust in their inability to respond to the suffering of Darnay, Lucie and the many unnamed aristocrats who die in the course of the Revolution and the book, but also because the intense singularity of the dead woman's suffering is figured neither through the largesse of detail and plenitude of speech that is the usual hallmark of Dickens's fictional characterization nor anything like Carton's idealizing self-projection, but through the anonymous and relayed voicing of a circular and potentially endless sequence of futile temporal enumeration.

Notes

1. Jacques Derrida, *Politics of Friendship*, trans. George Collins (London: Verso, 1997); *The Gift of Death*, trans. David Wills (Chicago: University of Chicago Press, 1997).
2. Derrida, *Politics*, p. 22.
3. Alex Woloch, *The One versus the Many: Minor Characters and the Space of the Protagonist in the Novel* (Princeton, NJ: Princeton University Press, 2003).
4. Thomas Carlyle, *On Heroes, Hero-worship and the Heroic in History* (London: Chapman & Hall, 1880), p. 27.
5. Thomas Carlyle, *The French Revolution: A History* (London: Chapman & Hall, 1880), vol. 3, p. 28.
6. John Stuart Mill, *On Liberty*, ed. Gertrude Himmelfarb (Harmondsworth: Penguin Books, 1974), pp. 59, 62; *Considerations on Representative Government* (Buffalo: Prometheus Books, 1991).
7. Mill, *On Liberty*, p. 62.
8. Mill, *On Liberty*, p. 76.
9. Mill, *On Liberty*, p. 68.
10. John R. Greenfield in his *Dictionary of British Literary Characters* 'counts some 11,663 figures invented by novelists writing between the later 17th century and 1890, 989 (approximately 8 per cent) of whom are Dickens's, a sum which puts him ahead of Scott (872), and gives him a commanding lead over all other Victorian novelists save Trollope'. *Oxford Reader's Companion to Dickens*, ed. Paul Schlicke (Oxford: Oxford University Press, 1999), p. 76. More ambitiously, George Newlin, in the most comprehensive examination of Dickens's naming practice, has identified 13,143 people mentioned by Dickens, of whom there are '2,640 "serious" surname usages, 410 named characters without surname (plus 65 surname or animal names), and 565 figures who bear sobriquets or names of parody'. George Newlin, *Everyone in Dickens: Volume I: Plots, People and Publishing Particulars in the Complete Works, 1833–1849* (Westport, CT: Greenwood, 1995), front matter.
11. Carlyle, *French Revolution*, vol. 1, p. 1. In the summer of 1851, Dickens reported to John Forster that he was 'reading that wonderful book the *French Revolution* again for the 500th time'. *Letters*, VI, p. 452. See also *TTC*, Appendix II, pp. 397–8. 'It has been one of my hopes to add something to the popular and picturesque means of understanding that terrible time, though no one can hope to add anything to the philosophy of Mr Carlyle's wonderful book.'
12. Georg Lukács, *The Historical Novel*, trans. Hannah and Stanley Mitchell (Harmondsworth: Penguin Books, 1969), p. 20.
13. Lukács, *Historical Novel*, p. 36.
14. Catherine Gallagher, 'The Duplicity of Doubling in *A Tale of Two Cities*', *DSA*, 12 (1983), 125–45.

15. Charles Dickens, *Little Dorrit*, ed. Harvey Peter Sucksmith (Oxford: World's Classics, 1982); *Oxford Reader's Companion*, p. 339.
16. See, for example, Christopher Harvie and H. C. G. Mathew, *Nineteenth-Century Britain: A Very Short Introduction* (Oxford: Oxford University Press, 2000), p. 64.
17. For Dickens's speech in support of the ARA, 27 June 1855, see *The Speeches of Charles Dickens*, ed. K. J. Fielding (Oxford: Clarendon, 1960), pp. 197–208, 200.
18. Charles Dickens, 'The Thousand and One Humbugs', Slater, III, pp. 292–8.
19. Charles Dickens, *Hard Times*, ed. Paul Schlicke (Oxford: World's Classics, 1989), p. 75.
20. Dickens, *Hard Times*, p. 72.
21. The countings of the novel to which we are bound as readers do not end with the boundaries of the text or with the explicit enumeration within it. It was published, for example, in 31 weekly parts, from 30 April to 26 November 1859, in eight monthly numbers (the final one being, as was Dickens's customary practice, a double one) from June to December 1859 and in one volume in the same year. For a sense of the need to mark dates in the novel's 'complex time-scheme', see Andrew Sanders, *The Companion to* A Tale of Two Cities (London: Unwin Hyman, 1988), pp. 24–9. For the enumeration necessary to understand its publication history, see Robert L. Patten, *Charles Dickens and his Publishers* (Oxford: Oxford University Press, 1978), pp. 276–8 and 456–7.
22. René Girard, *Deceit, Desire, and the Novel*, trans. Yvonne Freccero (Baltimore, MD: Johns Hopkins University Press, 1986); Eve Kosofsky Sedgwick, *Between Men: English Literature and Male Homosocial Desire* (New York: Columbia University Press, 1985).
23. Dickens, *Hard Times*, p. 28.
24. Gallagher, 'Duplicity of Doubling in *A Tale of Two Cities*'. More generally, on the 'compulsive and repetitive domination' of critical judgements on Dickens by 'an essentially uncritical mechanism of doubling and division', see John Bowen and Robert L. Patten, 'Introduction' to *Palgrave Advances in Charles Dickens Studies* (London: Palgrave, 2006), p. 6.
25. Geoffrey Bennington, 'Derridabase' in Geoffrey Bennington and Jacques Derrida, *Jacques Derrida* (Chicago: University of Chicago, 1993), p. 66.
26. In Dickens's 'The Bride's Chamber' in *A Lazy Tour of Two Idle Apprentices* (1857), co-authored with Wilkie Collins, the narrator meets a ghostly old man, whose fate is, at every strike of the clock, to be doubled into an exact copy of himself, so that 'at Two in the morning, I am Two old men. At Three, I am Three. By twelve at noon, I am Twelve old men, one for every hundred per cent of old gain.' Slater, III, p. 462.
27. Ian Hacking, *The Taming of Chance* (Cambridge: Cambridge University Press, 1990), p. 2.
28. Derrida, *Politics*, p. 22.
29. For John Lucas, it is Dickens's 'worst' novel. John Lucas, *The Melancholy Man* (London: Methuen, 1970), p. 287.
30. Lukács, *Historical Novel*, p. 292.
31. Peter Brooks, *The Melodramatic Imagination: Balzac, Henry James, Melodrama, and the Mode of Excess* (New Haven, CT: Yale University Press, 1995), pp. 81–2.
32. Derrida, *Politics*, p. 3.
33. Derrida, *Gift*, p. 9. See also Jan Patočka, *Heretical Essays in the Philosophy of History*, trans. Erazim Kohak (Chicago, IL: Open Court, 1996).
34. Derrida, *Gift*, pp. 5–6.

35. Walter Benjamin, 'Theses on the Philosophy of History', in *Illuminations*, trans. Harry Zohn (London: Fontana, 1973), p. 257.
36. Derrida, *Gift*, p. 8.
37. See Andrew Sanders, *The Victorian Historical Novel 1840–1880* (London: Macmillan, 1978), and Lukács, *Historical Novel*.
38. See Martin Heidegger, *Being and Time*, trans. John Macquarrie and Edward Robinson (Oxford: Blackwell, 1962), pp. 424–55; Stephen Mulhall, *Heidegger and Being and Time*, 2nd edn (London: Routledge, 2005), pp. 181–98; and Miguel de Beistegui, *The New Heidegger* (London: Continuum, 2005), pp. 76–7, 114–15. On the idea of 'thrownness' (*Geworfenheit*) in Heidegger, see *Being and Time*, pp. 135, 219–24; and Michael Inwood, *A Heidegger Dictionary* (Oxford: Blackwell, 1999), pp. 218–20.
39. Patočka, *Heretical Essays*, p. 112.
40. Patočka, *Heretical Essays*, pp. 98–9.
41. Patočka, *Heretical Essays*, p. 106.
42. Patočka, *Heretical Essays*, p. 112
43. Patočka, *Heretical Essays*, p. 113.
44. 'Carton enacts on that scaffold ... the most archaic, the most grandiose of all narcissistic fantasies.' John Glavin, *After Dickens: Reading, Adaptation and Performance* (Cambridge: Cambridge University Press, 1999), p. 137.
45. Patočka, *Heretical Essays*, p. 98.
46. Derrida, *Gift*, p. 10.
47. Derrida, *Gift*, p. 33. See also p. 21: 'every revolution, whether atheist or religious, bears witness to a return of the sacred in the form of an enthusiasm or fervor, otherwise known as the presence of the gods within us. Speaking of the "new rise of the orgiastic floodwaters" ... Patočka gives the example of the religious fervor that took hold during the French Revolution ... it might be said that all revolutionary fervor produces its slogans as though they were sacrificial rites or effects of secrecy.'
48. Gilbert Burnham, Riyadh Lafta, Shannon Doocy and Les Roberts, 'Mortality after the 2003 invasion of Iraq: a cross-sectional cluster sample survey', *The Lancet*, 368, no. 9545, 21–27 October 2006, pp. 1421–8.
49. 'Most of the characteristics falsely attributed to introjection in fact apply to the fantasmatic mechanism of incorporation.' Nicolas Abraham and Maria Torok, *The Shell and the Kernel: Renewals of Psychoanalysis Volume 1*, ed. and trans. Nicholas T. Rand (Chicago: University of Chicago Press, 1994), p. 113.

8

Mimi and the Matinée Idol: Martin-Harvey, Sydney Carton and the Staging of *A Tale of Two Cities*, 1860–1939

Joss Marsh

In 1899, Robert Baden-Powell, amateur actor and Boer War hero, put heart in his dwindling handful of troops at Mafeking by 'perform[ing] an impro-visation' of the hit play he had seen in London a few months before, *The Only Way*, a new version of *A Tale of Two Cities*, with Baden-Powell himself playing Sydney Carton.[1] In 1916, John Martin-Harvey, *The Only Way*'s star (some 2,000 performances later), put aside his notes for 'Shakespeare under Shell Fire' to give, instead, the impromptu performance that the Tommies in the trenches really wanted – 'their beloved *Only Way*', the 'popular mas-terpiece' of English theatre.[2] In 1925, now Sir John, he repeated the role on film (despite girth and age) to international acclaim; only forty years after the show took the Lyceum Theatre by storm did Martin-Harvey put aside Carton's artfully dishevelled costume and publish the play, with a final patriotic flourish.[3]

There had been Dickensian stage successes before: Lotta Crabtree in *Lit-tle Nell and the Marchioness*; Jennie Lee in *Poor Jo*; Irving in *Jingle*.[4] But at 4,000 performances between 1899 and 1939, *The Only Way* was not a play: it was a cultural phenomenon.[5] Harvey's Carton achieved cult status and made him (like Baden-Powell) an icon of Empire, this essay will argue, because the 'stirring and virile' stage vehicle 'machine-made' to drive him to stardom engaged powerful theatrical and cultural drives:[6] to restore – and rewrite – history, a founding fantasy of the Lyceum's 'archaeological' production style; to bask in celebrity presence; and – theatrically and with safety – to extend the baroque variations on gender to which nineteenth-century adaptations of *A Tale of Two Cities* gave rise. In what follows, I shall concentrate on those variations, while keeping other interests in view.

It is a critical commonplace that the 'inception' of *The Only Way* 'may be traced back to the time when young Martin Harvey ... and his wife', 'Nina', 'were on tour with Irving in America'.[7] They were searching for that first 'cast-iron' role on which every Victorian actor-manager founded

126

a career – 'some lovable, sympathetic creation', as Harvey put it, '*far out of the beaten track of heroes of dramatic drama*' (my emphasis).

> 'Then,' said my wife, 'you must have Sydney Carton.'
>   'There have been several plays on that subject,' said I, doubtfully, 'and they have not succeeded.'
>   'Because they were not good plays,' said she, emphatically. 'We must make a better one.'
>   'An old theatrical superstition considers the two periods of the French Revolution and the English Parliamentary Wars unlucky,' said I. 'Not that I have any faith in those old superstitions. Let's get a copy of *A Tale of Two Cities*.'
>   We . . . were riding in an open tramcar through the suburbs of St. Louis, Missouri. We got off at the first bookstore we sighted . . .[8]

All of these statements were untrue, except perhaps the mention of St. Louis: the tale as Harvey tells it and critics have repeated it is not a story of origins, but a myth of origin.

There followed several years' plotting and structuring (by Harvey and 'Nina'), and writing and rewriting (by two stage-struck clergymen). Then came the sudden euphoria of taking the Lyceum, with only one month to get the show on the stage; a nasty pause when it seemed Harvey would postpone the play – and his future – at Irving's request, unsentimentally squashed by 'Nina'; a gracious capitulation by Irving; and a not-so-gracious one by his manager, Bram Stoker. The rest was stage history: the sensation of the first night, 16 February 1899; Harvey's instant stardom; and (thanks to gruelling provincial and Canadian tours) the large financial returns required to keep 'The Martin-Harvey Company' afloat for the next forty years.

The stardom conferred on Harvey, unusually, meshed high-society *cachet* with mass celebrity. '[C]lad in the garments of Sydney Carton', for example, he posed for 'all-too-flattering' portraits by 'the gracious Violet, Duchess of Rutland'.[9] But fans of a different order offered homemade tributes: an embroidered copy of John Hassall's famous poster, hand-stitched by Mrs Hunter of Hove; 'a night-dress case, and a brush-and-comb bag' cut down from a lace curtain.[10] In Sheffield, Oldham, Erdington and Cardiff girls called Edie, 'Cussie', Nell and Kit exchanged postcards of 'Martin' in *The Only Way*, *Rouget de L'Isle* (1900), *A Cigarette-Maker's Romance* (1902), *The Breed of the Treshams* (1903) and *The Last Heir* (1908), inscribed:

Another one for our 'set' picked up in Bournemouth!

Sorry I cannot get any in 'The Only Way.' Hope you will like these.

This is the nearest I can get to the one of mine you liked. I hope you have not one like this already.

I have not yet been able to get any cards of 'The Breed of the Treshams' but these are very good.
We must see him in this play next time he brings it here.

I do hope you will like this card of your favourite.

I hope that your good people at home will not object to my sending so many cards at once. But I couldn't decide which was the nicest.

'[Mr Martin-Harvey] has asked me to send you this,' scribbles Ethel from Hull, in September 1909:

& tell you how delighted he is to know that you will be here to see him. He says we are to go alone . . .

Eileen writes to a chum in Derby:

Oh! those 'pools of inky blackness'!!!! . . . I managed to get this for you this afternoon.

'D.A.' writes to Miss Gunnell of Glasgow, October 1907:

Another faggot for the fire.

'Isn't it good of him[?]' Ethel asks Nellie in 1908: a question one does not ask without having seen the star in person. And see him they did: in the same plays, over and over again. If the play was not scheduled, they begged for it. At His Majesty's Theatre, Aberdeen, for example:

In consequence of numerous requests
and the widespread expression of regret
at the omission from programme of
THE ONLY WAY
MR. MARTIN HARVEY has arranged to
present this play on
Saturday, 11th April, 1908.[11]

Decades before Hollywood and the star system, Harvey understood its erotics, its need for presence and the physical guarantee of a 'REAL PHOTOGRAPH';[12] he serviced his fan-base graciously. His meaning for theatre history does not lie in his stage innovations, though he was not the dinosaur that his critical billing as 'the last romantic' makes him seem – a fact made vividly clear by his production of *Oedipus Rex*, with Max Reinhardt, at Covent Garden in 1912.[13] It lies along the doubtful margin where theatre history meets film studies and cultural history meets literary analysis. (Harvey made at least four feature films besides *The Only Way*.)

The fans' adulation was a product of the play's focus, in all senses of that word. *The Only Way* was adaptation as star vehicle – like *Jo*, or *Jingle* or *Little Nell*. It belonged to that phase in adaptation when the practice of lifting a well-loved character from the plot that contained her gave way to reshaping the story around her. It achieved its success in 1899 by the same means as the MGM film of 1935 (with Ronald Colman) and the Rank version of 1958 (with Dirk Bogarde, 'Britain's Biggest Star') – by tackling the same problem, faced by any adaptation which straightens out the novel's chronology (as nearly all do): the late appearance of Carton.[14]

Act I is thus set entirely in Carton's own chambers. It begins with 'CARTON ... *discovered asleep in chair L., his head lying on table*'; it ends when '*He falls forward on the table as at discovery of Act*'.[15] All must be done in this room: here, for example, not in a tavern near the Old Bailey, we see the ill-assorted doubles toast and spar over Lucie Manette. And if it cannot be done, it must be said in that room. Thus the lawyer Stryver recaps Dr Manette's story and bids Carton help the villainous Ernest Defarge, who has come to London in search of Darnay. Defarge duly calls(!), and his presence allows Carton to learn Darnay's identity as Évremonde through his own mirror:

CARTON: ... What sort of a chap to look at is this Évremonde? (CARTON *is looking into glass on wall, scraping his pipe out.*)
DEFARGE: What do you see there? (*Pointing with pipe at glass on mantle.*)
CARTON: My own face, Defarge. The face of my worst enemy.
DEFARGE: I don't know that – you see the face of Évremonde.[16]

In short, Act I throws away action, invests Carton with surprising prescience, droops into talky longueurs (skewered by first-night critics) and altogether gives us too much 'Harvey Sauce; or His Own Way', as it was put in a disgruntled collaborator's 'burlesque programme' for Harvey's next play, *Don Juan Tenorio*.[17]

Acts II, III and IV are better: Darnay's love for Lucie and Carton's hopelessness grow up in the Manette garden in Soho; Darnay stands trial in Paris, before the Tribunal, (a transposition of the novel's Old Bailey treason trial, Book II, chapters 2–3), where Carton makes a heroic defence;[18] and Carton takes Darnay's place on the scaffold. (A Prologue also briskly dramatized the perfidies of the Marquis St Évremonde and his imprisonment of Dr Manette.) 'The structural shape of the play', which 'seemed to jump into ... mind, ... at once, and was never changed', absolutely achieved its objective – to make us intimate with Carton.[19] All film adaptations of *A Tale* followed its lead, whether they returned to the novel or were based, more or less, on

Harvey's play (as were a Vitagraph film of 1911 and the landmark Fox version of 1917).

More complex than the play's afterlife, however, was the real theatrical genealogy that Harvey's version of its inception tended to mask. It has much to tell of the psychic potential of Dickens's novel, and of what we have done (and continue to do) with it.

The Only Way is a 'romantic' play, a product of the mid-1890s swashbuckling boom, part of the 'Neo-Gothic Shakespear[ean]' repertoire of Alexandre Dumas, Walter Scott and Edward Bulwer-Lytton.[20] As such, it is the tale of a man of destiny – like Fabien dei Franchi on his mission of revenge in the paradigm 'romantic' play, *The Corsican Brothers* (1852); or Joseph Lesurques, the innocent man falsely accused in *The Courier of Lyons* (1854); or Napoleon in Harvey's less than successful *The Exile* (1902).

And as such it is an actor's play. Throughout his career, Harvey mounted, and commissioned, inferior works if they gave him grandstand roles – Lieutenant Reresby, the 'heroic rapscallion' of *The Breed of the Treshams*, for example.[21] He aimed at, and produced, effect. One Victorian newspaper critic exulted about his performance as Carton:

> Waves of emotion swept over me, thrilling every faculty of my mind, every filament of my nerves, every pore of my flesh.[22]

The 'Art of Acting', Harvey wrote in an elegant and influential 1912 lecture, drew on the forces of the mysterious subconscious, even the ancestral unconscious.[23] It was not 'impersonation' but 'possession': 'Sometimes,' he said, 'I feel Carton's sadness with an almost overwhelming force'.[24]

The genealogy of romantic theatre included not only Dumas, Scott and Lytton but the French Revolution itself: *The Only Way* was the culmination of a long tradition. *The Triumph of Liberty; or, The Fall of the Bastille*, a burletta produced immediately in the wake of 'this extraordinary event', and 'taken from the various newspapers of the day, assisted by . . . fiction', recalled the comedian Jacob Decastro in 1824, brought into being one of theatrical revolutionism's essential types, the 'silver-headed, emaciated, decrepid [*sic*] old man' brought blinking into the light after years of immurement, to 'involuntary bursts of enthusiastic and electric applause'.[25]

Later plays reflected the next generation's Terror-struck loss of faith in progress by elevating a second type – the self-sacrificing, aristocratic hero, pitted in 'individualist' combat (to use one of Martin-Harvey's favourite terms) against impersonal history and the brutal mob. His most surprising avatar was Robespierre. At the climax of Benjamin Webster's *The Destruction of the Bastille*, in 1842:

> *An explosion takes place, the walls and prison falling to discover Ernestine [the daughter Robespierre did not know he had] on the point of being executed.*

Robespierre staggers through ruins in time to save her. He bears her in his arms to C., and falls dead. Victor and the rest form a picture. . . . and the Curtain descends on the DESTRUCTION OF THE BASTILLE.[26]

The second type was inspired by Thomas Carlyle's account, in *The French Revolution*, of the 'noble' father who 'hurr[ies] to the [prison] Grate, to hear the Death-list read' and answers for his son. Bulwer-Lytton made the father a lover in his novel *Zanoni* (1842); Dickens's Carton, in his last moments (with disturbing libidinal effect), imagines himself the symbolic father of his beloved Lucie's unborn son; and in the overblown spectacle with which Henry Irving followed *The Only Way* at the Lyceum, in 1899, Robespierre (again) sacrifices himself for the son of the woman whose loss made him a revolutionary – who turns out, of course, to be *his* son.[27] At that junction where history meets the needs of the matinée idol, a pattern fulfilled for the next hundred years, crossing media from stage to screen, manliness spells sacrifice, potency demands symbolic expression and repression means revolution: so, David Lean's Dr Zhivago breathes his last on a vision of Lara, and her rejected sweetheart, Pasha, is reborn as the scarfaced Bolshevik strongman Strelnikov; so *The Scarlet Pimpernel* and *Casablanca* redeem First World War impotence and Second World War neuterdom; and so Martin-Harvey gave his 100th-night audience souvenir 'facsimiles' of both a *lettre de cachet* and the farewell letter to Lucie that Carton dictates to Darnay, in prison, as items of equal historical value.[28]

I pass over here, regretfully, *The Dead Heart*, which reached the stage just before the final numbers of *A Tale of Two Cities* arrived at the printer's in late 1859 – a possible source *and* a possible plagiarism, revived by Irving in 1889. Enough to say the *ersatz* revolutionary *mythos* of burial and resurrection, desire and self-sacrifice, struck a profound and reverberating chord with Victorian audiences.

'Of course, *they will make a play* of Dickens's new tale, "The Two Cities",' wrote the author of *The Dead Heart* to Webster.[29] And, of course, they did: extant playbills assert that Dickens 'in the kindest manner superintended the production of the Piece';[30] his martinet drilling of supernumeraries for the scene of the Carmagnole delayed the first night.

The producer was Madame Celeste, Webster's ex-partner, who had set up in rival management at the Lyceum. Like Webster, she was a seasoned theatrical revolutionist: this was her third 'Bastille drama'. Her doubling of the roles of Colette Dubois, the Marquis's erotic victim (who dies, verbosely, in the play's Prologue) and the sister who avenges her, Mme Defarge, was 'memorable', never excelled, critics recalled a generation later.[31]

The play's omission of the eccentric spinster, Miss Pross, Mme Defarge's comic nemesis, was one of their few complaints in February 1860. In her absence, Celeste's Mme Defarge meets her end in a struggle with her own husband. 'Thérèse – look up,' he cries, heartbroken, as she falls, struck by

her own bullet: 'It is Ernest your husband who loves you – Dead! Dead!'[32]
While this change may restore some gender balance of power, it also violated
Dickens's expressed intent in the novel. '[W]hen I use Miss Pross' to 'bring
about' that revolutionary female's death, he wrote to Bulwer-Lytton, in
arguably the most critically astute letter of his career:

> I have the positive intention of making that half-comic intervention a
> part of the desperate woman's failure; and of opposing that mean death,
> instead of a desperate one in the streets, which she wouldn't have minded,
> to the dignity of Carton's.[33]

By contrast, in the Celeste/Taylor version, Carton's death offstage is a deliberate anticlimax. When it came to effects and profits, Dickens did not regard
his own texts as sacrosanct.[34]

The play's ending pales in peculiar interest, however, beside the scene
which closed an un-'superintended' rival version south of the river, from
7 July 1860. In *The Tale of Two Cities; or, The Incarcerated Victim of the Bastille*,
Mrs E. F. Saville, the manageress of the theatre, doubled 'LUCILLE (The
Betrayed – The Dying Victim of St. Évremonde's Amour)' and the harpy
Defarge. Darnay, rescued, lies in a swoon while Miss Pross (restored) dis-
patches Mme Defarge, who makes full verbal use of the Victorian deathbed's
cultural authority. Finally, '*[s]he mak[es] an effort to reach Darnay*', but '*[f]alls
dead*'. As he comes round:

Dar. Oh, Lucy [*sic*], a heap of thoughts is flitting darkly before me. –...*[He
struggles to recollect himself –...]* Ha, I remember now – my friend Carton!
Where, where is he?

[*Lucy bursts into tears, and falls at his feet.*]

Lucy. He has sacrificed himself for us!

[*The noise of the Guillotine is heard faintly ... – Darnay shrieks aloud,
and starts with frantic energy.*

Dar. I know all now:...that sound has burst the spell – it calls my friend
to the grave, but he shall not die – he shall not die for me!
Lucy. [*Holding him back.*] Whither would you go?
Dar. To the Guillotine, my friend to save. Unhand me. Away!
Enter SYDNEY CARTON, *suddenly, at the door, R....– He is dressed in Barsad's
clothes. – All stand transfixed in wonder. – Darnay throws his hands back, as
if in search of support, his head thrust forward, regarding Carton with wild but
joyous terror.*
Dar. The victim, then, was –
Car. The traitor, Barsad!

Dar. Joy! joy! my friend yet lives, and is restored to us! Thank heaven! thank heaven!

> [*Music. – The Characters kneel in thankfulness to Providence, except Carton, who forms the centre of the tableau, as the curtain falls.*]
>
> THE END[35]

We will return to the implications of Darnay's desperation to save his 'friend'.

On 18 October 1875, the most fascinating of *The Only Way*'s precursor-texts opened at the Mirror Theatre, Holborn: *All For Her!* by J. Palgrave Simpson and Herman Merivale. It was revived in 1884 and again in 1897. Its influence was unadmitted but it is clear.

On the one hand, there was the model of John Clayton, its star, whose fortune it made, a fellow graduate of Irving's Lyceum, in whose company Harvey had made his debut in 1881. On the other hand, the play was a kind of back-formation of *A Tale of Two Cities*, reminiscent of the 1944 MGM *Jane Eyre*, inspired by Alfred Hitchcock's 1940 *Rebecca*, an adaptation of a Daphne Du Maurier novel inspired by Brontë's novel *Jane Eyre*.

All For Her!, set in 1746, 'illustrat[ed] the irresistible power of love' (raved the *Sporting and Dramatic News*, 30 October 1875), '– a love which, though hopeless and unrequited, is so pure, abiding, and deep-rooted as to effect, first, the regeneration of the hero, Hugh Trevor, the . . . supposed illegitimate brother of Lord Edendale [a Jacobite sympathizer], from a state of reckless dissipation . . . and then leads him into several acts of . . . heroic self-sacrifice, "all for her," the Lady Marsden, whom he so passionately and helplessly loves; she, however, is betrothed to his . . . brother Lord Edendale, whom he as strongly hates.' Hence the finale to Act I: Hugh 'gives himself up as the treasonable peer', declaring (a double-identity bluff, since he is the genuine heir), 'I am Lord Edendale' while 'the real culprit escapes over the wall'. In Act III, he drugs Edendale and swaps clothes with him in the prison. Then he faces the headsman's axe.

> (*He is led to the scaffold:*)
>
> HUGH. (*as the sun's rays struggle in*) So breaks my morning which shall know no night. And the last image which dims my earthly eyes sight is hers . . . . She will love him very truly but she will hold my memory dearer still. . . . It is a far, far better rest that I go to, than I have ever known.[36]

It is *A Tale of Two Cities* in different costumes, tweaked into somewhat greater erotic maturity and layered with a little more irony. Swathes of dialogue are lifted direct from the novel: they are very effective. *All For Her!* was a vigorous bastard child.

But it was an admitted bastard. A formal caveat was inserted in the programme, posters and press advertisements for the play: 'The authors wish it to be known that the part of Hugh Trevor has been adapted from the character of Sidney [*sic*] Carton, in *The Tale of Two Cities* [*sic*], by the express permission of the late Charles Dickens.'[37]

The degree of 'permission' is impossible to ascertain. Both authors were known to Dickens. One, Palgrave Simpson, who specialized in romantic and revolutionary drama, he knew well – he was a fellow member of the Garrick Club. The other, Herman Merivale, was an occasional contributor to *All the Year Round*.[38] Extending 'permission', however, certainly corrected the emphasis that early stage versions of *A Tale of Two Cities* had placed on Mme Defarge. Nevertheless, it was in terms of gender that *All For Her!* proved critical to the genesis of *The Only Way*.

Lady Marsden was a plum role compared to golden-haired Lucie Manette – a widow who radiates sexual charisma and loving affection, made safe by a watertight Victorian alibi, since Edendale was her childhood playmate: the change is an implicit criticism of Dickens's infantilization of women.[39]

Lady Marsden, however, is not the play's most interesting female character, nor did she influence *The Only Way*. *All For Her!* opens with Hugh Trevor's rescue of a bit-player based on a nameless character from the novel's last number – the little nameless seamstress accused of fabulous 'plots' who accompanies Carton to the scaffold, whose fears he comforts and who asks for a kiss before she dies. Readers had taken her to their hearts; and adaptation after adaptation has struggled to provide her with an adequate back-story and to extend her gentle presence forward into the action. Thus, in the 1893 *Sydney Carton*, another pre-Martin-Harvey version, first staged in Norwich, she is a waitress (Sophie Le Blanc) called as a witness at the Old Bailey. Later, she becomes the Manettes' family servant. In the 1958 Rank version, she becomes Gabelle's daughter Marie, vulnerable to the Marquis and his *droit du seigneur* (the lord's alleged right to sleep with all new brides), and was played by a French newcomer, Marie Versini, a publicist's curvaceous dream.

In *All For Her!* the 'little seamstress' becomes Mary Rivers, on whom a Jacobite plotter tries to force his attentions in Act I, scene i. Enter Hugh:

HUGH. Don't be afraid; you shan't be kissed if you don't like it.
MARY. Mr. Hugh Trevor! Oh! I'm safe now.

She recognizes him because he saved her from 'starving...in a garret' as a child, when her aged father, a Manette figure, was treacherously murdered.[40] As a result, the 'faithful maiden' 'secretly loves Hugh Trevor'.[41]

Mary is the ancestor of a key player I omitted from my synopsis of *The Only Way* – easily enough, since her job in the play is to *be*, not to *do*: 'Mimi', a street child of Paris, where Carton once studied, whom he has (improbably) rescued and installed as his domestic servant. 'Mimi' is 'secretly in love' with

'Mister Carton'. This was the role Harvey's wife 'Nina' played from 1899 to 1939.[42]

'Mimi' is no victim, however: *The Only Way* has no truck with the trope of rape, the woman's story, the initiating spring of Dickens's novel, which privileged the *actress*-managers of the 1860s, and (scaled back to forced kisses) raised the chivalric stakes of *All For Her!* and *Sydney Carton*. The lecherous Marquis is banished to the Prologue; Carton rescues Mimi from poverty, not assault. Most importantly, Mme Defarge completely disappears from Martin-Harvey's 'romantic' star vehicle and her violated sister is removed off stage. The 'dying heroines' of 1860 – the female victim and her female avenger – are replaced by 'the two Defarges' – the young Jean, who dies in the Prologue, and Ernest, the revolutionary plotter (played by the same actor).

Thus, in *The Only Way*, the new actor-manager not only steals the show, but the female victim story too. Following it, Carton's way of sacrifice became the only way *A Tale of Two Cities* could be imagined: Bransby Williams's music-hall 'Dramatic Sketch' *A Noble Deed*, 1899; *Sydney Carton's Sacrifice; Or, All For Her*, at the Camberwell Palace, 1907.[43]

The novel gave Harvey considerable justification. Written during Dickens's painful separation from his wife, from whom he fought hard to steal the victim's role, it is a text powerfully focused on *ending* and taken up with its male martyr. (It is, in a sense, an alibi in which, in the person of Mme Defarge, the female victim revealed herself as monster.)[44] 'I must say that I like my Carton,' he wrote to his close friend Mary Boyle, 'and I have a faint idea sometimes that if I acted him I could do something with his life and death.'[45]

In a sense, he already had: it was while he was winning plaudits for his 'fine impersonation' of bitter Richard Wardour, who dies ('all for her') to save his romantic rival, in the play he helped Wilkie Collins to write, *The Frozen Deep*, that Dickens 'first conceived the main idea' of *A Tale of Two Cities*.[46] The role gave him intense gratification. In Manchester, his daughter Mary was replaced as his beloved Clara by the professional actress Marie Ternan. (Ellen, her sister, later Dickens's mistress, played her friend.) When Dickens died with his head in her lap, 'her tears fell down my face, down my beard, ... down my ragged dress – poured all over me like rain'.[47] The role of Carton allowed Harvey something of the same investment in what the *Era*, with professional brevity, termed 'the great art of self-sacrifice'.[48]

Nothing would pack the house more: Harvey's Lyceum training had taught him that. There was one role in which his revered 'Master' Henry Irving most impressed him: 'our martyr-king', Charles I, first played 1872. When the piece was revived, Harvey watched his 'apparition' in the last act, against the rules, from the prompt-box:

I wonder if the author who wrote in his manuscript, 'Enter Charles' conceived such a spectacle of purged suffering as Sir Henry Irving presented at that moment? . . . it was an imperishable moment, illuminating the power of creative imagination aided by a faultless technique.[49]

When Harvey's wife, 'Nina', was asked to testify to Irving's impact, it was of this 'most perfect performance', a 'reincarnation' of the always-already dead king, that she chose to write.[50] *Charles the First* may have been a travesty of history – made more gross by the casting of the Lyceum's low comedian as a cardboard-villainous Cromwell, and inspired by the hackneyed melodramatics of *Black Eye'd Susan* – but it was the male-martyr play of the century, written (in sub-Shakespearean verse) by W. G. Wills, the brother of one of the pair of clerical hacks Harvey paid to write the words for *The Only Way*. Irving replayed its emotions in his 'poetic' and humourless revival of *The Dead Heart*, 1889, in which Harvey played a small role.

The Prologue of *The Only Way*, declared one reviewer, 'serve[d] no purpose except to make one feel miserable right off'.[51] No Miss Pross was allowed to compete for attention, and no comic Jerry Cruncher, whose fear of the 'gelatine' and other malapropisms had run away with the 1893 Norwich *Sydney Carton* (to which Harvey lost his preferred title).[52]

Nothing ever intervened between Harvey and the serious theatre business of death. He made his name as tragic, 'spiritual' Pelléas in Mrs Patrick Campbell's 1896 staging of Maeterlinck's play, and 'def[ied] history' to have Rouget de L'Isle, the neglected composer of the Marseillaise, die on stage of consumption.[53] *The Only Way* 'builds' inexorably to the end towards which Dickens had driven so hard. Its climax was celebrated in verse ('Behold him standing on the scaffold stair', etc.), and reproduced in paintings, cartoons and cigarette cards (besides embroidery).[54]

That climax was not simply an iconic image, summarizing the play, however: it specifically recorded its final *tableau*: it was a 'picture' based on a 'picture'.

'[F]or a long time', Harvey writes in the *Autobiography*, 'I clung to a symbolical ending' – two leaves dropping from a tree branch, in Japanese style: but an *avant-garde* gesture risked not 'get[ting] over'. 'So we decided to realise' Fred[erick] Barnard's 'fine drawing of Carton standing upon the scaffold', which 'inevitably' had 'swung into our vision at once.'[55] It was on this that Hassall's famous poster was modelled (see cover and Illustration 8.1).

To the theatrical *sophisticate* and knight of the theatre, writing his memoirs in 1930, '[o]f course, the final tableau' of *The Only Way* was 'an anticlimax'.[56] But it was rooted deep in the history of revolutionary theatre: *All For Her!* ended with the same disclosure of the sacrificial scaffold Hugh has to mount; and the 'national barber' was revealed with 'striking phantasmagorical effect' in *The Dead Heart*, 1859, and by 'misty' and 'almost imperceptible' degrees in Irving's revival, 1889.[57] Harvey's suave hindsight of thirty years masks the professional intelligence that created the cult of Sydney Carton.

Illustration 8.1   John Hassall, poster for 'The Only Way'

The speaking of Carton's last words was 'another faggot for the fire'. 'With 4,000 Echoes' as the *Daily Telegraph*'s Wilson Midgeley reported in 1939, they still kept their 'Thrill':

Last chance this week to hear some of the most famous words in our language spoken by the original voice [*sic*], for Sir John Martin-Harvey is at Brighton on his farewell tour. . . .

When I entered the Theatre Royal I felt like an atheist in church.[58]

Repetition, after all, is of the essence to ritual, and to cult.

Three conclusions.

First: Harvey was a devout believer in Empire; he worked vigorously for its defence during and after the Great War. (His knighthood, in 1919, recognized his services to recruitment.) He wrote in 1930: 'A critic lately said that in the light of the war we no longer are moved by the sacrifice of Sydney Carton. That cannot be true.' He was, I think, right. Carton's 'vicarious sacrifice' gave borrowed meaning to First World War slaughter: one individual's choice – no. 23 in the death-list – against the annihilation of vast numbers.[59] The Tommies in the trenches needed Sydney Carton.

And this takes us back where we began – 'before the Great War, when self-sacrifice was not so common as in the wonderful days of 1914–18', as Harvey put it in 1942.[60] Dishevelled Sydney Carton was not the odd choice of theatrical role that he at first seems for the obsessively well turned-out officer who stage-managed the Siege of Mafeking.[61] But for five weary months, Baden-Powell, his men and the dusty town faced not only punitive boredom but random danger: the siege saw one of the first uses of blanket shelling. Harvey's account of 'B.P.'' 's impromptu performance understood Carton's attraction for the 'Hero of Mafeking', and his hero's ritual and sacrificial Imperial usefulness. It is a potted account of how (as Tracy Davis puts it) the Victorian theatrical repertoire 'functioned as a trigger of the social imaginary'.[62]

The second conclusion concerns doubles. This theatrical convention sometimes dealt with the *raison d'être* of *The Only Way*: sacrifice. Thus, Louis dei Franchi, in *The Corsican Brothers*, dies in a duel that his unattainable lady's honour may live and is redeemed by his twin brother, Fabien. Twin roles also often allowed exploration of contrasts in likeness – thus Kean or Irving flipped instantly from Dubosc to Lesurques, from debauched killer to fated innocent, in *The Courier of Lyons*; or William Farnum became the solitary screen star to play both Carton and Darnay, in the 1917 Fox *Tale of Two Cities*.

Dickens was fascinated by what he called 'the dark twin at the window'. Haughty Edith is doubled by her fallen cousin in *Dombey and Son*, Lady Dedlock by her unknown illegitimate daughter and her murderous servant Hortense in *Bleak House*. *A Tale of Two Cities* goes further: it not only allowed variations on the double in performance, but was itself a meditation on the theatrical convention. *The Courier of Lyons* seems the definitive intertext here. A 'romantic' drama, based on a real-life case of 1796, a miscarriage of revolutionary justice, it concerns doubles whose similarity is a disturbance, not a revelation, of familial inheritance and divine design.[63] Lesser adaptations of Dickens's *Tale*, like the 1893 *Sydney Carton* (in which, '*Carton taking off his wig, . . . the sensation is renewed*'), miss the point.[64]

But there is still other potential in the double convention: homoeroticism. In Byron's *Manfred* and elsewhere, homosexual desire figures as incestuous longing (which also figures in its own right). Likewise, the accidental similarity of the two men, Carton and Darnay, suggests same-sex desire. 'Unhand me,' Darnay cries to Lucie, in the Surreyside *Tale of Two Cities*, 1860; 'Away!' And when Carton enters, Darnay's reaction of '*wild but joyous terror*' is elaborately foregrounded in stage directions. This is not only bad writing; it is a recognition of the structural implications of Dickens's novel, as a critic like Eve Sedgwick would see them. Carton and Darnay are two sides of the classic triangle of which Lucie is the third: she is not only the object of desire, but its conduit, the valued thing shared between men.[65]

Herein also may have lain the appeal of Sydney Carton for Baden-Powell. 'B.-P.' graduated to his impromptu performance of *The Only Way* from drag roles and Gilbert and Sullivan; the lifting of the Mafeking siege brought him agony, when a 'handsome young captain', his 'lifelong friend, "the Boy McLaren"', was found absent from Plumer's relieving column.[66]

Herein, perhaps, was Carton's appeal to Dirk Bogarde, whose annotated script, extant at the BFI, attests strongly to his commitment; Rank Corporation's publicity photographs for the 1958 *Tale of Two Cities* are all tight trousers and smouldering looks. Bogarde plays the role straight, but his performance is part of gay stage and screen history. So too might have been John Gielgud's: he abandoned a theatrical version 'in deference to Martin-Harvey' in the 1930s.[67]

And so too is Martin-Harvey's. He knew how dangerous was the territory of the homoerotic in the years following the Oscar Wilde débâcle.[68] The romance boom of the 1890s gave it some cover, while '[d]rama in modern clothes felt the effects of [Wilde's] horrible downfall'.[69]

The trope of sacrifice offered another. *The Only Way* has an unexpected affinity with Wilde's *Salome*, and the paintings of St Sebastian which Wilde fetishized: both allowed meditation on the martyred body of a man. Sebastian, late Victorian homosexuals' 'favorite saint', whose name Wilde took in his post-prison exile, dies pierced by arrows.[70] John, in whose refusal of Salome's love and in whose martyrdom Wilde (and Beardsley) encoded desire and frustration, is decapitated. The sacrifice of Sydney Carton for his 'friend' likewise both revealed and masked homoerotic desire: Darnay's reprobate lookalike was not only, all at once, potent and castrated (the symbolic sire of Lucie's son, the childless bachelor), he was also gay and not-gay. In Carton's sacrifice, the apparent opposites of Imperialism and Wildean 'Aestheticism' converged.

This is not to suggest that Martin-Harvey did not understand the Christian meaning of sacrifice. He was a sincere believer, who had 'never been reconciled to the exclusion of the spiritual in the Theatre'.[71] Carton's sacrifice appealed equally to Harvey the Christian and Harvey the actor-manager.

It is also not to suggest that Martin-Harvey was not homosexual, or – what is more important – that his theatrical persona, like that of many 'matinée idols' (a term which is almost a code-word; Harvey flirts with it in the *Autobiography*), such as Ivor Novello, did not allow identification and adoration by women and other men.[72] This is part of his 'extra-theatrical' importance.

'Little Jack Harvey' (as Terry called him), 'the boy Jack',played the Dauphin in Irving's *Louis XI*; in *The Courier of Lyons*, 1891, as a notice has it, he played 'the boy Joliquet' (a cheeky inn servant who misidentifies Lesurques as Dubosc) *'like* a boy'.[73]

But Joliquet was a woman's role. Harvey had ruffled theatrical tradition by taking the part. This second convention returns us, again, to *All For Her!* Mary Rivers's love for Hugh Trevor is 'as unrequited as that of Trevor's for Lady Marsden'.[74] In his last moments, *'[h]e kisses her, she faints'*, and Hugh calls to the commanding officer: 'Mr. Gardner, you will be careful of this boy'.[75] For, from Act II, Mary has 'followed [Hugh's] fortunes disguised as [a] soldier servant'.[76] The faint reveals her – to Hugh's executioners, that is, not the audience – when her hair tumbles down. We thus enjoy several illicit pleasures in the play: seeing a woman in trousers; seeing a man (in all visual appearance) kiss a boy; etc.

Mary Rivers was the kind of role in which Martin-Harvey's devoted wife 'Nina' specialized. To partner Harvey's 'unconventional Knight errant, Reresby' in *The Breed of the Treshams*, in 1903, for example, she (and he) 'created the part of the boy Batty', his 'self-appointed Squire'.[77] In *Charles the First* she played Irving's page. Martin-Harvey had first felt the attraction of N. De Silva, to give 'Nina' her full androgynous, professional name as she strode about the Lyceum Theatre in boots and breeches.[78]

Her 'Mimi', then, was an amalgam of Mary Rivers and the little seamstress. But the dynamics of the Martin-Harvey marriage and managerial partnership were other inspiration for N. de Silva's role as Carton's female equivalent, the invented waif. The *Autobiography* habitually refers to 'Nina' as 'Mimi': the usage is affectionate, but not all of its meaning is benign.

In *All For Her!* Mary watches while Hugh Trevor dies, lamenting 'I cannot die with him!'; in *The Only Way*, 'Mimi' takes her place at Carton's side. But Mary is promised fulfilment in heaven with Trevor; Mimi, though she dies with him, will never get her man. Just before their numbers are called, Mimi asks:

MIMI: Do you remember when you first found me in the darkness, you took me by the hand and led me home.
    [CARTON *rising, takes* MIMI *tenderly in his arms.*]
CARTON: And now upon the threshold of your everlasting home, another tenderer, stronger hand will lead you in.
MIMI: I shall stretch out my hands to you.
CARTON: God grant that I may find them. And she, still sheltered in that peaceful England, which I shall see no more, remembering all, will understand this was the only way. . . .
MIMI: You kissed her once.
CARTON: Yes: in her sleep.
MIMI: And I shall be asleep soon. Would you once kiss me? (*They kiss.*)[79]

The paean to Lucie occurs as interior monologue in Dickens's novel; its insertion in dialogue here turns the screw of exclusion and psychological cruelty. Production photographs show Carton and Mimi holding hands, ready to ascend the steps: he looks drearily off stage left (towards the scaffold); she looks direct at the audience.

Mimi's unrequited desire resonates through the Martin-Harvey repertoire: in *Rouget de L'Isle*, N. de Silva played the landlord's infatuated daughter, not the romantic lead; as doomed Ophelia, her flimsy costume was splashed with pathetic 'symbolical' cartoon hearts. It was an endless drama of unavailability.

Mimi's sacrifice extended to professional opportunities, too. Harvey had no luck in America, in 1903, the *Autobiography* records, but 'Mimi' made a hit, and the impresario A. M. Palmer 'offered her a series of similar parts in which to "star" for three years'. His 'one stipulation' was 'that I should not act with her!' This 'temptation' was stoutly resisted. And 'the self-sacrifice of my wife' gets a long exculpatory aside.[80] Only once did 'Mimi' balk – at playing Miss Havisham, in Harvey's other Dickens adaptation, predictably renamed first *The Convict* and then *The Scapegoat*, in 1935. She found the role 'repellent', Harvey's official biographer records, 'accepting it only at her husband's entreaty': 'Provincial playgoers praised her ardently. The more they admired her the more she flinched.'[81]

The audience's preference brings us back to the tributes the fans sent to Harvey. Many were aimed also at 'Mimi'. 'Little Valentine', a dying Liverpool child, sent a 'parting' post-mortem gift of a 'little diamond brooch' for 'her dear "Mimi" ... to wear always in remembrance'.[82] Husband and wife took receipt, on another occasion, of 'a copy of *The Only Way*, written out from memory by a brother and sister'.[83] The 'demented' brother later dragged Mimi, then Harvey, to a garret off Piccadilly to see the sister's dead body, the impoverished girl's 'dying wish'.[84] Such tributes indicated the incapacity of simpler audiences to separate actor from role, Harvey from Carton, Mimi from N. de Silva. But they indicated also the fans' understanding of the complex of desire, sacrifice and homoeroticism that fuelled Martin-Harvey's success (as later it did that of the greatest heart-throb of the silent cinema, Rudolph Valentino): the meaning of his star image, calculated to sustain obsession. Neither Little Valentine nor Edith nor Ethel nor the dead sister could have him – but neither could anyone else, not even 'Mimi'.

Notes

1. *The Autobiography of Sir John Martin-Harvey* (London: Sampson Low, [1930]), p. 247. See Brian Gardner, *Mafeking: A Victorian Legend* (London: Cassell, 1966). 'Luckily', Baden-Powell remarked, 'my early play-acting instincts came in useful' (quoted in Gardner, p. 250), on which see Robert Baden-Powell, *Indian Memories* (London: Herbert Jenkins, 1915).

2. Martin-Harvey, *Autobiography*, pp. 478, 483; H. Philip Bolton, *Dickens Dramatized* (London: Mansell Publishing, 1987), p. 399.

3. 'THE ONLY WAY ... marks a gigantic forward movement in British film production', trumpeted *Variety*'s London reporter, 30 September 1925. 'Never in the history of a picture shown in this country has an audience deliberately refused to leave the theatre and called insistently for the leading actor and producer [i.e. director].' For the published version, see Lt.-Col. The Rev. Freeman Wills and the Rev. Canon Langbridge, *The Only Way: A Dramatic Version in a Prologue and Four Acts of Charles Dickens'* A Tale Of Two Cities (London: Frederick Muller, 1942). Langbridge's co-authorship was unknown until 1926, his bishop disapproving of his spare-time activities.

4. Harvey played the Fat Boy in Irving's *Jingle* (based on *The Pickwick Papers*; 1871, revised 1878), and took his *Two Roses* (partly based on *Little Dorrit*, 1870) on tour in summer vacations (see below).

5. Harvey sometimes inflated the number to 5,000. Working from production records, Nicholas Butler estimates 2,475–2,500 performances (*Sir John Martin-Harvey* (Wivenhoe: N. Butler, 1997), p. 5). For comparison: no Gilbert and Sullivan operetta exceeded 1,000 performances.

6. Actually, these phrases are promotional and critical descriptions of Harvey's vehicles *The Breed of the Treshams* (*Martin Harvey: A Short Sketch of His Career* (Letchworth: Arden Press, 1914), p. 16) and *Rouget de L'Isle*, commissioned by Harvey in 1894 and revived 1900 (*Illustrated London News*, 26 March 1900). But the plays are essentially interchangeable (see below). Harvey served a fourteen-year theatrical apprenticeship as a supernumerary, 'young gentleman' and bit-player in Irving's Lyceum Company, graduating from the Fat Boy to Sam Weller when Irving toured America in *Jingle*, and scoring a hit as Osric in *Hamlet*, but by and large was starved of substantial roles; he gained experience in management and leading roles, 1888–94, running the Lyceum Vacation Company.

7. Malcolm Morley, 'The Stage Story of *A Tale Of Two Cities*', *Dickensian*, 51 (1954) pp. 34–40, p. 38.

8. Martin-Harvey, *Autobiography*, pp. 186–7.

9. Martin-Harvey, *Autobiography*, p. 232.

10. Martin-Harvey, *Autobiography*, p. 233; N. de Silva, quoted in Edgar, p. 249.

11. Handbill; Theatre Museum, London (hereafter TM) Personal Box 46. Many thanks to the staff of the Theatre Museum.

12. Legend on verso of embossed coloured postcard of Harvey in the 1925 *The Only Way* by Beagles of London ('FAMOUS CINEMA STAR' series). I am grateful to Ms Sandra Gonzalez for sharing with me her Harvey collection and her insights.

13. 'Martin-Harvey does not receive much attention from today's theatre historians,' as L. W. Connolly writes ('Martin-Harvey in Canada', in *Bernhardt and the Theatre of Her Time*, ed. Eric Salmon (Westport, CT: Greenwood Press, 1984), p. 225). See Willson Disher, *The Last Romantic: The Authorised Biography of Sir John Martin-Harvey* (London: Hutchinson, 1948); and Hesketh Pearson, *The Last Actor-Managers* (London: White Lion, 1950).

14. Rank publicity. My comments on the film versions of *A Tale of Two Cities* of 1911, 1917, 1925, 1935 and 1958 are indebted to the British Film Institute (BFI), the Library of Congress and Judith Buchanan.

15. *The Only Way*, p. 30.

16. *The Only Way*, p. 25.

17. Harvey quotes the burlesque in his *Autobiography*, pp. 240–2. He also sued for libel.

18. On the late inspiration for this speech, the 'apex' of the play, see *Autobiography*, p. 212n.

19. Martin-Harvey, *Autobiography*, p. 203.

20. Disher, *Last Romantic*, p. 60.

21. D. L. Murray, 'Foreword', in Disher, *Last Romantic*, p. 11.

22. Quoted in Wilson Midgeley, 'The Genius of Sir John', *Daily Telegraph*, 13 April 1939.

23. 'Some Reflections on the Art of Acting', in *The Book of Martin-Harvey*, ed. R. N. Green-Armytage [Lady Martin-Harvey] (London: Henry Walker, 1930), p. 52. See also 'The Romantic Actor', *Times Literary Supplement*, 16 October 1930, p. 818.

24. Murray, in Disher, *Last Romantic*, p. 13; Harvey, quoted in Disher, *Last Romantic*, p. 13.

25. *The Memoirs of J. Decastro, Comedian* (London: Sherwood, Jones, and Co., 1824), pp. 122–4. See also the discussion of the burletta in George Taylor, *The French Revolution and the London Stage 1789–1805* (Cambridge: Cambridge University Press, 2000), p. 28.

26. Quoted in Disher, *Last Romantic*, p. 55.

27. It was to protect *Robespierre* that Irving asked Harvey to defer production of *The Only Way*: both feature climactic trials before the Tribunal. See Martin-Harvey, *Autobiography*, pp. 220–5, and 'The Story of *The Only Way*', *Dickensian*, 23 (1926), 24–6. On *Robespierre*, see Jeffrey Richards, *Sir Henry Irving* (London: Palgrave Macmillan, 2005).

28. Midgley recognized the lineage, describing Harvey's Carton as 'the very latest type of cinema bad man' (*Telegraph*, 13 April 1939).

29. 2 June 1859; quoted in E[mma] Watts Phillips, *Watts Phillips: Artist and Playwright* (London: Cassell, 1891), p. 46.

30. Quoted in Bolton, *Dickens Dramatized*, p. 397.

31. John Coleman; quoted in Watts Phillips, *Watts Phillips*, p. 51.

32. Tom Taylor, *A Tale of Two Cities*, British Library, Lord Chamberlain's Collection of MS Plays, fols 23, 24. My thanks to Kathryn Johnson for her help in working with this collection.

33. 5 June 1860; *Letters*, IX, pp. 259–60.

34. Richard Pearson reports that Wilkie Collins, similarly, made drastic and surprising changes in adapting his novels for the stage (presentation, 'New Issues in Theatre Historiography', University of Birmingham, 7 July 2007).

35. Henry Rivers [F. Fox Cooper], *The Tale Of Two Cities; Or, The Incarcerated Victim of the Bastille* (London: Davidson, 1860), pp. 61–2.

36. *All For Her!*, BL, Lord Chamberlain's Collection of MS Plays, fol. 58.

37. Advertisement for the performance of 1 December 1875, in the *Daily Telegraph* (undated cutting in TM file).

38. Dickens wrote to Merivale, *de haut en bas*, suggesting extensive changes to a theatrical article ('The Last of the Low Comedians') on 3 March 1869: his letter is a sparkling specimen of adroit editorial management, packed with minute details of theatre history. See *Letters*, XII, p. 302.

39. The hero of *The Dead Heart* is similarly stirred by a 'sweet, grey-haired mother, still beautiful' (*Souvenir of 'The Dead Heart'* (London: Cassell, 1889), p. 5): another criticism of Dickens's gender preferences. Even Taylor's Lucie muses knowingly: 'Poor Carton! . . . Ah! – Why am I not free to attend and nurture [him]?', p. 8. See Watts Phillips, *The Dead Heart: A Story of the French Revolution*, 1860; rev. Walter

H. Pollock (London: S. French, 1889). Martin-Harvey played in Pollock's revised version, produced for Henry Irving.

40. *All For Her!*, pp. 5, 6.
41. Unidentified cutting, TM file.
42. 'Nina' was replaced in Wilcox's film by Madge Stuart: the film medium demanded a younger woman.
43. A 'Romantic Play' called *The Angels; Or, Mortals of Sacrifice*, was copyrighted in New York in 1873, and the five-act *Sacrifice* in 1876 (Bolton, pp. 399, 400). Dr Manette's Bastille martyr story remained a popular focus of American dramatic versions through the 1870s and 1880s.
44. On the subject of gender politics: Lucille La Verne, who played The Vengeance in the 1935 MGM *Tale of Two Cities*, reappeared on screen as the Wicked Witch of the West in *The Wizard Of Oz*.
45. 8 December 1859; *Letters*, IX, p. 177.
46. Arthur Waugh, 'Introducing *A Tale of Two Cities*', *Dickensian* 23 (1926), 13; *TTC*, Appendix II, p. 397. At Manchester, Collins remembered in 1874, 'He electrified the audience'. Quoted in S. J. Adair Fitzgerald, *Dickens and the Drama* (London: Chapman & Hall, 1910), p. 47.
47. Edgar Johnson, *Charles Dickens*, rev. and abridged edn (Harmondsworth: Penguin Books, 1977), p. 446.
48. *The Era*, 18 February 1899.
49. Harvey, 'Art of Acting', p. 49.
50. 'Irving as Charles I', in *We Saw Him Act*, ed. H. A. Saintsbury and Cecil Palmer (London: Hurst & Blackett, 1939), p. 59.
51. *Sporting and Dramatic News*, 11 March 1899.
52. T. Edgar Pemberton, *Sydney Carton*, BL, Lord Chamberlain's Collection of MS Plays, 10.
53. Martin-Harvey, *Autobiography*, p. 13.
54. Poem by Henry Knight (*Dickensian* [1906], 99). The climactic moment was a main focus of publicity for the 1925 film.
55. Martin-Harvey, *Autobiography*, p. 210n.
56. Martin-Harvey, *Autobiography*, p. 210n.
57. Watts Phillips, *Watts Phillips*, pp. 42, 60.
58. *Telegraph*, 13 April 1939.
59. Martin-Harvey, *Autobiography*, p. 238.
60. Martin Harvey, 'Apology', *The Only Way*, p. xi.
61. Martin-Harvey, *Autobiography*, p. 282.
62. Davis, 'Repertoire', keynote presentation, 'New Issues in Theatre Historiography'.
63. In real life, Lesurques was guillotined; in English stage adaptations he was sometimes reprieved. The case was 'a familiar topic all over the world for more than one generation' (Charles Oman, *The Lyons Mail, being an account of the crime of April 27 1796 (Floréal 8 an IV)* (London: Methuen, 1945), p. 75). Charles Reade's English version of *Le Courrier de Lyons* (1850), starring Kean, was a sensation in 1854. Like Harvey's Carton, and by special permission from the French government, Lesurques wore white clothes for his execution. Other suggestive elements in the case and Reade's play include startling recognition scenes, Dubosc's 'sardonic wit' (Oman, p. 184), his use of a wig, Lesurques's possession of two passports, neither his own, and his dictation of letters from the condemned cell.
64. Pemberton, *Sydney Carton*, p. 25.

65. It might also be applied to *The Corsican Brothers*. I am grateful to Joe Bristow for encouraging me to pursue this line of inquiry. This essay has benefited generally from conversations at the Maison Française and at University of Birmingham.
66. Thomas Pakenham, *The Boer War* (London: Abacus, 1992 [1979]), p. 409.
67. Morley, 'Stage Story', p. 39. Gielgud did play the role on the radio.
68. See Martin-Harvey, *Autobiography*, pp. 240–2.
69. Disher, *Last Romantic*, p. 122.
70. Beside Keats's grave in Italy, 'the vision of Guido's St Sebastian came before my eyes', Wilde wrote, 'a lovely brown boy...bound by his evil enemies to a tree and...pierced by arrows'. Quoted in Richard Ellmann, *Oscar Wilde* (New York: Vintage Books, 1987), p. 74n.
71. Quoted in Disher, *Last Romantic*, p. 242. Harvey's explicitly Christian production, in 1923, of *Via Crucis* (*Everyman*), took courage and drew hostile criticism (Disher, pp. 242–4).
72. Female fans' desire was thus made safe. Nicholas Butler spends some time 'outing' Harvey. His analysis of Harvey's fabricated adolescent love for 'The Youngest Miss Howard', however, strikes home. Butler, *Sir John Martin-Harvey*, p. 167.
73. Terry, quoted in Harvey, 'Story of *The Only Way*', p. 26; review, quoted in Disher, *Last Romantic*, p. 108. Irving revived the play under the title *The Lyons Mail* in 1877. Harvey was between 5'3" and 5'6" tall.
74. Unidentified cutting in TM file.
75. *All For Her!*, pp. 56, 58.
76. *Sporting and Dramatic News*, 30 October 1875.
77. *Short Sketch*, p. 16.
78. Butler, *Sir John Martin-Harvey*, p. 30.
79. *The Only Way*, p. 87.
80. Martin-Harvey, *Autobiography*, p. 229.
81. Disher, *Last Romantic*, pp. 253–4.
82. Martin-Harvey, *Autobiography*, p. 234.
83. Martin-Harvey, *Autobiography*, p. 228.
84. Martin-Harvey, *Autobiography*, pp. 234–5, 236.

9
Sanguine Mirages, Cinematic Dreams: Things Seen and Things Imagined in the 1917 Fox Feature Film *A Tale of Two Cities*

Judith Buchanan with Alex Newhouse

In the June 1917 issue of the American movie fan magazine *Photoplay*, the reviewer of the Fox feature film *A Tale of Two Cities* declared that the film's artistic qualities and impressive dimensions 'came surprisingly as a shot from a dark doorway'.[1] Knowledge of the film's production stable (Fox), director (Scotsman Frank Lloyd) and cast (including the star William Farnum as both Sydney Carton and Charles Darnay) did not, that is, prepare its audiences for the visual appeal and emotional power of this particular film. The conjured image of the unanticipated eruption of deadly sniper fire from surprising quarters perfectly captures the impact the film makes on its spectators. In its performances, technical control, spectacular dimensions, eloquent editing and purposeful varying of perspectives, it is a film of ambitious reach and considerable subtlety. As an interpretive adaptation, moreover, it shows noteworthy courage in reading the novel against the sentimentalized grain of its interpretive moment.

At the heart of Dickens's novel lies a pitting of public acts and utterances against private hopes and fears. While grand historical event played out in the public setting of courtrooms, marketplaces and, in due course, scaffolds provides the engine for the drama, acts of protective and conspiratorial 'enclos[ure]' that would keep secrets within 'darkly clustered houses' and, more intimately yet, within the 'beating heart' of individuals form its darkly animating force (*TTC*, I, iii, 14–15). The 1917 film, we argue, engages purposefully with this central opposition as it narrates and cinematically investigates the inherited tale in both its ranging account of dramatic public event and its intimate engagement with private lives. In particular, it searches out and intrusively exposes hidden spaces, occluded corners and even complex interior worlds, thereby breaching the various bounds – of both architecture and selfhood – that would seek to 'enclose' the novel's secret realms of memory, conspiracy, imagination and prophecy. As the film cross-cuts between the spectacular display of material effect on the one hand and the tenacious teasing out and exposure of secrets on the other, an incrementally revealed, progressively illuminating discourse is established between the two.

*

In the marketing puff for the 1917 *A Tale of Two Cities*, the Fox Film Corporation shamelessly announced: 'This is a far, far better production than Fox has ever done before.'[2] The use of the Dickensian misquotation was both corny and commercially purposeful. It traded flatteringly on its target audience's ability to recognize the provenance of the line. And in doing so, it encouraged a wry smile in that audience as they identified the commercial appropriation and irreverent adjustment of the quotation. In this way the tagline succeeded in trailing, and simultaneously in tempering, the picture's literary credentials; this was a production able to draw on the elevated associations of the status of its source while distancing itself slightly from some of the cultural, and related market, constrictions that might accompany too sincerely courted a reflected literary kudos. The tagline also had the (supernumerary) virtue of being true: the production was indeed a more significant, more ambitious and, arguably, 'better' production than any Fox had yet released.

Adapting Dickens was, in the context of the silent film era, not just a commercial project, nor even simply an artistic or interpretive one: from the perspective of those for whom such things mattered, it was also an undertaking with a perceived moral worth. As early as 1910, for example, Frank L. Dyer of the Edison Manufacturing Company had written:

> The producing men ... realize [the potential for] the ultimate development of the art to a position of dignity and importance. When the work of Dickens and Victor Hugo, the poems of Browning, the plays of Shakespeare and stories from the Bible are used as a basis for moving pictures, no fair-minded man can deny that the art is developing along the right lines.[3]

Fox were fully conscious of the valuable image boost (and concomitant market share) that could be acquired by aligning themselves with the campaign to help the industry develop 'along the right lines'. By 1917, they had already proved their stripes in this respect through releases such as *Anna Karenina* (1915), *A Man of Sorrow* (1916) and *Romeo and Juliet* (1916). Soon after the release of *A Tale of Two Cities* in April 1917, they produced two more thematically related productions – an adaptation of Hugo's *Les Misérables* (again directed by Lloyd and starring Farnum)[4] and a version of *The Scarlet Pimpernel*. This run of films of revolutionary France across the same year, drawing on the same story pool, historical backdrop and dominant aesthetics, enabled the company to extract maximum returns from their considerable investment by recycling their lavish late eighteenth-century Parisian period sets and properties.[5] And, in the process, it enabled them to ride the wave of the public's interest in cinematic tales of the French Revolution. As these films played to both the American and the British markets through 1917 (in April of which year America entered the Great War), however, they also provided a narrative space, usefully removed in time, through which audiences could reflect on the societal values that were worth fighting for and, in particular, on the meaning of personal sacrifice in the context of larger historical movements. It was a cinematic interest in setting, scale and theme that had been influentially pioneered by the Dickensian film. The renewed popularity of the film on its re-release in February 1920 suggests, moreover, that it was an interest whose appeal proved lasting.[6]

In the first half of this chapter, we consider the camera's rapt attention to the objective matter, and considerable substance, of the narrative's outer world, with a concentration on the impact of the teeming crowd scenes and the cinematic presentation of the two central male characters. But the camera, in this film, also unsparingly intrudes on more private spaces to see how domestic, secret and otherwise occluded realms (the neglected, the hungry, the imprisoned, the downtrodden and in due course the conspiratorial) can relate to public event and mass spectacle. The film's investigative impulses that seek to root out and document the more topographically and emotionally secluded corners of this fictional world are at their *most* intimately exposing on the occasions when the camera does not just penetrate the walls of living spaces but, beyond this, also the secret interiority of characters themselves. In the second half of this chapter, therefore, we turn our attention to the camera's accounts – sometimes empathetically visualized, sometimes brutally exposing – of the subjective domains of memory, fantasy and prophecy. The key moments when aspects of characters' mindscapes are given temporarily visualized expression are: Dr Manette's memorial reconstruction of the events that put him in the Bastille; Sydney Carton's self-contemplation in the mirror when he imagines that it is Darnay whom he sees looking back at him; and Carton's final prophetic image of how the future for which he is dying will look. Since the film is not currently commercially available, we make it part of our project to put an account of the film into critical circulation. For this reason we include more descriptive reference to *mise-en-scène*, cinematography and editing than we would if a detailed knowledge of the film could be assumed.

Substance

Dickens's account of the storming of the Bastille describes the '[h]eadlong, mad, and dangerous footsteps' of 'Jacques One, Jacques Two, Jacques One Thousand, Jacques Two Thousand, Jacques Five-and-Twenty Thousand' as they reach for 'every weapon that distracted ingenuity could discover or devise'. '[A]s if there were an eternity of people', he writes, they act with the force of a 'living ocean'. In this 'sea' of Jacques, individual names are lost, individual voices dissolve into 'ten thousand incoherencies' and, as thousands of private grievances are absorbed into one common purpose, all are 'armed alike in hunger and revenge' (II, xxi, 222, 224, 223, 225, 227, 223, 224). The cinematography in the 1917 film is peculiarly responsive to the language of surges and oceans, choosing to see the vast crowd as a segmented single organism with a single will and a unified impulse. Bristling with improvised weapons, successive waves of revolutionaries are seen pouring through street after street in an irresistible cascade of collective energy (in ways closely reminiscent of the Parisian scenes of the 1572 St Bartholomew's Day Massacre in D. W. Griffith's spectacular and influential *Intolerance* of 1916). Over bridges, round corners, scaling walls, ramming the gates of the Bastille, overwhelming the Bastille guard by sheer force of numbers – the composite creature that is the crowd swarms across the screen, dividing and flowing and reconvening in ways that serve to eliminate the significance of the individual parts that make up the terrifying collective. The scenes appear as an overwhelming and extensive coalescing of myriad private griefs and motives for anger into one collective grief and mass act of unified anger. And in the crowd's surging, they pass rapidly in and out of shot, thus always alluding to the off-screen space from which they come and into which they disappear. Their constant movement into space beyond the frame borders evokes an immeasurably extensive imaginary further body of people currently out of shot. Moreover, the pace of the edit, cutting swiftly (for its moment) between different views of the crowds' activities, confirms the sense of an event that can be impressionistically sketched at some speed but that is too overwhelming in scope to be comprehensively caught in the containing parameters of the film frame. In these ways, the film takes this awe-inspiring outpouring and multiplies the effect of each scene further by offering it as a mere gesturing towards the full scope of the event. Not surprisingly, it was a scene that struck reviewers at its first release. The account given in *Photoplay* in June 1917, for example, may be taken as characteristic:

[T]hese gaunt and fantastic people, yapping at the heels of the Bourbon soldiery, are more than a crowd of energetically-driven supers. Almost as in the pages of Carlyle, we feel ourselves swept on the crest of the greatest awakening since Christianity.[7]

The immensity of the effect is well conveyed by this response, and the reference to Thomas Carlyle reminds us of both the indebtedness of the novel to *The French Revolution* (1837) and of the fact that subsequent audiences for *A Tale of Two Cities* continued to identify and acknowledge that debt. Despite *Photoplay*'s reference to Christianity in this context, however, as it appears on screen the surging force that is awakened and unleashed at this point seems more diabolic engine than holy uprising.

But the film also does here what the novel does not, and relates this scene of impressive, exhausting collective dynamism to another scene of a quite different character. For as the quasi-hedonistic energy of the crowd reaches its height, the sequence cuts away from the freneticism to a small, dark place within the Bastille, where one frail and distracted old man with a long white beard is working at a shoe lathe. This is a man whose name is not lost in a sea of Jacques: he himself may subsequently only be able to identify himself by his cell number, 'One Hundred and Five, North Tower' (I, vi, 44), but we know his name. Dr Manette (Joseph Swickard) pauses and looks up, struck by an unfamiliar noise, or level of noise, from outside his long-familiar cell in the North Tower. We know him from earlier encounters and see that his fate will now be decided by the surging anonymous mass intent on breaching the walls of his prison. We cut back to the exterior shots of soldiers firing on the crowd and of bodies falling from the battlements, of the criss-cross patterns of raised pikes and agricultural implements held aloft and the massed effect of a body of people rushing across the drawbridge to enter the Bastille. This exterior world is a world without individual faces, and despite the excessive choreography of bodies falling from crenellations and into moats, of bodies being tipped over walls and of bodies collapsing theatrically from gunshot wounds, it is a world seen almost exclusively in long-shot, apparently without concern for personal destinies.[8] In terms of frame composition, of the visual poetry of the moment and of the overriding political impact of the scene, it is the *pattern* and the *quantity* of the falling that matters; the identity of those who fall does not register among the film's interests at this point. By conspicuous contrast, however, the dawning consciousness that something is changing for one frail old man is an individualized story. His reaction to the unfolding drama as it incrementally approaches his space is both highly particularized and, to some extent, representative, standing as synecdochic expression of the fates of individuals caught within the terrifying dimensions of this sweeping drama.

Eventually the two planes of action converge as the crowds breach the defences of the Bastille. At this point another recognizable presence, Defarge (Herschel Mayall), emerges from the anonymized mass to rush to the North Tower and reclaim his old master. Bemused about his own release, Dr Manette is carried out on shoulders into the crowd as an uncomprehending trophy of the people's liberation. Here he is not, that is, simply 'recalled to life' (I, ii, 12, etc.) but, in his sudden exposure as an item of public display, invested with representative weight and meaning by those who are thus recalling him. Initially lost to sight in depth of field among the density of the heaving crowd viewed in panoptic long-shot, he is subsequently carried forward towards the camera, where it becomes apparent that he has, in effect, been elevated to the status of revolutionary totem (Illustration 9.1).

The novel provides the following prompt that has inspired this scene:

> Seven faces of prisoners, suddenly released by the storm that had burst their tomb, were carried high overhead: all scared, all lost, all wondering

Illustration 9.1   Dr Manette is carried forward from behind the incarcerating grid of the raised weaponry to be hailed as revolutionary totem

and amazed, as if the Last Day were come, and those who rejoiced around them were lost spirits.

(II, xxi, 229)

The film presents the novel's anonymous faces carried high overhead out of their living tomb but focuses attention exclusively on the one from among them that – in this adjusted telling of the tale – is known. Frank Lloyd's working script for the film instructs at this point: 'CLOSE UP MANETTE. He is stunned, bewildered and dazed.'[9] The film as released denies us the full close-up that Lloyd had originally envisaged, but gives us the dazed bewilderment. And so it is in the film that the crowd raises their weaponry around the iconized figure of Dr Manette as a way of hailing their own triumphant achievement in releasing the prisoners. The intention of the crowd at this point is clearly celebratory (the working script declares them 'delirious').[10] The film, however, allows itself to interrogate that intention and, in its frame composition, implicitly tells a prophetic story which carries another charge. Ominously, therefore, in the moment of ostensible liberation, when Manette is first seen in depth of field, he appears framed and contained by a forest of intersecting pikes and scythes. The film does not, as the novel does, suggest that the prisoners have been dragged from their tomb directly into a hellish afterlife. Rather, its symbolism is suggestive of future acts of earthly imprisonment. As we see Manette caught, almost incarcerated, within the network of shafts and handles of improvised weaponry by the very agents of his liberation, the film therefore allows itself to engage somberly with the narrative's *telos* which will see the same crowd eventually incarcerate others, including one innocent man and close relative of the man here conveniently serving as the emblem of their revolutionary cause.

The imagery's suggestive hint of further, future entrapments is the cinematically expressed equivalent of the verbal advertisements of a teleology conspicuously trailed in the novel. The seeming innocence of the 'rude carts, bespattered with rustic mire, snuffed about by pigs, and roosted in by poultry' at the opening of the tale, for example, is, we are told, a merely temporary state of affairs: these same carts have already been predestined in due course to become the 'tumbrils of the Revolution' (I, i, 6). Here, and throughout, the story's ending is inscribed into the fabric of its tale and of its telling. The film inherits this keen awareness of narrative destination and writes its own knowing retrospection into several of its intertitles. The opening scene-setting intertitle may be taken as representative in this respect:

> In Saint Antoine, where the frowning walls of the Bastille reminded the people of their woes in the threatening days that preceded the French Revolution.[11]

As in Dickens, so in the 1917 film, the story throughout carries with it the burden of the inexorable direction in which it tends. And this burden of foreknowledge is communicated, portentously and explicitly, through the intertitles and, more subtly and symbolically, through the action played out before the camera. So it is that, encoded in the entrapment-evocative visuals of the moment of Manette's liberation, lies the prophetic hint of the future threat that will in due course emerge directly from this very act of release.

The overwhelming impact of the spectacular crowd sequences showcases the impressive scale and materiality of the film's pro-filmic arena in its uncompromising display of sets, properties and extras. The force of such moments is enhanced within the overall scheme of the film through being offset by a series of differently modulated visual effects. Of these, the doubling of William Farnum playing both Carton and Darnay produces some of the most arresting visual moments.[12] The impression created by the dual presence of one actor on screen is, of course, of a different and far quieter order from that generated by the mass spectacle of a heaving crowd. However, in its unnerving departure from the extra-cinematic laws of nature that dictate that a body should have but a single instantiation, it is equally memorable. In a series of moments of cinematic wizardry, Carton and Darnay appear in shot together and are even seen interacting with each other closely. In the London courtroom, outside the court, across the dinner table, at the garden gate of the Manettes' London home, and finally in Darnay's prison cell where one cinematic expression of the shared actorly body is, through a composite piece of film trickery, brilliantly substituted for the other: Farnum's on-screen encounters with his other self are part of the film's dynamic repertoire of visual *coups*.

The shooting of these scenes required some impeccably executed performance timing in order to sustain the illusion of two separate characters coexisting in common space.[13] Lloyd was ambitious about what could be achieved through double exposure of this kind. Thus it is that the two characters become interlocutors who respond precisely to each other's movements, toasting each other at dinner and Darnay visibly starting at the precise moment when his companion then tosses his glass to the ground. But even as an audience takes stock of the daring choreography and precision timing of the encounters of the two characters, it is also simultaneously registering the unsettling challenge to the singular integrity of an actor's body that the doubled presence of Farnum on screen necessarily constitutes.

In 1917, many members of a contemporary audience would still have been able to remember the pioneering days of cinema and the sheer oddity of the effect of first seeing a recorded *version* of a person projected onto a screen and moving with lifelike accuracy. Removed as it was from the flesh and blood body it remembers, the cinematically animated recording of a person seen in his or her absence had elements of the disquieting about it, as several contemporary commentators remarked.[14] But to see the same person moving simultaneously with lifelike movement *twice* on screen makes a yet more troubling intervention into the meaning of screen presence. The effect is uncanny in that it challenges – as perhaps to the casual observer identical twins also do in the real world – the commonly held sense of an absolute relationship between the singularity of appearance and the meaning of individual selfhood. And it is, of course, precisely this challenge that the Dickens novel itself issues in depicting the (literal) interchangeability of its central characters. Farnum's twin presence on screen therefore both creates some bravura moments of technical cinematic artifice ('double exposure scenes have never been done better', enthused the *Moving Picture World* in March 1917)[15] and, simultaneously, plays on the kinship between the characters of Carton and Darnay richly suggested by the novel. The film, in tune with its novelistic source, constantly finds itself caught between differentiating between and aligning the two men. The appearance and performance of Farnum's maverick, dissolute and slightly haunted Carton on the one hand, and of his upright, urbane and dignified Darnay on the other, are, therefore, both expressively mimetic and beautifully counterpoised. Farnum's 'two distinct personalities' in the film were described by one contemporary reviewer in the following terms:

Darnay, the suave and silent aristocrat, direct and elegant as an arrow of silver in his discourse and his lovemaking; Carton, the rum-wrecked genius, abased to a gutter hell by his sloth and his appetite, fired with the passion of heaven by the eyes of Lucie Manette.[16]

There was, that is, considerable pleasure to be gained for an audience simply from observing the differing performances given by the same actor. Moreover, the conspicuous on-screen symmetry between the two gives an additional, and piquant, charge to the keenly tormenting sense nurtured by the novel's Carton of Darnay as a man unnervingly like himself but one whose moral sensibilities, social grace and romantic good fortune will always elude his more clouded 'counterpart' (II, iv, 86).

Shadow

The details of Farnum's performances (facial expression, gesture, stance, gait) are expressively communicative about the emotional and psychological landscape of each character he plays. However, the film's engagements with the inner workings of a mind transcend the interrogation of mood made possible by simply scrutinizing exterior performance detail. In order to explore interiority with greater intimacy, in this film the camera is additionally licensed to identify specific images from within a character's mind-world and to put these graphically before the cinema spectator. Ontologically, the images that result from this process of psychological intrusion, appropriation and revealing exhibition are as real and as unreal, as substantial and as insubstantial, as those that narrate events. Referentially, however, the two are clearly distinguished, in that some dramatize the narrative's outer world of occurrence and some the inner world of the imaginary. The occasions when exhumed subjectivities are put on cinematic show necessarily arrest the temporal flow of present-time sequential action. In the context of an inexorable and lavish cinematic take on the inherited tale that mostly privileges *what happens next*, these occasional forays into the secret interior worlds of characters inevitably render themselves conspicuous. Each incursion into a subjective domain uses its resulting visibility in interpretively pertinent ways. The first such moment we consider takes us back to Carton's tormented contemplation of Darnay and to our transfixed contemplation of them both.

The film engages directly with Carton's sense of Darnay as his more desirable double in the scene in which Carton contemplates himself in the mirror. In the novel, Carton 'survey[s] himself minutely' in the 'glass that hung against the wall' while muttering dejectedly to his own image. Darnay, he says accusingly to himself, 'shows you what you have fallen away from and what you might have been!' (II, iv, 89). Darnay, that is, has become for him his idealized alter-ego and is consequently loathed for inadvertently and uncomfortably reminding him of standards in moral rectitude and social grace he feels to be beyond him. The 1917 film takes the prompt, lifting Carton's line of self-address from the novel for an only slightly adjusted intertitle ('Today you have met a man who shows you what you have fallen away from and what you might have been') and capitalizing on the cinematic potential lying latent in the scene. Thus it is that as Carton leans against the mantelpiece barely able to raise his eyes to look at his own reflection, the face in the mirror transmutes through a dissolve into Darnay's, the implicitly accusing figure of the man Carton 'might have been'. Both the figure of the gazing Carton and the figure of the gazed-at Darnay are simultaneously visible in shot, the one contemplating the other in order to feed his own self-contempt the more.[17] But, once again, it is not only on the character that the spectator's eye rests in this scene, for the apparatus of cinema constantly invites us to see the star visibly present behind and within the role. Thus it is that, from the perspective of the audience, the scene carries the additional extra-textual interest of showing one expression of Farnum gazing at another, apparently in order to rue the distinctions between his part-alterized, part-identified on-screen selves. As the narrative is temporarily frozen to allow the spectator to gaze at Farnum's transmutation from one version of himself into another and then back again, in the terms of cinema spectatorship the shot constitutes a rare moment of *photogénie* – an invitation to the spectator to indulge in the absorbed contemplation of the photographic image of the star, momentarily undistracted by other ongoing plot considerations.[18] Farnum is doubly and, therefore, emphatically present in the frame as the only point of rest for our contemplative and interrogating gaze. We might even say that he is *too much* present in it, compromising all usual understandings of selfhood. The nature-defying presence of his doubled body thereby points up the artifice of the production of the cinematic body, sufficiently mutable and disconnected from its flesh-and-blood counterpart to be multipliable in this way. And so the irony is that the overemphatic presence of Farnum's body in this scene ultimately draws attention to its very absence from the performance space of the film – to, that is, its status as merely a projected trace of the real man.

Carton's subjective vision in the mirror allows us to see the psychological tenor of his inner world. An earlier excursion into a subjectively conjured world takes us into the realm of memory. The subjectively remembered images are conjured by Dr Manette from within his cell in the Bastille. In the novel we must wait until Book III, chapter 10 ('The Substance of the Shadow') to discover Manette's (written) account of the events of the 'cloudy moonlight night ... in the year 1757' which constitute the hidden well-spring of much of the novel's action (III, x, 331). It was usual for literary adaptations of the silent era to iron out a-chronologies from their sources in the interests of narrative clarity: explanatory back-stories that erupt into the flow of present-time narrative were often presented as chronologized action.[19] It is no surprise, therefore, that *The Only Way* (Herbert Wilcox, 1925), another adaptation of *A Tale of Two Cities*, opts to clarify the story's central narrative by opening with the accout of the Evrémondes' rape of madame

Defarge's sister and related summons of Dr Manette, to clarify the story's central narrative impetus. The Fox film, however, resists this clarifying tendency. Rather than converting the remembered story of abuse, contempt, murder and injustice into a piece of present-time action, seamlessly absorbed into the ongoing flow of chronologized narrative, the Fox film retains the tale *as a memory* painfully dwelt upon and scratched out at a later moment from within the prison cell. However, it moves the account of that memory from its late novelistic positioning as a document that is read to the beginning of the film, where we see it as a document in the (costly) process of being written. Eschewing the option of incorporating the story into the linear progress of chronologically sequential moments retains the retrospective filter and so underscores the aching chasm of time that has opened between then and now. In doing so, the film nimbly acknowledges the lasting significance of this story as the unbearable recollection from whose ongoing polluting influence the present tide of lived moments seems unable to free itself and to which innocent and unwitting lives tragically continue to be in thrall.

And so it is that at this early stage in the film an iris opens on the frail, ancient, white-bearded figure of Dr Manette hunched over a little table. He is brightly, almost spiritually lit from above (as he will be again during the later scene of reunion with Lucie) and, in its age and seemingly transfiguring character, his presence carries almost Old Testament weight. The shot cuts to show us the paper before him on the table. Snippets of his harrowing tale are legible: 'That awful night when I was called from the side of my wife and child...'. Like an accelerated rehearsal of the processes of literary adaptation itself, the words then cross-fade into the visualized version of the story they tell, the images apparently summoned into being by the written memorial account. It is a process that is repeated. At the close of each visualized snippet of the remembered story, the scene cross-fades back Manette's form feverishly engaged on his writing, or sitting looking ahead in horrified stupefaction as if at an imaginary screen showing him a graphic rerun of his painfully conjured recollections. Thus the remembered scene plays out episodically, punctuated throughout by the visual reminder of Manette as the subjective summoning imagination of the unfolding drama.

The first image his imagination conjures is one of unalloyed domestic bliss. Unlike in the novel in which he is walking 'on a retired part of the quay by the Seine' (III, x, 331) when the Evrémondes' carriage picks him up to take him to the dying girl, here, more emotively, he is called upon when comfortably at home. The working script accurately anticipates the scene of the finished film: 'Doctor sitting beside wife in front of fire, his little daughter Lucie, with little dog on hearth rug...Doctor and wife laughing...'[20] It is a scene without a tonal cloud upon it. In fact, the tableau seems to be on offer as the valued cameo from an idealized memory. But the domestic scene is then disrupted. A knock at the door makes Manette turn his head away from his wife, vacate his place beside her to answer the door and in due course leave in response to the Evrémondes' terrible summons. External agency has intervened to take him away from, and then permanently deprive him of, the uncomplicated contentment of his home life. Once the series of episodic scenes from Manette's memory ends, the ancient prisoner rests his head on his arms to sob at the vividness of his recollections and at the remembered sweetness of the life that he will never know again.

The perfection and precise choreography of this imagined domestic tableau from the opening of the film would not be worthy of quite this degree of attention were it not then deliberately reprised, though now in noticeably adjusted form, as the final shot of the film. This closing imagined domestic tableau once again shows a husband and wife sitting together by a fire with their child. In both shot set-up and *mise-en-scène*, it deliberately recalls the earlier scene. Tonally, however, the moment has been transformed. Whereas the earlier tableau was a memory, summoned from the past partly in order to torment a doomed man with its remembered sweetness, the second is a prophecy, fantasized about the future in order to console a doomed man about the legacy he will leave behind. The doomed man is Sydney Carton who, in the closing moments of the film, stands on the steps of the guillotine fortifying his mind against his imminent fate.

This moment on the scaffold was, in fact, the visual moment through which the film was sold. The centre-spread of the film's press book privileges the image of Carton ascending the scaffold and looking skywards in a moment of near-transfiguration. The same image was used on all the advertisements placed in trade papers. It is a central heroic image that directly and deliberately echoed the promotional material for the highly popular stage version of *The Only Way* (discussed in Joss Marsh's essay in this volume). In referencing the iconic image of John Martin-Harvey as Carton in their own marketing materials, Fox therefore both aligned their production with the resounding success of the popular stage production that preceded it and simultaneously implied that they were summoning a similarly heroic picture of the character as that on offer in the closing moments of *The Only Way*.[21]

That implication is, however, daringly problematized in the closing moments of the 1917 film. Here the Fox adaptation aligns itself far more closely with the psychological ambiguities of the novel than with the idealized Carton of *The Only Way*'s final scene. Carton's final, unuttered thoughts in the novel carry a striking charge. Their 'unpronounced form of enunciation' generates what Garrett Stewart terms 'inner predictive speech'.[22] They read thus:

> I see that I hold a sanctuary in their hearts, and in the hearts of their descendants, generations hence. I see her, an old woman, weeping for me on the anniversary of this day. I see her and her husband, their course done, lying side by side in their last earthly bed, and I know that each was

not more honoured and held sacred in the other's soul, than I was in the souls of both.

I see that child who lay upon her bosom and who bore my name, a man, winning his way up in that path of life which once was mine. I see him winning it so well, that my name is made illustrious there by the light of his. I see the blots I threw upon it, faded away. I see him, foremost of just judges and honoured men, bringing a boy of my name, with a forehead that I know and golden hair, to this place – then fair to look upon, with not a trace of this day's disfigurement – and I hear him tell the child my story, with a tender and a faltering voice.

(III, xv, 390)

This self-consoling imagery which precedes his act of self-sacrifice provides a resonant echo of Darnay's vision, of the good that he thinks he might do by returning to Paris:

that glorious vision of doing good, which is so often the sanguine mirage of so many good minds, arose before him, and he even saw himself in the illusion with some influence to guide this raging Revolution that was running so fearfully wild.

(II, xxiv, 252)

Dickens is plainly suspicious of Darnay's 'glorious vision of doing good', and with reason. It is, we are told, a 'sanguine mirage', a willed delusion about his own magnanimous influence. The suspicion that attaches to Darnay's motivation here also inflects the final page of the novel, acting as an interpretive filter through which we can read Carton's hopes for the good that *his* sacrifice might achieve. Carton's final actions in the novel are nobly intended, masterfully enacted and considerably moving. But as John Glavin has persuasively demonstrated, his vision of their impact is also keenly and strategically self-serving.[23] In that vision, Carton sees Darnay, the man with whom he could not compete in life, soundly routed and unmanned – both domestically and dynastically. It is Carton's forename not Darnay's that the child will bear, and into Carton's profession that the child will go. It is Carton's name not Darnay's that will be 'made illustrious' through the child's future fortunes, and over Carton's memory that Lucie will weep and her son's voice falter. The vision is, in fact, one of appropriated paternity, Carton symbolically and triumphantly assuming the place of the man he 'might have been' and securing his influence down future generations. And in this way, Darnay is written out of his own family's ongoing legacy. Moreover, there is no domain of the actual marriage between Lucie and Darnay (for which Carton ostensibly dies) that he then imagines immune to the impact of his sacrifice. He even, therefore, foresees his honoured memory being cherished in their 'last earthly bed' – an image which, though literally a reference to their grave, inevitably calls to mind their earlier earthly bed also. Being chastely cherished may not have been precisely the presence in Lucie's bed that Carton might most have wished for in an ideal world; on the other hand, his hallowed presence in it is unlikely to bolster the physical fortunes of the man who is actually there. Inserting himself into every aspect of their married life is part of the consolation he offers himself for the sacrifice he makes. His prophecy acts, in effect, as the dastardly fulfilment of the promise he had extracted from Darnay in Book II, chapter 20 that he should be allowed free passage into their home (II, xx, 216). In his dream, he claims the previously offered 'privilege of coming in uninvited' on a permanent basis, taking up residence, it seems, in their very 'souls' (II, xxi, 219; III, xv, 390). Without wanting to detract from the scale of the sacrifice he makes for them, it is nevertheless difficult not to read Carton's dream of their sobered future devoted to his memory as founded on a quiet satisfaction at having outmanoeuvred his rival so irreversibly.

The 1917 film was made at a time when the American film industry was already known for its strong preference for happy endings. In 1916, a British spoof of *Macbeth* entitled *The Real Thing at Last* was made by Lloyd's fellow Scot, J. M. Barrie. Barrie's film had impishly imagined an American production of Shakespeare's play in which the action was parodically sensationalized and sexualized and the final intertitle card read: 'The Macbeths repent and all ends happily'.[24] It is testimony to how securely established an American predilection for neat narrative resolution already was that it could become a subject of gentle mockery in a British film and, moreover, that audiences could be relied on to be sufficiently familiar with the tendency to appreciate the joke. But at a moment when neat narrative resolution was already the preferred industry norm in America, and in response to a novel which has proved itself the excuse for generating just such an idealized and heroic ending in subsequent film adaptations,[25] the 1917 film of *A Tale of Two Cities* resists both the market pressure and the interpretive temptation in this respect. Instead, it draws directly on the equivocal twists of the novel itself for the character of its closing scene.

The pressure to steer the film to a harmonious closure was not, however, just external: the collective will for such a thing is also acknowledged within the narrative and thematic patterning of the film itself, thus making its subsequent refusal the more noticeable. The precise configuration of the earlier domestic tableau is part of the teasing establishment of an expectation that will then be strikingly denied. The function Carton's final imagined tableau *ought* to fulfil is the healing of that earlier imagined domestic tableau – the restitution of the family unit that had been broken in Manette's conjured picture of familial disruption. Where Manette remembers being torn from his wife and child, we might have expected Carton to see Manette's daughter enjoying the restoration of her husband to her. Where the ominous knock at the door requires Manette to look *away* from the scene of fireside tranquility and bliss, Lucie might be allowed the luxury of looking attentively and lovingly *towards* hers. This is the healed imagery which the earlier broken tableau craves. And since Carton's final thoughts do indeed posit a husband, wife and child (Lucie, Darnay and their son) sitting in close proximity by a fire, the skeletal architecture seems to be in place to answer this craving. The shading and detail of the scene, however, drain it of potential joy, decisively denying the possibility that this reunited family might symbolically mend the fracturing of the earlier disunited one. The ostensible togetherness of this family has been purchased at an unbearable cost to another (whose imagination produces the image) and the scene is made to bear the scars of that costly knowledge: this is a family burdened by mordancy and marked by tonal disjuncture. Eerily side-lit, Lucie (Jewel Carmen) attempts a smile at her husband but is clearly distracted by thoughts of the man who has died to make possible her family life. In her case there is no extrinsic call on her attention away from her family as there was for her father. Nonetheless, as Darnay kisses her hand, she looks wistfully away in the closing moments of the film in a melancholy absorption, preferring to separate herself from the family unit as she considers the sacrifice made on her behalf. The family may be together, but the rhymed blocking of the comparable acts of looking away across the two tableaux makes the implication clear: there is a corrosive influence that compromises the unity of this family too. More subtly, and more insidiously, however, this time the corrosion is intrinsic. Therefore, Carton's final, exquisitely consoling image is of a family weighed down by the enormity of the thing that has been done for them and of Lucie extracting herself from intimacy in order to dwell on it.

There is, however, no provision for this imagined tableau in Lloyd's working script. The film as configured in that late script draft ended thus:

```
SCENE 498.    SHOOTING FROM GUILLOTINE, SHOWING CROWD
BEYOND (PACKED)

Carton mounts steps and comes to foreground near
executioner - crowd yell with glee - Carton looks
around with slight smile -

SCENE 499.    CLOSE- UP OF CARTON.

        He looks from crowd to sky and says:

SUBTITLE "IT IS A FAR, FAR BETTER THING THAT I DO THAN I
        HAVE EVER DONE; IT IS A FAR, FAR BETTER REST
```

> THAT I GO TO THAN I HAVE EVER KNOWN."
>
> SLOW FADE.
>
> FINISH.[26]

The envisaged end thus leaves Carton on the block, his calmness and nobility intact and his intentions unsullied. The streamlined simplicity of the working script becomes yet more explicitly an appealingly altruistic heroism in the official plot synopsis given in the Fox press book:

> With a smile on his face he ascended the platform and in a second had made the supreme sacrifice for the woman he loved but could not have.
> He had sent the one she loved the most to the one he loved the most.[27]

Until the final seconds of the released film, it remains fully complicit with the film's script and the company's marketing in celebrating the undiluted self-sacrificial altruism of the moment. In relation to Darnay and to the seamstress ('Dorothy' in the working script, changed to 'Mimi' in the film to bring it into line with the equivalent character in *The Only Way*), Carton is the height of considerably affecting, self-denying nobility. But these things are dependent only on the outer world of action and social demeanour and, in production, the possibility of the final imagined tableau presented itself as a late-in-the-day addition and was duly shot and appended. This allowed the film to stray into another dimension of its central character, delving into 'some of [the] imaginings' of a 'beating heart' that were 'secret' to all else. In breaking the bounds of 'enclos[ure]' and making public the intensely private and self-consoling vision it finds there, it renders plain the interior mindscape (I, iii, 15). And the exposure of that mindscape complicates the moral tenor of the moment by challenging the impression of uncompromising heroism generated by the action-based scenes that precede it. Carton's pose on the scaffold may, therefore, be heroic, but his thoughts that find form in the film's coda, like those of his novelistic counterpart, are not entirely so. The insertion of this late-appended scene provides a purposeful, book-ended counterpoise to the Manette-conjured tableau that had seemed to beg an antiphonal response. Its interest lies in its obdurate refusal to provide precisely the sort of restorative answering imagery for which the earlier tableau implicitly yearns. It is a sensitive reading of the psychological ambiguities of the novel's final page and, moreover, in its eschewing of industrial market forces, a significantly daring one for its moment.

*

When Dickens's Sydney Carton ascends the steps of the guillotine, his death is offered to the crowd as a moment of public theatre, a spectacle for the voyeuristic gaze and collective appreciation of the crowd. The novel's narrator even reminds us that some of those destined to be 'the day's wine' for the ever-thirsty guillotine demonstrated their awareness of the grisly performance role allocated to them for this public event by 'cast[ing] upon the multitude such glances as they have seen in theatres, and in pictures' (III, xv, 384–5). Taking the story of an individual's death out of the quiet, familial, private spaces in which it should properly belong and exposing it as a public show for the assembled masses is part of the revolutionary project. The women knitting at the foot of the guillotine create an implied rhyme with the domestic environment. That rhyme, however, is unsparingly ironic since the scaffold is no private hearth where clothes are darned and broths made, but rather the theatrical set for a violent one-act drama that keeps reprising itself.[28]

There is, of course, a long-standing historical relationship between stage and scaffold, theatrical performance and the choreography of institutionalized death: they are comparable sites of salutary and diverting public show and have historically proved to be comparable modes of public entertainment.[29] The Lloyd film, through its own medium identity, also has an incidental affinity with the executioner's scaffold. It too takes a private narrative, a tale traditionally told through the domesticated medium of the novel in this case, and exposes it to wide public view through the processes of mass exhibition. A public execution, to which the crowds come and at which they gawp in horror and fascinated, voyeuristic delight, has points of correspondence with the exhibited public event of a projected work of cinema in both its formal and sociological aspects. In each case, the massed crowd is motivated by a keen interest in observing the fate of others and enjoys being able to watch the unfolding spectacle apparently with impunity. And in each case, attendance is accompanied by the twin desires to see the expected story unfold in the expected way, and to see something disruptive or surprising occur (a break from generic patterning, interpretive trend or usual star persona in the cinema; a falling wig, a witty or hysterical final remark, a head that obstinately refuses to be severed, a moment of unseemly struggle or desperation at the moment of execution).

The Fox *Tale of Two Cities* satisfies precisely the twin cravings for a familiar and reassuring outworking of a known story on the one hand, and a wish to be surprised by a radical moment of intervention into or divergence from that story on the other, which the crowd at an execution also ghoulishly desired. Here there is no unseemly struggle or falling wig, but there is a far more radical reading of the novel than the script had anticipated or the company's safer press book brief, peddling as it did undiluted, uninterrogated heroism, would have the market believe. The film, that is, was both planned and sold on simple truths about a Christ-evocative act of self-denying sacrifice. Having conservatively wooed its audience thus, however, the ending the film actually delivers is of a more challenging, and, we would argue, a more intuitively Dickensian hue. It is an ending by which the film seems to have been mugged while in production, an idea that emerged from the fabric of the narrative as it was being enacted. It is, after all, not with Sydney kneeling nobly by the block, but with his imaginary picture of Lucie's pained and poignantly disquieting act of turning away from Darnay that the screen fades to black. As sniper fire from dark doorways goes, it is a daring and a welcome ambush.

Acknowledgement

We are grateful to John Bowen for commenting helpfully on a draft of this chapter.

Notes

1. Julian Johnson, review article, *Photoplay* 12.1 (June, 1917), pp. 91–2. Reproduced in *Selected Film Criticism, 1912–1920*, ed. Anthony Slide (Metuchen, NY and London: Scarecrow Press, 1982), pp. 250–2, p. 251.
2. Advertisement in *The Bioscope*, 17 May 1917, p. xxxii.
3. Frank L. Dyer, 'The Moral Development of the Silent Drama', *Edison Kinetogram*, 15 April 1910, p. 11.
4. When the film was re-released in February 1920, it was sold thus: 'The Great VICTOR HUGO wrote it. The Great WILLIAM FARNUM enacts it. The Great FOX ORGANIZATION produced it. And every theatre is great during the run of LES MISERABLES.' *Moving Picture World* (*MPW*), 43.7 (14 February 1920), Fox insert supplement between pp. 1010 and 1011.
5. Fox's scenery for *Two Cities* was so detailed and robust, it was retained at Fox's West Avenue studios to be used in successive future productions, allegedly as late as the 1960s. See *Magill's Survey of Cinema: Silent Films*, ed. Frank Magill (Englewood Cliffs, NJ: Salem Press, 1982), vol. 3, p. 1089.
6. See the Fox advertisement for the re-release when, once again, Dickens's name received top billing: 'The great author CHARLES DICKENS. The great actor WILLIAM FARNUM. The great drama A TALE OF TWO CITIES'; 'No greater play. No greater author in the history of screen or stage. A proved and continuous success of yesterday, today and tomorrow.' *MPW* (14 February 1920).
7. Johnson, *Photoplay*, June, 1917. Reproduced in Slide, *Selected Film Criticism*, pp. 250–2.
8. With a similar sort of impressionistic energy, the *Working Script* describes the moment thus: 'AT DRAWBRIDGE. Crowd swimming in moat and scaling walls – some falling in water – Draabridge [*sic*] falls with a crash – crowd surge over it forcing one another in to the moat – they press on into the courtyard – ' scene 133, p. 30. In similar vein, at other times the script instructs 'AD LIB flashes . . . AD LIB SCENES OF FIGHTING AROUND BASTILE . . . Flash of fight – ' Scenes 127, p. 29; 130, p. 30; 138, p. 31. Frank Lloyd's working script was deposited at the Library of Congress (13 March 1917) for copyright registration. It comprises 99 unnumbered loose pages in typescript on thin typing paper: *A Tale of Two Cities. A Photoplay in Seven Parts . . . From the story by CHARLES DICKENS: Working Script for Lloyd no. 3*. Motion Picture, Broadcasting and Recorded Sound Division, Library of Congress call no. LP10375. Hereafter *Working Script*.
9. *Working Script*, scene 143, p. 33. Shots are given as scenes in all Fox scripts of this period.

10. *Working Script,* scene 144, p. 33.
11. This deviates from the opening intertitle on the Working Script (preceding scene 1), which is given as: 'Saint Antoine: a wretched and vicious district of Paris near the Bastile [*sic*]'. The knowing inscription of narrative destination must therefore have been added at a late stage. However, in the script Lloyd has left a note to himself by this intertitle to 'Put on footnote', clearly feeling it needed something additional in terms of historical weighting.
12. In the 1911 Vitagraph film of *A Tale of Two Cities,* separate actors – Maurice Costello and Leo Delaney – had played the parts of Darnay and Carton. Advances in double-exposure techniques since then had made possible the double casting of Farnum. This notwithstanding, the doubling in casting has not been repeated in sound era productions made for the big screen.
13. This was achieved by shooting each scene twice. For the first take, Farnum would be in role as one character, engaging with a clearly designated space on set which his other screen self would in due course occupy. For the second, in which Farnum took the other role, either the film would be rewound in the camera and the scene reshot onto the same strip of negative, or it would be shot onto a clean strip of negative and then a master positive printed from the two strips together, with both characters now present in the scene. One contemporary reviewer declared: 'the double exposure work sets a new mark for accuracy of timing'. *Variety,* 46.3 (16 March 1917), 34.
14. See, for example, Maxim Gorky's assertion that a screen person was 'not life but its shadow . . . not motion but its silent spectre . . . It is terrifying to see, but it is the movement of shadows, only of shadows.' From 'The Kingdom of Shadows', widely anthologized. See, for example, *Authors on Film,* ed. Harry M. Geduld (Bloomington, IN and London: Indiana University Press, 1972), pp. 3–7. These quotations, pp. 3 and 4. It was an impression that did not entirely fade even as the medium matured. In 1913, for example, Georg Lukács argued that the key difference between cinema and theatre was the cinema's ability to turn the real substance of the world into 'a life without a soul'. Lukács, 'Thoughts on an Aesthetic for the Cinema', *Framework,* 14.1 (Spring 1981), 3. This pulseless presence was regarded as the unnerving force of the medium.
15. Edward Weitzel's review, *MPW,* 31.13 (31 March 1917), 2118.
16. Johnson, *Photoplay* (June 1917). Reproduced in Slide, *Selected Film Criticism,* pp. 250–2.
17. The Working Script anticipates the scene thus: 'He finishes speaking line [*sic*] looking at his image which slowly changes to that of Darnay who looks proud and haughty – it fades back to Carton's image – Carton shrinks slightly at comparison – slowly reg[isters] disgust for himself – he looks again at image . . . suddenly reg[isters] rage against himself – storms at his own image and in drunken rage he raises wine glass to dash at his own image – pauses – looks at wine glass, slowly becomes maudlin and drinks – wine glass drops from his hand – he slowly leans on mantelpiece and drunkenly starts to sob – SLOW IRIS' (scene 244, pp. 52–3). The realized film omits the moment of near-rage and enhances the mood of maudlin resignation.
18. Laura Mulvey, *Death 24 x a Second* (London: Reaktion, 2006), p. 164.
19. On the body's mutability in early cinema, see Judith Buchanan, 'Celluloid formaldehyde? The body on film', ch. 16 in C. Saunders, U. Maude and J. MacNaughton (eds), *The Body and the Arts* (Basingstoke and New York: Palgrave Macmillan, 2008), pp. 260–76.
20. Working Script, scenes 12–14.

21. Early commentators explicitly compared the productions and the central performances. One, for example, found a 'spiritual exaltation' in Harvey's Carton which was 'lacking' in Farnum's. See Weitzel's review, *MPW* (31 March 1917), 2118.
22. Garrett Stewart, *Dear Reader: The Conscripted Audience in Nineteenth-Century British Fiction* (Baltimore, MD and London: Johns Hopkins University Press, 1996), p. 227.
23. See John Glavin, *After Dickens: Reading, Adaptation and Performance* (Cambridge: Cambridge University Press, 1999), pp. 144–5.
24. *The Real Thing at Last* is discussed in detail in Judith Buchanan, *Shakespeare on Silent Film: An Excellent Dumb Discourse* (Cambridge: Cambridge University Press, 2009), ch. 6.
25. The 1925 film of *The Only Way* shows Carton ascending the scaffold and looking skyward in a moment of spiritual transfiguration. His thoughts tend towards heaven rather than being directed towards his own earthly legacy. (We are grateful to Joss Marsh for access to a recording of this film.) The 1958 film starring Dirk Bogarde has Sydney in voice-over rejoicing that his life has not after all been entirely wasted. The 1980 BBC mini-series omits Darnay from Carton's interior monologue about the future he imagines for Lucie. As the blade descends, it then cuts to a still image of Lucie sitting in a garden in front of a big oak tree looking at her small son playing on the grass next to her. This image too implicitly writes Darnay out of the future. In the 1989 animated feature of the novel, there is no final visionary image. Only the 1980 version, therefore, allows for such an image, and then only a still.
26. Working Script, pp. 98–9. Spacing, capitalization and punctuation are given here as in script. This script erroneously lists titles as 'subtitles'. Other Fox scripts of the same era describe them as 'titles'.
27. The Fox press book for the 1917 *A Tale of Two Cities*. On microfiche at the BFI, London.
28. For a discussion of the various symbolic meanings of *La Guillotine* in 1790s France, see Regina Janes, *Losing Our Heads: Beheadings in Literature and Culture* (New York and London: New York University Press, 2005), ch. 3, pp. 67–96. Domestication is discussed briefly on p. 83.
29. See, for example, Molly Smith, 'The Theater and the Scaffold: Death as Spectacle in *The Spanish Tragedy*', *Studies in English Literature*, 32 (1992), 217–32.

10
Two Cities, Two Films

Charles Barr

According to the website of the British Film Institute, the 1958 British film of *A Tale of Two Cities* is 'certainly a faithful adaptation, following in a simple, straightforward manner (thanks to screenwriter T. E. B. Clarke) the narrative line of the book'.[1]

The film, like the novel, opens with a stagecoach on the road to Dover, carrying Mr Jarvis Lorry of Tellson's bank. But its passengers also include Sydney Carton. As in the novel, Lucie Manette is already on her way to meet Mr Lorry at Dover. But the passengers in her coach include not only her companion, Miss Pross, but Charles Darnay (*aka* Evrémonde), and the spy, John Barsad. In the novel, we do not meet, or hear of, Carton, Darnay or Barsad until the first chapter of Book II, which is set five years later. So, whatever it is, the adaptation is hardly simple or straightforward.

This is one of the two major adaptations of the novel for cinema of the sound period, as distinct from silent films and television versions, the other being the Hollywood production of 1935. Both are ambitious A-pictures with high production values and a top romantic star in the role of Carton: Ronald Colman (1935) and Dirk Bogarde (1958). Both are the work of high-profile producers and production companies: David O. Selznick for MGM in 1935, and the experienced team of Betty Box and Ralph Thomas for the Rank Organization in 1958. Both offer an intriguing blend of respect for the novel with radical changes – changes motivated both by the perceived requirements of the film medium and the film audience, and by the historical contexts in which they were made.

A Tale of Two Cities offers a more formidable challenge to the adapter than any of the other Dickens novels to which cinema has been repeatedly attracted, for reasons of both form and subject-matter. The adapter has to work hard to extract a clear and cohesive narrative line; and the subject-matter is the potentially incendiary one of popular revolution. Films can hardly avoid dramatizing the storming of the Bastille and showing what provoked it, but have to be very aware of the vigilance of the censors: these two films were made in the period when cinema was still the dominant medium

of mass entertainment (even though by 1958 it was in the process of yielding to television), and at times of intense anxiety about Soviet power and
influence.

In 1935 at least, it was impossible to focus on the French Revolution of
1789 without evoking the Bolshevik one of 1917, which had already been
re-enacted on film with incomparable vividness by V. I. Pudovkin and Sergei
Eisenstein. Both had made films in 1927 to celebrate the tenth anniversary
of the Revolution, respectively *The End of St Petersburg* and *October*, having
previously dramatized anticipatory episodes of revolt set a few years earlier:
Mother (Pudovkin, 1926) and *The Battleship Potemkin* (Eisenstein, 1925). These
Soviet films, shot silent but with stirring musical accompaniment, made a
profound impact in London and in Hollywood, less for their politics than for
their formal daring, though it was hard to separate the two.[2] The impact in
Hollywood of the rapid montage techniques used by *Potemkin*, in particular,
to dramatize oppression and revolt was so great that it would have been difficult for any film-maker, less than a decade later, to avoid showing awareness
of it when filming 1789. And the 1935 film-makers, as we shall see, in their
core action sequence do unmistakably take *Potemkin* as a model.

This is exciting but dangerous: the film has to avoid seeming to have Red
sympathies. Censors in both countries were nervous of the Soviet films and
of their inflammatory potential. In Britain they did not try to stop them
being screened to groups like the Film Society in London, made up mainly
of middle- and upper-class intellectuals, but both they and local authorities went to great lengths throughout the 1930s to block not just public
screenings – *Potemkin* did not receive a censor's certificate until 1954 – but
screenings to workers' associations.[3] If a film of an ultimately unsuccessful
1905 revolt in Russia, prefiguring the successful Revolution of 1917, might
seem to risk encouraging unrest in the West in the 1930s, might not the same
apply to a film of 1789 in France? It seems very possible that the 1935 film
of *A Tale of Two Cities* was censored in Britain for this reason. The records of
the British Board of Film Censors show that the film was indeed cut when
submitted to them early in 1936, but no details are available of how much
footage was removed or from what part of the film, though the montage of
the storming of the Bastille seems by far the likeliest. In contrast, the 1958
film was passed without any cuts, its central sequence being considerably
shorter and tamer.[4]

These sequences are considered in more detail below; the point here is to
establish at the start one of the special challenges posed to film-makers by
this novel and to foreground the figure of Sergei Eisenstein.

Eisenstein and Dickens

Eisenstein wrote about cinema with the same intensity as he made his films,
and more prolifically. His essay 'Dickens, Griffith and the Film Today',

published in 1944 and much reprinted, remains a seminal document in film theory for its pioneering analysis of the affinities and continuities between cinema and the nineteenth-century novel, Dickens in particular.[5] It focuses both on the comparable role of the two media in their time in communicating with a massive popular audience and on the devices with which they do so: interweaving of public and private stories, and formal devices such as close-up and cross-cutting. Eisenstein takes delight in finding what seem to be anticipations of such tropes in Dickens, as in the Griffith-like 'dissolve' that opens the final chapter of *A Tale of Two Cities*:

> Six tumbrils roll along the streets. Change these back again to what they were, thou powerful enchanter, Time, and they shall be seen to be the carriages of absolute monarchs, the equipages of feudal nobles, the toilettes of flaring Jezebels, the churches that are not my father's house but dens of thieves, the huts of millions of starving peasants.[6]

Grahame Smith builds extensively on this essay in his vigorous book on *Dickens and the Dream of Cinema*, and cites another suggestive passage from the novel (*TTC*, II, xv, 173), in which Defarge conducts a comrade to Dr Manette's old room:

> 'Come, then! You shall see the apartment that I told you you could occupy. It will suit you to a marvel'.
>   Out of the wine-shop into the street, out of the street into a court-yard, out of the court-yard up a steep staircase, out of the staircase into a garret...[7]

Surely to read this, or to hear it read, many decades before the emergence of cinema itself must already have been to 'see' in the mind's eye a rapid sequence of images, which will be so easily translatable when the time comes into visual montage, just as to read the passage about the tumbrils is to 'see' the dissolve. Neither Eisenstein nor Smith says much more about this novel, both using *Oliver Twist* (1838) as their main case study (the novel for Eisenstein, the 1948 David Lean film for Smith), but other passages leap out from the text if one reads it with their perspective in mind. A prime reference point for Eisenstein is the long section of *Oliver Twist* (chapters 14–15) in which Oliver, entrusted by Brownlow and Grimwig with cash to take to the bookseller, is recaptured and returned to Fagin, and we 'cut back' repeatedly to the two men as they wait vainly for Oliver to return. *A Tale of Two Cities* uses exactly the same trope, close to the end, when Lucie and her child are still not out of danger. Miss Pross and Jerry Cruncher engage in protracted conversation, while all the time 'Madame Defarge, pursuing her way along the streets, came nearer and nearer'. Four times in all Dickens 'cuts away' briefly like this, in a suspense passage for which the term Hitchcockian seems quite appropriate.

As it happens, none of these three tempting passages is lifted and translated by the film-makers in 1935 or 1958, not because they are too obtuse to see the opportunity, but because their narratives have other priorities – neither of them, for instance, wants to keep Jerry hanging around chatting. The affinities between the media go deeper than isolated opportunities for exact transfer: both films, made in the orthodox 'classical' style, find their own opportunities for suspense, quick montage and dramatic or intimate cutting. One great value of the Eisenstein essay is that it makes questions of close 'fidelity' in adapting a text seem petty. He is concerned not with specific adaptations but with the overarching affinities between the Dickens novels and popular cinema of his time, and between the expressive economy of their respective systems for communicating, verbally and audiovisually, with mass audiences across boundaries of nation and class. He celebrates Dickens's energy in reaching out to audiences and adapting his own work for different contexts such as public readings, and would assuredly have been sympathetic in principle to the project of adapting and compressing *A Tale of Two Cities* into a two-hour narrative for an interwar or postwar audience. It would be fascinating to have his response to the 1935 film and to the fairly clear *homage* to his own form of montage cinema at its centre, but if he ever saw it, his response is not on record.

Structural reworking

For Selznick and MGM, *A Tale of Two Cities* followed on directly from the commercial and critical success, the previous year, of *David Copperfield*.[8] Betty Box and Ralph Thomas had not engaged with Dickens before, but there had already been five British adaptations of his novels since the end of the Second World War, financed mostly by the Rank Organization, including the most enduring and distinguished of the five, the David Lean film of *Great Expectations*.[9] A compulsive generator of memoranda, Selznick left a clear record of the difficulty he encountered in moving from one novel to the other. Writing to his script editor Kate Corbaley, he notes:

> I am astonished myself at the fact that the more I work on it, the more I feel the difficulties of getting on screen what you and I both like to think is in the book. It is amazing that Dickens had so many brilliant characters in *David Copperfield* and so few in *A Tale of Two Cities*. There are twenty or perhaps forty living, breathing, fascinating people in *David Copperfield* and practically none in *A Tale of Two Cities*.[10]

The fact that *David Copperfield* is, like *Great Expectations* (1861), told in the first person makes things altogether simpler: starting from a childhood perspective, both books provide an array of idiosyncratic and memorable characters, and the adapter can condense incident ruthlessly to fit a two-hour running time while relying on the momentum of a strong and clear story-line centred on the adventures of the hero. The four other British films of the postwar decade, although not based on first-person novels, are all able, likewise, to foreground a central character in their titles and in their narrative line – Nicholas Nickleby, Oliver Twist, Scrooge, Pickwick – and have no shortage of colourful characters to draw on.[11] Only *Oliver Twist*, with its complex back-story about Oliver's family, poses any real structural problems, but these are minor compared with *A Tale of Two Cities*.[12]

One immediate and understandable strategy is to bring it into line somewhat with the other narratives by making it more like the 'Life and Adventures of Sidney Carton'. The pattern of stage adaptations is followed in the creation of strong starring roles for Ronald Colman and, even more so, Dirk Bogarde: while it is not until over twenty minutes into his film that Colman appears, Bogarde does so in the first scene, in the seventh shot, and a glamorous star entrance it is, with a light shining on his sleeping face and causing him to turn and face the camera as he wakes. Yet even with such a starting point, there is no way in which a whole film can centre on Carton, as on David or Pip, if the narrative is to remain recognizable as Dickens's *A Tale of Two Cities*, and this is what both Selznick and Box were committed to, trading on the continuing status of the book as a popular classic.[13]

In what follows, I label the two films primarily by the names of the two producers, David O. Selznick and Betty Box, both of them powerful operators. This is in preference to studio, director, writer or star, all of whom could lay claim to a share in the films' authorship. Both producers ran their own units within MGM and the Rank Organization respectively, though of course ultimately being answerable to them. Jack Conway (1935) was an efficient journeyman director, mainly of action films, who worked very much under orders, as Selznick always required, and he had to cede the central scene of the film, the storming of the Bastille, to a separate unit. Ralph Thomas (1958) spent almost his entire career in partnership with Box, and one should perhaps label the film Box/Thomas, but no one has ever claimed a distinctive directorial style or signature for him, any more than for Conway; like the other films of the partnership, it seems a producer's film more than a director's.[14] As for the writers, both are solid English professionals, linked, as it happens, through their affiliation with that most craftsmanlike of English studios, Ealing, during the twenty-year leadership of Michael Balcon (1938–58). T. E. B. Clarke, who has sole credit in 1958, was Ealing's most prominent writer during the postwar decade, responsible for several of the most famous comedies, including *The Lavender Hill Mob*, which won him a script Oscar in 1952. W. P. Lipscomb is jointly credited in 1935 with S. N. Behrman. Selznick writes of relying on Behrman for dialogue,[15] so Lipscomb presumably had laid down the structure; he had already worked with Balcon at Gaumont-British before moving to Hollywood on the strength of his hit play *Clive of India* (filmed by Twentieth Century at around the same time), and he returned to work with Balcon at Ealing in the 1950s.

Both films, then, have the novel reworked for the screen by quality English writers who can be trusted to do a respectful, pragmatic job. The films, strongly cast, come right from the heart of the commercial industry of their respective times and countries. The structural challenges to the adapter can be focused through three main issues: the double, time-scale and authorial voice. Their solutions are so different that there is no question of the first film being a remake of the second.

The double

Colman was evidently reluctant at first to accept the role of Carton because he did not want to double it with that of Charles Darnay, and assumed that this would be part of the deal.[16] But such doubling is by no means the norm. The British silent film of 1928, *The Only Way*, with John Martin-Harvey – a far freer, stage-based adaptation than the Box or Selznick ones, discussed in Joss Marsh's contribution to this volume – does not double the parts, but, like every adaptation, it is has to deal with the early scene at the Old Bailey (2, iii) in which the corrupt agent Barsad, who claims to have witnessed the treasonable handover of secret papers, is confounded by the extraordinary resemblance between the two men, and thus has his confident identification of Darnay as the culprit thrown into question, 'The upshot of which was to smash this witness like a crockery vessel, and shiver his part of the case to useless lumber' (p. 77). The producers of *The Only Way* seem to have searched for the closest lookalike they could find for Martin-Harvey, irrespective of experience or acting ability, and the courtroom scene is thus quite effective on its own terms, with intercutting between the two faces and the amazed reactions of others; and the weakness of the actor, painfully evident in all his other scenes, does have the effect of setting off all the more strongly the charisma of Carton and of the star for whom the book has been reshaped as a vehicle: he gives, for instance, long and dramatic speeches to the Tribunal. But neither Selznick nor Box is ready to follow that extreme strategy.

As Darnay, Box casts Paul Guers, one of only two French actors in the film, in what remains his only British appearance; he is clearly chosen for his broad resemblance to Bogarde.[17] As noted above, both men appear right at the start, in the two coaches that converge upon Dover. Lucie has already met and been charmed by Darnay when she enters the inn at Dover and sees Carton slumped in a chair, his face turned away from her in drink-induced sleep. Her quick greeting to him, 'Oh, Mr Darnay', is neatly and plausibly managed, and sets up an affinity that is, as in Dickens, useful both thematically and, looking ahead to the court scene, pragmatically. In court, the film contrives a long shot with both characters in frame together, in profile, so that the witness (in this case Cly), the court and the viewer can register the similarity, but they are hardly doubles, nor, wisely, does the film make everything rest on the likeness in itself, there being other circumstantial evidence; and the verdict remains genuinely in doubt till the last minute.

Illustration 10.1   1935: Donald Woods as Darnay, Ronald Colman as Carton

Illustration 10.2   1958: Paul Guers as Darnay, Dirk Bogarde as Carton

Contrast the Selznick strategy. There is no facial similarity at all between Colman as Carton and Donald Woods as Darnay, nor is there any effort to approximate one by make-up or camera trickery. Yet when Carton stands up in court and shows himself, the witness, Barsad, is indeed at once 'smashed ... like a crockery vessel', and the Not Guilty verdict becomes a foregone conclusion.

How is this made plausible? By the preceding scenes, which have no equivalent in the novel. When Stryver tells him the details of the forthcoming trial, Carton recognizes the name of the informer, Barsad, and resolves to track him down – which he does, using his familiarity with London low-life to insinuate himself as a drinking companion of Barsad and to elicit confidences from him about his role in framing Darnay. Thus, Carton needs only to show his face to him the next day in court to make Barsad realize that his perjury will be exposed, and to cause him at once to retract his evidence.

Dickensian purists were no doubt offended by this invention, but it can be seen as a triumphant instance of bold reworking. The courtroom coup, based on facial similarity, was never going to be easy to make convincing, as indeed it hardly is in the original: so, the film finds an alternative that *is* convincing.[18] The stratagem has the advantage of enacting Carton's familiarity with low-life and drinking dens more vividly than the novel does through its baleful hints. It also, for better or worse, establishes Carton as, from the start, a more active and positive figure than in the novel, appropriate to Colman's star persona and to the whole goal-oriented thrust of the 'classical Hollywood' model.

Time-scale and back-story

The Selznick contrivance over the lead-up to the trial is only one instance of the radical reconstruction that both films recognize as necessary. The papers left by Box's writer, Clarke, contain disappointingly little on the film, but one thing they do offer is a thorough scene-by-scene breakdown of the narrative of the novel, as the raw plot material that had to be reworked.[19] Maybe somewhere else there survives a chart of the time-line distilled from it, which would look in outline something like this, in terms of Manette and family:

1755 Manette married
1757 Manette imprisoned; birth of Lucie
1767 Manette's letter hidden in the Bastille

1775 Manette recalled to life ... reunion, first meeting with Darnay
1780 trial of Darnay, leading to fuller acquaintance, then marriage
       (first appearance of Carton, in court)

1789   Revolution – main characters in England
1792   various trips to France
1793   death of Carton

Simplification and compression: these are intelligent strategies for a two-hour narrative, for an audience who have no chance, as the original readership did, to discuss and revisit the narrative as it unfolds, and who are so much further away in time from, and less familiar with, the historical events. Selznick simply opens with a title placing the film in 'the late 18th century', and Box has no specific date at any point. Everyone knows the date 1789, and the films are basically '1789, and events leading up to it'.

The 'Recalled to Life' moment is the starting point for both films, as for the novel, but neither allows a significant gap between then and the trial. Box goes further in compressing the time-scale: her 1958 film, apart from an early flashback, spans just two years in all.[20] Lucie is still pregnant with her first child when she goes to Paris, which provides Mme Defarge with a surpassingly strong motive for killing her and exterminating the Evrémonde line. Selznick retains the daughter and gets effective pathos out of her, which means she has to be given time to be born and grow; a slightly awkward five-year time gap is thus inserted in the dialogue between the killing of the Marquis and the approach of the Revolution. This also allows Carton to become close to the child and deepens his relation with Lucie, an absence that the Box film arguably suffers from.[21] Neither film, mercifully, retains the second child (who dies before the Revolution), and they likewise, just as sensibly, ignore the book's revelation that Barsad is Miss Pross's long-lost brother.

But however much they compress the main narrative, the films have to find ways of conveying the complex backstory: the acts of rape and murder by the Evrémondes; Manette's consignment to the Bastille for eighteen years to stop him revealing his knowledge of these acts; the fact that the surviving sister of the abused family was saved by Manette's servant Defarge and married him; Darnay's identity as an Evrémonde; and the document written by Manette ten years into his imprisonment and concealed by him behind a wall in his cell. There are three broad ways of handling the basic material of the outrage: prologue, flashback and dialogue. The film of *The Only Way* puts it in a prologue; Selznick does it by dialogue; Box by flashback, narrated by Lorry to Lucie before she meets her father. But whichever way is chosen – and all three have their advantages and disadvantages – this still leaves the considerable task of working out in detail the flow of information to both audiences and characters. When and how does Manette (and likewise Lucie and Carton) learn that Darnay is an Evrémonde? When do we learn that Mme Defarge is the surviving sister from the victimized family? When do we learn of the existence of a hidden document? The two films handle all these details in different ways, just as they give a different placement to, for instance, the scene of Manette's compulsion to return to the bootmaking of the days before his recall to life. Essentially, the two films use the building-blocks of the Dickens narrative, creating structures that differ from each other and from the novel, but that combine skilfully to tell the same basic story, and that lead via the same historical event, the Revolution, to the same outcome, Carton's substitution of himself for Darnay and his death on the guillotine while the family returns safely to England. It would be wearisome to trace the difference in the structures in detail, and here I simply refer to and endorse an essay by Brian Bialkowski: drawing on Roland Barthes's approach to the structural study of narrative, he uses the 1935 film, and in particular its handling of Barsad, as 'an excellent example of how certain major changes may be made without subtracting from the cohesiveness of the adaptation' and without being unfaithful in spirit, as opposed to detail.[22]

Authorial voice: Gabelle

> I am simply trying to point out to you the difficulties of getting the Dickens feeling, within our limitations of being able to put on the screen only action and dialogue scenes, without Dickens's comments as narrator.
>
> (Selznick to his script editor, Kate Corbaley)[23]

One clear way in which the film addresses itself to this difficulty is via the character of Gabelle – the agent who is left on the estate after the killing of the Marquis and is instructed by the absent Darnay to deal charitably with the peasants. He is crucial to Dickens's plot, in that it is his desper-ate appeal by letter to Darnay, whom he still knows as Evrémonde, that brings him to Paris and into mortal danger, but he remains a shadowy and colourless figure with no moral weight. Both films seize on Gabelle as a voice through which to articulate first opposition to aristocratic excesses and then dismay at the excesses of revolutionary vengeance. Where the novel's other characters necessarily have their actions and speeches cut, his are expanded: he is, in both films, introduced much earlier, and integrated into the Evrémonde household.

In the Box film it is Gabelle (played by Ian Bannen) who brings Dr Manette to the dying girl in the early flashback and who then takes him to see her dying brother, stabbed by the Marquis when he tried to defend his sister. The Marquis rebukes and strikes Gabelle for this, but does not dismiss him: it is Manette, not dependent on his patronage, who is the danger and who is therefore consigned to the Bastille. But Gabelle is established as a force of dis-sent from within, and articulates this in his second appearance, in the film's present time. Coming to inform the Marquis of the arrival of Barsad, who brings news of Darnay's forthcoming trial, he finds him embracing a young woman, whom we then discover to be Gabelle's own daughter. Outside the door, they exchange these concise lines:

Oh father, I hate . . .
    I know, child, I know – but as long as they have these rights, you know what it means to resist
    If only Monsieur Charles would come back

Later we see him, along with his daughter, protesting in vain against arrest by citizens. While we do not see him subsequently writing his letter of appeal to Darnay, his role as innocent victim, swept away despite his liberal views and actions, is carried forward through the daughter: she becomes the companion of Carton on his final journey to the guillotine, replacing the anonymous seamstress of the book, and of the Selznick film. Like the invented Selznick scene between Carton and Barsad before the Old Bailey trial, this substitution is an admirably bold, neat and justifiable screenwriter's device. But Gabelle himself has too little screen-time for the reworking to count for much in terms of authorial voice.

Selznick gives far more weight to Gabelle, in casting, in the plot and in dialogue. He is played by H. B. Warner, known above all as Christ in Cecil B de Mille's 1927 production of *King of Kings*, and his role here as a courageous martyr carries certain echoes of that one.[24] His Gabelle has become not just a managing agent of the Marquis, but tutor to his nephew. He has four scenes, all of them important:

1. The first time we see Darnay, he is in the company of Gabelle as well as Evrémonde, leaving the family estate for a new life in England. Gabelle bids him a warm farewell ('God bless you, Charles'), the Marquis a bitter one: he blames Gabelle for having introduced him to dangerous egalitarian ideas. But there is a teasing note to the Marquis's attack; as in the Box film, Gabelle is not perceived as dangerous.
2. Gabelle is with the Marquis on the night of his death, discussing rents, arguing the case of the starving peasants, but making no impression. We already know that Gaspard is outside the bedroom window, primed for killing: when the Marquis hears a noise, Gabelle investigates, but reports seeing nothing. In the novel, and in the Box film, it is Darnay who is on the premises that night, giving a sense that the killing is done in response to his unspoken wishes: here, it is like a punishment willed, and unconsciously abetted, by Gabelle for the rejection of his humanitarian arguments.
3. A dramatic screen-filling title makes a bridge across five years into the next scene:

    THIS WAS THE WARNING. IF ONE TYRANT COULD DIE,
    MANY COULD DIE. BUT THE APPROACHING FOOTSTEPS

OF A BITTER PEOPLE FOUND NO ECHO IN THE MINCING MEASURES OF THE MINUET

Again, Gabelle is centre-stage. In a lengthy scene, his impassioned plead-ing is received with contemptuous amusement by a roomful of complacent aristocrats as they wait to join the ladies after dinner. The elaborate *mise-en-scène* of their luxuriant indolence has, like the written title, the same repelling function as Dickens's set-piece at the start of the chapter titled 'Monseigneur the Marquis in Town' (II, vii), and Gabelle's oratory spells out what is surely the essence of Dickens's perspective on the Revolution – that the aristocrats could and should have avoided it by concessions, but got what they deserved, unleashing forces that would become uncontrol-lable. 'You may laugh, gentlemen, but revolution is in the air . . . all the people ask is justice . . . only the Jacquerie are extremists . . . give the people bread, reduce their taxes . . . Correct your errors, or the flood will come, a flood that may sweep us all away forever.'

4. Shortly after this comes the onset of that flood, the great set-piece of the storming of the Bastille, followed directly by Gabelle's fourth and final scene, in which he is himself swept away forever. He is held and taunted by the film's core Jacquerie quartet: the Defarge couple, the Vengeance, Gaspard. If he is indeed a friend of the people, a tutor who taught egali-tarian philosophy to Darnay and implemented it on his estate, let him summon Darnay to England to speak on his behalf. So Gabelle writes the letter; it is seized and brandished triumphantly; protesting, he is stabbed to death by Gaspard. In the next scene, we see Darnay receiving the letter and acting on it, walking into the trap.

The film thus again extrapolates from what we are given in the book, the arrival of the letter, to construct a strong new sequence that is consistent with the logic of the story. Gabelle's four scenes play out an exemplary Dickensian trajectory both through what he articulates and through the arc of his story: urging the right humanitarian course, not listened to, then falling victim to the vengeful mob, just like those who had ignored him.

The scenes get additional force not only from the strength of the actor's performance, but also from his remarkable similarity to Dr Manette. It is as if the theme of the double, ignored in the casting of Darnay and Carton, has been displaced onto this pair. The actors, born less than three years apart, are uncannily alike even in name: H. B. (Harry) Warner as Gabelle and, as Manette, Henry B. Walthall, one of the great film actors of his time, who died not long after this film was made, but who is remembered for his work with D. W. Griffith and the young John Ford.[25] Both men, as senior character actors, have a moral stature, based on a string of preceding roles, which most audiences of the time would at some level recognize, and which comes through even for modern audiences, who may know nothing of those roles,

Illustration 10.3   1935: Henry B.Walthall as Manette, H. B. Warner as Gabelle

on the basis simply of what is on screen. Their facial similarity is enhanced by parallels in stance, framing and delivery. Both pen a document which is then exploited against their wishes by Mme Defarge and her associates, in order to trap Darnay: this parallel is there in the book, but buried: the film brings it out, and increases the pathos of Dr Manette's story by having a second worthy white-haired man bewildered by the tide of events in which he is caught up.

'. . . a period very like the present' (from the introduction to the 1935 film)

Of course, this building up of Gabelle's role is more than simply the solution to a structural problem: it carries a message for the 1930s, warning government of the need to avoid provoking revolution, and warning the people of the dangers of unleashing it. In the words of Pierre Sorlin: 'historical films are concerned with the problems of the present even if that concern is expressed only indirectly.'[26] One thing that gives the Lean film of *Great Expectations* such an enduringly high rank among Dickens adaptations is the way it constitutes such a meaningful fable for its historical moment in 1946, and draws energy from that topicality.[27] At the other extreme, the 1989 TV adaptation of *A Tale of Two Cities*, widely disseminated internationally via TV and then DVD, has the twin handicap of having no other *raison d'être* than a dutiful bicentenary one, and being a Franco-British production (French director, British writer, appropriately mixed cast), thus further inhibiting the development of a distinctive angle: any political meaning is drained off, leaving only scraps of effective melodrama.[28] It is time to look more closely at the 1935 and 1958 films in this perspective, in relation to their time.

The first image of the former is of a page being turned to reveal these initial lines (the ellipsis is the film's, not mine):

> It was the best of times, it was the worst of times, it was the season of Light, it was the season of Darkness, we had everything before us, we had nothing before us … in short, it was a period very like the present.

Generating the film out of an initial printed page is a conventional strategy of the period, used also by Selznick in *David Copperfield* and by Lean in 1946: an assurance that we are about to see a respectful version of the classic text. Here, we can note that Selznick has made the 119 words of the novel's first paragraph more digestible by condensing them into 44, and has, in so doing, thrown a stronger grammatical and rhetorical emphasis onto the comparison with the present. *Qua* photographed page, the words refer us to Dickens's 'present' of the late 1850s; *qua* opening caption, they refer us to the film's 'present' of the mid-1930s. In the words of Jason W. Stevens, 'Within its first few seconds [the film] invites a parallel between 1785 and New Deal-era America in the process of recovering from its crisis of authority'.[29] The 1958 film not only has no such initial book-page (by then a less common device), it also seems less interested in any contemporary meanings.

Selznick 1935: politics

Stevens's essay astutely draws out the 1930s parallels. On the one hand, the film creates sympathy with the Revolution, tapping into memories of both the American Revolution and recent anti-Hoover unrest. On the other, it warns that mob violence inevitably gets out of hand and leads to 'a transgression of family and God'. Better to trust the government of Roosevelt, who has followed the policy articulated by Gabelle, that of defusing unrest by action against hunger and poverty. But Stevens goes too far in ascribing to the film a 'simple, conservative message', one that is 'opposed by the novel itself'.[30]

One factor is the way the film builds upon the novel's brief early allusion to George Washington, making him a key reference point in a scene that is central in both timing and importance. An invented dinner party at the family home bridges the gap between Gabelle's elaborate warning to the aristocrats and the storming of the Bastille. Present are Manette, Darnay, Carton, Lorry and Stryver. Carton and Stryver argue; the other three simply express feeble trust that moderation will prevail.

> STRYVER: The trouble is the aristocrats weren't firm enough. They should hang a few hoodlums, and that's all the revolution there will be.

CARTON: That's the kind of talk that cost us the American colonies.
STRYVER: We lost the colonies because they fell under the spell of that upstart Washington.
CARTON: Well, the time may come when the upstart Washington is remembered as a better Englishman than George III.[31]

This last line is picked up from the much earlier Old Bailey scene in the novel, where Lucie recalls Darnay having spoken it, five years ago, 'in a jesting way'. It has incomparably greater weight when spoken seriously in close-shot by Colman-as-Carton on the eve of Revolution, and juxtaposed with the habitual reactionary rant of Stryver. No amount of subsequent Terror can obliterate the careful parallel that has been spelled out. Nor can the Terror retrospectively cancel out the force of the 'revolutionary sequence' itself.

Among the initial credits we read: 'Revolutionary Sequences Arranged by Val Lewton and Jacques Tourneur'; in effect it is a single long sequence. Young film-makers with European roots, Russian and French respectively, Lewton and Tourneur later collaborated on a classic series of low-budget horror films such as *Cat People* (1942). Here, they deliver an intense set-piece lasting seven and a half minutes, a self-contained 'montage sequence': the storming of the Bastille, plus its build-up and aftermath. These are some of the ways in which it clearly, and exuberantly, draws on the example of Soviet silent montage cinema, and of Eisenstein's *The Battleship Potemkin* in particular:

- There is no dialogue, apart from a rallying-cry at the start from Mme Defarge.
- The cutting rate is extremely fast. The average shot length for the film up to this point has been a relatively sedate 10 seconds: for this sequence, it is 2.8 seconds.
- The trigger for the rising is anger over the denial of meat. In *Potemkin*, the sailors complain about their meat ration being made inedible through infestation by maggots; here, the starving people watch meat being fed by servants to their masters' dogs and break down the gates in protest – a scene that has no equivalent in Dickens.
- A key moment of suspense follows the arrival of troops to quell the violence. Will they fire on the crowd? No. Instead, they take their side, and the people exult. The tempo is very like the two scenes in *Potemkin*, one early and one late, in which Russian troops refuse to fire on rebels.
- The realization that they are not to be fired on is registered by a very rapid montage of close-ups of happy faces, a pattern that recurs several times in these seven and a half minutes: anonymous faces, ordinary people, sad or happy, but subsumed within the mass.
- Other images recall *Potemkin*: long shots of massive crowds (no CGI here), brief low-angle shots of troops wielding weapons.

Illustration 10.4   1935: WHY [should we endure it]? – the fourth in the series of titles, larger each time

- Written titles are used in an agitprop style akin to that of the Soviet films. Echoing Mme Defarge's cry to the people 'Why do you endure it?', the word WHY? is superimposed on the action five times, every time larger (Illustration 10.4).

It is hard to imagine any audience not being caught up in this sequence, exhilarated by it, rejoicing in the storming of the Bastille, as in the storming of the Winter Palace in *October* and *The End of St Petersburg*. To be sure, the montage ends with admonitory screen-filling titles about how the violence goes too far, culminating in this:

SO HATRED AND BLOODLUST
WERE THE INEVITABLE
ECHOES OF THE FOOTSTEPS
THE NOBLES FLED OR DIED
AND THE MOB RULED.

Yes, 'inevitable'. But compare here the 1958 British film of *Dracula*, recently, as it happens, restored and re-released by the BFI.[32] The film's conservative ideology, based on a simple good/evil polarity, is often emphasized by commentators. At the end, the women, whose sexuality has been so startlingly and so vividly (for the period) aroused by Dracula, are safely dead or, in the case of Mina, restored to wifely decorum: the natural order has been restored.

But why do people go to see the film, what do they remember of it, and why do they return to it? Unquestionably, the thrill of the release, not the conventional clamping down. This is an extreme case of an operation common to genre films, indeed to a wider range of narratives, and *A Tale of Two Cities* fits the pattern. To put it schematically, the storming of the Bastille is stirringly positive, in spirit like a combination of 1776 with the Roosevelt New Deal itself, and the hatred and bloodlust are an addendum, easily detachable by audiences. The film indeed has it both ways.

Any such reading is ultimately speculative; what is undeniable is that the Selznick film does engage seriously with these issues. It is unmistakably aware of the four historical reference points: the American and Bolshevik Revolutions as well as the French one, and the turbulence of the 1930s. In contrast, the 1958 British film, understandably, makes little of the American parallel, nor does its 'revolutionary sequence' evoke Eisenstein; it is half the length of the Lewton–Tourneur montage and much less forceful. Although the cutting rate is roughly the same, it is less of a contrast with what precedes it, since the average shot length up to now has been only seven seconds, compared with ten; and it makes repeated use of superimposition, for instance close-ups of cannons over faces, a distancing and aestheticizing device that works against the visceral involvement promoted by Eisensteinian montage cinema. The Box film clearly does not want to provoke such an involvement, whereas Selznick does. It has no equivalent of the scene where Gabelle's pleas to the aristocrats to show mercy to the people are scorned. Selznick first, with that scene, screws up the frustration and anger against that whole class, and then releases it in the montage of revolt. Box has no other representative of the oppressors than Evrémonde, now dead, and his associate Foulon; the film is angled much more towards family melodrama. It comes from a context of greater tranquility, and a cinema of much less dynamism, than the Selznick film: Britain, and the British cinema, of the 1950s.

Robert Giddings makes this connection, in an essay that complements that of Stevens on the 1935 film:

> *A Tale of Two Cities* has the fingerprints of the 1950s all over it and the film sits comfortably in its historical moment. The film's main action is placed in the context of threatening revolutionary change, but its narrative style ... is timidly conformist ...
> Britain in the 1950s may have had its drab side, but it afforded a safe view of European intensities.[33]

Box 1958: sexuality

Comfortable, conformist, safe: Giddings's words are appropriate, evoking the drab England, and southern English cinema, that Lindsay Anderson wrote about so impatiently in 1957.[34] Of course, things were soon to change, indeed were already changing, but Box and Thomas were not the kind of film-makers to be alert and responsive to this. Three years later they would film a political novel by the Labour MP Wilfred Fienburgh, *No Love for Johnnie* (1961). In her autobiography, Box writes:

I personally wasn't interested in the colour of our hero's politics; I thought Fienburgh had written an absorbing contemporary story with good characters and I didn't wish to lean on the political side of the piece – it was intended to be entertaining, which is what movies are supposed to do.[35]

The same thinking permeates the Dickens film; her chapter on it, dealing solely with production anecdotes, could not be more of a contrast to the urgency of the Selznick memoranda. Dirk Bogarde summed up the political side of it neatly: 'It did not transfer to the screen of the late fifties. It was not of its time.'[36]

Where the 1958 film still does have life and tension, and relates to its time in a more organic way, is in two performances: those of Bogarde himself and of Christopher Lee.

Lee brings to his brief role as Evrémonde exactly the aristocratic disdain and sexual ruthlessness that made his Dracula, soon after, so scarily definitive. Images like his preying upon Gabelle's daughter, and his dead body with a stake-like dagger through the heart, are directly evocative of that film, which had its premiere only four months later, in May 1958. Its power, and its impact on audiences, clearly relate to the thrilling way it was able to dramatize the return of the repressed in sexual terms, after a decade of mainly restrained and repressed British films. So this small corner of the 1958 *Tale of Two Cities* is a reminder of what was a more productive topical concern for British cinema at that moment than the story of the French Revolution.

As for Bogarde, he is by far the most of interesting of the British stars of his generation, not least for his subversion of the conventional images of masculinity offered by the likes of such contemporaries as Kenneth More, Jack Hawkins and Richard Todd. Andy Medhurst has traced the way in which, around the turn of the decade, he extends this subversion through a series of roles that are either implicitly or – with *Victim*, in 1961 – explicitly homosexual.[37] Medhurst's essay does not mention *A Tale of Two Cities*, which was hard to see at the time he wrote it, but it fits his argument well. Colman in 1935 comes across as so uncomplicatedly heterosexual that it seems strange for Lucie to enter so innocently into an intimate friendship with him: the film shows her alone with him more often than with her husband. Bogarde is different, repeatedly insisting in words and manner to Lucie that he is no potential sexual threat. The crude term that suggests itself for Dorothy Tutin's Lucie, as never for Elizabeth Allan's in 1935, is 'fag hag'. Interestingly, the same applies to the Anglo-French TV version of 1989: Carton is played by James Wilby, who had recently risen to fame in the title role of the film of

E. M. Forster's *Maurice*, which broke new ground in 1987 in its explicit and positive representation of a homosexual relationship. With both Wilby and Bogarde, there is a strong sense of continuity between the overt and highly publicized homosexual roles (*Maurice* shortly before, *Victim* shortly after) and the way they play Carton.

How far this can be argued to derive from a subtext present in Dickens's novel is a big and interesting question which I have no space to consider here, but it does underline the sheer fertility of the novel as a text that can be reworked at different times and from different perspectives. Giddings claimed that the 1958 film has 'the fingerprints of the 1950s all over it' in terms of its political detachment; at the same time, it shows the fingerprints of its time in the tensions throbbing in the performances of Lee and Bogarde. But jump forward ten years, and one can imagine alternative versions that could match or surpass the political urgency of the Selznick film: a 1968 *Tale of Two Cities* directed by the Lindsay Anderson of *if . . . .* or the Michael Reeves of *Witchfinder General* – set at the time of England's own Civil War – or indeed, crossing the Channel, the Jean-Luc Godard of *Weekend*. All of these films belong to 1968; in different ways they tap into, and feed into, the violent events and the radical spirit of that time, and the urgency and dynamism of their styles are very far from the 1958 film's conservatism.

Though it never happened in 1968, there will surely be later occasions when producers, turning again to Dickens, find that his work speaks as urgently in a new political context as it did for Lean and Cineguild in 1946, and for Selznick and his team in 1935. *A Tale of Two Cities* may have serious cinematic life left in it yet.

Notes

1. David Parker, entry on the film at www.screenonline.org.uk/film/id/455971/ index.html [accessed July 2007].
2. In *The Nation*, 15 September 1926, Ernestine Evans reported on a sensational private showing in California to 300 guests. 'Max Reinhardt and Douglas Fairbanks unite in saying that it is great art, the best motion picture either has ever seen . . . . Whether the public sees the picture or not, it will before long experience the influence of the new technique.' Reprinted in *American Film Criticism*, ed. Stanley Kauffman (New York: Liveright, 1972), pp. 181–3.
3. Much contemporary detail of the suppression of *Potemkin* in Britain in the 1930s is given in *Traditions of Independence: British Cinema in the Thirties*, ed. Don McPherson (London: BFI, 1980). The website of the British Board of Film Censors indicates that the film was considered on 30 September 1926 and rejected outright. www.bbfc.co.uk/search/index.php [accessed July 2007].
4. The BBFC website shows that the Selznick film was passed on 6 January 1936: 'cuts were required but details are not available'. In 1940 the BBFC offices in Soho were bombed and many records lost, so we may never get full information, nor is the film mentioned in any of the standard histories of film censorship. Other possible candidates for censorship are the late pair of scenes surrounding the Darnays'

young daughter, who is petted in sinister fashion by The Vengeance, and is later found by Sidney to be playing happily with the gruesome toy she has been given – a miniature guillotine; and the derogatory references to Britain's treatment of the American colonies. Cuts may, of course, have fallen in more than one place.

5. Sergei Eisenstein, 'Dickens, Griffith, and the Film Today', first published in Moscow in 1944, and in English translation in 1949, in the Eisenstein essay collection *Film Form*, ed. and trans. Jay Leyda (New York: Harcourt, Brace, 1949).

6. This dissolve through time is especially evocative of Griffith's historical epic of 1916, *Intolerance*, which moves back and forth between four stories set in different historical epochs, and which had a huge influence on film-makers in and beyond Russia.

7. Grahame Smith, *Dickens and the Dream of Cinema* (Manchester: Manchester University Press, 2003), p. 8.

8. *David Copperfield*, MGM 1935, directed by George Cukor. First shown in January 1935, almost a year before *A Tale of Two Cities*, it made much in publicity of having an English adapter in the novelist Hugh Walpole, who also played a cameo role as a clergyman. Only two actors are in both: Elizabeth Allan (David's mother and Lucie) and the magnificent Edna May Oliver (Betsy Trotwood and Miss Pross).

9. *Great Expectations*, a Cineguild production, 1946, directed by David Lean.

10. *Memo from David O. Selznick*, ed. Rudy Behlmer (New York: Viking, 1972), p. 83. This memo dated 3 June 1935.

11. *Nicholas Nickleby*, Ealing Studios, 1947, directed by Alberto Cavalcanti. *Oliver Twist*, Cineguild, 1948, David Lean. *Scrooge*, George Minter Productions, 1951, Brian Desmond Hurst. *The Pickwick Papers*, George Minter Productions, 1952, Noel Langley.

12. The best of all versions of *Oliver Twist*, for me, is one that tackles the back-story head-on rather than, like Lean and others, watering it down apologetically: the 1999 mini-series first broadcast on the ITV network in 1999. The adapter, Alan Bleasdale, only reaches the birth of Oliver at the end of the first of the three episodes. Directed by Renny Rye, the series is available on DVD.

13. Writing to Nicholas Schenck of MGM on 3 October 1935 about how to promote the film, Selznick told him to 'bear in mind that the book *A Tale of Two Cities* would [even] without Colman have a potential drawing power equalled only by *David Copperfield*, *Little Women*, and *The Count of Monte Cristo* among the films of recent years because only these books have an even comparable place in the affections of the reading public. This is ... a book that is revered by millions – yes, and tens of millions of people here and abroad.' Behlmer, *Memo*, p. 86.

14. 'Along with Michael Balcon at Ealing, [she] can be called the dominant British feature producer of the early postwar years.' Charles Barr, entry on Box in *The International Dictionary of Films and Film-Makers*, 4 vols. (Andover: St James Press, 1996), III, p. 96.

15. 'As to Sam Behrman, I think he is one of the best of American dialogue writers ... he is especially equipped, in my opinion, to give us the rather sardonic note in Carton.' Behlmer, *Memo*, p. 84.

16. 'Colman disliked dual roles and felt audiences would not believe Colman sacrificing himself for Colman.' Sam Frank, *Ronald Colman: A Bio-Bibliography* (Westport, CT and London: Greenwood Press, 1997), p. 100.

17. The other French member of the 1958 cast is Marie Versini, as the young woman who is with Carton at the end. She too has made no other British film.

18. Radio, of course, has less of a problem with the matter of the double. *A Tale of Two Cities* was among the novels dramatized by Orson Welles's Mercury Theatre of the Air (25 July 1938): Barsad reacts to the courtroom appearance of Carton by acknowledging they are 'like two peas in a pod'. Welles himself provides an original angle on the theme of doubling by playing both Manette and Carton. The recording can be accessed from the website www.mercurytheatre.info [accessed July 2007].

19. Box 3 of the T. E. B. Clarke papers, purchased after his death in 1989 by the Lilly Library at Indiana University, Bloomington.

20. At the tribunal in the 1958 film, Dr Manette speaks of having been released from the Bastille 'nearly two years ago'.

21. Two previous Bogarde roles had involved touching friendships with young children – *Hunted* (1952) and *The Spanish Gardener* (1956).

22. Brian Bialkowski, 'Facing up to the Question of Fidelity: the Example of *A Tale of Two Cities*', *Literature Film Quarterly*, 29 (2001), 203–9.

23. 3 June 1935: Behlmer, *Memo*, p. 84.

24. According to the Internet Movie Database: 'ever since being cast as Jesus in *The King of Kings* (1927), he was typecast into playing only dignified characters'. www.imdb.com/name/nm0912478/bio [accessed July 2007].

25. Starting in 1908, Walthall had made some 200 short films with Griffith, before playing Colonel Ben Cameron in his *Birth of a Nation* (1915). The year before *A Tale of Two Cities* he played a heroic militant churchman, the Reverend Ashby Brand, in Ford's *Judge Priest* (1934). He died in 1936.

26. Pierre Sorlin, *The Film in History* (New York: Barnes & Noble, 1980), p. 71.

27. The 1946 *Great Expectations* plays like a fable of the changes Britain had lived through during the war, when it was forced to realize afresh that prosperity, and indeed survival, depended on the labour of the working class. Both Estella and, after his sudden rise in society, Pip, are complacent in their roles as idle rich, and are patronizing at best towards working people. At the end of the film, as they head tentatively into the sunlight, they and we know that the wealth of each has derived not from Miss Havisham but from Magwitch, now revealed as Pip's benefactor and as Estella's father; for many years, and for nearly an hour of the film's running time, he has been absent from view and from memory, buried 'down under', but working ceaselessly. The great scene in mid-film where he makes himself known to Pip as his benefactor thus enacts the Return of the (political) Repressed, and evokes, for me at least, the irruption of the trade union leader Ernest Bevin into the political limelight in 1940 as Minister of Labour, a key role, both practically and symbolically, in the Coalition administration Churchill set up to replace the one-party government of Tory patricians. In build and features Finlay Currie, who plays Magwitch, is very much the same type as Bevin, whose bluntness and cragginess were a shock to some at first, but who soon came to be widely accepted and admired. In 1945 the country showed that it had, as it were, taken Pip's lesson to heart by electing a Labour government.

28. *A Tale of Two Cities*, Granada TV, 1989. Mini-series written by Arthur Hopcraft, directed by Philippe Monnier.

29. Jason W. Stevens, 'Insurrection and Depression-Era Politics in Selznick's *A Tale of Two Cities* (1935)', *Literature Film Quarterly*, 34 (2006), 176–93.

30. Stevens, 'Insurrection and Depression-Era Politics', pp. 177, 189.

31. Bizarrely, Stevens substitutes Richard III for George III, and discusses the signifi-cance of Richard in a footnote. It is, of course, George in the film, as in the novel;

Carton's remark would otherwise lose half its point. Stevens also gives a most inaccurate version of the film's initial quotation, though it is just possible that there are varying prints.

32. *Dracula*, Hammer Productions, 1958, directed by Terence Fisher.
33. Robert Giddings, 'A *Tale of Two Cities* and the Cold War', in *British Cinema of the 1950s: a Celebration*, ed. Ian McKillop and Neil Sinyard (Manchester: Manchester University Press, 2003), pp. 168–75.
34. Lindsay Anderson, 'Get out and Push', in *Declaration*, ed. Tom Maschler (London: Jonathan Cape, 1957), repr. *Never Apologise: the Collected Writings of Lindsay Anderson*, ed. Paul Ryan (London: Plexus, 2004).
35. Betty Box, *Lifting the Lid* (London: Book Guild, 2000), p. 202.
36. Quoted by Giddings, '*A Tale of Two Cities*', p. 173.
37. Andy Medhurst, 'Dirk Bogarde', in *All Our Yesterdays: 90 Years of British Cinema*, ed. Charles Barr (London: BFI, 1986), pp. 346–54.

11
Afterword

Michael Wood

Many narratives, perhaps most, offer a curious simulation of destiny. From the start of the story – the fairy tale, the joke, the film, the biography, the novel – the storyteller knows the ending. What happens *has* to happen not because it is fated but because it has happened already, and yet this is just what we are ordinarily not supposed to think. The very notion of suspense, or even standard narrative interest, relies on a strategic double denial, an imitation of freedom from history and time: the narrator won't spill the beans, except by a little cautious foreshadowing now and then, and the listener, viewer or reader will not interrupt with questions or fast-forward to see how it all turns out.

When Dickens's David Copperfield says he doesn't know whether he will be the hero of his own life, or, more eerily, when Esther Summerson, in *Bleak House*, says she is having trouble starting on her portion of the book, we recognize and enjoy the game.[1] Dickens is using an unknowing subject, a fictional, day-by-day memoirist, as a screen for his own full knowledge of the unfolding tale. Similar structures are in place even when a writer like Dickens really doesn't know what will happen in the next episode of a serial publication, or changes his mind between issues. The moment he writes in the past perfect tense – 'the factitious tense of cosmogonies, myths, histories and novels', as Roland Barthes says[2] – he either has the knowledge he didn't have a moment ago or is imitating a figure who does have such knowledge.

There are famous exceptions to this rule, one of them being Dickens's *A Tale of Two Cities*, but not all that many, and each of them, as far as I can see, has a strong philosophical or historical agenda in tow. The point in Diderot's *Jacques le Fataliste*, for example, is to use the idea of writing and the already written book to question the very concept of freedom, to mock both determinism and its too cheerful opposites. The point in Tolstoy's *War and Peace* is to remind us that historical knowledge belongs only to hindsight – no one in the novel knows what is going on at Borodino or any other battle, and no participant knows what the consequences of the invasion and evacuation of Moscow will be. And the point in García Márquez's *One Hundred Years of Solitude*, which contains some of literature's most elaborate play with the notions of text and destiny, is to paint a detailed picture of Latin American fatalism and to wonder whether there is any cure for it – perhaps to wonder whether fatalism is a disease that swallows up the very possibility of cure.

Dickens has an agenda too, but a different one. It is borrowed initially from Carlyle, but soon takes on a quite different life. Very broadly, Dickens uses the basic narrative convention I described above, the unimpeachable authority of the past tense, to create a logic so easy and apparently self-evident that by the time we fathom its falsity we shall have been hooked, or robbed of our arguments. First (tautological) principle: what happens happens. There was a French Revolution. Second (ambiguous) principle: what happened had to happen. The Revolution may once have been avoidable, but it isn't now, since it has already occurred. It takes only a little sleight of hand to turn this indisputable temporal claim into a forceful, if flawed, causal one. The Revolution, certainly inevitable now it is over, was always inevitable, lying in wait like the resolution of the plot of a novel.[3]

If the French Revolution was the inevitable effect of certain identifiable causes, Dickens's argument seems to go, then the reappearance of those causes in another time and country cannot fail to produce the same effect. Does Dickens believe this? He believes it is worth saying, worth dramatizing in a novel, precisely because of the ambiguity of the argument about inevitability. This is what he means, I think, by suggesting 'no one can hope to add anything to the philosophy of Mr Carlyle's wonderful book' (*TTC*, Appendix II, 398). The philosophy is one thing and its possible application is another. As several of the contributors in this volume make clear, and as Dickens's title itself indicates, life in London is as much at stake in the work as life in Paris. Sally Ledger reminds us that 'In the first trial of Charles Darnay, at the Old Bailey, the viciousness of the mob of spectators is barely distinguishable from the mob attending his subsequent trials before the revolutionary tribunal in France.'

Dickens says he hoped 'to add something to the popular and picturesque means of understanding that terrible time' (*TTC*, Appendix II), and he certainly does that. But the 'times' he evokes on his first page are consistently doubled by a second set: the explicit eighteenth-century dates look forward to the always implicit date of the time of the writing and publication of the novel. 'The political difference between Dickens and Carlyle', Gareth Stedman Jones remarks earlier in this volume, 'did not consist solely in their different readings of the past. It very directly concerned their reading of their own epoch.' And John Bowen cites an 1855 letter in which Dickens sees 'in the present time' both an 'alienation of the people from their own public affairs' and a smouldering 'discontent . . . extremely like the general mind of France before the breaking out of the first Revolution'.

What happened in France can happen in England, but causality has many paths, and there is a chance that the language of prophecy (this will happen) may function as if it were the language of warning (this will happen unless). The inevitability of the French Revolution, if I may put this a little cryptically, is a crucial argument in the case for the avoidance of a second English Revolution.[4] Dickens's line of thought here is witty, sly, cogent and passionate, and worth looking at in a little detail.

The perspective, the invasion of the known future into the unknowing past, opens on the first page of the novel, with an impeccably false assumption ascribed to both France and England: 'In both countries it was clearer than crystal to the lords of the State preserves of loaves and fishes, that things in general were settled for ever' (I, i, 5). We don't need any theory of destiny or history to recognize this delusion and its dangers, but Dickens's next move in this direction is more intricate. It appears on the novel's second page, and is echoed six pages from the end. Referring to the case of the Chevalier de la Barre, a young man tortured and burned alive in 1766 for failing to kneel before a procession of monks, and to the new, humane invention of Dr Joseph Ignace Guillotin, Dickens imagines that 'rooted in the woods of France and Norway, there were growing trees, when that unfortunate sufferer was put to death, already marked by the Woodman, Fate, to come down and be sawn into boards to make a certain movable framework with a sack and a knife in it'. Similarly, Dickens suggests, there were no doubt carts sitting in country sheds then 'which the Farmer, Death, had already set apart to be his tumbrils of the Revolution' (I, i, 6). At the end of the novel the tumbrils reappear as the failed instruments of a reverse fairy-tale:

> Change these back again to what they were, thou powerful enchanter, Time, and they shall be seen to be the carriages of absolute monarchs, the equipages of feudal nobles, the toilettes of flaring Jezebels, the churches that are not my father's house but dens of thieves, the huts of millions of starving peasants! No; the great magician who majestically works out the appointed order of the Creator, never reverses his transformations. . . . Changeless and hopeless, the tumbrils roll along.
>
> (III, xv, 385)

This is a complicated and disorderly trope, a modest synecdoche being much overworked. It is easy enough to imagine the tumbrils as carriages, more of a stretch to see them as churches and huts, let alone toilettes; but the suggestion of the enchanter's double helplessness is important. Not only can time not reverse its magic, turn the pumpkin back into a coach, but the pumpkin never was a coach, only a country cart with other uses. The hidden logic of the figure is that the carriages of the extravagant and heedless rich – we recall that St Evrémonde, the first time we see him, runs over a child in the street – were always paired with the scarcely used carts of the poor, so that both sets of vehicles can merge in the unchanging tumbrils, the first as a metaphor, the second as a metonymic origin. Everything was always headed here, just as those trees were marked for their use in building the guillotine.

But time is not the enchanter; or time is only the enchanter, the visible on-stage illusionist whose secret partner is historical causality, in Dickens's language the order of the Creator. All kinds of things happen to trees and carts in time, carriages in many ages travel the roads without any sign of magical transformation. What makes for change here is long abuse, ending in violent reaction. The evil deeds of the rich beget the evil deeds of the poor. 'I see the evil of this time', Sydney Carton says in the unspoken thoughts attributed to him at the end of the novel, 'and of the previous time of which this is the natural birth' (III, xv, 389). And Charles Darnay's description of *ancien régime* France is eloquent and beyond appeal: 'it is a crumbling tower of waste, mismanagement, extortion, debt, mortgage, oppression, hunger, nakedness and suffering' (II, ix, 130). 'Monseigneur as a class', Dickens says of his personification of this system, 'had, somehow or other, brought things to this' (II, xxiii, 236). 'Somehow or other' seems a little strange, since Dickens usually claims to know exactly how. Perhaps he is miming the casual self-ignorance of the class. Or perhaps – this is a stronger suggestion in the full context of the novel – he is mounting two quite different arguments at once here.

The first is the moral argument I have just evoked, and it is the one everyone sees. It drives a good deal of the plot on both sides of the Channel. The emphasis is on the wrongs done by the old order, and the comeuppance, however excessive, is morally deserved. In Darnay's indictment, the words 'extortion', 'oppression', 'hunger', 'nakedness' and 'suffering' all point in this direction, and because of the build-up towards the end of the sentence the whole claim seems to tilt that way.

But 'waste', 'mismanagement', 'debt' and 'mortgage' suggest different dangers, and Dickens's second argument is practical rather than moral – simply empirical, one might almost say. What afflicted the ruling classes of France, he says, was a 'leprosy of unreality', since the agents of government were 'totally unfit for their several callings, all lying horribly in pretending to belong to them'; and many others, not connected with government in any way, were 'equally unconnected with anything that was real, or with lives passed in travelling by any straight road to any true earthly end' (II, vii, 110–11). Here were 'military officers destitute of military knowledge; naval officers with no idea of a ship; civil officers without a notion of affairs; brazen ecclesiastics, of the word world worldly ... doctors who made fortunes out of dainty remedies for imaginary disorders' (II, vii, 110). 'The greatest reality' in this world was the *fermier-général* since in spite of, or because of, his luxurious life he 'pretended to do nothing but plunder and forage where he could' (II, vii, 110).[5]

Of course, there are firm moral implications in words like 'brazen' and 'lying' and in the metaphor of the straight road, and I am not suggesting that Dickens kept the moral and practical arguments separate. Indeed, it was very much in his interest not to. But it is clear that the line of causality is quite different in the two cases. The moral argument requires us to believe, if not in the triumph of good at least in the downfall of evil – in time and in this world.⁶ The practical argument merely asserts that reality will set in sooner or later, that worlds of fantasy must ultimately collapse because their very foundations and structures of support are illusionary. The first argument belongs to theology and fable and pious hope; the second seems to rest on common sense, to call for no particular kind of belief, and is the ground of the novel as a genre from Cervantes to Proust and Conrad, even Nabokov.⁷

So that when, in a quotation already discussed by the editors of this volume in their introduction, Dickens brings together 'Monseigneur as a class', in the form of a group of refugees in England, and what he calls 'native British orthodoxy', and tells us that it is 'too much the way' of both elements 'to talk of this terrible Revolution as if it were the only harvest ever known under the skies that had not been sown – as if nothing had ever been done, or omitted to be done, that had led to it' (II, xxiv, 246–7), he is simultaneously reverting to the simple irony of his first page ('things in general were settled for ever'), carefully pitching his book between fable and novel, and conjuring up a whole complex and mischievous claim about history.

'As ye sow, so shall ye reap.' The familiar moral admonishment becomes first a sturdy tautology (no reaping without sowing), then a stick to beat all disavowers of moral responsibility (sowers denying their undeniable seeds), then an invocation of the reality principle (who is going to say that leprosy is not a disease?), and finally, because all these events are now in the past, an assertion, or mock-assertion, of historical inevitability. To talk as if there were unsown harvests, we read in the continuation of the passage I have just quoted, is to talk 'as if observers of the wretched millions in France, and of the misused and perverted resources that should have made them prosperous, had not seen it inevitably coming, years before, and had not in plain words recorded what they saw' (II, xxiv, 247). Dickens is thinking of Arthur Young and his *Travels in France*, and the logic, once again, paradoxically pairs inevitability with the possibility of an alternative, the prosperity that might have been. And although the warning for the England of Dickens's day is clear enough, we cannot, because Dickens is writing a novel/fable rather than a tract, paraphrase it into simple propositional terms, or even get much beyond the overall sense that something must be done – since '*laissez-faire* complacency', as Stedman Jones puts it, is deeply harmful, and the failures of the judicial system, as Mark Philp suggests, may be providing dissidents 'with the same ammunition of grievance through imposture as mobilized the French in 1789'. The fear is general, and so is the portrait of danger. This is how Dickens's 'popular and picturesque means' work, and it is no accident that the book has had such a fortune in the theatre and the cinema – the logic of popular culture is often multiple and hard to act on in just this way. What is inevitable will happen – unless we prevent it. 1859 in England is just like 1789 in France, except for the difference in time and place. I don't think we can make sense of these claims by sheltering their contradictions in some sort of halfway house between destiny and freedom, or between difference and identity. It was in their contradictions that they mattered in 1859, and they continue to matter to us in the same mode. Dickens wanted his readers to be rattled and puzzled as well as entertained. The warning consists, then, of a hyperbolic and shadowy but constant relation between the two cities and the two times, and a running reminder that both parts of the contradiction are true in their way: if we fail to prevent it, the inevitable will indeed have happened, and the French Revolution will have occurred in England. As perhaps it did, in its way. In a recent essay on Robespierre, Christopher Prendergast argues that modern democracies rest on what they see as reason rather than virtue. 'This is not what Robespierre wanted, altogether too "impure", but it is by and large what we have got. The unfathomable causal question is whether, without Robespierre, we would have got it at all.'[8]

Notes

1. 'Whether I shall turn out to be the hero of my own life, or whether that station will be held by anybody else, these pages must show.' Charles Dickens, *David Copperfield* (New York: Washington Square Press, 1958), p. 1. 'I have a great deal of difficulty in beginning to write my portion of these pages, for I know I am not clever.' Charles Dickens, *Bleak House* (London and New York: Penguin Books, 1994), p. 13.
2. Roland Barthes, *Le Degré zéro de l'écriture* (Paris: Éditions du Seuil, 1953), p. 47.
3. There is an interesting uncertainty in Aristotle's argument on this subject in the *Poetics*. He offers the familiar tautology – 'what has happened is manifestly possible: otherwise it would not have happened' – but then goes on to say, rather strangely, that 'there is no reason why some events that have actually happened should not conform to the law of the probable and possible'. He cannot mean that what has happened was always probable as well as possible, but he does seem to be suggesting – the topic is the use of actual historical figures in tragedy – that what has happened brings with it a plausible if unreliable trail of the probable. This, it seems to me, is just how Dickens's strategy works. See *Poetics*, trans. S. H. Butcher (New York: Hill & Wang, 1961), p. 69.
4. G. K. Chesterton, *The Victorian Age in Literature* (New York: Henry Holt, 1913), pp. 17–18. 'It is no idle Hibernianism to say that towards the end of the eighteenth century the most important event in English history happened in France. It would seem still more perverse, yet it would be still more precise, to say that the most important event in English history was the event that never happened at all – the English Revolution on the lines of the French Revolution.'
5. Dickens takes almost all these instances from Louis-Sébastien Mercier's *Tableau de Paris*, 12 vols. (Amsterdam, 1782–88).

6. 'A very wholesome and comfortable doctrine', Henry Fielding said, 'and to which we have but one objection, namely, that it is not true.' *Tom Jones*, Book XV, chapter 1 (Oxford: Oxford University Press, 1996), p. 887.
7. Mark Philp's invocation of Chesterton is nicely relevant here with his suggestion that Dickens 'did not feel exactly that he was "in revolt"; he felt if anything that a number of idiotic institutions had revolted against reason and against him.'
8. Christopher Prendergast, 'From Arras to Thermidor', *New Left Review* 43, January/February 2007, p. 157.

Bibliography

Unpublished material

Lloyd, Frank, *A Tale of Two Cities. A Photoplay in Seven Parts . . . From the story by CHARLES DICKENS: Working Script for Lloyd no. 3*. Motion Picture, Broadcasting and Recorded Sound Division, Library of Congress call no. LP10375

Pearson, Richard, 'New Issues in Theatre Historiography', presentation, University of Birmingham, 7 July 2007

Pemberton, T. Edgar, *Sydney Carton*, British Library, Lord Chamberlain's Collection of MS Plays

Taylor, Tom, *A Tale of Two Cities*, British Library, Lord Chamberlain's Collection of MS Plays

Unsigned, *All For Her!*, British Library, Lord Chamberlain's Collection of MS Plays

Published material

Abraham, Nicolas and Maria Torok, *The Shell and the Kernel: Renewals of Psychoanalysis Volume 1*, ed. and trans. Nicholas T. Rand (Chicago: University of Chicago Press, 1994)

Ackroyd, Peter, *Dickens* (London: Sinclair-Stevenson, 1990)

Aldridge, Alfred Owen, *Man of Reason: The Life of Thomas Paine* (London: Cresset Press, 1960)

Andress, David, *The Terror: Civil War in the French Revolution* (London: Little, Brown, 2005)

Andrews, Malcolm, *Charles Dickens and his Performing Selves: Dickens and the Public Readings* (Oxford: Oxford University Press, 2006)

Aristotle, *Poetics*, trans. S. H. Butcher (New York: Hill & Wang, 1961)

Asfour, Lana, 'Movements of Sensibility and Sentiment: Sterne in Eighteenth-Century France', *The Reception of Laurence Sterne in Europe*, ed. Peter de Voogd and John Neubauer (Bristol: Thoemmes Continuum, 2004)

Baden-Powell, Robert, *Indian Memories* (London: Herbert Jenkins, 1915)

Barcelona, Antonio, ed., *Metaphor and Metonymy at the Crossroads: A Cognitive Perspective* (New York: Mouton de Gruyer, 2000)

Barrell, John and Jon Mee, *Trials for Treason and Sedition, 1792–1794* (London: Pickering & Chatto, 2006)

Barthes, Roland, *Le Degré zéro de l'écriture* (Paris: Éditions du Seuil, 1953)

Behlmer, Rudy, ed., *Memo from David O. Selznick* (New York: Viking, 1972)

Ben-Israel, Hedva, *English Historians in the French Revolution* (Cambridge: Cambridge University Press, 1968)

Benjamin, Walter, trans. Howard Eiland and Kevin McLaughlin, *The Arcades Project* (Cambridge, MA: The Belknap Press of Harvard University Press, 1999)

—— *Illuminations*, trans. Harry Zohn (London: Fontana, 1973)

Beiser, Frederick C. *The Fate of Reason: German Philosophy from Kant to Fichte* (Cambridge, MA and London: Harvard University Press, 1987)

de Beistegui, Miguel, *The New Heidegger* (London: Continuum, 2005)

Bennington, Geoffrey and Jacques Derrida, *Jacques Derrida* (Chicago: University of Chicago, 1993)

Bent, John, *The Bastille* (London: Lowndes, 1789)

Bentham, Jeremy, *The Works of Jeremy Bentham*, 11 vols., ed. John Bowring (Edinburgh: W. Tait, 1843)

Bialkowski, Brian, 'Facing up to the Question of Fidelity: the Example of *A Tale of Two Cities*', *Literature Film Quarterly*, 29 (2001), 203–9

Bindman, David, *The Shadow of the Guillotine. Britain and the French Revolution* (London: British Museum Publications, 1989)

Bisson, André and Meg Villars, 'Le Jour de Gloire', *La Petite Illustration*, no. 811. Théâtre. No. 207, 27 February 1937.

Bolton, H. Philip, *Dickens Dramatized* (London: Mansell Publishing, 1987)

Bowen, John and Robert L. Patten, eds., *Palgrave Advances in Charles Dickens Studies* (London: Palgrave, 2006)

Box, Betty, *Lifting the Lid* (London: Book Guild, 2000)

Burnham, Gilbert, Riyadh Lafta, Shannon Doocy and Les Roberts, 'Mortality after the 2003 invasion of Iraq: a cross-sectional cluster sample survey', *The Lancet*, 368, no. 9545, 21–27 October 2006, 1421–8

Brannan, R. L., ed., *Under the Management of Charles Dickens: His Production of 'The Frozen Deep'* (Ithaca, NY: Cornell University Press, 1966)

Brantlinger, Patrick, 'Did Dickens Have a Philosophy of History? The Case of *Barnaby Rudge*', *DSA*, 30 (2001), 59–74

—— *Rule of Darkness: British Literature and Imperialism, 1830–1914* (Ithaca, NY and London: Cornell University Press, 1988)

Brooks, Peter, 'Melodrama, Body, Revolution', *Melodrama: Stage, Picture, Screen*, ed. Jacky Bratton, Jim Cook and Christine Gledhill (London: British Film Institute, 1994)

—— *The Melodramatic Imagination: Balzac, Henry James, and the Mode of Excess* (New Haven, CT: Yale University Press, 1976)

Buchanan, Judith, *Shakespeare on Film* (Harlow: Longman-Pearson, 2005)

—— *Shakespeare on Silent Film* (Cambridge: Cambridge University Press, 2009)

Burke, Edmund, *Reflections on the Revolution in France*, ed. Conor Cruise O'Brien (Harmondsworth: Penguin Books, 1969)

Butler, Judith, *Gender Trouble: Feminism and the Subversion of Identity* (New York: Routledge, 1990)

Caplan, Jane and John Torpey, eds., *Documenting Individual Identity: The Development of State Practices in the Modern World*, (Princeton, NJ: Princeton University Press, 2001)

Carlyle, Thomas, *Chartism* (London: Chapman & Hall, 2nd edn. 1842)

—— *Critical and Miscellaneous Essays*, 5 vols. (Chicago and New York: Belford, Clarke & Co., 1899)

—— *The French Revolution: A History*, 3 vols. (London: Chapman & Hall, 1880)

—— *The French Revolution*, ed. K. J. Fielding and David Sorensen (Oxford: Oxford University Press, 1989)

—— *Latter Day Pamphlets* (London: Chapman & Hall, 1850)

—— *On Heroes, Hero-worship and the Heroic in History* (London: Chapman & Hall, 1880)

—— *Past and Present* (London, 1843)

Cash, Arthur H. *Laurence Sterne: The Later Years* (London and New York: Methuen, 1986)

Collini, Stefan, Richard Whatmore and Brian Young, eds., *Economy, Polity and Society* (Cambridge: Cambridge University Press, 2000)

—— Richard Whatmore, and Brian Young, eds., *History, Religion and Culture: British Intellectual History 1750–1950* (Cambridge: Cambridge University Press, 2000)

Collins, Philip, 'A Tale of Two Novels: *A Tale of Two Cities* and *Great Expectations* in Dickens's Career', *DSA* 2 (1972), 336–52
—— ed., *Charles Dickens: The Public Readings* (Oxford: Oxford University Press, 1975)
Collins, Wilkie, *The Frozen Deep and Other Tales* (London: Hesperus, 2004)
Collison, Robert, *The Story of Street Literature* (London: Dent, 1973)
Decastro, J., *The Memoirs of J. Decastro, Comedian* (London: Sherwood, Jones, and Co., 1824)
Delattre, Floris, *Dickens et la France. Étude d'une interaction littéraire anglo-française* (Paris: Le Gattre, 1927)
Deleuze, Gilles and Félix Guattari, *A Thousand Plateaus: Capitalism and Schizophrenia*, trans. Brian Massumi (London: Athlone Press, 1988)
Derrida, Jacques, *The Gift of Death*, trans. David Wills (Chicago: University of Chicago Press, 1997)
—— *Of Grammatology*, trans. Gayatri Chakravorty Spivak (Baltimore, MD: Johns Hopkins University Press, 1976)
—— *On the Name*, ed. Thomas Dutoit, trans. David Wood, John P. Leavey, Jr and Ian McLeod (Stanford, CA: Stanford University Press, 1995)
—— *Politics of Friendship*, trans. George Collins (London: Verso, 1997)
Dickens, Charles, *Bleak House*, ed. Nicola Bradbury (London and New York: Penguin Books, 2003)
—— *David Copperfield* (New York: Washington Square Press, 1958)
—— *Le Conte des deux villes* [*A Tale of Two Cities*], trans. C. Derblum (Monaco: Edition du Rocher, 1989)
—— *Un Conte de deux villes* [*A Tale of Two Cities*], trans. E. Bove and intro. Olivier Barot (Paris: Criterion, 1991)
—— *Espoirs et passion: un conte de deux villes* [*A Tale of Two Cities*], trans. L. Terelli (Paris: J'ai lu, 1989)
—— *Great Expectations*, ed. Charlotte Mitchell and intro. David Trotter (London: Penguin Books, 1996)
—— *Hard Times*, ed. Paul Schlicke (Oxford: World's Classics, 1989)
—— *Little Dorrit*, ed. Harvey Peter Sucksmith (Oxford: World's Classics, 1982)
—— *Le Marquis de Saint-Évremond, illustré de 47 photos* [*A Tale of Two Cities*], trans. Mme Tissier de Mallerais (Paris: Delagrave, 1938)
—— *Le Marquis de Saint-Évremond, illustré de 47 photos* [*A Tale of Two Cities*], trans. Mme Tissier de Mallerais (Paris: Bibliothèque Juventa, 1959)
—— *Le Marquis de Saint-Évremont. Paris et Londres en 1793* [*A Tale of Two Cities*], trans. unsigned (Paris: Le film complet no. 1931, 1937)
—— *La Petite Dorrit. Un Conte de deux villes* [*Little Dorrit. A Tale of Two Cities*, trans. Jeanne Metifeu-Béjeau and ed. P. Leyris (Paris: Gallimard, 1970)
—— *A Tale of Two Cities*, ed. Richard Maxwell (London: Penguin Books, 2003)
Disher, Willson, *The Last Romantic: The Authorised Biography of Sir John Martin-Harvey* (London: Hutchinson, 1948)
Dyer, Frank L., 'The Moral Development of the Silent Drama', *Edison Kinetogram*, 15 April 1910, 11
Edmondson, John, ed., *Dickens on France* (Oxford: Signal, 2006)
Eisenstein, Sergei, 'Dickens, Griffith, and the Film Today', *Film Form*, ed. and trans. Jay Leyda (New York: Harcourt, Brace, 1949; repr. 1977)
Eliot, George, *Adam Bede* (London: Blackwood, 1859)
Ellmann, Richard, *Oscar Wilde* (New York: Vintage Books, 1987)
Falconer, J.A., 'The Sources of *A Tale of Two Cities*', *Modern Language Notes*, 36 (1921), 3

Fielding, K. J., ed. *The Speeches of Charles Dickens* (Oxford: Clarendon, 1960)

Fitzgerald, S. J. Adair, *Dickens and the Drama*, (London: Chapman & Hall, 1910)

Ford, George H. and Lauriat Lane Jr, ed., *The Dickens Critics* (Ithaca, NY: Cornell University Press, 1961)

Foucault, Michel, *Discipline and Punish: The Birth of the Prison*, trans. Alan Sheridan (New York: Pantheon, 1978)

—— *Madness and Civilisation: A History of Insanity in the Age of Reason*, trans. Richard Howard (New York: Pantheon, 1965)

Fraenkel, Beatrice, *La signature: genèse d'un signe* (Paris: Gallimard, 1992)

Frank, Sam, *Ronald Colman: A Bio-Bibliography* (Westport, CT and London: Greenwood Press, 1997)

Gallagher, Catherine, 'The Duplicity of Doubling in *A Tale of Two Cities*', *DSA*, 12 (1983), 125–45

—— *The Industrial Reformation of English Fiction 1832–1867* (Chicago and London: University of Chicago Press, 1985)

Gardner, Brian, *Mafeking: A Victorian Legend* (London: Cassell, 1966)

Gaskell, Elizabeth, *Mary Barton* (London: Chapman & Hall, 1848)

Gatrell, Victor, *The Hanging Tree: Execution and the English People, 1770–1868* (Oxford: Oxford University Press, 1994)

Geduld, Harry M., ed., *Authors on Film* (Bloomington, IN and London: Indiana University Press, 1972)

Giddings, Robert, '*A Tale of Two Cities* and the Cold War', *British Cinema of the 1950s: a Celebration*, ed. Ian McKillop and Neil Sinyard (Manchester: Manchester University Press, 2003), 168–75

Gillray, James, *New Morality* (London, 1798)

Girard, René, *Deceit, Desire, and the Novel*, trans. Yvonne Freccero (Baltimore, MD: Johns Hopkins University Press, 1986)

Glavin, John, *After Dickens: Reading, Adaptation and Performance* (Cambridge: Cambridge University Press, 1999)

—— ed., *Dickens on Screen* (Cambridge: Cambridge University Press, 2003)

Godwin, William, *Thoughts Occasioned by the Perusal of Dr Parr's Spital Sermon* (London: G. G. and J. Robinson, 1802)

Goodwin, Albert, *The Friends of Liberty: The English Democratic Movement in the Age of the French Revolution* (London: Hutcheson, 1979)

Graybill, Lela, 'The Wound and the Weapon: The Virtual Culture of Violence in the Age of Reform, 1757–1832' (PhD dissertation, Stanford University, 2006)

Green-Armytage, R. N. [Lady Martin-Harvey], *The Book of Martin-Harvey* (London: Henry Walker, 1930)

Gregory, Michael, 'Old Bailey Speech in "A Tale of Two Cities"', *Review of English Literature* 6 (1965), 42–55

Hacking, Ian, *The Taming of Chance* (Cambridge: Cambridge University Press, 1990)

Harlow, V. T. 'An English Prisoner in Paris during the Terror (1793–1794)', *Camden Miscellany* (London: Royal Historical Society, 1929), vol. 15

Harvie, Christopher and H. C. G. Mathew, *Nineteenth-Century Britain: A Very Short Introduction* (Oxford: Oxford University Press, 2000)

Haser, Verena, *Metaphor, Metonymy, and Experientialist Philosophy: Challenging Cognitive Semantics* (Berlin: Mouton de Gruyter, 2005)

Heidegger, Martin, *Being and Time*, trans. John Macquarrie and Edward Robinson (Oxford: Blackwell, 1962)

Hennelly, Jr., Mark M., ' "Like or No Like": Figuring the Scapegoat in *A Tale of Two Cities*', *DSA*, 30 (2001), 193–216

House, Madeline, Graham Storey and others, *The Letters of Charles Dickens*, 12 vols. (Oxford: Clarendon Press, 1965–2002)

Houses of Commons Home Affairs Committee, *Identity Cards: Fourth Report of Session 2003–4* (London Stationery Office, 30 July 2004), vol. 1

Iggers, Georg G., trans., *The Doctrine of Saint Simon: An Exposition: First Year, 1828–1829* (Cambridge, MA: Harvard University Press, 1958)

Inwood, Michael, *A Heidegger Dictionary* (Oxford: Blackwell, 1999)

Jakobson, Roman, *Selected Writings* (The Hague: Mouton, 1966–81)

Janes, Regina, *Losing Our Heads: Beheadings in Literature and Culture* (New York and London: New York University Press, 2005)

Jeanneney, Jean-Noël, *Google and the Myth of Universal Knowledge: A View from Europe*, trans. Teresa Lavender Fagan (Chicago and London: University of Chicago Press, 2007)

—— 'Quand Google défie l'Europe', *Le Monde*, 24 January 2005, 13

Johnson, Edgar, *Charles Dickens* (Harmondsworth: Penguin Books, 1977)

Jones, Colin, *The Longman Companion to the French Revolution* (London and New York: Longman, 1988)

—— *Paris: Biography of a City* (London: Penguin Books, 2004)

Jordan, John O., ed., *The Cambridge Companion to Dickens* (Cambridge: Cambridge University Press, 2001)

Kates, Gary, 'From Liberalism to Radicalism: Tom Paine's *Rights of Man*', *Journal of the History of Ideas*, 50 (1989), 569–87

Kauffman, Stanley, ed., *American Film Criticism* (New York: Liveright, 1972)

Keane, John, *Tom Paine: A Political Life* (London: Bloomsbury, 1995)

Kennedy, John M., 'What Makes a Metaphor Stronger than a Simile?' *Metaphor and Symbol*, 14.1 (1999), 63–69

Kilgarriff, Michael, ed., *The Golden Age of Melodrama* (London: Wolfe Publishing, 1974)

Kooiman, Dick, 'The Short Career of Walter Dickens in India', *Dickensian*, 98 (2002), 14–28

Kövecses, Zoltán, *Metaphor in Culture: Universality and Variation* (Cambridge: Cambridge University Press, 2005)

Lacan, Jacques, *Écrits: A Selection*, trans. Alan Sheridan (London: Tavistock, 1977)

Ledger, Sally, *Dickens and the Popular Radical Imagination* (Cambridge and New York: Cambridge University Press, 2007)

Lewis, Linda M., 'Madame Defarge as Political Icon in Dickens's *A Tale of Two Cities*', *DSA*, 37 (2007), 31–49

Lloyd, Martin, *The Passport: The History of Man's Most Travelled Document* (Stroud: Sutton Publishing, 2003)

Locke, John, *Two Treatises of Government*, ed. Peter Laslett (Cambridge: Cambridge University Press, 1963)

Lucas, John, *The Melancholy Man* (London: Methuen, 1970)

Lukács, Georg, *The Historical Novel*, trans. Hannah and Stanley Mitchell (Harmondsworth: Penguin Books, 1969)

—— 'Thoughts on an Aesthetic for the Cinema', *Framework*, 14.1 (Spring 1981), 3

Mackintosh, R. J., *Memoirs of the Life of Sir James Mackintosh*, 2 vols. (London: E. Moxon, 1835)

Magill, Frank, ed., *Magill's Survey of Cinema: Silent Films* (Englewood Cliffs, NJ: Salem Press, 1982), vol. 3

de Maistre, Joseph, *Considerations on France* (1797), trans. and ed. Richard A. Lebrun (Cambridge: Cambridge University Press, 1994)

de Man, Paul, *Allegories of Reading: Figural Language in Rousseau, Nietzsche, Rilke, and Proust* (New Haven, CT: Yale University Press, 1979)

Martin-Harvey, Sir John, *The Autobiography of Sir John Martin-Harvey* (London: Sampson Low, [1930])

—— 'The Story of *The Only Way*', *Dickensian*, 23 (1926), 24–6

Marx, Karl and Friedrich Engels, *Karl Marx and Friedrich Engels Collected Works* (London, 1975)

Maslan, Susan, *Revolutionary Acts: Theatre, Democracy, and the French Revolution* (Baltimore, MD: Johns Hopkins University Press, 2005)

Mason, Laura and Tracy Rizzo, eds., *The French Revolution: A Document Collection* (Boston: Houghton Mifflin, 1999)

Maza, Sarah, *Private Lives and Public Affairs: The Causes Célèbres of Prerevolutionary France* (Berkeley, CA: University of California Press, 1993)

McPherson, Don, ed., *Traditions of Independence: British Cinema in the Thirties*, (London: BFI, 1980)

Medhurst, Andy, 'Dirk Bogarde', *All Our Yesterdays: 90 Years of British Cinema*, ed. Charles Barr (London: BFI, 1986), 346–54

Mercier, Louis-Sébastien, *Tableau de Paris*, ed. under direction of Jean-Claude Bonnet, 2 vols. (Paris, [1794?])

Metz, Christian, *The Imaginary Signifier: Psychoanalysis and the Cinema*, trans. Celia Britton (Bloomington, IN: Indiana University Press, 1982)

Midgeley, Wilson, 'The Genius of Sir John', *Daily Telegraph*, 13 April 1939

Mill, John Stuart, *Considerations on Representative Government* (Buffalo, NY: Prometheus Books, 1991)

—— 'Of Names and Propositions', *A System of Logic Ratiocinative and Inductive, Being a Connected View of the Principles of Evidence and the Methods of Scientific Investigation*, 2 vols. (London: Longmans, Green, & Co., 10th edn. 1879)

—— *On Liberty*, ed. Gertrude Himmelfarb (Harmondsworth: Penguin Books, 1974)

Miller, D.A., *The Novel and the Police* (Berkeley, CA and London: University of California Press, 1988)

Monod, Sylvère, ed., *Charles Dickens et la France. Colloque international de Boulogne-sur-Mer, 3 juin 1978* (Lille: Presses Universitaires de Lille, 1979)

—— 'Une curiosité dans l'histoire de la traduction: *Le Neveu de ma tante* d'Amédée Pichot', *Études anglaises*, 4 (1961)

Moore, Grace, *Dickens and Empire: Discourses of Class, Race and Colonialism in the Works of Charles Dickens* (Aldershot: Ashgate, 2004)

Morley, Malcolm, 'The Stage Story of *A Tale Of Two Cities*', *Dickensian*, 51 (1954) 34–40

Morrow, John, *Thomas Carlyle* (London: Hambledon Continuum, 2006)

Mulhall, Stephen, *Heidegger and Being and Time* (London: Routledge, 2nd edn. 2005)

Mulvey, Laura, *Death 24 x a Second* (London: Reaktion, 2006)

Musto, Sylvia, 'Portraiture, Revolutionary Identity and Subjugation: Anne-Louis Girodet's Citizen Belley', *Canadian Art Review*, 20.1/2 (1993), 60–71

Nalbantian, Susan, *The Symbol of the Soul from Holderlin to Yeats: A Study in Metonymy* (London: Macmillan, 1977)

Nead, Lynda, *Victorian Babylon: People, Streets, and Images in Nineteenth-Century London* (New Haven, CT: Yale University Press, 2000)

Newlin, George, *Everyone in Dickens: Volume I: Plots, People and Publishing Particulars in the Complete Works, 1833–1849* (Westport, CT: Greenwood Press, 1995)

Oddie, William, 'Dickens and the Indian Mutiny', *Dickensian*, 69 (1972), 3–17

Oddie, William, *Dickens and Carlyle: The Question of Influence* (London: Centenary Press, 1972)

Oman, Charles, *The Lyons Mail, being an account of the crime of April 27 1796 (Floréal 8 an IV)* (London: Methuen, 1945)

Paine, Thomas, *Rights of Man, Common Sense, and other Political Writings*, ed. Mark Philp (Oxford: Oxford University Press, 1995)

Pakenham, Thomas, *The Boer War* (1979; London: Abacus, 1992)

Pankhurst, Richard K. P., *The Saint-Simonians, Mill and Carlyle: A Preface to Modern Thought* (London: Sidgwick & Jackson, 1957)

Parry, Jonathan, *The Politics of Patriotism: English Liberalism, National Identity and Europe 1830–1886* (Cambridge: Cambridge University Press, 2006)

Patočka, Jan, *Heretical Essays in the Philosophy of History*, trans. Erazim Kohak (Chicago, IL: Open Court, 1996)

Patten, Robert L., *Charles Dickens and his Publishers* (Oxford: Oxford University Press, 1978)

Pearson, Hesketh, *The Last Actor-Managers* (London: White Lion, 1950)

Philpotts, Trey, *The Companion to Little Dorrit* (Mountfield: Helm Information, 2005)

Pilbeam, Pamela, *Madame Tussaud and the History of Waxworks* (New York and London: Hambledon, 2003)

Porter, Roy, *London: A Social History* (London: Hamish Hamilton, 1994)

Prendergast, Christopher, 'From Arras to Thermidor', *New Left Review* 43, January/February 2007, 157

Price, Richard, *Political Writings*, ed. D. O. Thomas (Cambridge: Cambridge University Press, 1991)

Reichardt, Rolf and Hans-Jurgen Lüsebrink, *The Bastille: A History of a Symbol of Despotism and Freedom*, trans. Norbert Schürer (Durham, NC: Duke University Press, 1997)

Richards, Jeffrey, *Sir Henry Irving* (London: Palgrave Macmillan, 2005)

Dr. Rigby's Letters from France &c in 1789. Edited by his Daughter, Lady Eastlake (London, 1880)

Rivers, Henry [F. Fox Cooper], *The Tale of Two Cities; Or, The Incarcerated Victim of the Bastille* (London: Davidson, 1860)

Robespierre, Maximilien, *Oeuvres complètes de Maximilien Robespierre*, ed. Victor Barbier and Charles Vellay (Paris, 1910), vol. 1

Rosenberg, John D., *Carlyle and the Burden of History* (Oxford: Clarendon Press, 1985)

Rowell, George, *Nineteenth-Century Plays* (Oxford: Oxford University Press, 2nd edn. 1972)

Ryan, Paul ed., *Never Apologise: the Collected Writings of Lindsay Anderson* (London: Plexus, 2004)

Sadrin, Anny, ed., *Dickens, Europe and the New Worlds* (Basingstoke: Macmillan, 1999)

—— *Dickens ou le roman-théâtre* (Paris: PUF, 1992)

Saintsbury, H. A. and Cecil Palmer, *We Saw Him Act* (London: Hurst & Blackett, 1939)

Salmon, Eric, ed., *Bernhardt and the Theatre of Her Time* (Westport, CT: Greenwood Press, 1984)

Sanders, Andrew, *The Companion to* A Tale of Two Cities (London: Unwin Hyman, 1988)

—— *Charles Dickens* (Oxford: Oxford University Press, 2003)

—— *The Victorian Historical Novel 1840–1880* (London: Macmillan, 1978)

Schama, Simon, *Citizens: A Chronicle of the French Revolution* (London: Viking, 1989),

Schlicke, Paul, ed. *Oxford Reader's Companion to Dickens* (Oxford: Oxford University Press, 1999)

Schwartzbach, F. S., *Dickens and the City* (London: Athlone, 1979)

Sedgwick, Eve Kosofsky, *Between Men: English Literature and Male Homosocial Desire* (New York: Columbia University Press, 1985)

Sharpe, Jenny, *Allegories of Empire: The Figure of Woman in the Colonial Text* (Minneapolis, MN: University of Minnesota Press, 1993)

Sheppard, Leslie, *The History of Street Literature* (Newton Abbot: David & Charles, 1973)

Simpson, David, *Romanticism, Nationalism, and the Revolt against Theory* (Chicago, IL: University of Chicago Press, 1993)

Slater, Michael, ' "The Bastille Prisoner": A Reading Dickens Never Gave', *Études anglaises*, 23 (1970), 190–6

—— and John Drew, ed., *The Dent Uniform Edition of Dickens' Journalism*, 4 vols. (London: Dent, 1994–2000)

—— *Dickens and Women* (Stanford, CA: Stanford University Press, 1983)

Slide, Anthony, ed., *Selected Film Criticism, 1912–1920* (Metuchen, NJ and London: Scarecrow Press, 1982)

Smith, Grahame, *Dickens and the Dream of Cinema* (Manchester and New York: Manchester University Press, 2003)

Smith, Molly, 'The Theater and the Scaffold: Death as Spectacle in *The Spanish Tragedy*', *Studies in English Literature*, 32 (1992), 217–32

Smyth, W., *Lectures on History: Second and Concluding Series on the French Revolution* (Cambridge: J. and J. Deighton, 1842)

Sorlin, Pierre, *The Film in History* (New York: Barnes & Noble, 1980)

de Staël, Madame, *Considerations on the Principal Events of the French Revolution*, 3 vols. (London: [n. pub.], 1818)

Stedman Jones, Gareth, 'The Return of Language: Radicalism and the British Historians 1960–1990', *Political Language in the Age of Extremes*, ed. W. Steinmetz, forthcoming 2009.

Sterne, Laurence, *A Sentimental Journey through France and England*, ed. Melvyn New and W.G. Day, *The Florida Edition of the Works of Laurence Sterne* (Gainesville, FL: 2002), vol. 6

Stevens, Jason W., 'Insurrection and Depression-Era Politics in Selznick's *A Tale of Two Cities* (1935)', *Literature Film Quarterly*, 34 (2006), 176–93

Stewart, Garrett, *Dear Reader: The Conscripted Audience in Nineteenth-Century British Fiction* (Baltimore, MD and London: Johns Hopkins University Press, 1996)

Stierle, Karlheinz, *La Capitale des signes: Paris et son discours*, trans. Marianne Rocher-Jacquin (Paris: Éditions de la Maison des Sciences de l'homme, 2001)

Stonehouse, J. H., *Catalogue of the Library of Charles Dickens from Gadshill Place, June 1870* (London: Piccadilly Fountain Press, 1935)

Sucksmith, Harvey Peter and Paul Davies, 'The Making of the Old Bailey Trial Scene in *A Tale of Two Cities*', *Dickensian*, 100 (2004), 23–35

Swindells, Julia, *Glorious Causes: The Grand Theatre of Political Change, 1789 to 1833* (Oxford: Oxford University Press, 2001)

Tambling, Jeremy, *Dickens, Violence and the Modern State: Dreams of the Scaffold* (London: Macmillan, 1995)

Taylor, George, *The French Revolution and the London Stage 1789–1805* (Cambridge: Cambridge University Press, 2000)

Taylor, Tom, *A Tale of Two Cities* (London: Thomas Hailes Lacy, 1860)

Tennyson, Georg Bernhard, *Sartor Called Resartus: The Genesis, Structure and Style of Thomas Carlyle's First Major Work* (Princeton, NJ: Princeton University Press, 1965)

Tomalin, Claire, *The Invisible Woman: The Story of Nelly Ternan and Charles Dickens* (London: Penguin Books, 1991)

Torpey, John, *The Invention of the Passport: Surveillance, Citizenship and the State* (Cambridge: Cambridge University Press, 2000)

Madame Tussaud's Memoirs and Reminiscences of France, Forming an Abridged History of the French Revolution. Edited by Francis Hervé, Esq. (London, 1838)

Unsigned, *Biographical Sketches of the Characters Composing the Cabinet of Composition Figures Executed by the Celebrated Curtius of Paris and his Successor* (Edinburgh, 1803)

—— *Le Gazetier Cuirassé, ou Anecdotes scandaleuses de la Cour de France ... Auxquelles on a ajouté Des Remarques historiques, ou anecdotes dur le Chateau de la Bastille & l'inquisition de France. Le Plan du Château de la Bastille* ('Imprime à cent lieus de la Bastille, à l'enseigne de la Liberté', [1785?])

—— [Henri Masers de Latude], *Histoire d'une détention de trente-neuf ans, dans les prisons d'etat. Ecrite par le prisonnier lui-même* (Amsterdam, 1787)

—— [Mauclerc], *Le langage des murs, Ou les cachots de la Bastille dévoilant leurs secrets* (Paris, 1789)

—— *Mémoires historiques at authentiques sur Bastille, Dans une Suite de près de trois cens Emprisonnemens, détaillés & constatés par de Pièces, Notes, Lettres, Rapports, Proces-verbaux, trouvés dans cette Forteresse, & rangés par époques depuis 1475 jusqu'à nos jours, &c.*, 3 vols. ('A Londres et se trouve à Paris', 1789)

—— *Mémoires secrets pour servir à l'histoire de la république des lettres en France*, etc., 36 vols. (London [Amsterdam], 1777–89)

—— *Mémoires sur la Bastille et la détention de l'auteur dans ce château royal depuis le 27 septembre 1780 jusqu'au 19 mai 1782* (Paris, Libraire des Bibliophiles, 1889)

—— *Remarques et anecdotes sur le château de la Bastille, suivies d'un detail historique du siege, de la prise & de la demolition de cette Forteresse, Enrichies de deux gravures analogues* (Paris, 'De l'imprimerie de Grange. Et se trouve chez Goujon, Marchand de Musique, au Palais Royal', 1789)

—— *Remarques historiques et anecdotes sur le château de la Bastille* [n. p.] (1774)

—— *Remarques historiques sur la Bastille; sa demolition, & Revolutions de Paris, en juillet 1789. Avec un grand nombre d'anecdotes interessantes & peu connues*, ('A Londres', 1789)

—— 'The Romantic Actor', *Times Literary Supplement*, 16 October 1930, 818

—— *Temple Bar: the City Golgatha by a Member of the Middle Temple* (London, 1853)

Varouxakis, Georgios, *Victorian Political Thought on France and the French* (Basingstoke: Palgrave, 2002)

Voltaire, *L'Ingénu*, ed. Richard A. Francis, *Les Oeuvres complètes de Voltaire* (Oxford: Voltaire Foundation, 2006), vol 63C

Wallbott, H. G., 'Influences of Facial Expression and Context Information on Emotion Attributions', *British Journal of Social Psychology* 27 (1988), 357–69

Watts Phillips, *The Dead Heart: A Story of the French Revolution*, 1860; rev. Walter H. Pollock (London: S. French, 1889)

Watts Phillips, E[mma], *Watts Phillips: Artist and Playwright* (London: Cassell, 1891)

Waugh, Arthur, 'Introducing *A Tale of Two Cities*', *Dickensian*, 23 (1926), 13

White, Hayden, *Metahistory: The Historical Imagination in Nineteenth-Century Europe* (Baltimore, MD: Johns Hopkins University Press, 1973)

Wills, Lt.-Col. The Rev. Freeman and The Rev. Canon Langbridge, *The Only Way: A Dramatic Version in a Prologue and Four Acts of Charles Dickens'* A Tale Of Two Cities (London: Frederick Muller, 1942)

Wollstonecraft, Mary, *An Historical and Moral View of the Origin and Progress of the French Revolution* (London: J. Johnson, 1794)

Woloch, Alex, *The One versus the Many: Minor Characters and the Space of the Protagonist in the Novel* (Princeton, NJ: Princeton University Press, 2003)

Wynne, Deborah, 'Scenes of "Incredible Outrage"': Dickens, Ireland, and *A Tale of Two Cities'*, *DSA*, 37 (2006), 51–64

Young, Arthur, *Arthur Young's Travels in France during the Years 1787, 1788, 1789*, ed. Miss Betham-Edwards (London: George Bell, 1906)

Notes on the Contributors

Keith Michael Baker is J. E. Wallace Sterling Professor in Humanities at Stanford University. His books include *Inventing the French Revolution: Essays on French Political Culture in the Eighteenth Century* (1990) and he has edited *The French Revolution and the Creation of Modern Political Culture, vol. 1, The Political Culture of the Old Regime* (1987) and *vol. 4, The Terror* (1994).

Charles Barr is Emeritus Professor of Film and Television at the University of East Anglia. His publications on British cinema include *Ealing Studios* (1977) and *English Hitchcock* (1999). With Stephen Frears, he co-scripted the centenary history of *British Cinema, Typically British* (1995).

John Bowen is Professor of Nineteenth-Century Literature at the University of York. He is the author of *Other Dickens: Pickwick to Chuzzlewit* (2000) and the co-editor of *Palgrave Advances in Charles Dickens Studies* (2005). He is the current President of the Dickens Society and is a member of the faculty of the University of California Dickens Project.

Judith Buchanan is Senior Lecturer in Film Studies at the University of York. She is the author of *Shakespeare on Film* (2005) and *Shakespeare on Silent Film: An Excellent Dumb Discourse* (forthcoming, 2009).

Kamilla Elliott is a Senior Lecturer in English Literature at Lancaster University. She is the author of *Rethinking the Novel/Film Debate* (2003). She is working on a monograph entitled 'Face Value: Victorian Fiction and the Rise of the Picture-ID'.

Colin Jones is Professor of History at Queen Mary, University of London. His recent books include *The Great Nation: France from Louis XV to Napoleon (1715–99)* (2002) and *Paris: Biography of a City* (2004). The latter won the Enid MacLeod Prize of the Franco-British Society.

Sally Ledger is Hildrid Carlile Chair in English Royal Holloway University of London. Her most recent book is *Dickens and the Popular Radical Imagination* (2007). Her other works include *The New Woman: Fiction and Feminism at the Fin de Siecle* (1997) and *Henrik Ibsen* (1999).

Joss Marsh is Professor of Victorian Studies at Indiana University. She is the author of *Word Crimes: Blasphemy, Culture, and Literature in 19th-Century*

England (1998), and of essays on Dickens and film in the *Cambridge Companion to Dickens* and the *Dickens Studies Annual*. She has a book manuscript in hand called 'Dickens/Cinema: The Imitable "Boz" and the Persistence of Human Fantasy'.

Josephine McDonagh is Professor of English at Kings College London. Her books include *De Quincey's Disciplines* (1994), *George Eliot* (1997) and *Child Murder and British Culture, 1720–1900* (2003).

Jon Mee is Professor of Romanticism Studies at Warwick University. His books include *Dangerous Enthusiasm: William Blake and the Culture of Radicalism in the 1790s* (1992) and *Romanticism, Enthusiasm, and Regulation: Poetics and the Policing of Culture in the Romantic Period* (2003). He co-edited *Barnaby Rudge* for Oxford World's Classics (2003).

Alex Newhouse is researching a PhD on Dickens and silent film at the University of York.

Mark Philp is a University Lecturer in Politics and Tutorial Fellow at Oriel College, Oxford. His books include *Political Conduct* (2007), *Thomas Paine* (2007) and, as editor, *The French Revolution and British Popular Politics* (1991).

Gareth Stedman Jones is Professor of Political Science at the University of Cambridge. His books include *Outcast London: A Study in the Relationship between Classes in Victorian Society* (1971), *Languages of Class: Studies in English Working Class History, 1832–1982* (1983), *An End to Poverty?* (2004) and an edition of *The Communist Manifesto* (2002).

Michael Wood is Charles Barnwell Straut Class of 1923 Professor of English and Comparative Literature at Princeton University. The most recent of his numerous books is *Literature and the Taste of Knowledge* (2005).

Index